There Should Have Been Eight

TITLES BY NALINI SINGH

Psy-Changeling Series

Slave to Sensation
Visions of Heat
Caressed by Ice
Mine to Possess
Hostage to Pleasure
Branded by Fire
Blaze of Memory
Bonds of Justice
Play of Passion
Kiss of Snow
Tangle of Need
Heart of Obsidian
Shield of Winter
Shards of Hope
Allegiance of Honor

Guild Hunter Series

Angels' Blood
Archangel's Kiss
Archangel's Consort
Archangel's Blade
Archangel's Storm
Archangel's Legion
Archangel's Shadows
Archangel's Enigma
Archangel's Heart
Archangel's Viper
Archangel's Prophecy
Archangel's War
Archangel's Sun
Archangel's Light
Archangel's Resurrection

Psy-Changeling Trinity Series

Silver Silence
Ocean Light
Wolf Rain
Alpha Night
Last Guard
Storm Echo
Resonance Surge

Thrillers

A Madness of Sunshine
Quiet in Her Bones
There Should Have Been Eight

There Should Have Been Eight

NALINI SINGH

BERKLEY

NEW YORK

BERKLEY

An imprint of Penguin Random House LLC

penguinrandomhouse.com

Copyright © 2023 by Nalini Singh

Penguin Random House supports copyright. Copyright fuels creativity, encourages
diverse voices, promotes free speech, and creates a vibrant culture. Thank you for
buying an authorized edition of this book and for complying with copyright laws by
not reproducing, scanning, or distributing any part of it in any form without
permission. You are supporting writers and allowing Penguin Random
House to continue to publish books for every reader.

BERKLEY and the BERKLEY & B colophon are registered
trademarks of Penguin Random House LLC.

Library of Congress Cataloging-in-Publication Data

Names: Singh, Nalini, 1977– author.
Title: There should have been eight / Nalini Singh.
Description: First edition. | New York: Berkley, 2023.
Identifiers: LCCN 2023016611 (print) | LCCN 2023016612 (ebook) |
ISBN 9780593549766 (hardcover) | ISBN 9780593549773 (ebook)
Subjects: LCGFT: Thrillers (Fiction) | Novels.
Classification: LCC PR9639.4.S566 T54 2023 (print) |
LCC PR9639.4.S566 (ebook) | DDC 823/.92—dc23/eng/20230414
LC record available at https://lccn.loc.gov/2023016611
LC ebook record available at https://lccn.loc.gov/2023016612

Printed in the United States of America
1st Printing

Book design by Katy Riegel

There Should Have Been Eight

1

. . . around the cache of disturbing images found in the personal laptop of Judge Landis Beale. The judge has refused to speak to the media after his initial statement denying all knowledge of the images and declaring that his system had been hacked.

However, sources close to the investigation state that there is no evidence of hacking, and that it appears the judge has been collecting the images for close to a year.

Major media organizations continue to file appeals against the gag order that prohibits any description of the images.

—MORNING NEWS BULLETIN

2

━

But I'm afraid of the dark.

That was all I could think when the doctor looked at me, kind and gentle, and told me that I was going to go blind. A slow, steady road to relentless darkness. There were other words. Things like "best-case scenario" and "limited vision," along with "cutting-edge developments" and "chance to optimize your habits," but it had just been buzz, a swarm of disoriented bees in my head.

It's been a year since that day. I now knew far too much about the genetic time bomb inside me, and my night vision was gone. But I could still see in the light, so I brought the camera up to my eye as the wind whipped my hair back from the open window, and I snapped a shot of one of the myriad waterfalls that cascaded down the fern-covered rocks of this final stretch of the West Coast.

We'd turn soon, going inland and upward as we made our way to the remote alpine area that housed Darcie's family estate. I'd never had reason to visit that specific part of the country, but I'd heard that it was breathtaking, a photographer's paradise. Still, that unknown landscape could never compete with my love for the black sands, rainforests, and jagged cliffs of this coast.

"We're flying south for three days to walk one of the trails, then road-tripping up to the estate," my best friend, Vansi, had said. "You should come! Kaea's already on board and I'm going to ask Aaron and Grace, too."

My love for this region was part of why I'd tried so hard to fly home early, join the road trip. But only a small part. When Darcie's invitation had come and I'd realized everyone had said yes to the idea of a reunion, the key had turned, unlocking the bitter box of questions I'd kept stifled for nine long years.

All of us. Together again.

While I could still see, still judge their expressions.

It was time.

No more avoiding the one subject none of us could bear to talk about.

No more false cheer anytime we reminisced about the past.

No more pretending that Bea wasn't dead.

My chest compressed in on itself, my eyes staring unblinkingly at the landscape beyond the window.

In the end, I'd only made this final stretch of the road trip. I'd needed to see my family, imprint their visages on my brain. Because the disease that had slumbered in my cells all my life was now well and truly awake. It was rare, the doctors had told me, and while they had data from other cases, there were no guarantees when it came to the timeline of progression.

I was a walking case study on its unpredictability: I'd been asymptomatic until I hit twenty-eight years of age. Such late onset was as rare as the disease itself. Most with the same diagnosis only got to keep their sight until their teens, or early twenties at best. I'd made it to almost thirty.

A gift.

More than a quarter century spent in blissful ignorance.

No awareness that there would come a day when my world would go blurry . . . then blink out, leaving me with nothing but ghostly afterimages of the life I'd once lived.

The diagnosis had turned me into a hoarder of memories.

After five days with my parents, brother, and grandparents in the frenetic energy of metropolitan Auckland, I'd made my way to Fox Glacier last night. The cabin I'd booked at the last minute had been low on the amenities front and chilly to boot, but was nestled inside primeval native bushland.

Giant tree ferns had shaded my back door, beyond them a landscape curling with mist. Soft focus provided by nature.

I'd taken more photographs, hoarded more memories—but I'd been ready to go when my friends drove in at ten that morning. The mist had faded by then, the sky ablaze with cool spring sunshine.

Hugs, cries of joy, grins exchanged.

It had all felt so painfully familiar, their voices and faces writ on my very bones. I'd never forget the fine details of any of their expressions, no matter how fast the curtain fell. We'd been part of each other's lives at a pivotal moment, that breath between childhood and adulthood, when the whole world was full of possibility and our minds fearless.

But of course, it wasn't the same.

We'd learned fear. And lived a grief so serrated that the scars ached to this day.

"Do you think we'll ever be how we were again?" Vansi had asked me the night when part of me had gone permanently numb. The whites of her eyes had been red, her voice a rasp, and her skin such an ashen shade of brown that, for a second, I'd thought I was speaking to a mirage, a stealthy shadow of my friend.

I'd stroked the wavy mass of her hair with a gentle hand, hugged her close . . . and held my silence. Because we'd both known the answer to her question. There'd been no need to give voice to the agony of it.

Bea was dead.

Her body erased out of existence.

There was no coming back from that.

3

An hour and a half until we reached the estate where Darcie and Ash waited for us. A shorter time until we left the state highway that hugged the jagged rocks and wild green of this coast with its massive white-capped waves and deadly undertows. Even the plants were eerie at times, so ancient that they appeared alien growths transported from another planet.

Click. Click. Click.

The big SUV hummed alone through the alien wilderness, no other cars on this silent stretch devoid of human settlement, but the sun shone bright, the colors of the landscape vivid. A pop of red berries I barely caught as we rolled by, a shot of golden green leaves against the sooty black trunk of a tree fern, a capture of Vansi's laughing face as reflected in the side mirror.

"You'll have a thousand shots just from the road, Lunes." Kaea bumped my shoulder. "Control yourself." All big shoulders and wicked dark eyes set against glowing brown skin, I'd thought him the most beautiful boy I'd ever seen the first day of high school, when we'd ended up in the same form room.

I'd soon learned that he was also a player. The boy around whom trailed a line of slack-eyed groupies and—once he hit his late-teenage years—whose bedroom had a revolving door that spun so fast it was a health hazard.

Back when I'd shared a flat with him, Vansi, and Aaron during our university days, I'd met so many young women in the kitchen on weekend mornings that I'd given up even exchanging names with them. Poor things always thought they'd be back, but Kaea had an endless smorgasbord from which to pick—and no desire for a steady girlfriend.

"Relationships are too much work," he'd told me once. "I'm here to graduate in the top one percent of my class, get head-hunted by a major corporate law firm, and make my way to partner in under ten years. I don't have time to be the doting boyfriend."

Arrogant ass, I thought with an inward grin. Because while he might not do relationships, he was an amazing friend. A friend who'd shipped me a giant order of my favorite local supermarket chocolates after I admitted to being homesick after moving to London—even though, according to him, my love for the cheap chocolates was a "screaming chemical-laced affront to good taste."

Lifting the camera, I snapped a photo of his grinning face.

When I looked at the tiny image on the screen, he was as beautiful and as charismatic as ever, some part of him still the boy on whom I'd had a crush. Thank God that hadn't lasted; he'd have obliterated my heart. "So, no third Mrs. Ngata yet?" I asked, after snapping another shot, this time of the couple in the front seats of the big black SUV that was our ride.

Another rugged vehicle—this one a dark green, per the recent photo in our group chat—hugged the road some three hours north of us.

Driving down as we drove up, our destination the same.

Like me, Aaron and his new fiancée, Grace, hadn't been able to join the hiking detour the others had organized. We'd link up at the estate. I hadn't yet met Grace, as Aaron's romance with her had taken place while I was out of the country, but Kaea and the others had reported that she was a sweetheart.

"What about his family?" I'd asked Kaea privately. "Any pushback there?" I knew that they'd expected Aaron to end up with someone from the African diaspora.

"I saw a photo he put up of her heading to church with his family. Huge smiles on everyone's faces, and his grandmother was holding Grace's hand. Fact Grace shares their faith will have been a major point in her favor. And she's just like Aaron, you know? Generous and warm, just the kind of person they'd want for him."

Trust Aaron to find a woman with a nature as gentle and kind as his own. Back when we'd flatted together, Aaron had always been the one most likely to organize a pick-me-up if one of us was struggling, or to make dinner for us all. He'd even packed me lunch one semester after he realized I was exhausted from study and work, and as a result was barely eating.

I'd been overjoyed when he called me with news of his engagement.

Not only for the love, but for finding his place in life. Back at the huge high school where we'd come together as a group, where the diverse student body was a matter of school pride, Aaron had still managed to stick out. His parents had been refugees from war-torn Sudan, Aaron one of the first generation born on New

Zealand soil. The eldest son, the eldest cousin, the first child born a Kiwi.

He'd carried the weight of his entire family's expectations on his thin shoulders.

"They survived refugee camps and the loss of most of the members of our family to relocate to a place so cold that my haboba's kneecaps creak from it," he'd said in a speech for our senior English class. "The least I can do is make them proud."

I'd never understood whether he was being serious or ironic when he said things like that, whether the words were his or a repetition of those spoken to him by his family, especially his treasured grandmother with the knees that couldn't bear the cold. For all his sweetness, Aaron was in no way an open book.

Quite different from blunt and almost-too-honest Kaea.

"Situation is in progress," Kaea said today. "Wife number three. My soulmate, this time. I know it."

Phoenix snorted from the driver's seat, his voice overriding a radio report about a scandal to do with a high court judge. "Didn't you use that line in your first wedding speech?"

"No." Vansi turned to grin at Kaea. "He said they were destined to be, two hearts in sync."

"Destined for divorce court," Phoenix added dryly as the newscaster began to speculate about the spring weather.

Unabashed, Kaea threw out his arms. "Hey, hate the game, not the player." At twenty-nine, with two divorces behind him, he had the confidence of a handsome and intelligent man who knew women would never be a challenge for him. It was a kind of curse, I'd always thought, the ease with which he could charm lovers. He valued none of them because there were always more waiting in the wings.

"Wait, hear that?" Phoenix turned up the radio.

". . . *polar blast*. Farmers are concerned about the effect of the late cold snap on the lambing season."

"Only in New Zealand," Vansi said with a roll of the eyes that I heard more than saw. "Sheep news on prime time."

"Wouldn't worry about the weather," Kaea added. "Remember last year they were going on about a polar blast and it ended up a day of cold rain?"

Phoenix nodded. "Yeah, you're right. We'll be safe at the estate regardless. If the place has survived close to a hundred and fifty years in the mountains, it's not going to buckle under a bit of rain." Reaching forward, he switched off the radio. "Signal's starting to crackle anyway. Did Darcie ever answer my question about cell reception at the estate? I forgot to check."

"Yeah—apparently it's usually only available in a single high part of the estate's main house, though she says she gets the odd bar out by the bridge sometimes." Kaea shrugged. "Be a proper break, right?"

Phoenix's profile underwent a subtle shift, his skin no longer as taut. And I realized how hard it must be, to live life tied to the scream of medical emergencies. It was a wonder he'd been able to take this break; maybe the hospital had been forced to give their junior doctors more time off by some health and safety authority.

"Anyway, enough about that." Kaea shifted his gaze to me, waggled his eyebrows. "You never say much about your dating life in London, Mysterious Ms. Wylie. Anyone serious?"

"Just me and my camera." And my oncoming blindness.

A year after the doctors first ended my world as it was, I still hadn't told anyone about the diagnosis. It had a fancy name, but at the bottom of it, it was a time bomb with which I'd been born and hadn't known of until that fateful doctor's appointment. I'd gone in thinking the thin and bald man with brilliant blue eyes was going to tell me I needed glasses, come out to a world that would never be sharp again.

I'd always known I was adopted. Hard not to when my hair was black glass and my skin olive in comparison to my parents' much paler hair and "winter white" complexions—as described by themselves. Complete with my mother's big laugh and my father's deep chuckle.

My ancestry had never been a big deal to me. I'd never felt any desire to go to China, trace my roots. But . . . would I have picked up a camera had I known what lived inside me? The lens that was slowly going dark as tiny crystals formed in the delicate tissues of my eyes.

"Legal blindness is a certainty." The bald doctor whose name my brain refused to hold on to had taken off his glasses, his features soft and sympathetic. "But a more-than-negligible percentage of patients retain a measure of central vision. Saying that, I don't want to lie to you or give you false hope. Such vision retention isn't guaranteed—and where it is present, that vision is in no way clear."

All I could think as he pronounced that sentence was that his own eyes were as blue as Bea's had been before they stopped being anything at all. At least they hadn't rotted. Darcie hadn't given them the chance.

She'd burned her sister's eyes, burned Bea.

4

Countless road photos—and twenty kilometers on a spine-adjusting gravel road later—we came to a halt in the stark beauty of an alpine world wholly apart from the primal forests and crashing waves of the coast. Calf-length golden grass waved as far as the eye could see, the jagged peaks of the Southern Alps soaring beyond, their caps encased in ice. No green anywhere. Just gold and white and granite.

An old Land Rover sat on the other side of a bridge that looked like it had been built in the early nineteenth century, all dark iron and rust. As for the vehicle, its side was dented and scratches marred most of its light brown finish, but the tires looked new.

"Luna!" Darcie's voice rang out over the rush of the creek filled with pristine glacial melt. It was beautiful, frothing white at the top, crystalline blue-green below.

Nothing, however, could compare to Darcie's luminous beauty.

Back before she'd ended up with Ash, we used to joke that if she and Kaea had kids, those kids would be the most infuriatingly beautiful people in the world. But if Kaea'd ever had thoughts in that vein about Darcie, he'd kept them to himself. Friendship mattered to Kaea.

Him and Ash, teammates on the rugby field. Fullback and halfback.

And Ash with a thing for—

Don't go there, Luna. Only pain that way.

Darcie waved from the other side, all shining golden hair that rippled down her back and skin kissed by the sun, the gentle breeze ruffling the lacy white of her ankle-length sundress. I couldn't see her eyes from this distance, but I knew they were as blue as the summer sky.

Bea's had been a sharper, more penetrating hue, her hair a luscious chocolate.

"Is that thing even safe!" Phoenix's voice as he poked his head out the driver's side window and pointed to the bridge.

"We're engineers, you asshole!" was Ash's rejoinder.

He was tall and slender and as blond as Darcie; together, the two of them were the perfect magazine couple. Golden bookends. It would've been easy to say it was all a facade, but seeing them together three years after their gorgeous spectacle of a wedding, Ash's hand lying against Darcie's lower back, I realized it felt real.

"Let's do this, boys and girls," Phoenix said, then began to make his way across the old bridge.

It creaked ominously, the waters roaring around us.

"Wait! Wait!"

Phoenix came to an immediate halt at my cry. "What? Is the bridge falling apart?"

"No." I pushed open my door. "I need to get shots of you driving across."

"Jesus, Luna." Vansi pressed a hand to her heart. "You idiot!" But she was laughing as she said it.

"Sorry! Artistic temperament and all that."

I heard Kaea join in the laughter before I shut the door and scampered on ahead over the old wooden boards of the bridge. I wasn't sure the boards should be wooden, but what did I know? From what I could tell, the struts and everything else had been formed of metal, so the wood was likely window dressing to help make it a smoother drive.

Once in position halfway across the bridge, I made a "come on" gesture and Phoenix crawled forward. Had it been Kaea in the driver's seat, he'd have revved the engine and pretended he was about to race forward, but Phoenix had always been far more stolid and steady.

A calm foil to Vansi's more tempestuous personality.

Now, my best friend poked her head out the window on one side, while Kaea and Phoenix did it on the other, and I snapped away. I kept on walking backward as I did so, image after image layering itself into my mind. My visual memory had always been acute, and it might yet save my sanity.

Lifting a palm in a motion for Phoenix to halt, I turned and grabbed multiple images of Darcie and Ash from my vantage point on the bridge. The wind tugged at her hair and dress. The sun made his eyes sparkle. Just like it had that day at the campsite when I'd photographed him with Bea, their laughing faces side by side as she rode his back across a large patch of mud.

A hitch in my chest.

I shook it off, made myself carry on across the bridge.

The others followed.

There were hugs, exclamations, then Kaea said, "You two doing okay? The cops figure out anything new about what happened at your place? It's been, what, about three weeks now?"

Pressing her lips tight, Darcie nodded. "No actual suspects, but they think it was probably a group high on drugs—the detective in charge isn't treating it as a burglary, more as an attempted home invasion with the intent to harm."

"No explanation as to how they bypassed our security system," Ash added, "but that thing was glitchy for a week beforehand so it might just not have sent out an alert. Thankfully our insurance company is still covering all the damage."

"I don't really care about the stuff," Darcie said with a razored edge to her tone, "but why did the creeps have to vandalize our house? And the way they did it? Disgusting."

Ash squeezed her shoulders. "We've spent the time since at an Airbnb overlooking the water at Mission Bay, and with the cops all done, we've lined up tradespeople to come in while we're down here. Painters will sand off the graffiti, repaint, then in go the new carpets."

He pressed a kiss to Darcie's cheek. "It'll be fine, honey—we can get a few new pieces from that furniture designer you love. Place will be like a whole new house by the time we return. No bad memories."

Darcie's mouth remained pinched at the corners, but she allowed Ash to jolly her along, and the conversation soon moved on. I could understand why she was shaken up about it, though—Kaea had been with the two of them when they discovered the

break-in, and he'd shared that the vandalism had been "disturbing as all hell."

"Fuckers painted the word 'Judas' in dripping red paint right
above their bed," he'd said in the SUV on the way here. "I also
saw 'JUDGMENT' in all caps above the fireplace, and Ash told
me there was nasty stuff in the master bathroom. Living room
carpet was trashed, smeared with brown liquid that Ash said later
tested as blood.

"Intruders cut up a ton of their clothes, too, just took scissors
to it. Pure luck that they didn't damage any of the outdoor gear
the two needed for this week, or I'm sure Darcie would've can-
celed. She lost it. I mean, she had reason to—I'm dead certain I
saw a meat cleaver stabbed into their bed."

It didn't sound like any burglary I'd ever heard of. No wonder
the cops were taking it seriously. Frankly, I was surprised the
couple had agreed to carry on with the reunion, but I could see
the attraction of spending time far away from the ugliness and
returning to find it erased.

I did feel bad for them, but that didn't squelch my bubbling
anger. It had been building for nine years, was a passionate stew
of sadness, fury, and bitterness. Fifteen minutes later, as Darcie
laid out a picnic spread for us to pick at while we waited for Aaron
and Grace, I wanted to say Bea's name, wanted to scream at Darcie for stealing Bea from us with such finality.

But even that hadn't been enough for Darcie, had it?

In the end, she'd also stolen that which Bea loved most.

However, I wasn't so far gone that I didn't understand that
some of my fury was fueled by my own diagnosis. My worry that
they'd stop talking about me—*to* me—when I proved imperfect.

It was the thought that my anger had nothing to do with Bea, that I just wanted to ruin this week for selfish reasons, that kept me from spitting out the rage eating at me.

"How cold is the creek water?" I asked instead. "Can I dip my toes in or will I end up with ice blocks for feet?"

"Ice blocks," Darcie said. "But it's still fun. And not dangerous if you stick to the part with the rocks."

I wasn't surprised when Vansi bounced up to join me on my adventure, both of us deciding to leave our shoes and socks by the picnic blankets.

We didn't say much because it wasn't necessary, and it wasn't until after we'd screamed at the frigid burn of the water and taken seats on the sun-warmed stone to dry off that Vansi made a face and said, "This is weird. Don't you think it's weird? All of us pretending we're good and normal when we haven't been good and normal since that night?"

My smile faded. "Yes." Having chosen to sit on the other side of the eddy in the rocks where we'd tested the water, I stretched my legs into the sun. And despite Vansi's words, I didn't mention Bea. My best friend had always been jealous of my relationship with Darcie's younger sister.

"Bea takes people, Luna," she'd told me at nineteen. "Don't you see? She doesn't mean to, but she's so amazing it just kind of happens. She took all of Darcie's friends, made them hers. I don't want her to take you, too."

I'd never seen it that way, had seen us all as a single huge organism of friendship. Certain people closer to others, but no one left out in the cold, no one who wasn't especially tight with a certain other member of the eight.

"Something's wrong with me and Nix and I can't figure it out," Vansi blurted out, the words cracking the mirror of memory.

"What?" She'd said nothing, *nothing* about this during any of our phone or online conversations.

Leaning forward, elbows on her thighs, she thrust her fingers through her hair. "He's just . . . different. Distant."

"You did say he was at an intensive part of his training. How did he even get this many days in a row off?" Phoenix had completed the brutal journeyman years required of a junior doctor, but he wasn't close to done. Not when he intended to become a neurosurgeon.

Vansi threw up her hands. "I have no idea. That's just it. Nix used to tell me everything. He was the moody, silent type to everyone else, but to me, he was an open book. I always felt special. *His* person."

"You've asked him?"

"Yep. All I get is that he's tired, stressed. The same nonanswer he'd give you if you asked him. But I'm his *wife*, the supposed love of his life."

"Shit."

"Sorry to dump this on you." Vansi rubbed her hands over her thighs. "I thought this break . . . away from the stress of his work, from the expectations of both our parents, he'd loosen up, but he's still putting on an act, even with me, and I hate it."

"Hey." I reached across the small glacial pool to touch her hand. "We just got here. Give it a bit more time."

Lips pressed tight, Vansi nodded. "I know you're right, but I still want to scream at him, then shake him." Picking up a small pebble from in between the rocks, she threw it into the frigid water with vicious force. "I wonder if it's this reunion," she said, her voice hard without warning. "His behavior, it lines up with when Darcie sent out the invite. It makes me wonder—"

"What, V?" I frowned. "I *know* you don't think he has a thing for Darcie." Our friend might be beautiful, but to be quite blunt, she wasn't Nix's type.

"Oh, Lu." Dark brown eyes opaque, Vansi's expression . . . sad. "You never did see it, did you? How Bea was the flower around which everyone buzzed? Even you." A tight smile. "If she'd still been alive, I wouldn't be Mrs. Phoenix Chang, and I wonder if this reunion's brought that home to him."

The words were a punch to the mouth. "Bea would've never—"

"How would you know?" my best friend demanded, her hands fisting on her thighs and spots of heat on her rounded cheeks. "He might've been standing right next to me, might've been mine on paper, but all she would've had to do was crook a finger. You don't know because you never had a lover for her to steal."

She dropped her face into her hands before I could fully process her words. "Oh God, I'm so sorry." Wet eyes looking into mine across the water in which I now spotted flecks of ice. "I didn't mean any of that."

"It's okay. I'm not insulted—I've never wanted a permanent lover." It was the absolute truth. "I have other dreams." I was more frustrated by the rest of what she'd said, how she'd characterized sweet, bubbly, *loyal* Bea.

"Hey, you two!" Kaea yelled down from above, his hands cupped around his mouth. "We're going to play cards and need more players!"

There was no more time for private conversation after that, even had Vansi been willing to speak. We played cards, talked about the speed with which Aaron and Grace had become engaged—after only six months together—and Darcie teased us with stories about her "loony tunes" ancestor Blake Shepherd, the prospector who'd struck it rich and decided to build a grand residence on the edge of eternity.

Lit to a glow by the spring sun, all gilded limbs and easy smiles, my friends suddenly seemed exactly that. No hidden motives, just an old sorrow shared that had bonded us with a glue unbreakable. And for a pulse in time, I was content, with no desire to stir up the past, to push Darcie until she told us why she'd done it.

5

We heard Aaron's car long before we saw him, the crackle of the tires on the gravel of the unpaved road carrying through the trees and over the water. I had myself in position to take photos by the time his Jeep appeared around the corner, while the others stood waving.

Grace popped her blond head out the window just as I began to shoot. Where Darcie's hair was a sheet of silk, Grace's was all wild curls with streaks of a blond so sun-kissed it was white. She jumped out the instant Aaron brought the vehicle to a stop and I saw that she was even tinier than she'd appeared in the photos I'd seen.

Five feet tall tops, all of it dangerous curves and bounce.

I couldn't imagine her as a climber, but that was where she'd met Aaron—in a club for people who liked to battle the elements uphill and punish their knees scrabbling downhill. Aaron had told me of their courtship over a video call, laughing at himself as he shared that Grace had beaten him to the summit during their first climb together.

When I'd teased it must've been because he was focused on her butt, he'd looked so sheepish that I'd cracked up laughing.

"Oh my God! You must be Luna!" Grace jumped into my arms, her hug fierce and . . . good. Because some people just gave better hugs than others.

Like they really meant it.

"Hi," I said after hugging her back more awkwardly.

Unabashed, she whipped off her mirrored sunglasses and beamed at me. No one would call her beautiful—her looks were too quixotic for that. Eyes that were slightly too large, along with a mouth that was a bit too wide, paired with a slender nose. But taken altogether when she was this animated?

Wow.

Grace was the kind of woman who could be a movie star. All charisma and a wild energy that reminded me of Bea. I took more photos as she hopped around greeting everyone else as if they were old friends, while Aaron smiled his shy smile that now shimmered with quiet pride.

A flicker at the corner of my eye, a sinuous shadow.

Shifting on my heel, I swiped out a hand. But if there'd been a bug there, it was gone.

My fingers fisted into my hand, the nails digging in.

"Luna, you want to ride with us up to the house?" Grace's voice, bright and joyful and accented in a way that was difficult to pin down, thanks to what Aaron had told us was a peripatetic childhood.

I ignored the renewed flickering at the corner of my eye, the awareness of minuscule crystals eating up my peripheral vision. "You don't want to rest here a bit?"

No, they said, they were keen to see the old Shepherd place. As was I. So I jumped into their Jeep, the three of us at the end of the cavalcade making its way through the rustling grasses and toward the looming bulk of the snow-covered mountains.

The route took us slightly upslope, the estate hidden beyond the rise.

As I sat in the back, scrolling through the photos I'd taken, I frowned. Grace photographed like a dream, but there was something slightly "off" about the images at the same time. The camera didn't quite capture her eyes. Or it captured them in a shade of green that wasn't true to life.

I'd have to see if I could fix the issue in postproduction. Speaking of photographs, though . . . "I could do an engagement-style shoot of you two while we're out here," I offered impulsively. "We can style it with whatever clothes you've brought along, use the natural surroundings."

Grace squealed. "Are you *serious*?" She pressed her hands together. "I love your work. I secretly stalk your socials." A whisper. "That Renaissance wedding shoot you did for the two brides? I *died*."

Chuffed at the compliments, I said, "Consider the shoot officially booked."

"I love you," Grace said in a solemn voice. "In fact, I'm planning to dump Aaron and beg for your hand in marriage."

My shoulders shook. I liked her. Really liked her. She was . . . *so much like Bea.*

Gut tight, I busied myself pretending to look at my photos

again, all the while thinking of those final sun-drenched days with Bea. It had been our last summer together, all eight of us. Not here. Up north, in a hired wooden bach next to one of those lazy East Coast beaches.

Golden white sand, clear blue water, native palms against the sky.

Paradise.

Bea in her big floppy hat, the color ice-cream pink, and halter-neck swimsuit in meringue yellow. She'd looked like a glamorous movie star, especially after she slid on those big sunglasses of hers.

Not once during that glorious week had I glimpsed any hint of trouble in her. After . . . after, I'd done relentless research, discovered that mental health problems didn't always show on the surface, but her supposed suicide still hadn't made sense to me—because I hadn't been a random bystander. I'd been part of her life for years.

Why hadn't I seen?

Why had *none* of us seen?

Not even Darcie. Her big sister. Her supposed protector after their parents passed as Bea began her final year of high school. She'd been the youngest of her classmates, only turning eighteen in the last month of the school year.

"Well, just dress me in black and call me Jane Eyre."

6

Grace's colorful exclamation as Aaron brought the Jeep to a stop had me looking up.

I scrambled out the door the next minute, my camera already rising to my eye. I didn't bother to yell at those in the front vehicles to get out of the way, just went left into the grass—because there, rising against a backdrop of jagged peaks burning in the late afternoon sun, was a house straight out of a gothic romance novel.

"Are those *turrets*?" Vansi's excited voice. "Freaking turrets!"

"And jeez, an honest-to-God ruined wing?" Kaea whistled. "Maaaan."

I couldn't shoot fast enough. Clad with exquisite gray-black stone that might've been a dark variant of local schist, the house was set up in a classic U shape, with the central structure and the wing to my left in fairly good condition—albeit a bit run-down. Half-crumbled fences made of the same stone arched around from either side and to the back, and had perhaps once protected kitchen gardens or more formal landscaping.

Ivy bright with the green of new spring growth crawled up one side, feathering red veins left bare over winter, while the area in front of the house looked like it might've at one time been a garden.

It was now badly overgrown, but not with the golden grass all around us. Spiky purple thistle fought for space with what looked like a mass of raspberry bushes, while clusters of dandelion seed heads, delicate and ethereal, swayed in the breeze.

Lovely chaos.

But the true showstopper was Kaea's "ruined wing"—because it was exactly that. While the wing still stood for the most part, it bore marks of a brutal fire that had collapsed one of its turrets and burned long slashes of soot into the stone.

Silent phantom flames.

What windows remained were badly cracked, the rest gaping holes of nothingness. I couldn't wait to get out here at sunrise, shoot it in the ghostly light of morning.

"Lu!" Aaron called out, and only then did I realize how far I'd wandered into the grass. "We're driving to the top of the front drive to park! You want to hop in?"

I shook my head. "I'll get some shots of you driving up, then walk in!" I also wanted time alone to enjoy this mad structure out in the middle of the wilderness, plan the images I was going to take.

Most would be for my portfolio—but if we could borrow one of Darcie's floaty dresses and pin it in a way that fit Grace's shorter and curvier frame, get Aaron into a white or black shirt and black pants—or as close as possible—we were all set for a romantic gothic shoot.

Car doors shut, engines started, vehicles began to move . . . but I didn't end up alone in the aftermath. Ash had stayed behind. "Hey, hope you don't mind the company." He slipped his hands into the pockets of his beige slacks, which he'd paired with a sky blue polo with a distinctive logo on one side. "I wanted to show you something."

It took effort to hide my irritation. "Of course I don't mind."

He waited until I'd taken a few images of the departing vehicles, then pointed me to the right. "This way. We only have a small window of time."

Deciding I could come back to get the shots I'd wanted, I went with him to a spot that placed me at an angle from the ruined wing. "What—" Breath catching, I ignored him for the next five minutes as I fought to capture the incredible light show against the shattered glass of the burned part of the house.

The broken shards gleamed in the thick light of early sunset—neither too sharp, nor too red—that refracted off the glass in a way that made the building come eerily alive. My heart was pounding by the time the light faded, and I half expected to turn to find Ash had long ago given up on me and left.

But I found him seated in the grass not far from me, his eyes on the glass that was no longer afire. "Brilliant, isn't it?" He shook his head. "Saw it by accident yesterday while taking a walk, was hoping you'd have your camera on you so I could ask you to take a few shots. I knew my phone wouldn't capture it."

"You can have as many of my photos as you want," I promised, knowing that I'd captured a spectacular series. The kind of images that won awards and made names out of photographers.

Rising to his feet, Ash brushed off the seat of his slacks. The round face of his watch with its multiple dials caught the light.

"We'd better go in. Darcie wants to show everyone the place to-gether."

More than satisfied with the images I'd taken, I fell into step with him. "Seriously, Ash, thank you. My heart's still pounding."

A small smile from the member of our group with whom I'd always interacted the least. "I thought of you the instant I saw it."

I wasn't sure quite how to take that. These days, I never thought of Ash except in relation to Darcie. Not out of any sense of malice, but because we'd never been tight. Then again, he'd have had to be oblivious our entire acquaintance to not immediately associate me with the camera.

"I'm excited to look at the photos on my laptop," I said before it struck me that no one in the group chat had asked one vital question. "Does this place have stable electricity?"

"Generators. Jim—that's our caretaker—made sure they're fueled up. More than enough juice there to get us through the week. Jim and his son also stocked up the fridge and left us a gift of fresh deer meat in the freezer."

I winced. "We're eating Bambi?"

"Introduced species, remember?" Ash pointed out. "Without hunters, they'd collapse the ecosystem." He frowned, glanced over at where the others were milling around in front of the estate house. "Luna, I wanted to ask a favor."

The hairs at the back of my neck prickled. "Oh?"

"It's just . . . look, Darcie's pregnant."

My hands clenched on the camera. "Wow, congratulations."

"Thanks." A tight smile. "Thing is, she doesn't want to tell anyone until after the first trimester. She's only nine weeks in right now."

"Sure, I understand that. So why . . . ?"

Exhaling, he rubbed his face. "I think the hormones, the emotions . . . she's thinking about Bea a lot. It began after the break-in, with her saying Bea was haunting her, or that she could smell Bea's perfume. Past two nights, though, she's woken screaming Bea's name—says she hears Bea whispering to her in the night."

He folded his arms. "I figure it's her way of dealing with the fact that her sister's not here for this moment, but I'm worried."

I halted while we were yet a safe distance from the rest of the group. "Have you spoken to anyone about this?" I didn't know much about pregnancy, but I knew postpartum psychosis was a thing. Perhaps the same kind of thing could happen earlier in the process, too.

"I would've gone to her old family doctor, Daniel Cox, but he died two weeks ago. Freak accident. His car went off a cliff." Ash shook his head. "Poor old guy. They were close and it hit her hard."

He shoved his hands into his pockets. "Night of the attempted home invasion, she . . . It wasn't good. I wanted to take her to the ER but I knew she'd do better with Dr. Cox—and when I called him, he came over to help without hesitation. That was the last time we saw him. Six days later, he was dead."

"Oh God, how horrible that she lost him on top of what happened to your place." No wonder Darcie remained emotionally brittle.

"Thing is, she was already in a bad place even before the break-in. One of her mother's old law buddies, a man Darcie really looks up to, well, he's got some very serious stuff happening in his life and she's struggling to handle it. I think the break-in was just one pressure point too far. She shattered."

"I'm so sorry, Ash, I didn't realize how deeply it affected her." Kaea obviously hadn't, either—that, or he'd decided to maintain her privacy on the matter.

"After she woke up, she was embarrassed, didn't want to talk about it and definitely didn't want me to tell anyone. You know how she gets."

"Yes." Darcie did everything in her power to have the perfect life, and as a result, didn't deal well with deviations.

"I want to give her this week away from it all before I raise the idea that she talk to a grief counselor—because that's what this is, I think, grief over Bea that she never processed. With her pregnancy, the shock of the break-in, then losing Dr. Cox, it's the perfect emotional storm to have brought it all to the surface."

Guilt gnawed at me for what I'd planned to do, the questions I'd intended to ask, but mingled with that was a huge dose of frustration. He'd cut me off now. What kind of monster would rage at a psychologically fragile pregnant woman? I might be angry, but I wasn't that bad. "What would you like me to do?"

"Keep an eye on her, let me know if you notice symptoms of what might be a larger issue." He hunched in his shoulders as we started walking again. "I'm really hoping I'm being a worry-wart, but—"

I touched his arm, anger erased by a wave of empathy. Because regardless of all else, Darcie was Bea's older sister. "No, I understand. This place, it has to hold a lot of memories. I know Darcie and Bea spent summers on the estate as kids."

"I actually wasn't too sure about coming here after she began to say that stuff about Bea—but she was so excited. And, I thought maybe being here is exactly what she needs. A way to say a proper goodbye to her sister. She never got to do that."

My spine stiffened. Darcie had made sure *none* of us got to say goodbye.

The solemn memorial service in a tiny chapel had been a grief-stricken Aaron's idea. He'd done what he could, but the somber affair hadn't felt like Bea at all. No sparkle, no shine, nothing but the priest and the seven of us.

No body in a casket. No urn of ashes.

But at least Aaron had *tried*. I'd always loved him for that. Darcie, in contrast, had seemed to want to ignore Bea's death, throw her away in more ways than one. I didn't think I'd ever make my peace with Darcie's decision to cremate Bea so far from home, scatter her ashes into the ocean.

As for Ash, the man he'd been was divided into two parts in my mind. Ash with Bea, and Ash afterward. When Bea had chosen to take her life, she'd taken the best part of Ash with her.

Suicide.

My Bea.

No, I still couldn't accept it.

Hell, even all these years later, I could barely believe she was dead. None of us had seen her body, had we? In the deepest, darkest part of night, I thought about that, and I wondered what Darcie had needed to hide that she hadn't even given Bea a proper burial.

"I'll keep an eye on her," I promised past the grit of grief and anger that lined my throat. "I'm surprised you asked me, and not one of the others."

He grimaced. "Don't take this wrong, but it's because you're always watching people. Usually through the lens."

"It's true." I shrugged. "People are fascinating." And I'd much rather watch them than be watched.

A surprised smile that creased his cheeks. "I swear I never could figure out what you found so interesting about a bunch of uni students. Surely there're only so many photos of drunken nights out you can take."

"Oh, you'd be surprised." I thought of the photo I had of him dancing with Bea, the spotlight only on them, and the tassels on her glittery dress flying, her hair in motion—and Ash watching her as if she were a fallen star come to land in his hands.

7

I'd intended to gift the photo to Ash and Bea on their engagement because we'd all known where that relationship was going. These days, I kept a print of it in the same folder in which I
had a stunning capture of Darcie on the tiny porch of my student
flat, her hands cupped around a steaming mug of coffee . . . and
a tormented agony in her eyes.

Bea and Ash had been on the lawn in front of her at the time,
playing some silly game of lovers. And I'd taken the photo while
fiddling with my camera. I hadn't meant to spy. I never meant to
spy. But people reveal so much in the split seconds before they put
their masks back on.

"It might only be pregnancy hormones," I said to Ash today,
so far from that morning on the porch where I'd learned that
Darcie loved a man who'd never looked at her that way. "I've
heard they can be powerful."

Ash glanced over at where the others stood, all animated faces and waving hands. "I'm hoping this reunion will pull her thoughts into the present and away from the memory of grief."

I almost asked him about his own grief, swallowed the question as I had countless other times. Ash had found a way to move on—and now, he was going to be a father. Nine years after Bea's death, he'd healed to the point that he could focus on Darcie's pain and well-being rather than his own loss. I had no right to shake that up by reminding him of the woman who'd chosen to leave him, leave all of us.

She didn't love me enough to stay.

Whispered, broken words I'd heard by accident when I'd come to the front door at four in the morning, unable to sleep. Though only V, Aaron, Kaea, and I were on the lease, all seven of us had been in the flat that night. Shocked and distraught and unable to face the idea of being alone.

I'd thought no one else was up. I'd been wrong. I would never forget looking through the screen door and seeing Ash slumped on the top step of the house, while Darcie stood in front of him, holding his face to her stomach.

She'd been stroking his hair, the look on her face . . .

Triumphant.

It had nauseated me that night, sent me lurching to the wall in sickened silence, but after all these years, I wasn't sure what I'd seen. My memory was sharp, yes, but I'd been drowning in grief, my vision skewed. What if all I'd seen was two broken people comforting each other?

"There you are!" Vansi cried out when we reached the others. "Come see what I've found!"

It proved to be a moss-covered cupid, his eyes filmed with black mold. Kneeling down on one knee, I took an image eerie and striking. I didn't know what made me do it, but I reached out to touch the mold.

A clap of sound before my fingers could make contact with the black, Darcie waving us all over. "You can wander tomorrow! I want to show you the house before we lose this gorgeous natural light."

I rose, leaving the cupid buried in what I'd realized weren't raspberry bushes, but poisonous imposters. Vansi had already gone on ahead, so I walked into the house at the tail end of the group. It was chilly inside, the walls of the hallway dark wood paneling that seemed to reflect the cold back at us.

"What the fuck!"

Kaea, staring upward at a dropped part of the ceiling designed to hold a painting.

Following his gaze as Vansi backtracked to do the same, I sucked in a breath. The woman looking down at us from inside a chipped golden frame could've been Darcie in period costume, the neckline of her dress high and stiff, the shade a solemn dark green.

Her eyes stared straight at us, her lips curved upward.

I could hear the others talking, but couldn't make myself look away from the portrait. Something about it didn't sit right. Was that actually a smile, or was it a shaky falsehood worn by someone who didn't want to anger another person? Was that a sparkle in her eyes, or was it the sheen of tears?

Oh.

It was the tilt of the eyes, the angle at which she held her head, the subtle difference in the line of her jaw. This Shepherd ancestor might look like Darcie at first glance, but change the hair from gold to darkest brown and it was Bea who stared out at you.

"Really looks like Darcie, doesn't she?" Vansi whistled from beside me. "She told us about her—the woman in the painting—while you were taking photos: Clara Darceline Shepherd, cultured nineteen-year-old bride from England who thought she was coming to a grand home and ended up in this mausoleum in the middle of nowhere."

Grace joined us. "It does look like her . . . but I don't know, there's something not quite right. A jitter in the frame."

I wondered how only the stranger in the room saw what I had, how Vansi *didn't* see it. Confirmation bias? Or was I the one seeing things wrong, the shadows in my vision creating mirages out of nothing?

A quiet obsession given visual form.

"Come on," Darcie called out when we hesitated too long, "the living area is a trip!"

I was the last one to follow her command. My nape prickled as I turned away from Clara, a shiver rippling over my skin. Beatrice would've never worn a dress so formal and stiff, but the secrets in Clara's eyes? That had been Bea, hadn't it? Always the one with secrets.

I stepped into the living room doorway on that thought . . . and gaped.

A massive fireplace dominated the cavernous space, the ceiling so high that our voices echoed. The exposed beams were as dark as the stone of the outside walls and some of that stone outlined the large black maw of the fireplace. But what had sparkled with glints of silver in the sunlight looked flat and heavy on the inside.

Mounted stag heads—had to be at least ten—glowered down at us from above the fireplace, their dead eyes black and staring.

If that wasn't disturbing enough, an entire stuffed stag stood by the windows, its pelt moth-eaten and one antler broken in half.

"I think old man Shepherd got a two-for-one deal on stuffed heads."

Vansi, near enough to hear my muttered aside, snorted. "Don't look up but there's a bull's head mounted above you. Prize-winning stud, apparently."

Shuddering, I turned my attention to the walls. Tapestries covered many, and from the look of them, they were old. As in, they'd come straight from England in the time of Clara Shepherd, carried on the ship that had brought her to her new home. Threadbare patches on the edges, where hands big and small must've touched; indications of moth damage higher up.

"What a shame," Vansi whispered, brushing her fingers over an undamaged part. "These would be museum-worthy with a little care."

"V, am I seeing things, or is that a frolicking demon?"

"Ha! Someone in this house had a sense of humor."

I thought of the portrait again, of the woman with Bea's mischievous eyes. "It's well hidden, too, a secret joke."

"Hope this place has bright lights." Grace's bubbly voice. "Be dark as anything at night."

"Afraid not." Ash crouched by the fireplace, grabbing kindling from a wooden crate that he stacked neatly in the grate. On one side of the fireplace sat five fat logs ready for use. "Lots of atmospheric shadows." A glance at me. "You'll love the photo opportunities."

I wasn't sure I liked Ash's sudden friendliness. "Can't wait."

"The bedrooms we've chosen upstairs are cozier," Darcie

added, "with their own fireplaces. Plus, the cleaners Jim hired made them up with fresh sheets, vacuumed, the whole lot."

"But how old are the beds?" Kaea folded his arms. "How many decades of dust will we be inhaling?"

"Well, yours is an ornate four-poster. Mattress stuffed with rabbit fur."

"Bullshit, Darceline."

"Guess you'll have to wait and see, Mr. Ngata." With that, she tucked her arm through Aaron's and tugged him past a huge space that looked like it was meant to hold a dining table, and through a door into what I assumed must be the kitchen.

Vansi joined them, while Nix chatted with Ash as the other man tried to start the fire, and Kaea decided to walk toward the windows at the other end—the very front of the house.

Grace, meanwhile, wandered over to where I was taking a close-up photograph of a detail in a tapestry. "Darcie and Kaea, they always like that?" A sidelong look at Ash out of the corner of her eye. "Straddling that line between sniping and kind of flirting?"

I winced, was struggling to think of a response when Aaron called for her with delight in his voice. Not wanting to be stuck in the gloomy living area—complete with what I'd realized were ratty fur rugs on the floor—I went with her.

Into a kitchen straight out of a museum.

Enormous black woodstove in the corner, the manufacturer's markings on the front heavy metallic embossing. Copper utensils and pots hanging from a ceiling rack. Huge metal taps. Massive marble counters.

Those, I thought, wouldn't look out of place in a modern home.

I tapped my knuckles on the dark green stone with veins of gray. Not my kind of color, but I couldn't deny its beauty. "Where did this come from?"

"Italy." Darcie leaned a hip against one end, nothing of her pregnancy yet showing in the lines of her body or face. "Where else if you were a nouveau riche former prospector with a gold mine that was throwing out more wealth than any sane person could hope to spend in their entire lifetime. Old man Shepherd was *rich*. Too bad he lost his mind and a massive pile of his wealth toward the end of his life."

"Not enough to lose this place," I pointed out. "Land alone's got to be worth millions." One person's middle-of-nowheresville was a movie star's dream hideaway.

"True enough now," Darcie said. "But back then, without money, this place was a dead-end backwater. Even with money, Blake Shepherd wasn't much of an entertainer, though apparently he allowed a few parties to appease his pretty new wife."

She made a face. "Clara was twenty-five years younger than him. It can't have been fun being stuck out here all alone with a grumpy sod of a husband who—rumor has it—had all kinds of venereal diseases from his prospector days. A little too much nighttime fun, if you know what I mean."

"Ah, romance," Ash said, entering the kitchen from another doorway that I realized was the hallway entrance.

His tone was even, holding neither anger nor humor.

"What can I say?" Darcie quipped. "Loony Shepherd knew how to woo his wife." She dropped her voice to a conspiratorial whisper. "Though I don't think he really got to it until at least a couple of years into their marriage, because their first child wasn't born until four years in. She had three more in quick succession."

Aaron looked up from stroking the counter. "Could've been those diseases cramping his style."

"Ugh, true."

Brushing his hand lightly over Darcie's back as she grimaced, Ash walked over to the bookshelf in one corner and picked up a thick leather-bound tome. "Aaron, look at this. We thought you could try to make a dish using one of the old recipes if we had the ingredients."

"Wow." Aaron's hands trembled as he took the book. "This is a treasure, man. A true heirloom." While he waxed lyrical over the old recipe book, Darcie led us out to the main hallway, her intent to show us upstairs to our rooms.

But she paused at the bottom of the stairs to point out a sepia photograph on the wall directly opposite. "Clara and Blake Shepherd right after their wedding in England."

The painfully young woman in the image smiled with her lips, her eyes turbulent, while the much older man beside her looked on, grim faced. "He went all the way over there for her?"

"Guess it was the done thing for rich old men." She led us up the stairs.

"Luna, you're over there to the right," she said once we reached the top landing. "I know you love your soaks, so I put you in the only single room with a claw-foot tub." She pointed down the narrow hallway already dark with the press of oncoming night. "Grace, come with me. You and Aaron are next to Kaea."

I let their voices fade away, eager to check out my room.

The door was solid wood that opened without a single creak. Someone had oiled the hinges. I laughed at my own disappointment before stepping inside.

"Now, *this* is more like it."

Had we been paying to stay at the estate, my room would've been worth a premium price. First of all, it was spotless. The cleaners had done a stellar job. Second, though the bed was a single, it was a single with four posts and what looked to be an ancient canopy.

I hadn't even known that you could get single four-poster beds.

Walking over, I ran my hand over the smooth dark of the wood. The polish was dull, the wood marked with fine scratches. But other than that minor cosmetic detail, there was nothing wrong with it.

The bed itself was made with crisp white sheets and a white comforter.

I wasn't, however, so sure about the curtains tied to the posts. A heavy ruby brocade with swirling designs in black, they struck me as more theater than restful bedroom, and I was glad to see that the underside—the side I'd see from the bed if I pulled the curtains shut—was a simple black.

When I undid the tasseled black rope that tied the curtain to one of the posts, however, it was to get a faceful of dust.

Coughing, I waved a hand in front of my nose and took a few steps back. The cleaning service had clearly decided that laundering antique curtains was beyond their brief.

Once the dust quieted down, I retied the curtain back to the wood of the post and decided that I'd forgo the "romantic" experience of sleeping in a bed surrounded by curtains. I also decided to more carefully check the actual bedding on which I was to sleep.

Picking up a pillow, I took a sniff.

"Darcie told me they hired the bedding."

I jumped, turning to find Vansi in the doorway. "Shit, you almost gave me a heart attack."

My best friend was unrepentant. "Comes with the territory— spooky old house and all that." Then she nodded at the bed. "Ash knows a guy who owns a hotel. Borrowed the bedding, freshly laundered and all. Mates rates."

"Nice friend," I said, my heart yet racing. "Where are you and Nix?"

"All the way at the other end. I think you might be the only one on this side."

"It's the only single with a tub."

"Yeah? Let's go nosy at the other rooms."

Normally, I'd have jumped at the chance, but my head already felt heavy. "Tomorrow," I promised. "I know it's early, but I've been awake since four this morning." My body had decided I needed to be up with the birds. "I'm going to run the bath and sink—"

A sharp short scream reverberated through the house, slamming into the windows and making my heart knock against my rib cage.

8

Vansi and I arrived at the location of the scream at the same time as Aaron and Grace. He wore nothing but his jeans, while a barefoot Grace had on what looked to be a hastily pulled-on robe of silky black patterned with huge pink hibiscus flowers. What would've been scandalously short on a taller woman hit Grace only a few inches above the knee.

The four of us crowded into the doorway of the room just off the stairway landing to the left. As with my room, windows lined the back wall.

The space would be flooded with light in the daytime.

Right now, however, the air hung a dirty yellow, the old-fashioned lamps against the walls shaky in providing even that faint illumination. The muddy shade sank into the white of Darcie's floaty dress as she stood by a huge four-poster bed, one hand pressed to her mouth and her body trembling.

I'd somehow made it to the front of the group in the doorway.

Going over to Darcie, I said, "What's the matter?" because the way she was trembling, the look on her face—this wasn't about a spider or a mouse.

Her spine shook against the hand I ran down her back.

When she didn't answer, I followed the line of her gaze. And froze.

"Whoa." Grace's voice, the other woman having come to stand beside me. "What *is* that?"

My voice was thin when I answered. "Bea's doll." I stared at the doll's shiny white porcelain face and glassy blue eyes. She had perfect curls of chocolate brown, silky and not a strand out of place, her cheeks painted with dots of red. Across her nose and those rounded cheeks was a sprinkling of freckles.

Just like Beatrice's freckles.

"Darcie and Bea's parents had a doll made for each of them when Darcie was seven and Bea was six. The dolls were meant to mirror them." A fun little Mini-Me for each girl.

It should've been a cute idea.

Shivering, Grace tugged the panels of her robe tighter around herself. "Why is it creepy?" she murmured. "It shouldn't be creepy. I mean, it's wearing overalls over a floral T-shirt. There are tiny sneakers on its feet. But it's creepy."

I knew exactly what she meant. Back when we'd been teens and Mr. and Mrs. Shepherd alive, we'd all hung out at the Shepherd home, had grown up seeing the doll—and being disturbed by it in ways we couldn't articulate at the time.

Creepy Bea.

I didn't remember which one of us had given the doll that moniker, but it had stuck.

"It's an effect called 'the uncanny valley,'" I murmured, kneeling down beside the bed so I could look more closely at the doll without having to touch it. "Humans don't like artificial things that come within a whisker of looking human. Things that *do* look human at first glance . . . but aren't. It incites a kind of visceral revulsion in us."

The artisan who'd made this doll had been far too gifted. I'd seen photos of Bea when she was the age at which the doll had been created, and it was as if the doll maker had shrunk adorable six-year-old Bea down into doll form.

Darcie's doll, while beautiful, didn't incite the same cold nausea in the gut. It had either been worked on by someone else, or the doll maker had realized their mistake with the first doll and slightly altered her doll so that it didn't look like it was a breath away from coming to life.

"Who did this?" A shrill demand from Darcie. "Which one of you did this?"

I looked over my shoulder at Vansi, who'd kept her distance— not a surprise. Of the entire group, it was my best friend who'd been the least enamored with Creepy Bea. She'd refused to even take Halloween pics with it. "Dolls are creepy in general and *that* one is gonna come to life one day and stab someone," she'd muttered darkly.

Bea had laughed so hard she'd cried.

"Don't look at me." Vansi shivered just as Phoenix appeared behind her. "You know I could never stand that thing. No way would I voluntarily touch it."

"I thought it was your sister's?" Grace asked Darcie, hugging herself. "Did I misunderstand?"

I was the one to answer, Darcie's mouth a flat line and her eyes stark pools. "You didn't. That's definitely Bea's doll." I stared again at the thing, only now noticing that it was no longer in the close-to-pristine condition in which I'd last seen it.

Bea might've allowed photos with the doll, but we'd all known not to mess with it. Not because it was expensive but because it was Bea's most cherished possession from childhood. As a result, it had survived to adulthood all but unscathed.

Now, however . . .

A slight scuff mark on the neck. A tear on the strap of the overalls—or was that fraying? I'd have to get closer to make sure. My vision wasn't good enough at this distance, especially in this light.

"Somebody *had* to do this!" Darcie's scream held a ragged edge. "Bea had that doll with her!"

My eyes widened. "Darcie? Are you saying that you put the doll in the casket with Bea before the cremation?"

"What?" Darcie seemed unable to look away from the doll, but when she finally jerked her head toward me, I sucked in a breath. Her pupils were so huge they'd all but swallowed her irises.

"It was her favorite." Almost a plea. "I know she made fun of it, but it was still one of the things she wanted with—"

One of the things she wanted with her when she left us, I completed silently. Because that was what Beatrice had done. Left us all. Just packed up and taken off without a word. She hadn't told Ash or Darcie, but she had informed their family doctor—a friend and mentor—that she was leaving on purpose.

Oh.

Had to be the same doctor Ash had mentioned, the one whose death had devastated Darcie. Dr. Cox. He'd walked Darcie down the aisle, I remembered belatedly, standing in for her father—who'd been his closest friend. While I hadn't spoken to him at the wedding, I had a vague memory of strength and warmth.

Exactly the kind of man who would've stepped in to help Bea and Darcie in the aftermath of their parents' deaths. He'd also apparently tried to talk Bea out of her plans. When that hadn't worked, he'd contacted Darcie and let her know that her sister was taking off.

Darcie had attempted to call her, find out what was going on, received no reply. And the doctor hadn't known where she'd gone, just that she'd left of her own accord.

We'd been left in limbo, Bea gone without a trace.

Until one day, seven horrible months later, Darcie had received word of her sister's suicide. In a cabin in some remote South Island township. She'd left without a word, too, gone to Beatrice alone.

I knew her next decision had been made in grief, but I'd never forgive her for taking away my chance to say a proper goodbye to my friend. For cremating our cherished Bea so far from home, then scattering her ashes as if she deserved no ceremony, no celebration of a life dazzling and joyous.

"Darcie is broken, Lunes," a hollow-eyed Kaea had said to me at the time. "She'll regret her decision down the road, but right now, she's not all there."

I tried to remind myself of his empathic comment, tried to push away the surge of old resentment and gnawing questions. And failed. Beatrice *had* deserved a proper funeral, deserved to have a service where her friends told funny stories and reminisced about her love of pickles and peanut butter.

She'd deserved bunches of flowers and a montage of photographs on a big screen. She'd had so *many* friends, been in so many photographs. But when the time came to say goodbye to her, Darcie had done it all on her own. Leaving out even a bewildered and heartbroken Ash.

She'd told us *nothing.*

Not even the address of the cabin where Bea had died, so we could go and lay flowers in the bush around it.

I'd never understood who she'd wanted to punish with her actions: Bea for leaving, or us for not stopping her? That was one of the questions I'd intended to shout at her this week, one of the questions I now swallowed down past bile hot and sour.

Reminding myself that she was pregnant, vulnerable, I rose and tried to wrap my arms around her—but she shook me off with a jerking movement, stumbling backward toward the windows. "It had to be one of you." Fat tears rolled down her face as she spoke. "It had to be. How else . . . ?"

"What's going on?" Ash demanded, his question followed by the rumble of Kaea's voice in the background.

Darcie threw herself against his chest.

Jaw tight, he looked over at me.

"Someone put Creepy Bea in your bed." I pointed to the doll. "Darcie thinks it had to be one of us, but I don't know how it could've been. That doll disappeared with Bea." I knew because I'd looked.

Darcie had told us when the authorities finally returned Bea's belongings three months later, said she couldn't bear to look at any of it. Knowing what she'd done with Bea's body, I hadn't trusted her not to destroy the doll in a fit of rage.

So, one day, while she was hanging out in our flat with Ash

and Aaron, I'd snuck into her house using the spare key Bea had given me for emergencies and I'd searched with a clinical attention to detail. I'd even unscrewed the cover off a heating vent to ensure Bea hadn't stashed the doll in the wide tubing beyond.

I hadn't found the doll.

But I had found something else.

9

I lifted my hand to my chest, my finger touching the aquamarine pendant hidden below the fine gray wool of my sweater.

Bea's birthstone.

And her first gift from Ash. She'd had a habit of taking it off when she showered, but otherwise, it was around her neck. It would've made sense if I'd found it in the bathroom—but I hadn't. I'd located it in a lime-green handbag stuffed in the back of Darcie's closet.

Only Bea could've pulled off a handbag of that shade—and she had.

Live a little, Nae-nae. I dare you to choose any color but black, brown, or gray.

She was the only one who'd ever called me Nae-nae, as I'd called her Bee-bee. Silly girlhood nicknames that we'd allowed only each other. Hugging the handbag close in that house empty of the person who'd filled it with life, I'd sobbed, knowing the bag for what it was: part of Bea's property.

Returned to Darcie on Bea's suicide.

It had still contained the faint smell of summer sunshine and peach blossoms. Bea's signature scent. She'd happily worn inexpensive jewelry and carried fun but low-priced handbags, but she'd refused to wear any scent but the luxury one she'd first been given by her mother.

Later, after I'd recovered from my shock and the last lingering notes of her scent were only a memory, I'd searched inside and found her wallet—complete with her driver's license, credit cards, all of it. Also in the handbag had been a crisp white envelope, within it this necklace as well as a couple of pretty dress rings.

I'd taken the necklace.

I'd planned to steal her phone and journal, too. So many hours I'd spent reading while she wrote in the journal beside me. I hadn't wanted her secrets—I'd already known them. No, I'd wanted them out of Darcie's hands.

But I'd never found either.

Perhaps she'd given away or destroyed those items in her suicidal state, but one thing I knew—the necklace should've *never* been in the handbag. Darcie should've at least given Bea that when she died, cremating her with this treasured token of Ash's love.

I'd taken it without any sense of guilt.

I felt none to this day.

It gave me a feral pleasure that Darcie couldn't steal this from Bea.

Ash's eyes went to the bed, his skin paling and a tic in his jaw.

"It's a fucking awful joke. I don't care which one of you the fuck did it. Just get rid of the thing."

Driven by the need to protect it for Bea's sake, I plucked up the doll before anyone else could move, said, "I'll take care of it." I glanced at the others. "We should let Darcie and Ash be alone now."

No one argued, and I pulled the door shut behind us after we were all out.

"What are you going to do with that?" Vansi whispered from a safe distance away. "I love you, babes—enough that I'm willing to walk at least ten meters behind you while you go and throw that cursed object into the river. Or better yet into the fire."

"We are *not* throwing away Bea's doll," Aaron whispered, low and fierce, the muscles of his chest rigid beneath skin the shade of ebony. "She loved that thing."

"I'm with Aaron," I said. "And Creepy Bea never bothered me like it did you, V. I'll hang on to her tonight and we can sort it out tomorrow." I tucked the doll gently against my side. "Darcie will probably want it." Much as it pained me, I couldn't just keep it. "You know how unstable she is in a crisis."

Kaea shoved a hand through his hair. "Yeah. Remember how she used to cry about having nowhere to go to mourn her sister because Bea wasn't buried anywhere."

I'd honestly wanted to slap her during those breakdowns, even as I felt for her. Mother, father, sister, all dead. No wonder Darcie had gone a little mad. I could understand that, even hurt for her, and still hate her for depriving us all of one last glimpse of our Bea.

"But how did the doll get *on* the bed?" Grace said, chewing on her plump lower lip. "Or is there something I'm not understanding? Is Darcie . . . ?" She made a worried face.

"You mean, did Darcie orchestrate the whole thing?" Vansi frowned, while Phoenix looked at Grace with a little too much intensity for a married man. "Look, I'm not blind to her faults—girlfriend's got an ego bigger than Mount Everest—but Bea's death shattered her."

Though I agreed with Vansi, I also couldn't forget what Ash had said about Darcie's belief that Bea was haunting her. Was it possible she'd become unhinged enough to bring out the doll from wherever she'd hidden it, then not remember what she'd done?

"I think," Aaron said, one hand on Grace's shoulder, "right now, we're all too emotional to be rational. We'll talk about it more tomorrow.

"It might be as simple as that Beatrice came down here when she took off, and left the doll behind on purpose," he added. "Could be one of the cleaners found it and thought it would be cute to put on the bed. I mean, if you don't know who the doll looks like, it's just an unusual piece of art."

My shoulders melted, the burning sensation in my gut subsiding. "Of course," I said, relieved that we weren't going to have to deal with a psychotic break. "Darcie didn't say that she put it into the casket. I just assumed. What she said was that Bea had it *with* her."

Kaea was nodding, too. "It makes sense that Bea would've come out here if she wanted to get lost without being lost, if you know what I mean? A place no one could kick her out of, but that she knew really well."

I swallowed hard. "Do you think that's the reason Darcie would never tell us where Bea died? Because it was here?"

No movement, all of us frozen.

"No," Vansi said firmly, her cheekbones pressing hard against her skin. "I am not going to go to sleep in this monstrosity of a castle with that thought in my head. I'm going to go light a fire in our hearth, eat chocolate, bathe, and read a fucking beach novel."

"It's not a castle," Phoenix murmured, his attention no longer on Grace. "But I can pretend to be a dark knight chasing you through the halls if you like."

It had been a long time since I'd heard Nix crack a joke. His words snapped the frigid tension and made Vansi lean into him as they turned to walk back to their room. Aaron and Grace did the same, Aaron's arm around Grace's shoulders.

Poor Grace. She definitely hadn't signed on for this.

Kaea spoke up, stopping the others. "If you want a fire," he said, "the logs are stacked beside the living room fireplace. I'm not schlepping them up for you. According to Ash, the rooms are already kitted out with a full fire-starting set. Just add logs. Oh, and picnic leftovers in the fridge if you're hungry."

"Oooh." Grace rose up on her toes and beamed at Aaron. "We should definitely have a fire. Shall we go grab the logs now?"

At Aaron's nod, the two of them changed direction. "Careful, darling!" Grace clamped a hand around Aaron's forearm when he almost slid on the old Persian-style runner laid out along the wood of the hallway.

"Oops." A kiss pressed to Grace's cheek before the two continued on downstairs.

Vansi and Nix, however, kept on walking toward their room

and from the way they were whispering to each other, there'd be another kind of fire burning in that room soon.

Well, at least Vansi's marriage issues seemed to be working out.

"'Night, Kaea," I said, the thought of Beatrice dying in this cold and dark place stuck in my head like a tiny stone in a shoe.

But he fell into step with me. "I think my room's along here. Nix took my bag to put into my room when I volunteered to help Ash grab more logs from the barn." But when he tried each of the doors in turn, one proved locked, the second a toilet, and the third an empty shell.

"Has to be that one." I pointed out the room opposite Vansi and Phoenix's. "It's the only one left."

Hands on his hips, he frowned. "You don't mind being out here by yourself? You're on the far end of the hall. You can bunk with me if you want."

"You forget—I've heard you snore." We'd shared many a tent during our student days when we'd hired a van and driven out to the bush for a budget vacation. Hiking, swimming in the water holes along the way, cheap beers with equally cheap sausages.

Some of the best memories of my life.

"And I've heard you snuffle," he murmured darkly. "Snuffle snuffle, snort snort, snuffle snuffle, then a weirdo little giggle."

Laughing, I shoved at his chest with one hand. The worst of it was that he was right. I did make odd noises in my sleep. One boyfriend had taped me and played it back. I'd been mortified, but he'd told me I sounded cute and if I'd ever been meant to be in a relationship it would've been with him. But he'd deserved to be loved—and I'd only loved one person that way my entire life.

"Go to bed," I said to Kaea.

"Want me to grab a couple of logs for you?" He frowned.

"Don't tell the others. I'm only doing this because you're all by yourself at the end of a dark and badly lit horror hallway."

I rolled my eyes. "Don't strain your chivalry muscles. I'll probably go down to make myself a cup of tea anyway. I'll grab a couple of small logs then. Enough to warm up the room before I fall asleep."

Kaea gave me a small salute before backing off and heading toward his room.

I waited at the doorway to mine until he looked into his, then gave a thumbs-up to indicate it held his bag. Waving good night, I walked in and shut the door quietly behind myself.

Then I looked at the doll in my hand.

The doll that hadn't been with Bea's belongings.

10

My room had the same lighting as Darcie and Ash's, the entire space drenched in a dirty yellowish cast. Digging my phone out of my pocket, I turned on the flashlight function. Cold white light, crisp and bright. I'd been right about the new wear and tear on the doll. It definitely hadn't looked like this when Bea'd had it on the little shelf in her room.

"I never played rough with her." The memory of Bea's husky tones, the two of us sitting by the window in her room, sneaking a cigarette.

Neither of us had kept up the habit after the first week, but back then we'd wanted to be cool teenagers. I'd have invited Vansi, but I'd known she'd balk. My best friend might've strained against her parents' strict rules, but the only time she'd ever rebelled was when it came to her secret love affair with Nix.

Bea's full lips curved in my mind. "She was too pretty, and I didn't want to mess her up." Her eyes danced, so intense they seemed to see right through to the secret truth inside me. "My mom says that when I was younger I'd hide her anytime we had visitors. I didn't want anyone to damage her."

The doll had been all but spotless at that time. I'd had the chance to take another closer look at it some years later, about a year before Beatrice's disappearance. Still in pristine condition, with not even a coating of dust on her.

That was how I'd always known that even though Bea laughed along with the Creepy Bea jokes, the doll was important to her even in adulthood. Likely because it had been a gift from the parents who'd died in a fiery crash before her eighteenth birthday.

The others must've understood, too, because jokes or not, no one ever picked up the doll or threw it around. Creepy Bea always got a seat of honor on a table or chair in our annual Halloween photos.

Darcie wasn't as attached to her own doll. Last time I'd seen it was when we were around sixteen. If Bea's was pristine, Darcie's had been through the wars. Per Darcie, she'd brushed out her doll's hair, put makeup on its porcelain face, changed its clothes, and otherwise treated the handcrafted object like a department-store Barbie.

Tonight, I was sure that someone had played with Bea's doll after she vanished. Not as roughly as Darcie had played with hers, but it had definitely been handled.

If Bea *had* left it here, perhaps the caretaker or one of the regular cleaners had found it, taken it home for their children to play with. Could be they'd later realized it might be missed and made the decision to return it before Darcie could notice.

Gently patting the doll's hair, I decided to put her on the windowsill—facing away from the bed.

I might not be creeped out by Bea's doll, but that didn't mean I wanted it staring at me all night.

The outside world was charcoal gray, on the final verge before going pitch-black. Hands on the windowsill, I squinted to make out the view directly beyond my window. Blocky shadows, dark against the encroaching night.

Instinct had me leaning closer to the cold glass of the window—then jolting back.

A cemetery. My room looked out onto a cemetery.

Of course the place would have a cemetery. Where else would the Shepherd family be buried except on their own estate?

"It's probably stark and lovely in daylight," I said aloud, and went to pull the curtains closed.

The fabric tore off to lie in a crumpled heap of dusty red at my feet. I coughed, waved a hand in front of my face, then looked at the doll I'd placed on the windowsill.

She stared out at the graveyard.

I should've been disturbed, but all I could see was that she, too, now wore a patina of dust. Immediately picking her up, I blew away the debris with gentle puffs of air.

I couldn't bear not to treat her as Bea had done.

Deciding against the windowsill, I took her to the other end of the room and to the writing table tucked in the corner in front of a long and narrow window. Once again, I placed her so that she was looking away from the bed, but I made sure she wasn't looking outside.

Instead, she faced an oil painting of a bucolic country scene that looked far too placid to be New Zealand. I was no art critic but I'd bet good money the painting had come from England. Either with Clara Shepherd or due to Blake Shepherd's desire to clothe his house in the symbols of old wealth.

Doll taken care of, I returned to the window. The curtain rod was still up, but when I picked up the crumpled mass of curtain fabric, I saw that it had literally frayed away. Broken apart like cobwebs. Just old. Wasn't going to go back up anytime soon. And given the height of the windows, it wasn't like I could throw a towel over the rod, either.

I'd have to risk the dust of the curtains around the bed. Because the idea of sleeping exposed made the hairs rise on the back of my neck. It might be an old graveyard, and the reasonable part of me might know that there was zero chance of ghouls crawling up the walls to stare at me through the window—but I was afraid of the dark.

Logic wasn't my strong suit when ink-black chased the light from the world.

Still, though my mouth was dry and my heart thudded, I forced myself to look back out the window one more time . . . because I couldn't be afraid of the dark. I had to learn to live with it.

I could no longer make out any of the shapes I'd seen earlier. I told myself it was the result of a quick darkfall, the landscape beyond obsidian. But deep within, I knew I should've still been able to see vague outlines of the headstones. My world was slowly fading away. Getting smaller and smaller with every day that passed.

After deciding to grab a couple of small logs from the living room and leave the tea for later, I spent an hour in the bath. Peaceful—

after I'd gotten past the filling stage, which had involved clanking pipes, odd gurgles, and a bonus banging sound to boot.

Pipes in the place liked to make an impression.

As Darcie had promised, it was an old claw-foot thing, the fittings rustic bronze with patches gone a rough antique green. The cleaners had polished them, but no amount of shining would return them to their original glory—but that was part of the charm for me. I'd always been fascinated by aged things, objects and people with history.

"It's because you're adopted," an ex–school friend had opined. "You're obsessed with history because you don't have any."

There was a reason that person was an ex-friend. That didn't mean they hadn't been partially right. Only partially. Because I'd never felt any longing for my birth family, didn't even to this day. I'd thought maybe I was just weird in that, but a little research online and I'd realized that no, there were others like me.

I touched wet fingers to the edge of one eye.

This was the part of my history I wanted to know.

Had other people in my birth family gone blind?

Could I foretell my future journey by examining theirs?

Dr. Mehta, my postdiagnosis counselor, had suggested I trace them to request medical records even if I didn't want to make more personal contact. I couldn't tell her why I hadn't followed her advice, how I woke up sweat-soaked after night terrors in which I knocked on a door and the woman who opened it had my face—and no eyes.

The floorboards creaked.

I jerked, sloshing water over the side, and stared out the bathroom door I hadn't closed. The fire I'd started flicked warm shadows on the walls while the wind whistled beyond the windows. Even the dull yellow light seemed softer, more golden.

Nothing else moved.

Exhaling quietly, I settled back into the water and pretended I was a pampered old maiden lazing away the day. I even summoned up the energy to read a chapter of the paperback I'd brought along for the trip.

I really should've switched to an electronic reader—or even to reading on my phone. It wasn't that the printed text was difficult for me to see—not yet anyway. It was about preparation, about acceptance.

The idea of it made my breath speed up, my skin burn.

Books—heavy, physical books—had been an integral part of my life for so long that of all the small things I'd have to give up in the future, this was the one I'd mourn the most. Nothing Dr. Mehta could say could make me come to peace with the loss of my ability to read as I'd been doing since I was a child sounding out my first words.

My eyes scanned the print, my fingers brushing over the green ink Bea had used to make notes in the margins. I'd been horrified the first time I'd seen her do it, but she'd won me over to her side, made me agree that it was part of getting lost in the text. Becoming so caught up in it that I wanted to engage with it.

We'd begun to trade books—and margin notes. Hers in green, mine in dark purple.

My eyes burned, dry and gritty.

Dr. Mehta had suggested I learn braille, told me that I didn't have to stick to audiobooks if that wasn't my preference. I hadn't even read the brochures she'd handed me, much less booked myself in for a lesson, but every time I was in an elevator or at a pedestrian crossing with the raised dots below the written text, I closed my eyes and brushed my fingers over them.

Trying to see how it would be to read through my fingertips.

I couldn't tell one dot from the next, would soon open my eyes and give up on the small experiment. But one day, it wouldn't matter if I had my eyes open or closed. The world would remain the same formless black. Full only of the ghosts that would float across my vision, echoes of past sight.

I shivered, realizing the water had cooled and my fingertips were wrinkled. Tugging the plug chain with my foot, I allowed the water to gurgle down the drain with noisy enthusiasm as I got out and quickly rubbed myself dry.

Afterward, I pulled on my pajamas. No fancy silky robe like Grace's. The bottoms were a pair of fleece pants—pale blush with red hearts on them. New, for the occasion of this reunion, since I'd figured people were going to see me in them at breakfast. The top was a matching tee. Blush pink with a single red heart in the center.

I'd bought it for the texture, not the cutesy motif.

I'd become increasingly more aware of textures since my diagnosis, conscious that one day in the future, it was touch, weight, smell that would create the shape of my world, not colors and patterns. Dr. Mehta had told me that there were all kinds of assistive technologies now, including programs that would read out descriptions of items of clothing to me.

I didn't have to fear ending up dressed in a chaotic mishmash.

But the doctor had also been harsh with my initial refusal to consider any changes in my existence. "You won't be able to move forward until you accept that your life has changed on the most fundamental level."

I'd frustrated her. I knew that. I'd acted the child, placing invisible hands over my ears and refusing to listen. Still, she'd tried. "Instead of trying to force your old life into a shape it no longer fits, you can choose to create a life that suits who you are now, today."

The problem was that the Luna I was today was the same Luna I'd been yesterday and the same Luna I'd be tomorrow. The only thing that was going to change was my vision.

And I had *no choice* in that change.

Grabbing my favorite slouchy gray cardigan out of my bag, I shrugged it on, then pulled on thick woolen socks. The fire had warmed up the room, but I knew it would be freezing outside these four walls. I'd forgotten slippers, but the house was clean so I just padded out in my socks. I could see light from under the doors of all the rooms, but couldn't hear anything aside from the odd clank or gurgle as the others showered or otherwise used the plumbing.

The lack of any voices, the silence beneath the creaks and groans, made me feel a great deal of sympathy for the woman who'd been lured out here with the promise of a life as the social-ite wife of a wealthy gentleman—only to find herself trapped in what would've then been one of the most remote places on earth. Far from all polite company.

I made sure to skirt the slippery floor runner as I headed for the stairs.

Once downstairs, I poked my head into the living room to check if anyone else was down there, but it proved cold and life-less. Ash must not have started the fire after all.

The only light came from a single anemic wall lamp.

The stag heads glared at me.

My peripheral vision stirred with shadows, but at least I could see. Shaking off the chill of those cold dead eyes, I retreated back into the hallway, then followed it to the kitchen. Once at the archway that led into the large space, I reached in and moved my hand around, looking for the light switch.

A touch, papery and alive, on the back of my hand.

11

The only reason I didn't scream down the house was shock.

My fingers moved automatically to flick on the switch . . . scaring away the large moth that had landed on my hand.

Laughing at myself, I pressed a palm to my racing heart.

Get a grip, Nae-nae.

God, Bea would've cackled at my jumpiness.

I grinned as I looked for an electric kettle—but all I could find was a heavy old iron kettle that looked like it might whistle. Not wanting to make too much noise, I found a pot instead, filled it at the sink—deep, with softly squared edges and patches of rust in the corners—then placed it on the gas hob.

It took three tries before I managed to get it going, but then came sweet blue flame.

Inspired by the chill in the air, I went and found the milk in the old but sturdy fridge.

Vansi had taught me how to make chai back when we were in

high school, but I was usually too lazy to put in the effort. Now, however, with my mind far from relaxed, I had nothing but time. After adding the milk to the water, at the ratio that I preferred, I put away the container, then began to open and quietly close cupboard doors on the hunt for loose-leaf black tea.

I didn't have to hunt far. Whoever had stocked the kitchen had put most of the tea and coffee supplies in an easily accessible spot near the hob. No loose-leaf tea, but I spotted a box of strong black tea bags. That would do. Once the water and milk mixture came to a boil, I threw in the tea bags, then monitored the flame until I had it at a temperature where the mixture would simmer but not boil over.

I'd already grabbed a jar of honey from the hot drinks cupboard and set it beside the hob, alongside a mug. No hope of cardamom pods or chai masala, but it'd be nice plain, too. While waiting for my drink, I decided to snoop through the other cupboards, see what else we had. Maybe I could talk Aaron into making his fantastic green chili—*if* we had the ingredients.

When most of the cupboards proved empty, I went to the door opposite the hob that I'd previously assumed led to a cellar, and pulled it open. The light from the kitchen spilled inside to reveal neat rows of wooden shelving, on which sat equally neat rows of cans and jars full of nonperishable supplies. Included in that were bags of potato chips and boxes of cookies.

Painted directly on the back wall was a faded image of a plump woman kneading bread.

Faded though the paint might be, the brush lines were precise, nothing soft or fuzzy about the artist's style despite the placid domestic scene. The baker's hair had been painted strand by fine strand, and the flour on the board and around her hands was a fine spray that appeared in motion.

A hidden treasure.

The servants would see this, but never the master and mistress of the house. The baker's clothing looked like late nineteenth century to me, and I knew enough about how old houses like this had worked at the time to guess that the baker's employers were highly unlikely to even step into the kitchen, much less examine the pantry.

Who had painted this? A servant?

I'd come back in the morning light, I decided, take photographs of the piece. The only light in the pantry was a naked bulb that, when I turned it on, cast a lackluster glow at best. What was with this house and the bad lighting? Cost cutting, if I had to guess. No point in having it high-spec when it was rarely used.

Closing the pantry door for now, I wandered over to grab the recipe book Ash had showed Aaron.

Two minutes later, the chai was done and I'd hitched myself up on a stool by the counter, ready to leaf through the recipes. On the flyleaf in a beautiful script were the words: *To my dear daughter, Clara, on the occasion of your marriage. For you to fill with your and your family's favorite recipes. May your table be ever bountiful and your hearth never cold. With all my love. Mama.*

I lived as distant from my own mother as Clara had gone from hers, but it wasn't the same. Clara had been marooned in place after she arrived, with no hope of a quick trip over the oceans to see her family, and nothing but letters eagerly awaited to receive word from home.

I turned the page to the first recipe . . . and rubbed a fist over my aching heart: *Mama's Winter Stew.*

The handwriting was different from that in the flyleaf. Clara had written this; a cherished memory of her past life even as she began her new one.

What must it have been like to live in this alpine wilderness in the time of Blake Shepherd? If Clara had come from a well-off family, she would've been used to house parties and church gatherings at the least. Perhaps even dances or other larger engagements.

My knowledge of that part of English history came via the romances I read, and per them, even those in isolated country estates had enjoyed an active social circle. People had held elaborate dinners and hosted their friends for days or weeks at a time.

Even if none of that was correct, she'd had a full life with her family. Because below the title of the recipe was the note: *Beloved of my six younger sisters and I.*

It must've been a home bright with conversation and energy.

And then to come to this?

I looked around the kitchen again, so huge and hollow and cold. I wondered if she'd ever tried to set up one of her sisters with someone in the region—perhaps even one of her husband's wealthy associates? I wouldn't blame her if she had. At least then, she'd have had one person in the country who'd visit with her—and whom *she* could visit, leaving this remote heap behind.

The recipes were written in a lovely script, the kind that looks like water flowing across the page. No flourishes. Smooth and flawless, music without notes. I couldn't imagine how she'd done this at a time when she would've been writing with ink and a fountain pen. Not only that, but the recipes were illustrated—and Clara had been no journeyman artist.

I ran my finger over the stark beauty of the first line drawing.

She hadn't tried to illustrate the dishes themselves, but rather one or two of the ingredients in each. This was a delicately rendered sketch of a head of cauliflower. A partially sliced onion illustrated the bottom right corner of the next page.

The sharp precision of the lines, the attention to minute detail . . . I glanced at the closed pantry door, thought of the spray of flour in the air.

Clara had painted the baker. In a place her husband would never see.

The realization made my skin chill.

After taking a big sip of my chai, I turned back to the warmth and skill evidenced in the pages of the recipe book, immersed at this glimpse into the life of a young woman who'd had to become mistress of a grand house while barely out of childhood herself.

I didn't know what made me stop, frown at the large image that took up half of one page. It was of a groaning harvest table, not unlike an earlier spread which had featured spring greens bursting out of a large wicker basket.

Detailed work, but there was something . . .

Leaning closer, I stared, even as my vision flickered at the corners. I should've stopped, rested. But I couldn't let go, not now.

I dug my cell phone out of the pocket of my pajama pants. I always had it with me, a habit formed after I first realized the photographs I could take with it. Phone cameras these days could do far more than most people realized, and for a photographer who had to pick up day jobs to pay her rent, it was a boon to have a device that allowed me to indulge my passion in stolen moments.

Postdiagnosis, the phone also served as a security blanket

because it came with voice assistance. I'd used it prior to the day my life changed forever, so that was the one accessibility feature I didn't have any trouble utilizing. It gave me comfort to know I could call someone if I suddenly lost my sight in the middle of the day far from home.

The latter was a ridiculous fear. My vision loss would be a gradual thing, a slow erosion of the world of light and color. But fears were hardly rational things to begin with, and this one haunted me.

The world vanishing at the flick of an internal switch.

Mouth dry, I activated the trusty flashlight function and trained it on the page. I was sure now of what I was seeing, but I still couldn't quite make it out, my vision too damaged. Thinking fast, I switched to camera mode and took multiple pictures of the drawing from every angle, both as a whole and in pieces.

Then I used my fingertips to zoom into one of the pictures.

. . . cold and lonely and silent.

I hadn't imagined it. There were words hidden in the image. Words written in such a fine, *fine* script that it seemed impossible.

Heart thumping, I began to flick backward through the book, searching for more text. They weren't there at the start, I realized, only began to pop up about a third of the way through.

I began to shoot.

My neck hurt and my shoulders were stiff, my chai ice-cold, by the time I reached the end of Clara's concealed testimony— and my battery warned me it was at five percent.

Closing the book, I put it back where I'd found it. I wasn't sure I wanted to share my discovery with the others. It felt like a secret between me and the woman who'd arrived into this house as a new bride beyond unprepared for the life she was now expected to live.

Aaron was probably the only one who might look close enough to notice—but he was more interested in the recipes than in the sketches, so chances were high he wouldn't figure it out anytime soon.

Throwing away the rest of my forgotten chai, I did the dishes and left them draining on the rack. No dishwasher out here. I wondered what Vansi would make of that—if there was one chore my best friend would do anything to avoid, it was the dishes.

Everything tidy, I turned off the kitchen light only after I was in the doorway with the hallway light aglow in front of me. Darkness fell in the kitchen . . . just as the hallway light flickered and went out. The small lamp in the distance that illuminated the staircase followed a split second later.

I froze, a lump in my throat and my heart a thudding roar in my ears.

Spots of color floated in front of my eyes . . . and then there was nothing. Just black. My eyes would never adjust to the dark, never begin to pick up shapes. I'd lost that ability. Biting back a whimper, I stretched out my left hand and pressed it hard against the wall. I used that as an anchor as I tried to remember the layout of the hallway and how many steps I had to take to get to the stairs.

I had my phone, but it was almost out of charge. I'd need the light more on the stairs than I did now. *Breathe, Luna,* I told myself, but I couldn't stop the shallow, fast rhythm of my gasps. My eyes burned dry as the desert and as arid, my fingernails clawing into the wall.

The black air suffocated, wrapping itself around my throat, tangling in my hair.

"It's not real," I whispered and it was mostly air. "It's not real."

My parents had bought me pretty night-lights when I first moved into our university flat. A sweet gift for the daughter who'd never quite grown out of her childhood fear of the dark. Most of the time, however, I forgot about it. It was easy to do so in a city apartment with streetlights outside and constant activity on the roads.

But there was no light here. *None.*

A small buzz and then the light fixtures spluttered back into life.

Throat cracked and without moisture even as sweat trickled down my spine, I stared at the hallway lamp for a second before jolting into motion, racing up the stairs and almost falling to my knees when I slid on that damn floor runner. Catching myself barely in time, I powered on until I was behind the door to my room.

Safe, I was safe now in this contained space where the worst I could do was stub my toe.

Digging out my charging cable, I plugged it in and hoped the generator-run system wouldn't decide now was a good time to pack it in. I might devolve into a full-on panic attack if I lost my lifeline to a world that I could no longer trust to remain in vivid, sharp color. I might open my eyes tomorrow morning to another dark spot, another cluster of crystals eclipsing my vision.

But there were no surprises in the time it took me to stop shaking and gasping and get into bed—*after* I risked death by dust and undid the curtains around my bed. Only once I was under the duvet did I realize that I'd made it so I couldn't see anyone sneaking up on me until after they pulled back the curtains.

But my eyelids were already too heavy, my body coming down off the adrenaline high, all thoughts of Clara's hidden messages forgotten. And even though my heart kicked as it always did these days when I slipped into the dark, I was too tired to resist.

I fell.

12

I woke to a spray of grayish light.

Blinking, I stared at the bed-curtains, frowned . . . then began to giggle. The things were so freaking moth-bitten that they let in the sunlight in a shower of mottled stars.

It was weirdly pretty.

Grabbing my phone from beside my head, where it had been charging overnight—because no, I didn't care about anything blowing up while I was sleeping—I checked the time.

Eight a.m.

Wow, I'd had a solid night's sleep.

Yawning and feeling foolish for my fear in the night hours, I pushed the curtains aside and bit back a yelp. My room was an icebox, the windows frosted over and the air so cold that it turned my breath into chill smoke. "Ugh."

I quickly found the fluffy socks I'd kicked off at some point in the night, as well as a thick cable-knit sweater I'd had forever. A dark navy, it hung to my thighs and, together with my pajamas and socks, allowed me to retain a good percentage of my body heat.

My face, however, burned with cold.

Walking to the window, I managed to find a patch that wasn't frosted over, looked out.

"Holy shit!" Cold forgotten, I raced to grab my cameras, thrust a knit woolen hat onto my head, and shoved my feet into the boots I'd brought along after I researched this location. I surely looked like an idiot, but I didn't care.

Opening my door, I glanced up and down the hallway but didn't hear or see any sign of life. So I tiptoed—as well as I could in my clunky boots—down to the staircase, not going any faster until I was over halfway.

My nose twitched at the smell of coffee as I reached the kitchen, and the warmth told me that the woodstove was likely going, but the awareness was vague at best, my attention on getting outside. The kitchen door stuck for a second and I growled under my breath, pulled again.

This time, it came away from the jamb so fast it almost smacked me in the face.

Ducking around it, I stepped out and into a wonderland.

Frost coated every single blade of golden grass, every tiny dandelion flower, every leaf on every bush. The tree with the weird octopus branches I'd noticed yesterday was today a delicate sculpture.

I couldn't shoot fast enough—especially when the morning sun's pale rays hit the frost and lit it on fire. The beauty of it hurt. Frost so delicate and ephemeral, it was like out of a haunted old tale.

My knee was soggy from kneeling on the ground, my sweater covered in frost from brushing against it, and my nose running from the cold when I finally came to a stop and just stood there watching the sun burn a line of fire over the frost.

A creak of the wooden boards of the veranda. "I brought you coffee."

I startled, not at the voice, but at whose it was—I'd have expected Kaea, Vansi, almost anyone but Phoenix. "Oh, hey, thanks." Cupping my hands around it, I winced. The heat burned my frozen fingers, but I didn't let go, the steam a benediction against my face. "I didn't see you when I came through."

"I must've been in the lounge. Got the fire going. Ash mentioned it'll warm up as the day goes on, but I figured we could eat breakfast in the lounge. Woodstove in the kitchen is nice, but living room fire's bigger and we can sit around it."

"Good idea." I sipped on the coffee, surprised he hadn't already left to return to the house. The two of us had never been buddies, our friendship via Vansi. "Where's V?"

"Asleep." His profile was perfect in the morning light, the steam from his own mug rising to brush his skin, but where I would've thought nothing of taking Kaea's photo in the same situation, it was different with Nix.

"I couldn't sleep," he added. "Strange place, strange sounds, you know what it's like."

I nodded, though I'd slept like the dead. Probably my system crashing after the panic. "I thought my face was going to freeze off this morning when I got out of bed. I didn't realize it'd be *this* cold here."

His lips curved. "I restarted the fire before I left the bedroom. You know how Vansi is about the cold." No hint of any marital disharmony in his tone, so perhaps the two of them had made up last night. "Luna, I know your memory for faces is better than the rest of us. Can I ask you something?"

"Sure."

"Is it possible we went to uni with Grace? It's just that I feel like I've seen her before."

Relieved at the innocent explanation for how he'd stared at the other woman last night, I shook my head. "No, remember? Aaron mentioned she went to boarding school in Switzerland and stayed in Europe for her tertiary studies. I'm pretty sure he said she speaks French and Italian alongside English."

He winced. "To be honest, I can't keep up with the chat when I'm working."

"I get that." He probably craved sleep more than scrolling through the group's messages. "Hey," I joked, "maybe you ran into her during your backpacking adventure with V. You went through Zurich, right?"

"I'm pretty sure the closest Grace has been to a hostel has been seeing one outside the limo window," was the dry response. "V and I were on the bones of our arse during that trip. Survived on ramen, cheap bread, and bad chocolate." But he was smiling as he said that.

Thinking back to their shiny, happy faces after they returned, I smiled with him. "Is it possible you saw Grace at the hospital? Patient or visiting a patient?"

"Yeah, that's probably it," he said, then shrugged. "I'm looking forward to the day I become a specialist and stop having so many patients that they all blur together." He leaned one shoulder against the wooden support beam on one side of the veranda steps, his gaze on the view. "Worth the spinal adjustment on that gravel bit of the road."

"Absolutely." I watched the line of sunshine in silence. Soon, the frost would be gone, my photographs all that remained of this sublime and fragile teardrop of time.

The sound of the kitchen door opening.

"What're you two doing out here?" Arms hugging her own body, Darcie walked down the steps. "Oh, the frost." Dressed in pajama pants and a pink puffer jacket, her hair in a loose knot, she knelt down to touch her fingers to a lattice of frost on a patch of ground cover. "I'd forgotten how stunning it is on days like this."

She looked up, the bruises under her eyes almost purple against the pale hue of her skin. "You're lucky. Takes perfect conditions for this to happen." A tone soft with memory. "Bea and I used to sneak out of bed and crunch our way through the grass, but we found treasures, too. Once, Bea found a dandelion perfectly preserved in frost."

My entire soul keened in memory, but I fought not to push us back into the past. Darcie had obviously had a tough night. She didn't need me screaming at her about a decision she'd made in the maw of grief.

The aquamarine burned against my chest, a searing indictment of my choice to stay silent, as we'd all stayed silent for near to a decade.

"I took a thousand photos, I'm sure," I told her. "I don't know how I'll ever choose my favorites. It's days like this that make me realize just how much I love photography." Even if the knowledge twisted the knife deeper, made it even harder to face the future.

"I'll go start making breakfast."

Phoenix was gone before I could process the curt interjection. "Maybe he's not a morning person." Though he'd seemed perfectly happy to keep me company prior to Darcie's arrival.

"No, he likes mornings," she said in a tone that was too sure, before she seemed to shake herself out of it and rose to her full height. "Sorry for my freak-out last night."

"No, I got it. Me and the others, we were thinking maybe Bea came down here after she disappeared?" I didn't take my eyes off her. "Left her doll behind and could be a cleaner found it and put it there for you."

Darcie's face was an oil painting in the morning light, lovely and without movement. "Yes, that must be it." Flat words. "She probably thought I'd find it after, but I never came back down here. Not for years—and even after that, it was just day visits to make sure Jim was doing his job. It's only recently we've spent more time here."

Shivering, she rubbed her hands over her upper arms, over the soft bulge of her jacket. "God, I'd forgotten how cold it could get even in spring. I'll see you inside."

I stayed outside for ten more minutes after she left, not wanting to be stuck in the kitchen with her and Phoenix. Secrets, or just morning moodiness?

"People are weird," I said, my breath a plume of white. "Don't worry about them. You have your own issues."

I watched my breath, focused so hard on creating the memory that I didn't realize I was gritting my teeth until my jaw began to hurt.

Breathe, Nae-nae. You're such a serious little bug.

I inhaled and exhaled on the echo of Bea's advice, on the memory of her fierce hugs and even fiercer love. She'd seen me in ways no one had, not even Vansi. Right through to the core.

"I miss you." The loss of her was no longer an open sore, but it had never healed right, either.

She seemed to dance in the grass in the distance, not as I'd last seen her, but as the girl who'd played through this landscape with her sister. Wild and beautiful and as fragile as the frost.

I wanted to see more of her world.

Putting my empty mug on the veranda railing, I decided to explore the family cemetery that was no longer any kind of nightmare. It had featured in many of my frost-laden shots this morning.

Now, I walked through it in respectful silence.

Though it was tidy and clearly regularly maintained, the majority of the headstones were old and weathered. Only two remained shiny and black, bearing no moss or other signs of time. I knew whose they were before I knelt down to read the inscriptions.

I'd attended their funeral service in Auckland, watched the two somber black hearses depart for the airport.

Katherine Jenkins Shepherd,
beloved wife of Martin,
and adored mother of Darceline and Beatrice.
She sleeps with the angels now.

The next was for Martin Blake Shepherd and included the words "beloved husband of Katherine, and cherished father of Darcie and Bea." I gave a small laugh, surprised by the joy in this melancholy place. Mrs. Shepherd had hated that all her daughters' friends almost always used their nicknames, had insisted on calling Darcie and Bea by their full names, while Mr. Shepherd had been in favor of the nicknames.

No real tension to it, just the loving bickering of a longtime couple.

Kneeling down, I brushed off a couple of leaves that had fallen on the glossy black veined with gold, and looked instinctively to the right and then the left. But of course there was no Bea. She *should've* been here with her parents. All her ancestors were here. All her family was here.

My stomach tightened, my chest a hard knot. I told myself that Bea was here nonetheless, her spirit in every blade of grass, her laughter imprinted in the walls of the house, but God, I was so angry. If Darcie had buried her here, I could've talked to her, could've sat with her.

A prickling on the back of my neck.

I looked around, then up to the house—toward my room. Nothing. But movement flashed when I turned my attention to the other half of the hallway. A person shifting away from a window.

Frowning, I tried to work out who was in that room. Yes, of course, it was Ash and Darcie. Maybe Darcie had gone up there to get rid of her jacket now that it was warming up.

Talking of how much time had passed . . .

I wiggled my toes. Yep, they were on the road to going numb.

Consciously deciding to leave my anger in the graveyard where it wouldn't wreck the week or destabilize an already vulnerable woman, I wandered back. Because it didn't matter how much I screamed at Darcie; Bea was still dead. And Bea was the true target of my rage.

How could she have just *left* us? Just vanished without a trace? How could she have left me?

13

When I stepped into the kitchen after taking off my wet boots and leaving them on the veranda, I found it bustling. Phoenix was making eggs, while Darcie put on a fresh pot of coffee and Ash sliced what looked to be a fresh-baked loaf of bread.

"Where did that come from?" I asked, putting my mug aside as I took a deep breath of the yeasty air.

"Parbaked," Darcie said, her smile bright now. "We stocked up enough for the entire time we're here. Frozen. Just chuck the loaves in the oven for, like, fifteen minutes and yum."

My vision trembled, the brilliant life of this scene after the gray melancholy of the graveyard disconcerting. "I'll be back to stuff my face after I get out of my wet clothes," I managed to say. The frost had turned into water, damp seeping into my bones at my knees and on my face.

"Scrambled, right?" Phoenix asked. "With smoked paprika."

I stared at him. "How do you even remember that?"

He rolled his eyes. "Did you really think Vansi was a domestic goddess all those nights you spent over at ours? I was her secret kitchen slave."

Startled into a laugh, I left him to the eggs and headed up to change. I'd forgotten how often I had actually spent time with Nix over the years. Our quiet friendship, I realized, had become submerged under the deeper weight of my bond with Vansi—and my potent connection with Bea.

It was only after I'd pulled off my T-shirt that I realized that it couldn't have been Ash or Darcie at the window. Not given the timing. They'd both clearly been in the kitchen a while—I'd seen Darcie's pink jacket hanging off the back of a chair, and Ash had showed no signs of having raced down the stairs to take up position at the breadboard.

And yet I was certain I'd seen someone in their room.

My spatial sense might not be the best, but it wasn't hard to count windows.

I was still frowning when I came out of my room dressed in jeans, fluffy socks, and a fine cashmere sweater in black, my body warm again after a hot shower. Most of the doors were open now, and Grace emerged with Aaron around the same time as me.

The tight black curls of Aaron's hair glimmered with beads of water.

Grace waved, her smile pure bubbly energy. "Is everyone already up?" she asked, tugging the sleeves of her creamy yellow sweater over her hands.

"I think so." Vansi's door was also open, so she'd probably gone downstairs while I was in the shower.

"How's Creepy Bea?"

Aaron's question made me realize I hadn't even looked at the doll that morning. "Living her best doll life," I said, making him laugh.

The other two preceded me down the stairs.

I hesitated, said, "Give me a sec. I forgot my phone."

They waved and carried on, and I waited until they were out of sight before I went to Ash and Darcie's room. Poking my head inside, I looked around, searching for signs of disturbance.

A shimmer in my peripheral vision.

I jerked . . . and saw that their window was slightly open. Probably to air out the room.

That explained what I'd seen. A freaking curtain twitching in the breeze.

And since Aaron had reminded me about the doll, I decided to check in on her, too. I didn't know what I was imagining— that she really had gone walking about in the night? But Bea's doll sat where I'd put her, every hair in place and those frayed bits on her clothing silent evidence of an unknown child's play.

I wanted to tell myself that Bea would've been happy that the doll had been played with, but as warm and generous as Bea had been, she'd also had a possessive streak. But only for certain people and things.

Which was why I would've expected her to have this doll with her when she decided to take her own life. It had always been a comfort object for her. And yet she'd left it behind. For Darcie?

Still chewing over that fact, I decided to put the doll out of open view. Just in case Darcie came to visit me in my room. She might be ready to look at the doll one day, but that day definitely wasn't going to be today.

And my complicated feelings for her aside, I had no desire to torture her with memories of her younger sister. The easiest place to put the doll was inside the large closet—I hadn't properly unpacked the night before, so there was plenty of space. Even if I had unpacked, there still would've been plenty of space.

Placing the doll on the back of a shelf, I gently petted one shoulder. "Don't worry, I don't intend to leave you in here forever."

My stomach rumbled as I shut the door, and I'd suddenly had enough of twitching curtains, haunting graveyards, and creepy dolls. After making sure I had my phone on me, I grabbed my everyday camera.

I'd trained my friends to rely on me to document our gatherings, and it was a task I loved. As I skirted the slippery floor runner, I wondered if I should just roll it up out of the way. It was a menace this close to the staircase.

The thought decided me, and I put it into action then and there, leaving the rolled-up rug neatly against the wall. Then I ran down the stairs. When I heard voices in the living room, I snuck my head in to see Kaea crouched by the fire, feeding it another log, while Vansi stood next to him, whispering fast and low.

Her face was scrunched up small and tight, her eyebrows drawn together.

I wondered what that was about as I continued on down the hallway to the kitchen. V and Kaea got along most of the time, but if she was still having problems with Phoenix, then she was probably irritated at the world in general, and Kaea just happened to be in the line of fire.

Whatever it was, it would blow over quick enough. Kaea didn't know how to hold a grudge—and it was difficult to hold a grudge against someone like him, someone so bighearted and open. Oh, he had his faults, but when it came down to it, he was a good guy.

I took my first photograph from the main doorway of the kitchen. "Straight out of a *Country Living* magazine."

Phoenix waved a spatula at me. He now wore an apron of heavy brown fabric. Ash, meanwhile, was squeezing orange juice out of what looked like fresh oranges, while Grace had just walked inside with a bouquet of frost-damp wildflowers in her hands, and Aaron was already pulling trays of toast out of the old-fashioned oven grill.

"Maybe I can use that shot in my cookbook one day," Aaron joked. "I'll just pretend you're all my nonexistent kitchen staff."

"I demand royalties for the use of my image," Phoenix joked. "At least one batch of homemade pancakes per week."

He was in fine form again.

"Darcie went to collect more oranges," Ash said just as I was about to ask about the missing member of the group. "There's a big old tree around the side of the house. Heaps of fruit on the branches. We figured why not use them."

Even though my stomach was in full hunger mode, I couldn't give up the chance to photograph what might be an heirloom orange tree groaning with fruit against the gold of the grass and the stone of the estate, possibly the mountains in the distance. I hadn't even known oranges would grow in this kind of climate. I would've thought it much too cold.

Filching a piece of toast that Aaron had just buttered, I ran out the door while he was pretending to protest. My boots were right there; I shoved the toast in between my teeth so I could use both hands to pull them on. Only when I was halfway down the steps did I realize I had no idea *which* "side of the house" Ash had meant. I was turning on my heel to go ask when he called out, "Burned wing!"

This, I thought after a yelled-out "Thank you," was what I'd missed terribly while living so far from home. Friends who knew me inside out. And who didn't care about my quirks. No, that wasn't the way to put it. They cared but in the right way. Rather than being annoyed by my desire to capture the world in images, they enabled it.

It took a lot of effort not to be distracted by the silent dark flames on the walls of the burned wing, but I wanted to get photographs of Darcie gathering the oranges, so I forced myself to carry on. The rest of the week awaited for me to return to the ruins, lose myself to the silent story told by the shattered windows and gaping holes.

I'd finished off the toast and was puffing by the time I ran around the corner—I'd stopped my daily runs after my diagnosis and was definitely paying the price for it now. Dr. Mehta was right—I had to learn to deal or my life would go down the toilet. Because if I couldn't move fast, I couldn't shoot the world as I wanted to shoot it.

As I cleared the corner, my foot caught on something and I went flying.

"Fuck!" I scrambled to save my camera from smashing onto the cold ground, barely managing to hold my feet. Meanwhile, I could imagine my mother's face as she shook her head. Mum could be raucous, but she hated swearing and always had.

Once I was stable again, I turned to check what I'd tripped on. It proved to be a stack of bricks held together by mortar. The top ones were badly cracked and broken.

"Luna!"

Jerking up my head, I saw Darcie waving at me from around

the side of the curving wall that I'd spotted when we'd arrived, the pink of her jacket a bolt of color against the gold and black.

I jogged over to join her. "Almost tripped on a pile of bricks."

"Oh, I forgot about that. There was a small gatehouse there. Old Blake Shepherd apparently had plans to fence off his land at one point."

"From what?"

Darcie shrugged. "Who knows. Anyway, he ended up having the gatehouse pulled down after Clara died."

I sucked in a sharp breath. "She died first? But she was so much younger than him."

Darcie's eyes went to the ruined wing in a silent answer.

"The fire?" I whispered.

She nodded, a tight smile on her face. "I'll tell you about it another time. Just don't have the bandwidth today."

Though the hunger to know more about Clara gnawed at me, I knew Darcie well enough to understand pushing would achieve nothing. The eldest Shepherd sister was good at appearing flexible, but she only ever did what she wanted.

Watch out, Nae-nae. My sister will talk you into her plan to undertake a bank heist and have you believing that you were the one that came up with the idea in the first place.

Bea's long-ago advice whispered in my head as I followed Darcie around the wall. And stopped. Stared. "I don't believe it."

It was an orchard.

A central orange tree groaning with fruit, other trees just bursting into leaf, while tiny blooms of pink and white covered myriad branches. "How can all this stuff be growing down here?" I asked. "It's too cold for at least some of the trees, right?"

"No idea really." Darcie snagged an orange and put it in her basket. "Our guess is that they were protected by the walls as they grew and became acclimatized to the conditions. They're basically wild now, as the most Jim does in terms of care is dispose of the fallen fruit, but we have found a couple of records that suggest there was glass over the top at some point. Timing says it was put in place after Blake's marriage."

"A giant orangery or greenhouse for his bride?"

"Romantic, right?" Darcie flattened her lips. "I'm sure it made up for dragging her to the back of beyond."

My mind flashed to the cookbook. I wondered if Clara Shepherd had written anything about this garden.

"Anyway"—Darcie plucked another orange off the branch— "the trees have been here forever. The oranges are okay, but the cherries are spectacular, so juicy and sweet. I ask Jim to pick me a huge box once or twice during the season and ship it up to Auckland."

I'd been taking photographs as we spoke, and now Darcie laughed and put out a palm as if to block me. "If I'd known you'd catch me out here, I would've put on a nice dress." She dropped her hand, the blue of her eyes sparkling. "Instead, you're going to have photographs of me with a grandmotherly knot in my hair and pajamas over which I've put on a puffer jacket. Oh, and let's not forget my gumboots. Classy."

"The gumboots are the perfect touch," I argued. "I'll do more photos later if you want. Perfect for your social media." Darcie's profile, unsurprisingly, was one of those soft-focus, picture-perfect-life kinds of accounts. She was an influencer in lifestyle circles, had over a hundred thousand followers last I'd looked.

Not huge, but not tiny, either.

She also had an interesting circle of people she followed and promoted. Once, while I'd been bored and up far too late at night, I'd gone poking around and discovered that many of the accounts Darcie followed were far smaller than her own. Generous of her, I'd thought. Until I dug a little deeper and discovered that most of those accounts were linked to others far more powerful—whether by blood or by bonds of friendship.

Darcie making connections through the weakest link.

Clever, I supposed. And it seemed to be working for her.

As for her style, as a photographer for hire, I knew to give the client what they wanted, so that I'd get paid and get recommended for other jobs. My art was a thing quite apart from the bread-and-butter work I did to pay the bills.

Darcie's point of difference was that, as an engineer, she wore hard hats as often as she did her favorite floaty dresses, and—alongside the home and hearth–type images—she tended to take images of the structures with which she was involved in her work. Same with Ash; he was a familiar presence on her account, all square jaw and perfect suits except when he was on a site.

Time was, Ash had lived in jeans and rugby shirts.

"These are just for us," I added. "A true representation of a reunion where we all regress to our young adult years." Warmth spilled through my veins. "Do you remember going to the supermarket in our onesies at six in the morning to get pancake mix?"

Darcie's smile faded, her eyes hooded. "That wasn't me."

I went to part my lips to argue, right as I remembered that Darcie had never worn a onesie. She'd refused to get one when me, Bea, and Vansi had made the drunken decision to order them.

A unicorn, a mouse, and a tiger.

Instead of apologizing for inadvertently bringing up Bea, I chose to grab the opportunity. Even if I'd decided against raging at Darcie, I was tired of not talking about the girl who'd been such a huge part of all our lives. And surely it wouldn't hurt her for us to talk about her sister? After all, wasn't our silence part of the problem?

"I miss Bea." Lowering my camera, I met Darcie's gaze. "Can you imagine the fun she would've had this morning, racing around trying to organize us into an early morning adventure?"

Darcie's features moved in a way that was unnatural, too tight, too jagged. Fighting themselves. "It was mania, you know." Words twisted with pain. "How she used to get. She made me promise never to tell you. But she's gone, and what use is it?"

Her lower lip quivered. "She'd have manic phases and then she'd come down off them into flat depression. Never bad enough that you'd notice it as anything other than Bea being in one of her quiet moods, but she'd been on medication since she was twelve."

14

I stared at Darcie, her words simply not fitting into an understandable pattern inside my head. "What are you talking about?"

In response, she threw an orange hard against the trunk of another large tree, sending a shower of white blossoms floating to the earth. Then she collapsed into a sitting position on the ground, her hands pressed to her face.

Her shoulders shook violently, her sobs raw.

"Hey." Snapping out of my frozen state, I came down to cradle her against my body with one arm. Because even if I would always be angry with her for what she'd chosen to do with Bea's remains, Darcie was my friend, too. She had, in fact, been my friend first, before I ever met Bea. Seeing her in such pain . . . "Hey, Darcie. I'm here."

She didn't cry for long. It was like one of those thunderstorms that come in a roar, drench the landscape in water, then vanish without a trace. Wiping her face in the aftermath, Darcie began to breathe deep and even. "I don't want anyone else to know that I've been crying."

"Sure, I get that." I picked an orange off a low-hanging branch. "These are nice and cold. If you close your eyes, then put oranges on them, it'll probably make sure they don't puff up."

Darcie took the orange from me, paused for a second, then began to laugh. It held a slight edge of hysteria. "Can you imagine one of the others coming here and seeing me sitting holding two oranges to my eyes?"

I decided to help her pretend everything was all right, that she hadn't just cried hard enough that her throat was rough with it. "Hey, I was trying to help."

"I can't believe I'm doing this." But she put the cold oranges to her closed eyes. "I promised myself I'd take Bea's secret to the grave. You won't tell anyone, will you?"

"Of course I won't." I continued to struggle to accept the shape of her words. "But why was it a secret in the first place? It wouldn't have been a big deal in our group." We'd come of age at a time when our friends were dealing with depression and burnout and other mental health issues, therapy or pharmaceutical treatment no kind of taboo topic.

Darcie took a long time to reply. "It was our parents." Lifting the oranges from her eyes, she put them in the basket. "They didn't know what to do with a child who wasn't"—she hooked her fingers in the air to create air quotes—"'normal.'"

A shake of the head, the sun glinting on the strands. "I tried to do what I could, tell Bea she didn't have to hide who she was from our friends, but she just wouldn't have it."

I'd always thought the Shepherds the best of parents. "Did they get her counseling, other treatment?"

"Yes, of course. They weren't negligent." Sharp, hard. "To be honest, I think my mother was scared by the Shepherd family history. Blake wasn't playing with a full deck by the end, and there was also the so-called mad cousin of my father's. I was too young to know much, but he did something pretty awful, got himself committed for life."

She stared at the burned-out part of the structure that began their history. "I think, given time, my mother would've come to terms with Bea's needs, figured out the best way forward—but she didn't have that time. And we'd almost stopped noticing the problem; the medications worked *so* well while our parents were alive."

"I would've never guessed." Betrayal was a sour taste on the tongue. "Not in a million years." Beatrice and I, we'd had an understanding. I was the keeper of her hopes and her secrets, the one person she could trust to never speak those secrets.

Darcie's face softened. "She'd be happy to hear that. On her meds, she was the sister I grew up with. She was herself." A sudden passionate look. "Don't ever think that the girl you got to know wasn't the real Bea."

"I'd never think that." I brushed her hand with mine. "She must've been excellent about taking the meds if we didn't notice any fluctuations."

"She was militant about it. Remember that watch she used to wear with all the alarms on it?"

"The one she told us was for her vitamin regimen?" We'd teased her about her obsession, told her nothing would happen if she missed a dose of vitamin D or A.

"She did actually have a vitamin regimen." Darcie leaned back against the tree, her lips curving upward. "Got into holistic health at fourteen, had a crazy schedule of vitamins and minerals and herbal teas. At first, we thought it was a manic episode, the way she was so excited about it—but she kept it up."

"Never missed a day of yoga," I murmured, thinking of how she'd done it even when we'd all gone camping, her body fluid in the slow dance of the ancient practice. One of my favorite photos of all time was of her sliding between moves in a forest clearing, the sunbeams her spotlight.

I don't need anything special, Nae-nae. Just clear space and my breath.

"Yes." Darcie's smile faded. "But hidden in among the rest of it were the drugs she had to take to maintain her moods. It was *so* hard for me not to talk to you and the others about it, but I had to talk to someone. So I started calling our family doctor."

"Dr. Cox?" I said before I realized I probably shouldn't know that. Thinking fast, I added, "I think I might've chatted to him at your wedding? Name just stuck in my head for some reason."

"Yes, that was him," she said, with no indication that she found anything odd with my apparently infallible memory. "He used to accept calls from me outside of office hours, anytime I needed. Always said I could pay him in cookies." A shaky smile. "My parents asked me if I wanted a counselor, but I trusted Dr. Cox, could really talk to him, you know?"

Not waiting for me to respond, she said, "He suggested that perhaps the only way Bea could come to terms with her need for her medication was to think of them as another kind of mineral or vitamin."

Sitting with my arms on my knees, my back against the orange tree, shoulder to shoulder with Darcie, I said, "He sounds like a good person." I wasn't sure of the ethics there, talking to one sister about the diagnosis of the other, but it wasn't as if he'd revealed anything Darcie didn't already know. "No judgment, just practicality."

"He was a kind man—and he never told my parents about our talks, even when I was a minor." Darcie swallowed hard. "What he said? It's why I think our mother would've come around—she was a practical person, too. But what Bea remembered was the mum who told her that she must never, ever let anyone know about the special doctor she had to see."

Something about the way she'd put that made me frown, turn to her. "I thought you said she got medicated as a preteen?"

"She did. I didn't say the problems only began when she was a teenager." Rising to her feet on that, she brushed off the seat of her pants. "Come on, you can help me carry the oranges back."

Almost able to hear the door slamming shut on the subject of Bea and knowing I'd already pushed it today, I helped her load up the basket to a level she wouldn't have been able to carry back on her own but that we could manage easily between us. We didn't talk much more after that, and it was just as well because my mind was full to the brim already, awash in memories of my interactions with Bea.

So many images of her in my mental files, the vast majority of her laughing or smiling, or swooping in to give someone a big hug. Had she been too energetic at times? Too frenetic?

I dug and dug, but I couldn't see it. Perhaps because that was how I'd always known her to be. High-energy, enough to tire me out with it, but in no way unbalanced. Especially when she also had what Darcie had referred to as her quiet moods. Quiet but not withdrawn.

But Darcie had known her best of all; Darcie had lived with her.

My abdominal muscles tightened.

Suddenly, it made so much more sense that the sisters had lived together in that city-fringe villa worth upwards of two million rather than selling it, putting the money into an investment, and getting a smaller apartment. The upkeep and rates bill on the house had to have been significant.

But, for Beatrice, it had been a safe place; while I didn't know too much about her specific diagnosis, I could guess that a sense of being on stable ground was important for emotional regulation—especially in the wake of a tragedy like the loss of their parents. It could be that Bea's doctor had advised that they not change locations, that they try to keep things as static as possible.

I looked over at Darcie, who, to be honest, I'd often thought of as the most vacuous member of our group. Not a person with whom to have deep conversations. And yet, if I were to believe what she'd told me, Darcie had borne the weight of responsibility for her sister in more ways than one.

"Does Ash know? About Bea?"

"He didn't back then. But I had to have someone to talk to after . . ." She looked off to the side, her jaw set and her shoulders rigid.

It took her several long seconds to speak again. "I couldn't talk properly about her, grieve over her, without talking about her mental health. It was such an integral aspect of her nature. My too-bright, too-smart baby sister."

Once again, she'd avoided saying the word "suicide." But I heard it all the same. Beatrice's mental health had played a starring role in her death. Maybe that explained Darcie's secretiveness about the cremation. She'd been keeping her promise to her sister even then, making sure no one would figure out Beatrice's secret when her suicide had written that secret in neon.

But she was so happy.

It was a theme that had run through the comments after we found out what Bea had done. We'd been young, in shock, and that had been the first thing that had come to mind.

Now I'd been through my own bout with the abyss that blotted out all light and all hope—and wasn't sure I'd quite come out of it. I'd smiled for clients throughout, maintained my social media, complete with upbeat captions, and kept up the expected Luna Wylie facade with my closest friends. All the while the abyss yawned beneath my feet and my emotions flatlined.

Masks.

People were skilled at putting on masks. But Beatrice . . . She'd been *herself* for the entirety of our relationship. Surely no one could wear a mask for that long? Or had I simply been blind to my friend's inner pain?

Unless . . . Had she come off her medications at some point? But Darcie had said that she was militant about taking them, so what reason would she have to stop? It wasn't as if she'd had a major change in her life that might've precipitated it. She'd been with the same friend group, passed all her papers, and been on the way to an engagement with Ash.

Could that be it? A life change that wasn't negative but that shook her up all the same?

"Oh, by the way." Darcie's voice breaking into my thoughts. "Have you seen my phone? I couldn't find it last night." Though she attempted to sound casual, tension was a taut metal wire in every word.

I got it; I was surgically attached to my device. "No, sorry. When did you last see it? I can keep an eye out for it."

"I was sure I left it in our bedroom, on the bedside table. I definitely had it when we got here, because I asked Kaea to grab a quick photo of me in front of the house before we went in." She chewed on her lower lip. "But last night, after—" Shaking her head hard, as if to wipe out the memories, she said, "I couldn't find it. Ash even tried to call it, but we couldn't hear anything."

It didn't strike me as strange that she'd looked for her phone after her emotional breakdown. She'd probably wanted to numb her brain by playing a game or scrolling through her photos. An off-the-grid substitute for mindless online scrolling—of which I'd done plenty after my diagnosis.

"Clear case with pressed flowers inside, right?" Even her phone case matched her style aesthetic; that was why I'd noticed it. "It'll probably show up in a random spot like a shelf where you put it down while busy with something else. And if you had it when we arrived, it can't be too far from the main areas—we didn't wander much. You'll find it."

"Yes, you're right." She gave me an unsteady smile. "It's probably good for me to disconnect anyway."

"I thought you two got lost out there!" Ash called out from only meters away, his handsome face aglow in the morning light. "I was coming to hunt you down."

"Oh, you know Luna." Laughter in Darcie's eyes, no hint of the pain she'd revealed in the hidden orchard. "Snap, snap, snap."

Masks.

Bea wasn't the only member of the Shepherd family who was an expert at wearing one. Nausea swirled in my gut. Because what proof did I have of Darcie's claims?

Bea, after all, wasn't here to defend herself.

And Darcie was married to the love of Bea's life.

15

Ash took the basket of oranges with an "oof" of sound, but carried the load without trouble when he began to move. "Everything's ready. We can juice these later."

I trailed behind them as we made our way back to the kitchen, then through to the lounge. Bea's face, all the photographs I'd taken over the years, ran in a staccato slideshow inside my brain.

Not old memories these, not when I looked at snapshots of her almost every day.

Today, I focused on the ones where she hadn't been smiling— including a pensive image of her seated on Piha's glittering black sands, her hair flyaway under the knitted dark gray of her woolen hat, and her eyes reflecting a hint of the sunset fire on the water.

I'd taken that photograph about two months before her disappearance.

Bea, Darcie, Vansi, and I had gone to the beach that day. A

long way to go for a sunset followed by fish and chips for dinner, but it hadn't actually been about either of those things.

It had been about us. The friendship, the togetherness.

But there'd been something . . . not quite right that day. After all that had happened in the months to come, I'd thought I was making it up, seeing ghosts where none existed, but as I remembered that photograph, I remembered why Bea had been sitting alone on the sand rather than walking with us.

She and Darcie'd had a vicious fight. They'd been sniping at each other in the car the entire time, but that could be explained away as sisterly aggravation. Not that the two had often snapped at each other, quite the opposite, but they were sisters, after all. The odd tiff was inevitable. I'd seen the same with Vansi and her younger sister.

With my brother being five years my junior, we'd never had that kind of relationship. I didn't think it was because of our genders but rather the age gap. I'd always felt protective toward him, Cable forever the skinny two-year-old our parents had brought into the house when I was seven years old.

He was one of my closest friends, but he was also the kind of friend I looked after and sheltered from the world. That was just how it was between us. I was the big sister, and he the little brother. It'd be harder to share my diagnosis with him than it would be even with my parents.

Beatrice and Darcie's relationship, in contrast, had been of friends who saw each other as equals. Except Darcie had just told me that she'd been looking after Beatrice the entire time. I struggled to accept her portrayal of events. Especially because I remembered pieces of that vicious fight.

That day, we'd split to explore different areas of the beach while not going too far from each other. Vansi had decided to walk down to the water's edge to test the temperature of the waves, while I'd hiked up a dune to take distant snaps of my best friend silhouetted against the thick red light, as well as a few shots in the other direction. Capturing the changeable moods of the tangled bushland that rose up over the sands fascinated me as much as the water.

I hadn't realized that Darcie and Bea had walked behind the dune already, and was almost at the top when I picked up pieces of their conversation. I'd gone to call out, make myself known, then realized Bea was shouting—in a way that I'd never before heard from her.

The sea winds had whipped away many of her words, but I remembered her saying, ". . . not my keeper! You always want . . ."

Darcie's response had been unintelligible but for a single word: ". . . unstable!"

Then had come Bea's crystal clear reply. "You're the only one who thinks I'm unstable, Darcie. Did you ever wonder why?"

Those words rang around and around in my head today. Because while Darcie had known Bea better than any of us, we'd *all* spent years entwined in Bea's life. How was it possible that every single one of us had missed indications of mania and severe depression?

"You're away with the fairies this morning." Vansi nudged her shoulder against mine as the two of us sat on an overstuffed sofa of hunter green, our plates in our laps and the severed stag heads staring down at us with their dead black eyes.

I scooped up a forkful of scrambled eggs to give myself time to think up a reply. The flavors burst to life on my tongue, had my eyes going wide. I pointed my fork at Vansi. "Nix *did* make all those eggs for me back when I used to visit after you two got hitched!"

I expected Vansi to giggle, admit her small subterfuge, but she bit down on her lower lip, her eyes going over to where Phoenix stood by the fireplace talking to Darcie. He had a piece of toast in one hand, a mug of coffee in the other, while Darcie held a glass of orange juice.

"Did you ever notice how she has to have the attention of every single man in the room?" A quiet comment. "I never saw it before because, well, Phoenix always gave me his attention. But now . . ."

I took in the tableau by the fireplace once more, saw the distance between the two, the way they seemed more interested in the fire than each other. "I love you, chickadee, but at this point, you've accused both Bea and Darcie of having the hots for your husband."

Angling my body so I faced her, I said, "This isn't like you." She'd never done the jealous girlfriend thing. "So what's really going on?"

Vansi's mouth tightened at the corners, tiny lines flaring out from her lips—and I had the piercing thought that we weren't university students any longer. Closer to thirty than twenty now, with the odd glint of silver already appearing in some of our hair, the fine lines on our faces beginning to spread.

Only Bea remained ageless, untouched by time.

"You think I'm paranoid?" Vansi demanded in a low hiss.

"Of course not. But remember what we always said to each other—that it's the job of a best friend to tell the truth when no one else will. I'm going to tell you if you're acting off, the same way I'd tell you if you had your skirt tucked into your waistband after you came out of the bathroom or toilet paper stuck to your shoe."

Vansi didn't speak, didn't even look at me. Instead, she focused so tightly on her plate that I knew it was conscious. Surprised at her recalcitrance when we'd always talked openly to each other, I decided to give her time and tuned in to the conversation happening over to my right.

Kaea was talking to Ash about a possible hike.

Grace moaned from beside them. "I'll pass on that," she said. "My idea of a vacation involves reading a good book and maybe going for a leisurely walk."

"But you climb!" Kaea protested.

"Not this week," Grace said with cheerful stubbornness. "This week, I'm planning to do my best impression of a happy potato. Downtime before we rev up for the next climb."

Kaea looked across to where Aaron sprawled in an armchair across from Grace. "How about you?"

"I was hoping to take over the kitchen and make one of the recipes I saw in Clara Shepherd's book."

"Seriously?" Kaea threw up his arms, his white T-shirt stretching over his shoulders and his feet bare below the dark red and black plaid of pajama bottoms I was certain he'd only bought to wear outside the bedroom. "No one wants to hike with us?"

"I'll come," Darcie said from over by the fireplace. "And Nix was saying he wanted to see more of the area, too, weren't you?"

"Yeah." Phoenix looked over at Vansi. "You keen, sweetheart?"

Vansi's smile was faint. "I think I'll relax with Grace, maybe check out the orchard that Ash was telling us about."

Phoenix's eyebrows drew together. We all knew that Vansi was an avid hiker—she and Kaea had always been the first to suggest a tramp through one of the many tracks around the country. The persuasive tag team of Vansi and Kaea was the reason we'd ended up on camping holidays more often than not.

"Hell no, V, you have to come." Kaea pointed toward the hallway entrance into the lounge. "I found this old map on a wall in what Ash tells me might've been a study way back when, and the outlook from the top of the hike is going to be sick. I need my partner in hiking crime up there."

Vansi's leg tensed against mine before she smiled widely at our friend. "You've twisted my arm. What time are we leaving?" Rising, she moved to join the hiking group. I noticed that she positioned herself beside Kaea, with Phoenix on the other side of the small circle.

What the hell?

The sofa compressed next to me, Grace plopping down beside me on the couch. "You not a hiker? Only, no one asked you to join."

"They all know I'm itching to take photos of the estate." While I could handle a short hike even in my current physical condition, it was far from my favorite leisure activity. "I was thinking that since it'll be me, you, and Aaron here, we could do that engagement shoot."

If a person could bounce while sitting still, Grace did it right that moment. "Oh, I'm sure Aaron will be okay with that. If not, I'll work my wiles on him." A winsome and openly mischievous smile that made me laugh. "I'm guessing it won't take too long? He'll have plenty of time in the kitchen, right?"

"Two hours sound okay?" I tapped my fork lightly on my plate. "And you know, we could do a couple of cute shots in the kitchen, too. Him feeding you a treat he's baked up, for example.

I could come in and grab those shots later in the day, after he's done the cooking."

Glowing with excitement, Grace bounced off to tell Aaron my suggestion. She stood on tiptoe by the fire with him, her hands animated.

Cute, the woman was cute. But, crucially, not annoying with it.

As everyone chatted among themselves, I couldn't help but wonder if I knew my friends at all. I was keeping a huge secret of my own. What were the rest of them hiding? Because the undercurrents in this room? They ran as deep and dangerous as the glacier-fed creek we'd crossed to enter the estate.

Was Vansi right? Did Darcie crave male attention? Had Bea?

Right this moment, Darcie leaned against Ash, who had his arm around her waist. But when he glanced down at her while she wasn't paying attention, his expression was . . . flat.

As if the love and emotion had been the mask and this was the truth.

Then there was Phoenix. He had that inscrutable "surgeon" look on his face, the one that made me feel that despite our shared experiences, I no longer knew him. Vansi, too, was acting nothing like the friend with whom I'd been tight since we were eleven. She sat on the arm of Kaea's armchair, her smile huge as she ignored her husband.

Enough, Luna.

I hadn't joined this reunion to worry about my friends' marriage issues. If Vansi wanted to talk to me, she'd find me. If all she'd wanted was to vent, and I'd made a misstep by offering advice, then I'd make it up to her. It was always better to let her cool down before attempting to patch things up.

Looking away from the others, I mentally planned my own day. Grace and Aaron's photo shoot. Photos of the estate while it was all but empty. Then, late afternoon, I'd sit down to decode the messages Clara Shepherd had hidden in her recipe book.

But the first thing I did after we broke up was go to the cemetery.

Clara's gravestone was the oldest, weathered by time until no amount of maintenance could keep the lichen away. But that wasn't why I was there. I had a question. And the answer was on Clara's gravestone.

> Here lies Clara Darceline Shepherd,
> wife of Blake Shepherd,
> and mistress of the Shepherd Estate.

None of that was a surprise. But below that line were three more.

> Matthew Charles Shepherd
> Rose Matilda Shepherd
> Diana Beatrice Shepherd
> Forever in their mother's arms

The date of death was identical for all four people in the grave . . . or what remained of them after the fire. Which left Blake Shepherd and a child whose name I didn't know.

The sole survivors of a family of six.

16

It was as I was finishing up the first part of the engagement shoot that dark clouds began to gather on the horizon.

Grace had borrowed one of Darcie's floaty dresses, with Darcie generously offering her one of the three new ones she'd brought along for fresh social media images. Together, the two of us had managed to rig it so that it looked perfect from the front. A lushness of cream and lace. The back was Frankenstein's monster of bulldog clips, safety pins, and even paper clips, but photography could be all smoke and mirrors and I knew these images set among the golden grasses and on the rocks by the creek would come out breathtaking.

I had, however, also taken a couple of candids for their own personal archive of the two of them in hysterics over the look of the back of her dress.

Aaron, after some discussion, had opted to wear his own long-sleeved white shirt over blue jeans. Together, they looked romantic and playful, young and happy. I'd started with shots of them lying down—though those'd had to be quick because all those pins were poking into Grace—then had come photos of them running through the grass, along with portraits more formal and posed.

I'd also taken a small set with the Shepherd estate in the background, but the couple had quickly nixed that setup after taking a look at the resulting images.

"Too gloomy," Aaron had said. "There's something creepy about that place."

"I can't stop thinking about that poor woman who came out here expecting a grand estate and had to live a lonely life in a dismal pile." Grace shivered. "And have you been to the grave-yard? She's buried with *three* of her children. They all died in the fire. Rumor has it old Blake Shepherd started the blaze—he ended up badly burned all up one side of his body."

My eyes flared. "What? Did Darcie tell you that?"

"Oh, no." Grace waved a hand. "I love history and after Aaron told me we were invited here, I went down the research rabbit hole, found a couple of archived documents in the Central Library up in Auckland."

I was surprised that Blake Shepherd had been considered note-worthy enough for the archives—though I guessed it had to do with how successful he'd been as a prospector. What surprised me even more was that chirpy, happy Grace had been interested enough to dig that deep.

Then again, she was highly educated and well traveled—all I knew of her after such a short acquaintance was nothing but surface gloss. Though her cheerful personality was very much real; I saw that over and over again in the time that followed, my own heart blooming at seeing the two lovebirds interact.

A-dorable.

Now, lowering my camera, I put my hand to my eyes and glanced at the horizon. "Looks like we might get a bit of rain."

Aaron and Grace, having been posing on the bridge, looked over their shoulders.

"Damn." Aaron whistled. "Weather forecast did mention a polar blast, but they were saying there was a chance it'd bypass this region. Guess not."

I threw my camera strap over my shoulder, the back of my neck tired. "We're done as far as the outdoor shoot anyway. Cloudy light won't matter as much for the inside part. If it does rain, we can use the effect of rain against the windows to make it sweet and romantic."

"You're amazing, Luna. You made me feel like a movie star today." Beaming, Grace fell into step beside me, Aaron loping up to take position on her other side. "But I hope the others don't get drenched." A frown as she looked at the mountains beyond the estate. "How far did they say they were going to go?"

"I wasn't paying too much attention." The foot of the mountain at which the group had aimed itself was about two football field lengths away from the estate house. They obviously hadn't been planning to go all the way up—that would've required climbing gear.

"I think Kaea said that it was pretty much a full-day thing unless they pushed it. He also wanted to be back well before dark," Aaron said. "No one wanted to go hard, not even him."

"So conservative estimate is, what, six hours?" I zoomed in on the mountain using my camera lens, even though I had no hope of picking out five tiny specks against the stone and snow. "Three to go up, two to come down, with a lunch break thrown in there."

"It'd have to be something like that for them to be back before dark. Maybe seven hours at the most."

We all glanced at the approaching bank of clouds, which had already altered from murky and gray to gravid black. Below, the stalks of grass began to bend from the rising wind; the air temperature had also dropped sharply in the short time we'd been talking.

"If we can see the clouds, they will, too." I allowed my camera to drop to my side. "It's not like there's a ton of tree cover to block the view." What bush there was existed only at the bottom of the mountain, the rest more low-lying alpine flora.

"Yeah." Aaron put his hands on his hips. "Kaea'll turn the group around if it begins to look grim. This isn't a survival course."

We left it at that, but three hours later, as I was setting up to take the shots in the kitchen after having spent the time in between around the estate, the rain *thundered* down. The type of cold and drenching downpour that would get right through any outdoor jacket and soak you to the bone.

I looked out the window, in the direction from which the others would come if they'd turned around when the clouds grew black. "I hope they're not too far away." That was when it struck me that we'd been stupid—the others hadn't marked out a route map for us. A simple safety procedure we'd overlooked because this was meant to be an easy day hike.

"Kaea's very experienced," Aaron reminded me. "Even if he's out of shape by his standards, he's in great shape by any other standard. And he's always been safety conscious."

He was right. Kaea double-checked everything, from making sure that we had the appropriate gear for going into the bush, even if it was only for a summer weekend, to checking the use-by dates on the food we were bringing in. "Right, let's get this shoot done and then you can whip up something hot for them. They'll be freezing by the time they arrive."

All of us in agreement, we got to shooting, and I snapped what I had to say was a series of incredible pictures. While the estate might have looked gloomy from the outside, the kitchen was warm and cozy with the lights on, the old woodstove going, and Grace's laughter filling the space.

"You're a natural in front of the camera, Grace. You make even Aaron relax."

Aaron didn't take my words as an insult—back at uni, he used to make fun of his "robotic" expression in pictures. "Yeah?" he said now. "I'm not messing them up?"

"You both look gorgeous." Walking over, I showed him the images on the tiny screen of my camera—but they were still big enough for him to see the light in his eyes, the way his lips curved. "See?"

His smile creased his cheeks. "Thanks for doing this, Lu. I don't think I could've relaxed with any other photographer, even with my Gracie."

"He's right." Grace cuddled under his arm. "You're so non-judgmental and calming. If we have kids, I'm going to be booking you for our over-the-top matchy-matchy photographs. I'm talking identical family pj's and onesies here."

Laughing at the way Aaron slapped a hand over his face and groaned, I finished up the shoot, then left them in the kitchen. Aaron liked to cook alone—though it appeared he'd made an exception for Grace—and I wanted to work on their photographs using my laptop. A couple extra hours would make the gift so much more valuable to them, and if I did it straightaway, I could get it off my plate.

The rain continued to slam against the windows as I fine-tuned the images, though I kept on walking over to look in the direction of the mountains beyond the graveyard. My room was on the same side as the kitchen but farther to the right, so I had an excellent view in the correct direction.

Each time I looked out, I hoped to spot Darcie's pink jacket or the high-visibility stripes on Kaea's camo-green outdoor one.

Nothing, the landscape outside cold and desolate and hard.

My gut twisted.

Giving up on the photos, I paced in front of the window while using my phone to zoom in on some of the pictures I'd taken of the recipe book.

The first few hidden texts were similar—the lament of a lonely girl far from home, with a man that she barely knew. Slowly, however, the entries began to change. And I realized that they'd been made some time apart. The recipe book hadn't been put together in a month or even a year.

It had been the work of long, cold years.

My husband speaks to himself. I do not know if that is strange or not. Perhaps it isn't. He seems to simply be working out business matters—perhaps it is like writing things down but he wishes to speak them aloud.

As a person who often spoke to myself, I didn't make too much of that particular note until I read another one, which said:

He is still speaking to himself, but it is more in mutters under his breath now. I hear him inside his secret room where I am not permitted to go, and in other areas of the house when he thinks I am not there.

I do not know if he does it around the servants, but I know that they have begun to give him strange looks. I should not care what the servants think, but they are the only ones close to me.

I know I am their mistress, but there is no one of my station here. I have the servants alone as friends. One of them whispered to me that she found my husband's desk drawer full of spoons that had gone missing from the kitchen. The housekeeper had been about to blame one of the maids.

I surely do not understand why he would hoard his own silverware.

I quickly switched to the next photograph, the next piece of the entry, but it said nothing about Blake Shepherd's hoarding behavior.

My husband has cut the household staff in half. He says we have no need for so many people, that they get in his way, and disturb him when he is thinking. Now, it is only the housekeeper, the cook, and one maid.

I wished to keep on my private maid and closest friend, Laura, but he made the decision, and he retained only the older ones. They are fine enough workers, but I cannot talk to them. Without my babe, I think I would surely go mad.

Babe.

What had Darcie said? First baby four years into the marriage? So four years on and she'd still had no agency in her marriage or influence over her husband.

My eyes throbbed from concentrating on the tiny screen, and

I knew I should shift to the laptop, but I couldn't make myself walk away from the window. Because between every sentence, I'd look up to check for the others.

The clouds covered the entire sky now, a boiling black ceiling on the world, and the wind had picked up until the house groaned. No longer did I see any semblance of grass stalks, just a flat sheet of dull beige, and I was sure that some of the rain hitting my window held bits of that mushy ice that turned to sludge on a city street.

I distracted myself by reading more of Clara's secret diary.

Today, I came in after taking our children for a walk outside to find the entire house dark and cold. My husband had ordered the housekeeper to extinguish every single fire in every single hearth.

The flames hurt his eyes, he said.

I saw fear on the housekeeper's face, and I cannot blame her. He is changing in ways that scare me, too. At least he rarely comes to my bed. I should not say that. It is not for a wife to say. But where before, I could do my duty, now, I am afraid without knowing why. I pray for the day I fall with child again. He never came to me while I was gravid with our eldest, then again with Matthew.

I looked up again and was so used to not seeing anything that I almost missed the speck of pink in the distance. The instant I realized what it was, I dropped my phone onto the window seat, raced to grab my jacket—dark brown, hiplength, and full of deep pockets—and pulled it on as I ran down the stairs.

17

"They're back!" I yelled out to Aaron as I entered the kitchen.

But I was talking to empty air. The kitchen was silent but for the quiet rumble of the woodstove, everything tidied and put away. Of course it was. It had been at least three hours since I'd left Grace and Aaron. They were probably either upstairs or in another part of the house.

Zipping up my jacket, I went to run outside, only reconsidered what I was doing as I hit the edge of the veranda. I'd do better to get towels ready for the returning group. Stripping off my jacket on that thought, I dumped it on the back of a kitchen chair. The linen cupboard was just off the kitchen to the right, next to the laundry room—which I knew because Darcie had pointed it out.

Thanks to the cleaners her caretaker had hired to prepare the house, there was no shortage of fresh towels. Grabbing armfuls, I took them to the kitchen, the entrance through which the others would enter the house. I also piled up several blankets on the kitchen table, in case any of them wanted to strip down then and there.

Light footsteps on the stairs before Aaron and Grace walked into the kitchen hand in hand. "Lu, what—" Aaron hissed out a breath. "You spotted the others?"

I took one look at Grace's flushed skin and the languid look in Aaron's eyes and knew exactly what they'd been up to. "Yes. They're visible in the distance."

"I'll heat up the food." Aaron was already moving to turn on the stovetop. "Gracie, why don't you put on the coffee and start a pot of tea?"

"I'll get out the honey, too." Grace began to fill the kettle. "Sweet and hot, that's the ticket after being cold and wet. Oh, shall I add logs to the living room fire? It should still be going but is probably low."

"I'll do that," I volunteered.

With the distance the others had to cover, we had the lounge fire blazing and the kitchen warm with the scent of coffee by the time I got my first real glimpse of the returning group, the rain a sleet-gray curtain.

I frowned. "Kaea's not walking on his own." He was being supported by Ash and Phoenix, one on either side of him.

"Is he hurt?" Aaron's shoulder brushed mine in the doorway, his lanky body taut. "Should we go out?"

"No, we'll do better helping them once they get closer." There wasn't any point in us getting drenched and needing to dry off before we could assist them once they were inside. "Kaea looks okay except for his leg. Have you seen a first-aid kit around here?"

Aaron shook his head, but Grace piped up with, "I have an emergency one that I take when traveling. It's only small, though."

"Grab it anyway. If I know Kaea, he'll have one in his luggage, too—I'll get that." Given the situation, I didn't have any hesitation in racing up the stairs in the direction of his room.

I knew where he usually kept the kit, which meant I wouldn't have to rifle through his bag. Always in the side pocket of his pack—he'd drummed that piece of knowledge into all of us when we began to hike and camp together. Just in case something ever happened to him and he was unable to tell us where to find it.

The dark green backpack in his room looked identical to the one he'd had at uni, if a bit more battered, with more badges sewn into it from the places he'd hiked. The one from Glacier National Park, a trip he'd taken during our winter season, was pristine, the white threads that edged the badge clean of any accumulated dust.

Sewn on only recently.

As for the emergency first-aid kit, it was exactly where I'd expected it to be: in the square side pocket just big enough to fit the red metal tin he'd inherited from his pops.

I pulled it out—and accidentally pulled out something else that must've been at the bottom. A scarf, the gauzy fabric a faded purple with white flowers. My forehead wrinkled. Funny, but I could've sworn I'd seen that before. Shoving it back into the pocket with a shrug, I then got myself downstairs.

Kaea's group still hadn't made it to the door, and I saw that despite our earlier conversation, Aaron had gone out to help. He'd always had the softest heart of all of us, so it wasn't exactly a shock that he hadn't been able to stand watching them struggle.

Grace hovered in the doorway, twisting her hands together. "I feel like we should go out there," she said. "But I don't know what we could do. Aaron said he could at least take a couple of the daypacks off their hands."

"I know it's instinct to rush out. But they'll need us when they make it here."

And at last they reached us and it was all hands on deck. I ended up with Kaea, helping him strip off his top half while he sat on a chair. Vansi and Phoenix rubbed themselves off with rapid motions, then headed to their room, but Ash and Darcie decided to remove their outer layers in the kitchen.

"I don't mind if you want to get naked here," I said to Kaea. "I've seen you in your birthday suit before and lived to tell the tale." Such glimpses were hard to avoid when you lived together and certain people had a way of turning exhibitionist when drunk.

He grinned, but there was a wince to it. "I think I'll have to. Fucked up my leg."

Placing one hand on the table and one on the back of the chair, he pushed himself up slightly, the veins on his arms standing out and his biceps taut.

His breath was short, shallow.

Working as fast as possible, I tugged his pants off over his butt and down. I did, in the end, leave him with his black boxer briefs. But only long enough to throw the pants on the pile of discarded towels. At which point, I grabbed a fresh towel he could wrap around his waist so he could push down the briefs while maintaining his modesty.

He got them most of the way down, but I had to help with the final bit, which I didn't mind in the least. I was more worried about the makeshift bandage around his left knee, along with the deep abrasions along his shin. "What happened? Did you fall?"

"Sort of." He looked over at where Darcie and Ash were rubbing themselves dry, with Grace and a damp Aaron putting together everyone's hot drinks, then nudged his head so I'd lean in closer. "It's really weird, Lunes." Low volume, quiet words. "The stitching on my boot gave way on one side."

I frowned, looking over at where everyone had left their wet boots out on the veranda. Though the kitchen door was still open, I couldn't immediately spot his, so went out there on the pretext of closing the door and saw what he was talking about. The leather flapped on one side, creating a gaping hole.

"It wasn't bad manufacture," I murmured when I returned to him. "Not with that kind of a tear, and not with how you are in terms of buying and maintaining your outdoor supplies."

"I checked them before and after the tramp I did with Nix and Vansi on the way up here," he confirmed, still in that low tone that would reach no one else. "My boots were in perfect shape. The only way for it to have given way so significantly is for someone to have cut the stitching—and even then, the glue should've held it together. It had to have been cut almost but not quite all the way through."

My heart thudded, and the two of us held gazes for a moment, neither one vocalizing what we were thinking. That this had been done on purpose. But why? And by who?

"Make sure the boots don't get lost," he muttered, leaning close as we heard the sound of feet thundering down the stairs.

Phoenix entered the kitchen only seconds later, bustling over to look at Kaea's knee, with Vansi beside him. Given that he was a doctor, and she an ER nurse, I backed off.

Ash and Darcie headed upstairs to change at the same moment, as did Aaron. Grace, meanwhile, was walking out of the kitchen with a pile of damp towels and discarded clothing in her arms. Probably going to throw them in the washing machine.

No one was paying any attention to me.

Slipping outside, I took both of Kaea's boots and, running quickly around the veranda, hid them under an overgrown blackberry bush I'd photographed earlier that day. They'd stay dry due to the overhang of the house and no one would find them without going to that specific spot and crouching down to search under the bush.

I was back in the kitchen before the others who'd left.

When Kaea met my gaze, I gave him a slight nod. "I'll go find you dry clothes."

It wasn't a hard job—he traveled light and packed neatly. I picked out a pair of gray sweatpants along with a thick black hoodie. Easy for him to get on and off. And even if I knew Kaea wouldn't care, I didn't dig around in his underwear. He could go commando or ask one of the guys to grab that.

I was looking for a pair of socks when my eye caught on the edge of the scarf poking out of the side pocket of the pack. I spotted three pairs of carefully balled-up socks lined up by his sneakers a heartbeat later.

I should've left.

I didn't.

Walking over, I fingered the material of the scarf, images flashing behind my eyes until they screeched to a sudden halt— on a memory of Bea sitting by the campfire, that scarf wrapped around her hair and sunflower earrings hanging from her ears. As if she was some '70s hippie child born into the wrong era.

"No," I whispered, tucking the scarf back into the pocket. But I knew what I'd remembered and I knew it was correct. My memories were always correct when it came to the visual. But why did Kaea have Bea's scarf?

Maybe it had just been forgotten there all these years. If he was carrying around a pack from that long ago, then why not? Especially if he'd never managed to pull it out while checking on the first-aid kit. But even as I considered that, I knew it to be nonsensical.

Kaea was fanatical about maintaining his gear, would've gone over the pack multiple times by now. He'd also have pulled out and updated the kit prior to every single hike. Man was safety conscious to the point of being anal.

Yet his was the shoe that had broken.

Kaea was in the living room by the time I arrived, on one of the long and deep sofas with the low backs and cushions that might've once been hard but had softened with time and use. He had his legs stretched out in front of him, back braced against the arm, and a jerry-rigged ice pack on his knee.

". . . nothing is broken," Phoenix was saying as I arrived. "I'm fairly certain it's a bad wrench. You managed to save yourself."

"Doesn't feel like it." Kaea made a face, teeth gritted, as he shifted position to shrug into the hoodie I handed him. "Hurts like a bitch."

"It should calm down." Phoenix helped stabilize him so he could pull on the sweatpants under the cover provided by the towel around his waist, after which, I put on his socks for him.

"Thanks, guys." Already out of breath from the pain caused by the exertion, Kaea settled into an unmoving position.

Phoenix put the ice pack back where it had been. "If it doesn't stop hurting," he added, "we might need to take you in to get a scan. Something might've torn."

Vansi looked toward the windows, the rain slamming into the glass in tiny pellets. "Can we even get out of here? Or do we have a signal to call emergency services?"

Her words made me realize that my phone was upstairs. I'd left it because I hadn't wanted it to get wet when I ran outside, but now the lack made my muscles twitch. As I watched, my best friend pulled out her own phone, frowned. "No signal here just like on the mountain."

They must've tried to call us, I thought, tell us what was going on. "When did you injure yourself?" I grabbed Kaea's discarded towel. "On the way up?"

He shook his head. "I probably wouldn't have been hurt if it had happened on the way up. No, we'd turned around—I'd begun to worry about the weather. It happened on a slope with broken stones, made the entire thing worse." He held up his palms; both looked as if they'd been through a cheese grater.

"Good thing is I've got you two right here. Fucking A-team." He bumped fists with Nix and Vansi. "I should be fine if you can cobble up a crutch for me."

"I found it!" Darcie cried from the doorway.

I glanced over to see her holding up a carved wooden cane.

"I *knew* we had this around somewhere. My grandfather used it when he came down."

"Fantastic." Vansi smiled for the first time. "It's not as good as a crutch, but it'll do in the interim until we can figure out a better solution."

As I was closest to Darcie, I threw the towel over my shoulder and took the cane from her, examining the smooth curve of it. "It's beautiful work," I said before handing it over to Kaea.

His eyes met mine for a second before he took it, began to run his hand over it. I knew what he was thinking, understood he wanted to examine the shoes. But there was no way for either one of us to do so with everyone around.

Since it didn't look like Kaea's first-aid kit was needed, I picked it up from where it had been placed on the seat of an armchair. After putting it on the table beside the sofa, I threw the towel into the basket in the laundry room before heading back upstairs to grab my phone. I ran into Grace as she was coming downstairs, and she made a face at me. "Poor Kaea," she said. "Aaron told me he's the most active one of the friend group. He's going to hate being stuck in place."

I angled my head toward the narrow window that threw bleak gray light onto the staircase. "With this weather, we might all end up playing cards in the living room anyway." I could hear thunder now, rolling booms of it that seemed to make the windows rattle.

Grace shivered. "See you downstairs. Aaron made cookies."

"I'll be quick."

Once I reached the bedroom, I picked up my phone, grabbing my camera as well. Why not? I could wander around inside the house, get a few images of the internal architecture and oddities—such as that wall of stag heads. Might not be my idea of décor, but it'd make an excellent photograph.

I was halfway down the stairs when a short, sharp scream reverberated against the walls. This time it wasn't of terror but of what felt like blinding rage. Running to the living room, I found the others all there . . . with Darcie holding Bea's doll.

18

"You think this is funny, Luna?" A harsh demand, her fingers squeezing the doll until I was scared she'd break it. "To torment me with the reminder of my dead sister?"

I fought the urge to tear Bea's treasured possession from her grip. "I have no idea what you're talking about. I put that in the closet."

Darcie's entire face . . . shivered. Turning on her heel without warning, she lifted her arm and threw the doll into the fireplace. "The cursed thing can burn!"

"Jesus, Darcie!" Ash, closest to the fire, moved with unexpected speed. Picking up a fireplace poker, he dragged the doll out of the flames.

Her hair was on fire, the side of her face scorched. Beside him by now, I stamped out the flames using a rag that had been hanging on the same stand as the poker. Probably what the cleaners used to wipe away any lingering ashes.

The acrid scent of burned hair lingered in the air as Ash picked up the doll. At the same time that I understood that meant the doll's hair was real, was likely Bea's, I saw the macabre vision the doll had now become. No longer was she a perfect representation of six-year-old Bea.

Now . . . now she looked like the house. One half of her scorched and ruined, the other half perfect. A crack marred her singed cheek, and one hand was damaged, pieces broken away. And her hair, *Bea's* beautiful hair, was crisp and burned to the scalp on one side, blackened on the other, several of the strands seemingly melted into the porcelain.

"Why the fuck would you do that?" Ash's voice shook, red streaks on his cheekbones. "We talked about this. It's a memory of your sister and you know you'll regret it later on. You always act first and think later!"

"I don't want it!" Darcie's face was hot and pink, splotches mottling her picture-perfect glow. "I hate that doll. I've always hated it! *You're* the one who thought we should keep it to pass on to our children! You're the one obsessed with Bea!"

Sensing I wouldn't get my hands on the doll anytime soon, I moved out of the line of fire and found myself beside Vansi. "Where did she find it?" I muttered.

Vansi nodded to the dripping-wet daypack that sat half-open on the floor by one of the sofas. "In the bag she took on the hike. She was emptying it out while we sat around chatting, and all of a sudden that thing was in her hands." She folded her arms, met my gaze. "No question of it being on purpose. But who, and why?"

I appreciated that even though I was the last person to have had custody of the doll, she didn't even consider that it might've been me. Vansi knew I'd never go around torturing someone this

way—I'd wanted to confront Darcie face-to-face, not mount a
passive-aggressive campaign.

"That means someone went into my room this morning *after*
I put Creepy Bea in the closet, searched and found her, and put
her in Darcie's pack."

Face tight, Vansi nodded. "We were all moving around this
morning. You were outside taking photos of that weird tree for a
bit, remember? None of the rooms have locks. It could've been
any of the group."

I rubbed my forehead, while Ash and Darcie continued to
argue. They were doing so in whispers now, however, their faces
only an inch apart. Ash still held on to the doll.

And I thought of what he'd told me.

"Do you think . . ." I leaned closer to Vansi. "I mean, it sounds
crazy, but do you think there's a chance Darcie did it herself?"

Her eyes cut away from the tableau by the fireplace, her pupils
flaring. "Why?" A whisper. "To start drama?"

I shrugged, but didn't share what Ash had said about her recent unstable behavior.

Lips twisted, my best friend took a second to think. "I mean,
I don't like her, but she seemed sincerely freaked out. To be honest, more freaked out than she should be. I know it's Bea's doll,
but Bea's gone, has been for years. If anything, the doll should've
made her sad, you know? Especially since we've all kind of guessed
how it ended up at the estate, that Bea must've left it behind for
Darcie."

"But then who'd put it where Darcie would stumble on it?" I
murmured. "Who would dislike her enough to torment her?"

If it came down to it, Vansi was the only one I'd heard say
angry words about Darcie—and I knew beyond any doubt that

she'd never pull this kind of cruel prank. She wasn't a nurse just because it was a well-paying career. She was kind, and she liked helping people. She'd never consciously shove anyone into a place of pain and rage.

"I've had enough of this." Ash's announcement, unbending and blunt, caught our attention. "I'm going to put the doll somewhere safe, where no one else can find it. All of you stay in this room until I get back."

Darcie stared at him mutely as he strode out of the room. The words she spoke in the silence that followed were small and broken. "It'll never be perfect again even if we get it repaired." A sob broke out of her. "They used our real hair. Oh God, I burned Bea's hair."

Even though I'd already guessed, the confirmation rippled a shiver up my spine, made goose bumps break out over my skin. I wished I'd stroked that hair, taken the chance to touch a piece of Bea one last time.

"Okay." Vansi held up her hands. "I was creeped out by that doll before, but now I'm never, ever going near it and I will run in the other direction if I see it. What were your parents thinking?"

It should've been a horrifyingly insensitive statement, but the way Vansi had said it, the words held a gentle sympathy. They made Darcie sob out a laugh through the tears that had begun to roll down her face.

Grace went over, took her hand. Darcie didn't shake her off.

"I don't know," she said afterward, mopping up her tears on one sleeve of her loose gray sweater. "I think it was the thing to do in their circle at the time. A doll no one else would ever have. Truly one of a kind."

Vansi stepped over to hug Darcie, Grace releasing her hand so

Darcie could return the embrace. Because while Vansi could have a sharp tongue, she was also generous at heart.

"Well," my best friend said when she pulled back, "I think Bea would've enjoyed knowing that her doll is still causing a ruckus. We're all missing her spirit this week, aren't we? It was always meant to be eight of us."

A glance at Grace. "I didn't mean—"

"No, I understand." Grace squeezed her hand. "Aaron talks about how you named yourselves the Great Eight. I get it. I wish I would've made it the Prime Nine, that she was here still."

And, for the first time since the night our world fractured into seven damaged pieces, we began to talk about our Bea. Until by the time Ash returned to the room, we were all seated with fresh mugs of tea or coffee in hand, a plate of Aaron's peanut butter–chocolate cookies doing the rounds as we shared stories about the friend who hadn't made it to this reunion.

Ash looked stricken as he realized what was going on, but when Darcie reached out a hand, sorrow and apology on every inch of her face, he immediately walked over to sit next to her.

Tucking her against him, he ran his hand down her arm.

"Remember that time she talked us into toilet-papering that one teacher's car?" Aaron leaned forward, mug in hand and elbows braced on his thighs. "I mean, it was such a juvenile thing to do, but she made it hysterical. Until even I joined in, though I was the ultimate teacher's pet." A sheepish grin that had Grace dropping a kiss on his cheek. "My parents would've disowned me if it ever came to light."

"That asshole deserved it," Phoenix muttered. "He put our whole class into detention because he couldn't figure out who'd thrown a spitball in his direction, and none of us would talk."

He shook his head. "I mean, if that's not a sign of global dislike . . ."

"I can't believe we got away with it. Our lucky night," I said.

"No," Aaron argued. "It was strategy. See, Bea and Nix were top of their grades, and Darcie was student council president with a spotless record and thus above suspicion, which sort of carried over to the rest of us by association. Helped that Kaea kept winning rugby and athletics trophies. No one was ever going to look at the Great Eight."

Aaron's grin lit up his whole face. "Bea also made sure we did it on a night when the naughty kid most likely to be blamed had an airtight alibi—he was in theater practice. No scapegoat for them to point at."

"Beatrice was always smart like that." Darcie's throat sounded scraped raw, but a smile glowed in her eyes. "She could get around adults in a way I never could figure out. It was like she was born knowing how people's brains worked."

I shifted on the sofa, not comfortable with how Darcie was coloring her sister and not about to allow it to stand. Because it wasn't Bea who was the manipulative one of the two. "She never talked us into anything we didn't want to do," I pointed out. "She'd suggest, but it was always our call."

"That's right." Vansi swallowed a bite of cookie. "I bowed out a couple of times because the risk was too high my parents would ground me forever, and she never held it against me."

"Yeah, she was good like that." Aaron's smile held a weight of memory. "Must've been all that yoga and meditation. Remember that time she signed us up for that silent meditation retreat as a joke and made a bet that we wouldn't last the day?"

"I'd forgotten about that." Kaea grinned. "Jesus, what a trip. I could not believe that Bea, whose mouth moved like a train, beat us all!"

"I was runner-up," Vansi pointed out with a fist pump. "Meanwhile, my dark and handsome and taciturn lasted exactly three hours."

Phoenix's lips twitched. "That Zen garden was a beautiful place to propose. And what did you do when I spoke the romantic words I'd sweated over for days? Just nod yes and stick out your hand. I had to wait *hours* for vocal confirmation. Brutal, baby."

Vansi cackled, and suddenly we were all laughing as the rain smashed against the windows, the world outside pitch-black.

19

At some point, Aaron and Grace wandered into the kitchen after Aaron decided to add another dish to the food he'd cooked earlier, which we'd then have for dinner later on in the evening. With the hot drinks and cookies already eaten, no one was hungry for a meal.

"Not that I don't appreciate the coffee," Kaea said from the sofa, "but how about we get some real drinks going? Seems like the kind of night for it."

I groaned. "I'm getting flashbacks to many a night at the flat. I'll only drink if you swear not to strip and start doing the 'Y.M.C.A.' dance."

"I'm injured!" Kaea protested even as the room filled with laughter once more. "Your innocent little peepers are safe."

We scattered to carry down the bottles of alcohol we'd brought so that Ash and Darcie wouldn't have to bear that cost on top of what they'd already paid to get the place cleaned up for habitation. Despite their protests, we'd all chipped in on the money for the groceries, too. Everyone except for Aaron—oh, he'd tried, but we'd refused to accept.

We'd known he'd end up doing more than his share of the cooking. Because Aaron could cook the rest of us under the table any day of the week—*and* he liked having a group that he knew was game to try his more experimental creations.

The least we could do was pay for the ingredients.

After all, our accommodation was free and none of us were on the breadline. Of the entire group, I surely earned the least, but I'd also done barely any discretionary spending since my diagnosis. My bank account was healthier than it had been for a while. One positive, at least.

"I'll get yours," I told Kaea. "Where is it?"

"Closet. Thanks, Lunes."

I grabbed my own two bottles of wine first, passing Phoenix in the hall as he emerged from his and Vansi's room with the makings for a cocktail. I knew that without asking about the bottles in his hands, the labels of which I couldn't clearly see. Cocktails were Vansi's jam, and Phoenix was incredible at creating them.

"I'll wait for you," he said as I ducked into Kaea's room. "Ash and Darcie brought stuff, too, and already put it downstairs, and Grace is helping Aaron in the kitchen, so it's just us up here."

"Thanks." I made quick work of getting Kaea's whiskey, my gaze falling once again on the old green pack as I left Kaea's room. "That must've been scary when he slipped," I commented as we began to walk downstairs.

"Just between us, I have to admit I was worried he'd broken his leg," he said in that deliberate way of his. "With the lack of reception here, and the distance from any significant help . . ." He shook his head. "It wouldn't have been life-threatening, but the delay might've ended up causing an infection."

I hadn't considered what it might mean if one of us got injured all the way out here, but of course he was right. Even a surgeon-in-training could only do so much without equipment. "What do you think happened to his boot? It looked bad when I saw it."

A shrug. "Manufacturers are cutting corners these days, making things at lower quality. Just bad luck, I'm guessing."

The glib response was not what I would've expected from Phoenix, and I was frowning when we entered the living room. Ash waved at us from a corner that held a curving wall of wood that I belatedly realized was meant to be a bar.

"Darcie's ancestors were lushes!" he called out.

"Truth," Darcie confirmed. "Cellar is full of wine. I should've told you that, Luna. Since I have zero liking for the stuff, I'm not sure whether it tastes like vinegar at this point, or how old it can get until it's no longer drinkable, but you game to try one of the oldies?"

Startled at the friendly comment after the way she'd blown up at me, I decided to accept the olive branch. "Are you kidding?" I dumped my bottles on Ash's bar; all the alcohol was to be shared anyway. "Let's go!" Who knew what treasures lay dusty and forgotten under the house. "Wait, let me grab my camera. Will there be enough light to take photos?"

She waved her hand in that way that meant maybe, maybe not.

"Should we grab a flashlight?"

"Jim told us he stocked up the flashlights, but I haven't found them yet. Cleaners must've moved them from the usual spot. Probably thought they were being helpful." She rolled her eyes toward the ceiling. "There's a lightbulb in the cellar, so we should be okay for a first look."

"Sounds good." Dim lighting could work for mood, too. It might well be perfect for shooting an old wine cellar that—hopefully—hadn't seen a cleaner's brush for years. I knew exactly the corporate client to which I could pitch those images.

I mentally crossed my fingers.

Darcie didn't say much as she led me out of the living room and down the endless hallway to the left of the staircase. I busied myself taking in the surroundings, snapping the odd pic. More mounted animal heads, a preserved fish or two that seemed to be from her grandfather's time, a yellowed cross-stitch that was the most wholesome thing on the walls so far.

After that came a painted family portrait that I knew at once was of Blake and Clara Shepherd and their children. He was all clean lines and thick blond mustache, his hair cut sharp and neat, and his suit fitted to his athletic frame.

Blake Shepherd had been handsome.

Clara, however, was painted nowhere near as well as Blake; the only reason I recognized it as her was the dress she wore—the same one as from the portrait of her by the entrance to the house. Three of her children's faces, too, were smudged blurs. The sole child with a defined face was a teenage girl with blond hair and blue eyes. She stared at me with a faint smirk on her face.

Wondering if the artist had suffered a stroke midpainting to have done such a divided piece of work, I took another, closer look. My eyes widened. The faces of Clara and the three children had been smudged on purpose, extra paint used to wipe out their features.

Blake Shepherd destroying their images as he'd ended their existence?

Shivering, I turned away from the eerie painting that generations of Shepherds had left hanging, and caught up to Darcie. We were thankfully long past the portrait when she spoke. "Sorry about screaming at you." She rubbed her hands over her face. "I know you didn't do it. You were always the nicest of the group."

"Nope, that's definitely Aaron."

Snorting out a laugh that then made us both giggle, she dropped her hands to her sides. "I meant of us girls. I don't think I've ever heard you say a mean thing in my life."

I said plenty of bitchy things, but usually only to Vansi. Darcie and I weren't close enough that I'd ever vent to her. I'd never vented to Bea, either. That wasn't how our relationship had worked. I'd been content to just be near her, listen to her. If anyone else had realized how I felt about her, there was a good chance they'd have thought I wanted more, that she was leading me on.

Those people would've been wrong.

Bea's joy had been mine. Nothing had made me happier than seeing her shine and laugh and live a life glorious. I'd loved her beyond breath itself, but it wasn't the kind of love most people understood. It had no need for the physical, and no desire to possess.

All I'd ever needed was for her to see me, trust me . . . and never leave me behind.

"I should've hidden the doll better," I said now, to the sister of the girl who'd broken me when she broke herself. "I honestly didn't think anyone would go into the closet to grab her. I'm sorry about that."

"I've been racking my brain to figure out who it could've been." Darcie stared into nothingness. "Kaea used to play stupid pranks back when we were at uni."

"No, he wouldn't do this." Kaea's worst pranks had still only been about mischief. "He told us how bad it was with your break-in. He feels awful about it, would've never tried to ruin your week here."

Darcie's expression softened. "He was amazing that night, stayed with us until after the cops had come, even booked us into a suite at a nice hotel for a couple of days. You're right. He wouldn't try to hurt me."

Her chest rose and fell on deep, conscious breaths. "Whoever it was, I think I have to let it go. Someone probably thought they were being funny and setting up a jump scare, had no idea how I'd react."

Since she'd brought up the subject, I said, "Why *does* it affect you that way? You loved Bea."

A whispered darkness passed over Darcie's face. "The authorities don't make you identify bodies like they do in the TV shows," she said, her voice distant. "They knew who she was by the time I arrived, had identified her by dental records. But I wanted to say goodbye." Pressing her lips together when they trembled, she swallowed hard as she hugged her arms around her rib cage.

I didn't interrupt, didn't comfort. I needed to understand what had happened that long-ago midwinter when Darcie had vanished for a weekend and come back to tell us that Bea was gone, dead and cremated, her ashes scattered in the ocean.

"I should've listened to the undertaker when he told me it would be better if I didn't look at my sister, that they hadn't been able to do much. I'd asked the ho—" She swallowed again, the movement convulsive. "I'd asked that her body be transferred directly to the funeral home, and I went there to say my goodbyes.

"I should've listened. But I didn't, and now all I see when I think of my sister is the way she looked in that box. Her face all bloated up, and the marks from the thin rope she used cutting into her neck, the deep gouges in her skin from where she tried to struggle and tear it off at the end."

Tears spilled down her cheeks. "I can't remember my baby sister as she was, Luna. I remember her only as the mangled thing she became."

My heart thundered. I'd always imagined that Beatrice must've taken an overdose. But to commit suicide by hanging? For the girl I'd known, that was an act of violence, of rage. Especially when she had to have known that Darcie was likely to end up viewing her body and the damage she'd done to it.

"I'm so sorry." My fingers trembled as I stroked her upper arm. "Why didn't you bring even one of us with you? Why did you try to do everything on your own?"

"My therapist says it was shock and anger." Flat tone, flatter gaze. "I'm such a bad person that I wanted to obliterate all reminders of my sister and carry on as if nothing had happened."

Even though I'd blamed Darcie for her actions since that horrible weekend, I couldn't help but hurt for the naked depth of her grief. "I'm sure that's not what your therapist meant."

When she didn't respond, I said, "Come on. Let's go get this vintage wine so we can get drunk and weepy, and probably watch Kaea do the naked limbo under a broomstick."

Bursting into a wet laugh at the reminder of one particular night at the flat, she nodded, and led me to a right turn into another hallway. The cellar door proved to be the one at the very end—*far* away from the single weak wall lamp that lit up the windowless internal hall. Shadows converged thickly around the door through which we were to enter.

"No horror movie vibes at all," I muttered.

Darcie's laugh was forced as she opened the door and pushed the switch on the inside wall. And got a big fat nothing. "Bulb must've blown." She wiped her face on her sweater. "You were right. We should've looked for a flashlight."

"I have my phone." I turned on the flashlight icon, the resulting light revealing a set of narrow and dusty stairs that vanished into nothingness.

20

"Oh, hell no." Stronger, sounding more like herself, Darcie backed off from the doorway. "You wait here while I run back to the kitchen. I just remembered that Jim keeps his personal flashlight in the pantry."

I should've called after her, told her I wasn't staying there alone. But I let her go, her footfalls fading quickly as she broke into a jog. After a while, the only sound was my breath. The shadows coalesced into a near-physical presence around me, pressing down on my shoulders and whispering in my ears.

Because as I stared at the circle of light thrown by my phone, I had the chilling realization that this was my future. At least for the short term. A limited field of vision that would get progressively smaller . . . until all that remained was a blurry pinprick.

The doctors had been clear with me. While there was a slim chance that I might retain a small percentage of my vision, that percentage would be limited in the extreme. And even that droplet of vision might be restricted to one eye. It was equally possible that I'd have nothing, the visual world a complete blank.

"I know the temptation is to ignore it, but you can't." Dr. Mehta's kind but firm tone. "This *is* going to happen. Pretending it won't will gain you nothing. You have a brief window of time here—time that you can use to set yourself up to thrive in the years to come."

I hadn't wanted to listen to her, hadn't wanted to accept that my world would one day be smaller than the aperture of my favorite camera. I didn't know why today was different, why the realization settled heavy and solid in my gut.

I spoke the cold truth aloud. "I'm going blind."

There was nothing the doctors could do, no magic potion I could drink, no operation that'd fix me. I'd have to tell my family soon, my friends, too.

But first, I had to begin to live in the dark.

So despite Darcie's request that I stay there, I walked into the cellar and down the stairs. The first delicate strands of a spider's web across my nose and mouth made me shriek, but I was an old hand at tearing through them by the end. Once at the bottom, I should've switched off the light, made myself embrace the pitch-black, but I couldn't.

It wasn't about safety, about bumbling around in a room full of glass bottles. It was because I was afraid of the dark. I'd always been afraid of the dark. No matter my intention to accept the diagnosis, that fear wasn't going to vanish overnight.

My heart thudded, my tongue too fat in my dry mouth, but I was here. I'd walked into the dark and I wasn't screaming. As far as I was concerned, that was a win. Turning carefully to the left, phone light pointed in front of me, I sucked in a breath. Rows of wine bottles stretched out in front of me, the bottles stacked on shelves created for that purpose.

I discovered the same when I checked on the right.

Excitement took a big bite out of my fear. I was no wine snob or expert, but I could distinguish the different layers of flavor and appreciated complexity—but I'd never had the budget to try truly old wine. This week might turn out far better than I'd expected if I could go to town on this cellar.

I grabbed a couple of bottles at random, purely on the basis of which ones had the most interesting labels. I could always put them back if Darcie and Ash didn't want me to open a specific one.

Tucking both under one arm, I began to walk quickly back up the stairs.

The door slammed shut.

I froze. "Darcie!" Barely able to hear myself over the thudding drum of my pulse, I tried again. "Darcie, I'm down here!"

Silence from the other side.

"Ha ha, very funny." My face was hot, sweat blooming in my armpits. "It better not be locked."

I raced up the remaining steps, my phone held in a death grip. Putting the bottles down on the landing at the top, I wrenched at the door handle. And almost sent myself careening down the stairs when it came open without a problem.

"Fuck!" Though I managed to catch myself in time, I dropped my phone.

The light blinked out.

Terrified of losing my lifeline, I dropped onto my hands and knees and patted the area. Dust was grit on my palms . . . No, there, the slick black of my phone case. "The dust will go nicely with the cobwebs in my hair," I muttered in throat-drying relief, not even concerned that I might've picked up an eight-legged hitchhiker.

Wanting out of there, I took everything with me into the hallway. Only once I'd pulled the door shut did I examine my phone.

The screen came on at my first touch.

Shuddering, I bent over, my hands braced on my knees. I knew this wasn't good, that I couldn't become reliant on a device to the point of having a panic attack if I ever couldn't find it, but there was only so much I could handle at once.

It took time to be able to breathe again.

When I could, I looked at the cellar door. It must've swung shut on its own. But . . . Chewing on my lip, I looked up the hallway. The air was deathly still, no airflow at all, nothing to nudge the door shut.

"It's an old building," I said, more than ready for my wine. "I bet it has quirks aplenty." With that, I grabbed the bottles, both of them dusty and marked with my fingerprints. I didn't know if it was seeing the dust that set me off, but I sneezed five times in quick succession.

I sounded like a chipmunk.

Laughing at myself, I began to retrace my steps. I figured I'd either run into Darcie at some point or—if she took a different route back—she'd turn back as soon as she'd confirmed I wasn't in the cellar. Anyway, girl was taking way too long to get a flashlight. Likely she'd gotten caught up in a conversation and I'd find her with the others.

I almost got lost a couple of times, was saved by my visual memory for the paintings that lined the hallways. I just followed the trail of glum landscapes and emotionless, staring portraits. At one point, I thought I heard rustling *in* the walls, shuddered. "I hope this place doesn't have rats," I muttered, knowing that was likely to be a false hope—it was an old, barely maintained pile.

As I hurried on, I made very certain not to look at the painting with the blurred faces.

"How long does it take to get a flashlight?" I called out as I entered the living room.

Kaea looked up from the couch. "Come again?"

I scanned the room. "Where is everybody?"

"A couple of people went to the tower to download their emails—though I'd be surprised if they have reception even up there, what with this weather. I think someone else went to get their laptop, or maybe it was for a quickie." A waggle of the eyebrows. "I, meanwhile, am lounging around drinking this fine whiskey that Ash poured me." He raised a cut-glass tumbler, the amber liquid within jewel-bright in the firelight.

"Very Lord of the Manor." I walked toward the bar.

"You have cobwebs in your hair," he pointed out helpfully. "And dust imprints of what I assume are your own hands on your butt."

"Ugh." I put the bottles on the bar. "How's my face?"

When he tapped one cheek, I used a paper serviette I found on the bar to wipe it off.

"You going to open up one of those?" he asked while I finger-combed my hair to get rid of the cobwebs. "I'll try it with you."

"I thought I'd wait for Darcie, make sure I haven't accidentally taken a thousand-dollar bottle." I halted, stared at him. "How long do you think everyone will be gone?"

He went motionless, the tumbler held partway to his lips. "No idea." Lowering his glass to his lap, he said, "But it might be long enough for you to go out and get some photos even if we can't look at the goods themselves."

I was outside less than a minute later. Rain fell in a torrent, but it wasn't angling in under the overhang despite the wind that slapped me in the face like a living hand. The world turned invisible a bare few steps out from the house, nothing but roiling black cracked with flashes of broken white fire.

Despite the angry downpour, the light that fell from the house was enough for me to find my way to where I'd stashed Kaea's boots. I quickly took multiple high-definition photographs, hid the boots again, and was on my way back across the wooden boards of the veranda when Phoenix appeared out of nowhere.

I screamed and stumbled backward onto the veranda railing. It creaked under my weight. "What the hell, Nix!"

Wincing, he held up his hands. "Sorry, sorry." A second later, he opened his mouth while leaning way too close to me. "Can you smell it?"

About to ask him how much he'd already had to drink, I suddenly had a brainstorm. "Have you started smoking again?" I asked in a harsh whisper. "Oh my God, Nix! V will bug out!" Her father, a longtime smoker, had barely survived lung cancer and it was the one vice about which she was not in any way rational.

"I tried really hard not to"—he shoved his hands through his hair, pulled at clumps of it—"but fuck, sometimes I feel like my head will explode."

Dropping his hands, he began to pace back and forth but only went about three steps before repeating the loop. A mouse in a trap about to gnaw off its foot to escape. Worried now, I tried to stop his pacing by touching his shoulder, failed. "Nix, what's going on?"

21

Instead of answering, Phoenix pulled out a travel-size bottle of blue liquid that I recognized as high-strength mouthwash. "I brought this along to try to get rid of the smell. And I've mastered it so that the smoke doesn't come toward me or sink into my clothing. Lu, please, will you sniff me?"

That was the last thing I'd ever thought Phoenix would ask of me, but I did it. "A touch of smokiness, but that could be from the fire. You're safe." Stepping back afterward, I said, "You know I have to tell her. She's my best friend. I can't be keeping secrets from her."

"She hates smoking. I gave up the smoking or I gave her up, that was the deal." More pulling at his hair, more jagged pacing. "Can you give me this week? I'll sort it out with her, tell her everything."

Since I had no desire to get in the middle of their marriage, I nodded. "She knows something is wrong." And no matter her antipathy for smoking, she might well be relieved that it was only him sneaking cigarettes. But still . . . "You know how she is about honesty in a relationship."

"I promise I'll fix it." He stared at me, seeming to realize the incongruity of my presence for the first time. "What are you doing out here? Don't tell me you've taken up smoking, too."

"Hardly." I held up my camera. "Was hoping to take a set of storm pictures, but the light's no good for it." The lie came out smoothly; it was one I'd used often over the years when discovered in a place I wasn't supposed to be.

Of course it wouldn't have worked had Darcie figured out I'd broken into her place to look for Bea's doll, but other times? It was astonishing how often people just took others at their word. I could've pulled off many a heist by now if I were so inclined, but I wasn't about stealing.

I was about watching.

"We should get back inside." Phoenix swept his hand through his hair, his movements firm now as he tried to tidy himself up. "Kaea mentioned doing a toast, so they'll notice if we're not around."

As it happened, we weren't the last ones to arrive. "Where's Darcie?"

Ash glanced over with a frown. "I figured you knew."

"What? Why?"

"You two went off together." Abandoning the drink he'd been making, he walked around the side of the bar.

Everyone else had stopped moving, was staring at me.

My mind flashed to the doll on Darcie's bed, then in her hands. Flaming strands, a burned face. An intent to torment. It hadn't been a prank gone wrong, no matter if she'd tried to play it off that way. One of us had been torturing her. And now no one had seen her for at least a half hour, maybe even forty-five minutes. I hadn't looked at the clock when we'd left, had to go off instinct.

"She came back to get a flashlight," I said. "I was supposed to wait for her, but I decided to use my phone flashlight to go down and check out the cellar. She said Jim's flashlight was in the pantry." I glanced at Aaron. "You didn't see her?"

"No, and I was in the kitchen until about ten minutes ago. But let me go check the pantry just to be certain."

No one spoke until he came back through the door from the living room to the kitchen. Face grim, he held up a heavy-duty black flashlight.

"Maybe she's upstairs?" Vansi jumped to her feet. "I'll run up and see. On the hike, she was laughing about getting dolled up tonight. Could be she decided to do that."

It was a flimsy hope, as was Ash's thought that she might be feeling ill and was holed up in one of the toilets. We all went to check the various toilets and bathrooms, even our own, but came up empty.

"Okay." Ash pressed his fingers to his temples after we returned to the living room. "We split up." He dropped his hand. "Everyone take a part of the house and search. Place has a ton of nooks and crannies. She could've fallen if she decided to take a shortcut on the servants' stairs, or if she slipped someplace nearer to the cellar."

"Take your phones if we can't find the flashlights," I blurted out. "I've noticed the lamps flicker—they might go out without warning."

Aaron confirmed the flashlight from the pantry worked, and Kaea proved to have two in his pack, which I ran up to get. Grace also dug out a slimline one that she kept in her travel bag. "Here, Luna," she said. "You take this one. It's light but strong. I'll be with Aaron and he has the heavy-duty one. That leaves two for Ash, Vansi, and Nix."

"We all stay in pairs," Ash said before we could split off. "Luna, you're with me."

"I can keep track of what's been searched." Kaea's skin was taut over his cheekbones, his hand digging into the back of the sofa. "If you pass by this way, check in with me and let me know."

I squeezed the rigid line of his shoulders. "We'll keep you in the loop."

"This is weird, Lunes," Kaea said softly as Ash began to divide up the search zones. "First that stupid doll, then my shoes, and now Darcie goes missing?" He stared up at the mounted stag heads. "I'm almost starting to believe this pile is haunted."

"It's more likely something in the house gave way." I wasn't willing to see ghosts when I already lived with shadows every day of my life. "It's an old place, and hasn't been maintained as well as it should."

"Luna." Ash's voice was clipped, a command.

Given the situation, I felt no sense of irritation, just joined him as he led me down the corridor toward the wine cellar. "We're going back to where I last saw her?"

He nodded, his jaw working. "You're sure you saw no sign of her on the way back?"

"Yes." And because I didn't like the tone of his voice, added, "I have no reason to lie."

A muttered expletive. "I know. Shit." He punched a fist against his thigh. "This fucking house. So many ghosts."

Something about the way he said that made the hairs rise on the back of my neck. "You're not talking about the metaphysical kind, are you?"

"That burned-out part of the house?" He jerked his head in the direction of the ruined wing. "It's not all historical. Darcie just prefers to let everyone believe that because explaining the truth is harder."

"What? I thought Clara Shepherd and three of her children died in the fire?"

"They did, but that fire was contained to a small section of the wing—the four of them just happened to be trapped in a room without an exit. Servants managed to put out the fire and save the rest of the wing, but Clara and her kids had already died from smoke inhalation by then."

My pulse beat in my mouth. Having read what I had of Clara's hidden diary, I wasn't certain any of that had been an accident. But that wasn't the most important thing right now. "Neither Bea nor Darcie ever mentioned a fire."

"It would've been before you met. Darcie was eleven, Bea ten. Down here for a family summer—ended up being the last summer they spent here together."

The cellar door appeared in the gloom in the distance. "What happened?"

"No one knows for sure, but Darcie told me it had to be Bea. She had a fascination with fire, likely set it while playing with matches." His jaw was so tight the tendons looked as if they might snap. "They had a nanny who used to come down here with them. She was in that wing when it went up."

"Oh my God." I didn't need to ask if she'd survived, not with what he'd said about ghosts.

"Darcie says fire starting is a sign of disturbance, and that her parents should've got Beatrice help then. But they didn't, not until much later." A pause before he swore again. "Do you believe it? That Bea was that unhinged?"

"No." I never would. "We would've noticed *something*. And I know she's your wife, but Darcie's the only one saying anything about Bea being unstable. What other proof do we have?"

"Bea killed herself."

A denunciation so angry that I knew why Darcie had screamed those words about obsession at him: Ash was still in love with Bea.

Having reached the cellar, he pushed open the door and called out Darcie's name while lighting up the space with the beam of his flashlight. There was no sign of movement, and when we walked down to search among the aisles, I stopped him and pointed to the floor with my own flashlight. "Look."

Only a single set of footprints in the dust. Obviously mine due to the distinctive tread pattern on the bottoms of my sneakers—which I'd decided to turn into house shoes for the duration of this week.

Regardless, we did a full search. Nothing.

Once back in the hallway, we aimed ourselves toward the living area, but didn't go in a straight line. Instead, we checked every side door and room that Darcie might've passed on the way. We were close to the smudged portrait—close to the area where I'd heard rustling in the walls—when I noticed a tapestry that was hanging in a way that shouldn't have been possible. At a permanent angle to the left.

Frowning, I walked over.

My mouth went dry the instant I tried to lift the tapestry . . . and found it was caught in a seam in the wall that shouldn't be there. "Ash, there's a door behind here."

22

I tried to turn the latch cleverly inlaid into a hollow in the door—so that the tapestry would lie flat against it. It wouldn't budge. I tried again.

Roughly pushing aside my hand, Ash twisted with his own. "It's locked." A grim line to his jaw, he told me to hold back the tapestry, then he put his shoulder to the door and banged into it.

Once.

Twice.

A cracking sound on the third.

The fourth broke it away from the jam and sent him tumbling inside.

Motes of dust danced in the beam of my flashlight as I began to search the secret space. I was moving slowly but still almost missed her. She looked like nothing, a discarded piece of clothing in a corner behind an old chaise longue with a curved back and once-golden arm dull with dust.

It was the glint of pale blond that alerted my subconscious, the shine of her hair the most brilliant thing in the room. My light hitched, returned to her, and then I was running over. "Darcie!"

"Jesus, baby! Darceline!" Ash fell onto his knees beside her, cradling her in his arms while I checked desperately for a pulse in her wrist, then in her neck. My own was so loud in my ears that it took me multiple attempts.

"She's got a pulse," I said, not adding that it felt sluggish to me. I was no expert. "We should get her to V and Nix."

Ash rose shakily, Darcie in his arms.

I went ahead to make sure the broken door didn't get in his way, and the two of us made our way to the lounge as quickly as possible. I called out as I went, yelling that we'd found her and needed Vansi or Phoenix. Even if they couldn't make out what I was saying, the fact that I was shouting should sound the alert.

I heard Kaea yell from the living room even as the sound of running feet vibrated through the house from various directions. A winded Vansi made it to us just as we reached the living area. Ash immediately placed Darcie on a sofa, and Vansi got to work checking her vitals.

It was only when I turned to look at Ash, say something, that I saw the blood on the pale blue of his shirt. Against the edge of one side of his chest and over one of his biceps. He looked down when I gasped, saw what I already had. "She's bleeding."

Thinking of how he'd held her, I said, "Her head, it has to be her head."

Phoenix ran in just as Vansi began to examine the back of Darcie's head. "Head wound," she said in a clipped, professional tone. "Vitals are steady. Bleeding seems to have stopped."

Phoenix came down beside her, the two of them speaking

quietly to each other as they checked Darcie over. Not knowing what else to do, I went and found a clean towel to place under Darcie's head, while Grace went upstairs to bring down a blanket.

"It doesn't look too serious," Vansi said after she got to her feet, Darcie now resting under the blanket. "Hopefully, she's just stunned and will come out of it soon."

"You sure?" Ash's voice was sandpaper, his face white. "We don't know how long she was in there. If it was since she left Luna . . ."

Phoenix, his hands on his hips, glanced between us. "Where exactly did you locate her?"

After we laid it out, he frowned. "Could she have locked herself in there by accident?"

"And what?" Ash demanded. "Knocked herself on the head, too?"

Phoenix was unflustered, his tone that of the doctor who dealt with countless injured patients and stressed relatives day after day. "The site of the injury suggests it could've been sustained if she fell against the wall or onto the floor at the wrong angle."

"I think I saw another door in the room." I wasn't sure I trusted my vision, but I couldn't hide something that might offer an insight into what Darcie had been doing there. "What if that door leads to a shortcut through the house?" It'd explain why she'd told me to wait; she hadn't wanted to share the route outside the family.

"A secret passageway!" Grace's eyes rounded. "We should go check it out, answer the question so we can stop thinking one of us tried to hurt Darcie on purpose—because if she decided to go in there, the accident theory makes the most sense."

Stomach churning, I nodded. "Yes, that's a good idea."

Aaron and Grace came with me, the others staying put in the

living area—though Kaea caught my gaze as I exited. He mouthed, *Be careful.* His hair was mussed up, five-o'clock shadow heavy on his face, and his whiskey abandoned on the table beside him.

I promised myself I'd give him a full update once we were back.

"It's not the fun reunion we all expected, huh?" Aaron said softly after we were out of earshot of the others. "Sorry, Gracie. I promised you a great time."

"Oh, sweetheart," she murmured, squeezing his arm as she leaned against him.

It struck me then that Grace was the unknown here, the one person whose motives we couldn't hope to guess at—we didn't know her well enough. Wouldn't that be easy? Just blame the newcomer in our midst like we were in some incestuous backwoods settlement that went around kidnapping hitchhikers.

I rolled my eyes at myself, because the truth of it was that poor Grace had no horse in this race. She was just an innocent bystander caught in the currents that tied the seven of us together.

"It's not your fault," she continued now. "It's this house. Bad juju all around."

"I'm beginning to agree with you." All the tiny hairs on my body were standing up, taut and alert. "It's as if it's holding on to all the bad energy from the past." I thought of Clara's tight script, the painstaking work she'd done to hide the ugly reality of her life.

I knew deep in my gut that she'd shared none of that with her family back in England. It would've only hurt them—they were helpless to do anything for her. And so she'd dealt alone with this life of whispering madness that could well have led to murder.

A glimpse of the eerie family portrait up ahead.

"This is it." Turning consciously away from that unnerving piece of art, I pointed out the tapestry that covered the now broken door.

Pulling it aside, Aaron turned on his flashlight. "Wow, apologies, Lu, but I almost didn't believe you on the secret room."

"I saw it and I still hardly believe it." I entered with him, while Grace hovered outside.

"You can wait there, Gracie," Aaron said with his customary gentleness, then mouthed "afraid of the dark" to me.

Bile burned my throat, but I just nodded. If only I could stand outside the dark, too, but the dark was coming for me.

There would never be any escape.

"No." Grace's shoulders rose, her face set. "I'm more frightened standing out here by myself. Especially if we *do* think someone did that to Darcie. Do we?"

"It was an accident." Aaron took her hand with a smile of encouragement. "It's only us eight in the house, remember?"

That was exactly the problem, though, wasn't it? It was only the eight of us in this house. And unlike Aaron, I wasn't so sure that I could trust all of my friends. Poor Grace. She didn't even know most of us that well, and she was now stuck with us in a house straight out of a gothic novel.

Wanting to hurry this up for her and for myself, I flashed the beam of my light at the spot I thought I'd seen a door. Air rushed out of me. "There it is."

"Did you see these bookshelves?" Grace said from my right at the same time. She pulled out a slim volume as Aaron went to check the door handle.

"It's in Latin," she muttered, sliding it back while I was still digesting the fact that she could make out anything in this light. "I think I recognized the word 'demon' from school."

I wanted to ask what kind of school taught Latin in this day and age, then remembered that she'd been educated at boarding schools in Europe. Answer had to be rich people schools.

I wondered idly if that meant Grace was rich. Be nice for Aaron if she was; if anyone deserved a break in life, it was him. He'd worked all through high school and university, and was currently doing a ton to support his younger siblings through higher education.

"It's open." Aaron pushed the door into empty space on the other side.

The smooth transition made me frown. "The door to this room was locked." I glanced back at the splintered edges that were a silent testament to what it had taken to get in. Ash was going to be paying the price for that in a few hours.

"Darcie must've locked it after she came inside." Grace slid back another book. "Did you check her pockets for a key?"

I shook my head.

Though Grace's words made sense, I couldn't understand why Darcie would've locked up when she was the only one who knew about the secret passage in the first place.

"This one is in English," Grace muttered, shifting to catch more of the glow from my flashlight.

The pages blazed a painful white to my eyes.

"It's a book of spells. Dark stuff. Cursing-your-neighbor kind of thing." Shuddering, she shoved it back onto the shelf. "Luna, do you mind if I go after Aaron into the passage?"

The weight of the dark at my back was suffocating. "No problem." I fell in behind her.

"Gah!" Aaron made a jerking motion, paused. "Uh, sorry. Cobwebs." He sounded so sheepish that it broke the tension, had us giggling. "At exactly the height of my face."

"It doesn't count unless a spider sets up home in your hair," I said.

"I hate you," he muttered without force, while Grace patted his back and said, "It's okay, sweetie. Spiders prefer other nesting places."

Not listening to Aaron's rumbled response, I ran the beam of my flashlight on either side of me. "Narrow." Not enough to be uncomfortable, but meant for single file.

"Yeah." Aaron coughed into the crook of his elbow. "I'll stay up front—unless you want to swap? You did find this place."

"No, go on." A few steps in, I couldn't help glancing back at the door through which we'd entered, my neck prickling.

"What if it *isn't* just us eight?" Grace whispered. "I mean, if there's one secret room, there could be others, right?"

My entire face went cold, her words giving shape to the primal fear in my gut.

I snapped my attention back to the other two.

"We'd have noticed," Aaron argued. "We've been all over the house. *I'd* have noticed if a ton of food went missing. Ash and Darcie might've stocked it, but they asked me to make the shopping list."

I hadn't known the latter, though it made sense. "Place is huge," I said, wondering why the hell I was adding fuel to the fire when it was the stuff of nightmares. "And one person wouldn't need a lot of food."

"How would they even have got here?" Aaron said, his voice a whisper, too.

As if the walls were listening in.

Stomach lurching, I remembered the rustling I'd put down to rats—then later to Darcie. But what if it hadn't been either of those two? What if the walls *were* listening?

"Could be a squatter," Grace said. "Like that case in America where that person lived in someone's attic for years and only came out at night."

"That's an urban legend," I said, though I wasn't so sure.

"I'm saying the estate sits empty most of the time, right? Perfect place to stay if you don't care that you're in the middle of nowhere. Plus, there's a pantry stocked with nonperishables."

"But they'd have to go out *sometime*," Aaron said, his tone firm. "I'm not buying that the squatter's happy to sit in isolation forever. They couldn't eat out the pantry, for one. The caretaker would notice."

I didn't want to say what I did next. "Easy enough to hide a vehicle in the bush at the foot of the mountains. Jim's got no reason to go out there. He's only responsible for the house and making sure any fallen fruit is cleaned up."

"That's it," Aaron muttered, "I'm separating you and Gracie the minute we're out of here. You're dangerous together."

"Sorry, sweetie." Grace patted his shoulder again. "It's this house. It's getting to us."

I allowed the topic to drift away, but I wondered if part of the reason Grace and I had clung to it was that it'd be less of a horror to have it be a stranger behind the odd occurrences. Because if there was no squatter . . . then it had to be one of us.

23

o you see anything?" I asked Aaron after several minutes of walking. From what I could tell, we'd turned the corner, but that was it. This place had no other markers, no helpful arrows on the wall.

My jaw ached, my neck stiff.

"Nothing." Thirty seconds or so later, our breathing loud in the silence, he said, "Hold on. I think I see a sliver of light. Switch off your flashlight."

Sweat broke out along my spine. "Grace, you okay with that?"

Grace's voice was unsteady as she said, "If it's only for a second or two."

"Here, take my hand. There you go. You're good, Lu."

With no escape hatches left, I forced myself to press down on the button that turned off the beam of light.

Spots flickered in my vision, fiery flashes of fading sight, and I had to place my hand against the wall to keep from screaming.

But it did nothing to stop the mental babbling: *Oh God. Oh God. Oh God!*

"Oh, I see it, too!" Grace's hand brushing my shoulder as she reached back. "Look!"

I could see easily enough over her diminutive height, but Aaron had to duck down to clear the sightline. And sure enough, there it was, a thin line of light beneath what had to be a doorway.

Air returned to my lungs in a stagnant rush.

Neither Aaron nor I turned on our flashlights as we headed toward that light. I still couldn't see anything except for when I caught a glimpse around Aaron, but just knowing that the light was there, that we were getting closer to it, stopped me from panicking.

A voice at the back of my brain whispered that I was a fool, that I had to accept that there would be no light in my future, nothing but the cold embrace of the dark.

Get used to it, it said. Or you'll go stark, raving mad.

Unable to deal with that while stuck in this damn passageway with its flat, stale air, the dust grit under my teeth, and no doubt a new crop of cobwebs in my hair, I focused on Grace's scent. She used either a body spray or shampoo with lavender as a base ingredient.

It was a scent I knew to the bone after growing up with masses of the blooms in our yard at home. Mum had always had grand plans to dry them and make potpourri, but two active kids and a joyous social life kept her too busy to ever quite get to the task. So the lavender thrived unchecked, our yard abuzz with bees who loved the tall purple stalks.

The birds had brought other seeds, and I'd mischievously sprinkled a packet of wildflower seeds through the yard one spring. Over time, Mum's wild garden had become a thing of stunning beauty, until the neighbors believed she'd planned it that way on purpose. Some of my first photographs had been of the garden in bloom as my parents sat on our little porch with cups of tea in hand and Cable zoomed around with his toy airplane.

Dad had hung one of those photographs in the hallway after having it professionally framed. It was still there, in among my brother's sports certificates, the little shrine of trophies he'd collected over the years—and all the other photos of mine that my mum and dad had framed.

My parents knew how to love both their children, and I'd never appreciated the true gift of that until just now, when I thought of how Bea's mother hadn't been able to accept her daughter's divergence. If there even *had* been a divergence.

Again, I had only Darcie's word for Bea's problems.

"I hope that door's unlocked." Grace's voice wobbled. "Otherwise, fair warning, I'm gonna scream."

I hadn't even thought about that, but she was right. It would be a bit much to come this far and then find the door locked and have to make it all the way back . . . all the while trying not to think about the phantom squatter who might've decided to somehow block us in on that end, too.

My heart beat so fast it hurt.

But when we reached the light at last, the door swung smoothly open under Aaron's hand . . . to a clanking rattle of sound.

"What the—"

The three of us stood in the pantry. The sounds we'd heard had been cans falling off the shelf attached to the back of the door we'd opened. Chickpeas, tomatoes, beetroot, corn, spaghetti, baked beans, more baked beans, mackerel in red sauce, sardines, and beside it, a can of black cherries.

I also spotted rice nearby, a bag of flour, dried fruits and nuts. More cans.

And the painting on the far wall.

My face dropped, my skin melting. "Her eyes weren't like that before."

Glancing over his shoulder, Aaron blurted out an expletive I'd never before heard come from his lips. Grace, meanwhile, had her hand over her mouth, her eyes awash in tears. She ran out of the pantry the next second, Aaron behind her.

I stayed, stared.

And took a photograph of the painting's bloody, scratched-out eyes.

"Lu," Aaron hissed from the doorway. "Get out of there."

A niggle at the back of my mind, I nonetheless followed, all the way through the door from the kitchen to the lounge—behind him and a pale Grace. She'd dried her eyes, but they remained rimmed in red.

"That was quick." Kaea looked at my hair, winced. "Um, Lunes, it's not just a cobweb this time."

I forgot everything, would've given in to the urge to flail and scream like a little girl, but Grace reached up to gently collect whatever it was that had decided to live on my head. "It's only a wee thing," she said, her voice soft. "I'll go put it somewhere it won't bother anyone."

I stared after her.

Aaron's pride was squared shoulders, a curve of the lips. "She's not scared of bugs, any bugs." A grin as he watched her take the bug out of the living room. "She wanted to be an entomologist as a child, but life took her in a different direction. My girl still loves bugs, though."

Grace walked back in right as Aaron and I finished explaining about the secret passageway. "He's got a nice cozy spot now," she said, dusting off her hands. "And it looks like we proved our theory. Darcie must've been taking the shortcut to the pantry when she slipped, hit her head."

No hint of our squatter theory. I didn't bring it up, either—we had no proof, had been telling ghost stories in the dark.

Vansi frowned. "What position was Darcie in when you found her? Did it look like she'd fallen?"

I glanced at Ash slumped in an armchair, his face in one hand, and figured he must've been too distraught to give them anything useful. Flicking backward through my mental snapshots, I stopped at my first glimpse of Darcie's crumpled form, the way her hair had lain around her in a halo.

"She could have," I said slowly. "She was on her side on the ground, in a position it'd be natural to fall into in terms of the space."

"I just . . ." Kaea chewed his lower lip. "It's weird, that's all. For her to injure herself that way when it's obvious she knows the house inside out."

"Freak accidents happen." Phoenix's pragmatic contribution.

Vansi nodded. "You'd be surprised how many people come into the ER because of household accidents. Slipping on a puddle of water in the laundry and getting a skull fracture from the edge of the washing machine, forgetting a step that's been there for three decades and breaking a leg, grabbing the scalding handle of a cast-iron pan, we see it all."

"Our bodies are far weaker than we think." Phoenix put one

arm around Vansi's shoulders, hugging her to his side. "One mistake away from catastrophic failure."

Hard to argue when they put it in such stark terms.

A rasp of air. "Uh . . ."

All our attention snapped immediately to Darcie. Ash dropped to his knees beside the sofa, took one of her hands in his. "Darceline?" A gentle touch to her hair, Ash careful to avoid the wounded area.

It took several minutes for her to come out of it, and she did so with a grimace. I'd moved to the end of the sofa by now, trying not to crowd her but also wanting to see how she was. When she opened her eyes, it was with a look of confused blankness . . . that turned to biting rage. "They hit me!"

Everyone froze.

"It's okay, darling," Ash soothed. "You're safe. You're with us."

Darcie looked around wildly, whimpered. "My head . . ."

"You took quite a blow when you fell." Phoenix took her wrist, fingers on her pulse. "Do you remember what happened?"

"Fell?" Darcie's voice rose at the end in a questioning upstroke.

"That's what we think happened," Vansi began.

"Hold on, guys." Kaea's voice, firm and authoritative as he hobbled over using his cane.

I gave him my shoulder and he braced the heat of his muscular body against mine.

"She said someone hit her," Kaea continued. "Didn't you, Darcie?"

Rubbing at her forehead, Darcie struggled to sit up. Ash helped her.

Smeared red marked the checked blue-and-white fabric of the towel that had been under her head. Grace, closest to it, picked it up and slid it out of sight behind her back. Catching her gaze, I nodded in agreement. Darcie was barely holding it together as it was. The last thing she needed was to get upset by the sight of her own blood.

"I—" She squeezed her knees with her hands. "I was so sure, but it's gone now." Her voice trembled. "I c-can't—"

"Don't worry about it," Phoenix said. "You took a hard blow. Your memories will settle after a while."

I knew that was comfort, not truth. Sometimes, the memories never returned. It had been like that with me when I'd had one of those stupid household accidents V had described and whacked my head on the edge of an open cupboard door in my kitchen. I remembered standing up from looking inside the lower cupboards . . . and then I was waking up in the hospital.

Yet, at some point during that time, I'd staggered to the cell phone I'd left on the little table beside my sofa. I'd called emergency services, and had apparently opened the door to them, too.

When I'd finally come home, it was to a trail of blood around my apartment. It'd looked like a crime scene. Complete with fingerprints in blood and photos pulled off the walls as I staggered around. Later, I'd learned that when I spoke to the paramedics, it was with my Oyster card in hand. I'd had a conversation with them, insisted I could take the Tube to the hospital.

I had zero memory of any of that, and even though I knew it was stupid, a small part of me continued to wonder if it was the head wound that had caused my eyes to go dark. I knew it was a genetic disease. I *knew*. But it was easier to blame a physical injury. It gave the diagnosis chasing me heft and shape.

"Will I remember?" Darcie's eyes were huge and wet. "Later?"

24

Phoenix patted her on the shoulder. "Don't stress about it. Like I said, things will settle down, be clearer after you've had time to recover."

"Here." Vansi held out a couple of pills with an empathetic smile. "They're painkillers from my own personal stash for migraines, bit stronger than the usual over-the-counter meds. No side effects other than a little bit of dry mouth."

Intercepting the pills, Ash whispered in Vansi's ear. From her sudden intake of breath, he had to be asking her if they were safe to take during pregnancy. He might have fudged things by saying they weren't sure yet but had been trying. Whatever Vansi said in response seemed to satisfy him and he put the pills in Darcie's hand and gently urged her to take them.

Darcie obeyed with childlike compliance, swallowing the medication using the water Vansi had given her; she even finished the glass when instructed. And though she refused to go upstairs to rest in her room, she allowed Ash to sit next to her and cuddle her close.

Probably a good idea to have her in sight of others. Head injuries could be unpredictable. The doctors had refused to allow me to go home until I'd called up a friend to come stay with me for a couple of days.

I hadn't spoken to that friend—that good, kind person—since my diagnosis.

Slowly, things began to settle again. Kaea, back on his sofa, pointed out the pack of cards left from an earlier game, Aaron served us a nourishing stew that was all about comfort, and Grace put on music. We all groaned when Rick Astley's mellow tones poured out of the portable speakers Aaron had brought along.

"My '80s playlist is extensive," Grace boasted with a grin, waving her phone in the air, so of course, we had to make requests.

With the fire flickering in the hearth, the good food, and the music that Grace kept at a volume that didn't overwhelm the quiet conversation, even Darcie began to smile.

At one point, after Ash got up to use the bathroom, I went to sit next to her. "How are you feeling?"

"Like an idiot," she muttered, raising a hand to the back of her head but stopping before she touched the wound. It wasn't bleeding anymore, but her hair was matted and rusty with the dried fluid. I didn't point that out to her; she'd figure it out on her own, and by then, it would hopefully be safe for her to take a shower.

Because Darcie would *not* rest easy once she knew, far less go to bed in that state.

"Ash told me where you two found me. I must've decided to take the shortcut to the pantry." A pained smile. "Bea and I used to run wild through the passageways—at least until our parents put a stop to it. They locked all the entries they could find. Said it was for safety, but I think it was really because they were scared we'd see or hear something we shouldn't if we accidentally ended up near their bedroom."

"I wondered if there was more than one hidden passage."

Darcie shook her head at my implied question. "It's our secret, mine and Bea's. To be passed on only to our children." A hitch in her breath. "I haven't even shown Ash most of them."

It took effort not to drop my eyes to her abdomen. "You obviously got the keys to the locked doors at some point," I said, still queasy about the idea that there might be a hidden way into my bedroom; I knew what I'd be doing tonight, and that was checking every wall and cupboard for concealed doors.

"Not all of them. Beatrice . . ." Darcie stared at the crackling flames. "We found the keys after our parents' accident, made a copy so that we'd both have access to all of the house."

Her throat moved as she swallowed. "I never found her set. She was possessive of them even though we rarely came here, used to tell me that hiding the keys in a secret spot was her homage to the man who designed the house—Blake Shepherd."

I ran my hand down her back even as a small part of me hungered to discover this lost piece of Beatrice. I'd known her better than anyone; if I put my mind to it, I was certain I could unearth her keys. Because I didn't think she'd have taken them from this house.

Bea's sense of mischief wouldn't have seen the fun in that.

Darcie twisted her hands together, the movement of her throat convulsive.

Reminded all over again that no matter their problems, they'd been sisters first and foremost, I made a conscious effort to change the subject. "How's your head?"

It took her several long breaths to reply and when she did, it was with a shaky smile. "Those pills V gave me are magic. Dull thud at the back of my head, but that's about it."

She looked longingly at the tumbler half-full of sparkling clear liquid on the coffee table by Grace, who sat cross-legged on the floor with a small bowl of pistachios, chatting away to Kaea. "I could murder a vodka on the rocks, but Nix told me that alcohol is definitely not a good idea with a head wound."

"Don't worry—it won't ruin your night." I sank back into the sofa, wondering if Darcie had forgotten her pregnancy for a moment, or if she was just saying the words to make conversation. "Remember that weekend we got stuck in that disastrously 'rustic' cabin Kaea hired out in the middle of nowhere? When Aaron forgot the cooler with the beers *and* I dropped the only bottle of wine on the floor?" It had ended up one of my favorite trips ever, even with all of us stone-cold sober.

"Oh my God, that trip!" Her laughter drew the attention of the others, and of course everyone wanted to know what we were on about.

The walk down memory lane was bittersweet.

Because there was no Bea to giggle with me about how the two of us had woken in the night with the urge to use the bathroom and, dressed only in our sleep T-shirts, had tiptoed to the tiny wood-paneled room using a flashlight—only to exit screaming when we found not one but *three* giant wētā sitting on the seat, antennae twitching.

Later, after the screams had turned into laughter, she'd said, "I

THERE SHOULD HAVE BEEN EIGHT

know they're harmless, but seriously, they look like bugs straight out of the prehistoric era. I swear that first one was the size of my hand!"

But there was no laughter now.

As there was no Bea to remind me to "Have fun, Nae-nae. We only live once. Unless we're zombies, then we live once and shamble the second time around."

Opening one of the old wines that Darcie had told me meant nothing to her, I made a silent toast to our missing friend. *Miss you, Bee-bee. Hope you're not a zombie.*

Her ghostly laughter was pure delight in my head. Because Bea, *my* Bea, had always had a sense of humor that could be silly and sharp and wicked all at once.

It wasn't until we were about to head to bed, and the others—sans Darcie, who was already upstairs—had gone to clean up the kitchen, while I tidied the lounge, collecting any stray glasses and plates, that Kaea said, "Don't you think that was weird?" A low whisper. "The way Nix immediately put it into her head that it was all an accident—even after what she said when she first woke up?"

"I figured he was doing the doctor thing—you know, trying to calm her down." I stood up with a glass in one hand and a couple of small bowls in the other. Pistachio shells filled both of the latter.

Kaea made a face. "I suppose. But she sure looked certain when she woke up and said that someone had hit her on the back of the head."

"Well, the one person we know couldn't have done it is you."

I widened my eyes at him. "Can you say the same about me?" I added "dum, dum, dum" music in my most dramatic tones.

"Firstly, you're tipsy." He pointed a finger at me, his grin wide. "And secondly, you? The woman scared of bugs who almost passed out when she had to get a blood test?"

"Hey! I hadn't eaten that day!"

He snorted. "Thirdly, if you were ever going to do something nasty, Lunes, you'd be smarter about it. Probably slip a little poison into your enemy's drink, maybe inject them between the toes while they weren't conscious."

I stared at him. "Dude."

Shrugging, he said, "I've been sitting on the sofa with a lot of time to think." He threw back the last of his whiskey. "I can't see any reason why Phoenix would bash Darcie over the head. Unless he decided to try his luck one last time, she turned him down, and he lost it."

I blinked like an owl.

Kaea groaned. "Seriously, Lunes, sometimes, I think you're so used to being behind the lens that you don't see what's happening right in front of you. Our resident doc had a big old thing for her after they first met."

"He was already with Vansi then." I frowned, thought about it. "Yes, V met him first. At that after-school science club."

"I'm not sure about that. Darcie mentioned a shared riding lesson once, and she gave up riding at twelve, I think." He shoved up the sleeves of his hoodie. "Anyway, Darcie wasn't interested, always had her eye on Ash." His fingers tightened on his empty tumbler. "I figured Nix was over it, what with Vansi and all, but who knows."

I was beginning to regret that third glass of excellent old wine. The edges of my thoughts were fuzzy and I felt very much like an idiot when it came to the emotional undercurrents between my friends. "I certainly knew who you were sleeping with," I muttered with a scowl.

The slightest shift of his eyes, before he grinned and threw out his arms. "That's because I'm an open book. Why hide it when I can flaunt it."

Even fuzzy-headed, I knew I hadn't imagined that momentary pause, but I'd had too much wine to cross-examine my friend who happened to be a high-powered lawyer. Especially since Kaea could hold his liquor far better than me; his mind was no doubt still razor-sharp.

"I'm taking these dishes to the kitchen and we'll finish this conversation when I'm not addlebrained, Mr. Kaea Ngata Fancy Pants, Esquire." I waved a finger at him like a schoolmarm straight out of an old film.

His shoulders shook. "I love you, Lunes."

"As you should. I'll tell the guys to come back and help you upstairs to bed."

"Nah, don't bother. I think it'll be easier all around if I stay down here. The couch is big enough and there's a bathroom just down the hallway. Close enough for me to hobble to, and less pain than trying to get up and down the stairs. I do need a few things from my room."

"I can grab that for you." Walking into the kitchen after he told me what he needed, I dropped off the dishes. "Kaea's going to stay in the lounge tonight."

Phoenix paused in the act of drying the pot Aaron had used

to make the stew. "Probably for the best." A short nod. "Less chance of jolting his knee for no good reason. He should be feeling better by tomorrow if he rests up."

Once upstairs, I knocked gently on Darcie's door. "You okay in there, Darcie? I can get you a cup of chamomile tea if you want."

She'd had a habit of ending a night out with that back when we'd been at uni; drunk Darcie making her chamomile tea was one of my favorite memories of her. All her walls down, no sophistication or manipulation. Just silly, happy Darcie trying to add honey to her cup while her coordination was shot and the entire world was hilarious.

No sound from Darcie and Ash's room.

After a short internal battle, I decided to open the door and peek inside. I still wasn't too sure about her being alone with a head injury, but she'd been insistent on coming upstairs about thirty minutes ago, saying that she wanted to rest. She'd also refused to let Ash come up with her, arguing that she'd feel guilty if he ended the night early on her account.

The bed was empty, the sheets mussed, but steam curled out from the open bathroom door.

I struggled with what to do next, my thoughts wrapped in cotton wool. I certainly didn't want to walk in on her, but what if she'd collapsed in there?

A thudding sound, followed by, "Damn it!"

It took my inebriated brain a lot longer than usual to process that she'd dropped her soap or shampoo. The size of that thud indicated a small thing, not a person.

Backing quietly out, I shut the door behind myself, then

walked to Kaea's room. Instead of digging around in his pack, I just grabbed the entire thing. He'd always packed light, so it wasn't hard to carry.

"Lunes, my Lunes," he'd drawl when picking up my backpack to throw into the back of whatever vehicle we'd hired for our latest adventure into the bush. "You don't have to bring the entire library, you know."

"That's what you think" had been my usual response.

Now, as I walked into the lounge, I thought about the scarf I'd found in his pocket. Perhaps it was the wine, but the words just slipped out. "Why do you have Beatrice's scarf?"

25

Kaea's face stilled for a second before his shoulders kind of hunched in and he pressed his hands to his face. When he dropped them, it was to reveal an expression raw with grief.

"She left it in my room once, while we were hanging out playing video games. I kept on meaning to give it back to her, never quite got around to it . . . And then . . ." He dug his fingers into the back of the sofa. "I couldn't let go of it. I should've left it at home this week, but I didn't—because she should've been here for this.

"She should've been roasting me about my love life, should've been helping Ash mix drinks, should've been sneaking bits of Aaron's creations while he threatened to chase her out of the kitchen. We can pretend as much as we want, but it's not right without her. It'll never be right again. *We'll* never be right again."

Eyes hot with emotion, he looked over at where Ash had sat for much of the night. "Bea made him *better*. Darcie's made him what she always wanted. Like he's a doll and she's maneuvering his limbs so he behaves in certain ways. Preppy, polite Ash who holds her hand and wears coordinated clothing she picks out."

My throat thick, I sat down on the coffee table and held his gaze. "Yes." It came out ragged, rough. "Be honest with me. Did you play that prank with the doll?" His anger altered the equation, made it far more likely that he'd struck out.

He made a face. "Believe it or not, I have grown up. That was just mean, the whole doll thing." A hesitation, his lips pressed together among all that dark beard stubble that just made him more handsome.

"What?"

"Leave out my sabotaged boot and it's all been done to Darcie, did you notice? And unlike Nix, I do think someone is behind it. Just a few too many coincidences."

My temples throbbed. "But who?" I hissed under my breath, glancing over at the door that led from the kitchen to the lounge.

Unflexing his hand, he held it in that taut, stretched position for a long breath before exhaling. "I don't know. While you were searching the house, I got to wondering whether we're all alone here after all."

His dark eyes met mine. "I mean, how hard would it be to hide in this huge pile, and only come out when none of us is looking? Not a single one of us has been over to the ruined wing. We have no idea if parts of it remain habitable."

A chill crept over my spine, the tiny hairs on my arms standing up. "We talked about that," I admitted. "In the passageway. It seemed ridiculous once we walked out. Ghost stories around a campfire."

Kaea's gaze flicked to the kitchen door again, back to me. "I've been thinking about that break-in at Darcie and Ash's. There was something really ugly about it, just *off*. What if it wasn't drug addicts? What if it was personal and that person followed them here?"

My face was flushing hot and cold, hot and cold. It was an anxiety response, one I'd had forever. Pressing my fingers to my temples, I tried to still the roar in my head, the sloshing in my gut. "But if Darcie is the target, why come after her now? And here? It's a long way to go for a stalker. Much easier to wait until she's back in Auckland, carrying on with her regular routine."

"Who knows? Darcie is very good at keeping secrets." His voice shook, the muscles in his forearm standing out as he clenched his hand into a fist against the brocade of the couch. "I never thought she'd do it to us, though. I saw her lie with glib ease to others, but I never thought she'd do it to us until she did."

My mouth dried up. "What are you talking about?"

"You should ask her about Professor Hammett sometime," he said just as the door from the kitchen opened with a small creak of sound.

The others spilled into the room, laughing and talking among themselves.

"Nightcap, anyone?" Vansi asked, lifting a pretty cut-glass bottle. "I have butterscotch liqueur."

"I'm out." I got up with a wince. "I'm too old and decrepit to handle my liquor. Good night, my young friends."

Their laughter followed me to the hallway and up the stairs, but it was Kaea's voice that rang in my head, his words tumbling around and around in my skull. I remembered Professor Hammett. A middle-aged man with pallid white skin, brown hair, and round spectacles, his body pudgy around the middle and his jaw soft.

I'd only known of him because Darcie and Bea had dragged me along to a public lecture of his. What had it been? History of Engineering? No, more esoteric, but to do with their shared major.

"Engineering runs in our blood," Darcie had said during one of the times when she and Bea had been as thick as thieves. "Dad, Granddad, Aunt Helene, and now me and Bea. We're going to open our own firm, aren't we, Triss? Shepherd and Shepherd."

Triss.

I'd forgotten that, how Darcie always called Bea by her childhood pet name when they were getting along. I hadn't heard it for at least a year prior to Bea's suicide. But they'd been tight when we'd gone to that lecture.

My hand slid up the last bit of the banister as I gave up attempting to recall the exact subject of the lecture. Most of it had gone over my head, but Bea and Darcie had been enthralled. I'd taken several photographs of Hammett. There'd been something about his eyes. Such an ordinary-looking man, but with such depth in his eyes.

What the hell had Kaea been talking about?

I pushed through into my bedroom, wishing we hadn't been interrupted. I'd get it out of him tomorrow, I thought as I kicked off my sneakers and began to undress. And while he might believe me oblivious, I knew secrets, too, things Kaea would never know.

No one but Vansi and I knew that Vansi had suffered an early-in-pregnancy miscarriage at twenty-one. Phoenix hadn't even been aware she was pregnant. She'd still been deciding what to do about it. Then her body had made the decision for her in a gush of blood.

She'd been so strange that night, my best friend. Hollow-eyed yet resolute. "I want him to be with me because he loves me, Luna." Her fingers bruising on my wrist. "I don't want him to be forced into it."

That wasn't the only secret I kept.

Walking naked to the window, the air in the room a chill second skin, I pressed my hand to the glass while looking out at the graveyard obliterated by the darkness and the rain. All I could see were the droplets on the glass, fat little globes that rolled at a speed that should've worried me for what it indicated about the weather.

But it was Bea on my mind.

Bea who'd kissed girls as well as boys. Never me. I hadn't been interested and for some reason, that had made my love for her all the more precious to her. I'd wanted nothing from her but her mere presence.

Bea, who was no angel and all the more lovable for it.

Bea, who'd like to steal little things and keep them in a treasure box in my room. Stupid things. Cheap things. The joy in the sleight of hand. Her favorite acquisition a pen from the desk of the banker who managed the trust left behind by her and Darcie's parents.

Bea, who'd snorted white powder off a glass table in front of me one night in a club, then later told me the high wasn't worth it. Her pupils had been dilated at the time, her hair spread out in a fan below her head as she lay on my bed, her fingers stroking my cheek. "Nae-nae, my Nae-nae, you'd do anything for me, wouldn't you?"

"Yes."

A tilt of her head, a funny little smile. "Why?"

"Because I love you." My world was simple, my needs simpler yet.

When she'd brushed her fingertips over my lips, I'd gently pulled away her hand. "You need to sleep."

Tense muscles, a stark gaze. "What do you want from me?" she'd demanded in a soft whisper. "Why don't you want anything at all?"

"That you exist in this world? It's enough." I'd never found a word to define my sexuality or my needs. None that existed in the world quite fit. All I knew was that Bea was the only person I had ever loved that way, and would ever love. The only one who'd lit me up on the inside, made me comprehend what Vansi meant when she talked about her love for Phoenix, and why Darcie looked at Ash that way.

For the first and only time in my life, I'd understood why my friends did frankly insane things in the grip of love. And I'd felt sorry for Darcie. Because Ash was never going to give her what she needed; Ash had already chosen his person and it wasn't Darcie.

I'd never been jealous of him. He might have Bea, but I was the only one who *knew* Bea.

"Tell me something, Nae-nae," she'd murmured sleepily after I'd finally got her stripped and tucked into bed.

"Hmm?" I'd curled around her, my intent to keep her warm and protected through the night.

"Would you bury a body for me?" Curved lips.

My answer hadn't been a joke at all. "Yes."

Later, after her breathing evened out and her body went lax, I'd added the rest. "I'd do far worse for you, Bea."

26

I woke to the sound of feet slamming down the staircase and raised voices that turned into shouts. Rain continued to pelt the windows. Still dazed from sleep, my head thick from a wine hangover, I stumbled out of bed in my pajamas—fighting my way past the curtains—and wrenched open my door.

"What's going on?" I yelled to the only person in sight—and she was running to her room.

"Kaea's throwing up." Grace tightened the tie of her beautiful silky robe. "It's bad. Aaron found him when he went down to make pancakes. Looks like he's been sick most of the night."

Not bothering to grab a cardigan, I ran down in my bare feet.

It was the smell that hit me first—that thick, sour scent that could only be old vomit. While Kaea was bent over a bowl right now, he'd clearly not made it to the toilet or found a bowl earlier in the night. Regurgitated whiskey and stew splattered the floor beside where he would've been sleeping.

Thank God he hadn't choked.

Able to breathe now that I'd seen him—he looked gray as hell, but he was sitting up on his own—I ducked into the laundry, found the mop and other cleaning supplies, and got to work. A shirtless Phoenix, his lower body covered in a pair of black sweat-pants, was beside Kaea by then, checking his temperature, pulse, and whatever else he could, given the limited supplies he had available.

I passed over Kaea's emergency kit when Nix asked for it, but otherwise stayed out of his way.

"I'm sorry," Kaea groaned after Nix was done.

I patted his knee. "It's not the first time I've cleaned up after you." I hated the drawn look on his face, the sunken shadows under his eyes. "Nothing will ever beat the rager you had for your twentieth." Afterward, I'd told him to consider my cleaning ser-vices his birthday present.

To his credit, he'd shamefacedly admitted that he'd overdone the celebrations, and had made it up to me by taking me to the fanciest restaurant in town. A dinner we'd both raved over for weeks, but that neither one of us could've afforded if he hadn't used a chunk of his birthday money.

He was a good friend.

Now, he tried to smile, but shudders wracked his body before he could make it. He bent over the bowl again, dry-retching so painfully that it hurt me to watch him. I stroked his back, brushed his hair off his feverish face, and was about to ask Phoenix if there was nothing else we could do, when Vansi walked into the room, Aaron and Grace behind her.

While Aaron was dressed in his day clothes, my best friend wore powder blue shorts and a matching camisole, over which she'd thrown on a haphazardly belted gray fleece robe. Her feet were as bare and no doubt as cold as mine.

"I've checked our own emergency kit as well as the little one that Grace has," Vansi told Phoenix. "There's nothing in either to stop him from throwing up. You have any luck with Kaea's kit?"

Frowning, Phoenix shook his head. "I think we should let him get it out of his system anyway. It looks like food poisoning."

"Shit," Aaron muttered, "it had to be something I cooked."

But Grace, who'd taken a clean rag from the supplies I'd gathered, and begun to wipe dry the area I'd mopped, said, "You were eating things on the trail, weren't you, Kaea? Berries and leaves?"

He nodded, but couldn't speak.

I could see Grace's point, but I didn't believe it. Kaea had forgotten more about bush tucker than the rest of us would ever know. He'd given me tons of things to nibble on during our hikes over the years, from the tips of fern fronds to pieces of chewy bark, and not once had I ever gotten sick.

First his shoes and now this.

Kaea was right; it was one too many coincidences. But I couldn't see a connection between Darcie and Kaea that would lead to them both being targeted. It definitely wasn't a clandestine affair—that was Kaea's line in the sand. He was a serial monogamist, didn't cheat. Ever.

He didn't help others do it, either.

"We need to get liquids into him," Phoenix was saying. "Aaron, could you make a thin but nourishing soup?"

"I could do a bone broth with pureed vegetables." Aaron rubbed his hands on his thighs. "No chewing required, and I can season it according to what Kaea can stomach."

Phoenix nodded before turning to his patient. "I need to monitor how much you're taking in and throwing back up. If it gets too bad, we'll have to drive to an area with a phone signal and call for a rescue helicopter. Dehydration is the main threat."

Kaea groaned. "I'm sure I look like death, but it's either a stomach bug or food poisoning, and I've survived both before." No longer wracked by spasms, he nonetheless clenched the bowl close to his chest. "I need a shower."

"You need to rest," Phoenix began, but Vansi interrupted with, "No, let him shower. He'll do much better after." She held her husband's gaze. "I'm telling you this as a nurse."

Phoenix gave a curt nod before shifting his attention back to Kaea. "But you are not going to be alone in the shower. Aaron and I'll both go with you, and we'll turn our backs, but that's about it."

"I'm not shy," Kaea said, and the next few minutes were taken up with Aaron and Phoenix getting him up off the couch. Slinging one arm around each of their shoulders, both men placing one arm behind his back to brace him in turn, Kaea winced as he began a slow hobble to the closest shower.

Our cleanup complete, Grace and I returned the mop and bucket to the laundry after using the rain to rinse them out, threw the used rags into a bucket of soapy water to soak, then washed our hands. Afterward, while Grace was pulling out a pile of finished laundry to throw into the must've-been-an-antique dryer, I decided to go into the kitchen and open the back door a fraction to refresh the place.

I propped open the door to the living room as well, so that the crisp air would circulate and clear out the lingering smell from

Kaea's illness. It would do him no good to walk out of the shower fresh and clean only to find the air ripe with the memory of his awful night.

Vansi, dressed in skinny jeans and a thick roll-neck sweater in dark green, was already in there, struggling with the stiff windows. "They don't open far." She pointed to a latch that locked each window in place after about a handsbreadth.

"Those don't look period appropriate, do they?"

Vansi shrugged, neither one of us a history major. "I'm guessing Darcie's parents or grandparents put them in—maybe because the weather down here can get so bad. No chance of a window being left wide open when the snow flurries hit."

"Makes sense." I glanced through the door into the kitchen to see Grace stepping outside, trailing a blanket cape.

Curious, I followed.

She stood on the veranda, her eyes trained on the lightning that cracked within the black of the rain clouds. Though it was morning, the gloom made it appear like twilight. And yet I couldn't deny that it was stunning, too, a kind of voracious beauty that'd devour you without hesitation.

The sound of the downpour was so deep it created an echo in my bones.

My fingers itched for my camera, but from the looks of it, the storm wasn't going to pass anytime soon, so I'd have plenty of other chances. Might as well enjoy the sight.

"Here." Grace opened up one side of the blanket. "We can freeze together while we enjoy the show Mother Nature's putting on for us."

I wasn't a toucher, not like Darcie, but it was icy out, I had no cardigan or sweater, and my feet were slowly going numb.

"Thanks," I said, tugging the blanket closed on my side while she did the same on hers.

"No problem."

I felt engulfed by a sense of unexpected comfort as we stood there . . . comfort carried on the scent of lavender. *Oh*. Grace, I realized, smelled like home, like my mum. Maybe that was part of why I liked her, but most of it was because of how she treated Aaron. With affection and love and an open heart—leavened with a sense of mischief that made my straitlaced friend loosen up.

Bea would've liked her.

"I wonder if we should think about getting out of here," I murmured, my heart aching for a meeting that would never happen. "The water level in the creek has to be rising. We won't be able to cross the bridge if it gets too high, and then we'll be stuck here."

Grace wrinkled up her nose. "I was waiting until we were all together to share, but I did actually pick up a signal early this morning. I get insomnia," she confessed, "and mostly I read while Aaron sleeps, but today I decided to walk up to the tower. Tire myself out, you know?"

Having experienced more than a few restless nights myself, I nodded. "Good signal?"

She shook her head. "Blip at best. I managed to download one email and what do you know, I'm just the right customer for a penis enlargement." A glare that made my lips twitch. "But my phone's set up to download breaking news articles automatically, and I synced that with the local paper before we arrived."

"Smart."

A delicate lift of the shoulders. "I traveled a ton as a kid, got used to adapting. Anyway, paper says there's been a slip on the road out of here. About a twenty-minute drive from the bridge in normal weather. Entire side of a large slope just came down onto the road—it's a mess of boulders and mud. Total blockage."

I groaned. "Seriously?"

She nodded, her lips turned down at the corners. "I don't have all the details because only half the article came through before the signal cut out again, but it's bad. Like that slip out in Kaikoura after the quake, the one that cut off the entire town. I took a screenshot in case the app blanked after the signal cut out."

Removing her phone from the pocket of her robe one-handed, she brought up the image. Below the headline was the image of a tumble of soil and rocks and broken trees. The road had vanished under the mass. On one side of which was the hillside, on the other a sheer drop.

No way around it.

The first few lines of the article also made it clear that nothing could be done until the storm passed. It was too dangerous out there right now.

We were stuck.

27

Damn it." Even my photographer's heart was fast falling out of love with this house and its remote location; the idea of being stuck here for far longer than planned was a nightmare. "I hope it is just food poisoning then, because if Kaea's really sick . . ." I didn't want to say it, didn't even want to think it.

Grace chewed on her lower lip. "Do you think I should tell the others? I showed Aaron already, and I did want to tell everyone at breakfast, but with Kaea and all, I'm second-guessing myself. I think it'll stress everyone out even more."

I agreed with her. "Maybe hold on to it until someone brings up the idea of leaving." No point in putting an even bigger downer into the mix.

Exhaling, as if my agreement had given her the confidence she needed, Grace slipped away her phone. "I know it wasn't Aaron's food," she said, her tone passionate. "We all ate the same thing. It had to be something Kaea had on the track."

"But that would mean it took over twelve hours to set in."

"I don't think that's that long," Grace argued. "One time I ate fish at lunch that didn't agree with me, and didn't get sick until early morning the next day."

Since neither of us were physicians, I dropped the subject. "Let's hope the worst is over for today, and the rest of it will be smooth sailing." My chest shivered, the chill working its way into my bones. "We can stay warm and cozy and eat tons of Aaron's delicious food. And if he gets sick of cooking for us, Nix and I aren't too bad."

"Are you kidding?" Grace's expression softened. "He's been itching to cook for a larger group for ages. Most of the time it's only me and him."

She nudged me with her shoulder. "I love how you're so supportive of his dream of opening his own restaurant. He never discusses it with his family—to them, he's a suit-wearing accountant who cooks as a hobby. His mum is always boasting to her friends about how he's going to make partner at the firm."

"You understand why that is?"

Grace nodded. "Oh, yes. I don't judge them for it. Especially when it's obvious they adore him. I think they'll be fine with his shift in career direction once the restaurant is actually in place— a physical symbol of success, with him as the owner. It would be much harder to sell them the dream."

It struck me that I wouldn't have expected such insight from a woman who'd had a life wholly different from Aaron's. "You have a good heart, Grace."

When she put her head against my shoulder, her curls tickling my neck, I realized I didn't mind it. "I come from money," she admitted. "All I've seen my entire life is how people use it to control others, woo others. I knew I loved Aaron the instant we met, but I didn't know how to make him love me, so I tried to give him enough to start his business."

"He wouldn't take it, would he?"

"No, and I thought that was the end of us, that he didn't want me. I thought my only value lay in my trust fund. Messed up, huh?" A wry laugh. "Aaron is so proud, but that's part of what I love about him—that he stands on his own hard work, no one else's. And the irony is that my capitalist monster of a dad *also* loves that about him. I'm pretty sure he likes Aaron more than his own sons."

I went to reply . . . only my teeth began to chatter uncontrollably.

"Oh God, you're freezing! So am I. Do I even have feet?"

Giggling, the two of us stumbled into the warmth of the kitchen, startling Aaron. "What the hell were you doing out there!" Hand cupping the back of Grace's head, he pressed a sweet kiss to her nose. "I can see Lu sneaking out to take photos, but you're meant to be a good influence, Gracie."

"Since when?" Grace teased and kissed his jaw.

Cheeks creasing, Aaron just shook his head. "You two should take the chance to have a quick shower. You know how the pressure gets. I did it first thing before I came down, and from how quiet the pipes are, I don't think anyone's using the water just now. Vansi and Phoenix are in the living room with Kaea, helping him get settled."

"Did Ash and Darcie come out at all?" I asked, wondering if they'd slept through the entire kerfuffle.

But Aaron nodded. "Ash stuck his head out of the bedroom when I first ran up to get Phoenix. He told us to grab him if we needed him, but otherwise he'd stay with Darcie. She's not feeling the greatest."

"We're dropping like flies," I muttered under my breath. "I think Grace is right—this house is cursed."

Aaron put his hands on his hips. "Don't even hint at such a thing around my grandmother. She'll be flying down to drag me out of here before you can say boo."

"I notice that you didn't disagree with me about the whole cursed thing."

"Hard to disagree at this point." He nuzzled his chin into Grace's soft curls when she cuddled to his side. "I was thinking blueberry ripple pancakes. Along with eggs and bacon. How does that sound?"

"It sounds like I wish you two lived next door so I could mooch food off you daily." I wasn't entirely joking; while I was a passable cook, I hardly ever took the time to put together a proper meal. "Burnt toast is a good day for me. Otherwise, it's grabbing a quick coffee on the way to a shoot."

"I've told him that I'll become his food stalker if he ever divorces me," Grace said with utmost solemnity. "Of course, I'm never letting him go in the first place." An enthusiastic kiss on the lips. "No one is touching my gorgeous love."

Aaron's cheeks heated, his old shyness still there, beneath the adult confidence. "Shoo, go use the hot water before it runs out."

"You two are adorable," I said, not teasing them about their goo-goo eyes, because honestly, with how this week was going, I could do with light and joyous—and their delight in each other was infectious.

———

Aaron had been right to tell us to hurry up. The water pressure was incredible, the heat stellar. I allowed myself the luxury of just standing under it for a few seconds, letting the thin needles massage my scalp.

The aim was to forget, to float.

But that nibbling sensation in the back of my brain, it wouldn't go away. I kept on thinking about Kaea and how he was the only one who was sick when—as Grace had argued—we'd all eaten the same food. Because Kaea wouldn't have made a mistake about anything he'd eaten on the trail. I wasn't budging on that.

It *was* possible that he'd been bitten by an insect or that he'd picked up a stomach virus on our last stop—a no-frills café designed to fuel long-haul truckers. But . . . it just didn't feel right. Especially when it had occurred to me that Kaea was the only one who'd openly questioned Darcie's apparent fall.

"So what, Luna?" I muttered as I shampooed my hair. "Now you think Phoenix poisoned Kaea so that he'd stop asking questions?" Put that way, it sounded dramatic and on the edge of lunacy, but that didn't eliminate the bad feeling in the pit of my stomach.

If I had my way, we'd get the hell off this accursed estate, but driving out into the strengthening storm would be a nightmare, one with no end in sight with that massive slip blocking the road. Far more sensible to wait it out.

However, since Grace had managed to get a signal that morning, I decided I'd go up to the tower early tomorrow. Just in case. If nothing else, we could call emergency services and get advice about Kaea, let them know that he was in the area and that we were cut off.

The water began to cool down as I was rinsing out the shampoo so I quickly soaped my body and had just managed to wash it all off when the water switched to freezing without warning.

Yelping, I jumped out, then reached in to shut off the shower. Which was now scalding. "Ugh." Old house, old pipes.

After drying myself off, I looked in the mirror, which wasn't totally steamed up, likely due to the relatively short time I'd spent under the water, and I began to wonder if the edges of my reflection were blurry because of the steam or because of the minuscule crystals eating away at my eyes. I was a photographer by trade, but I did art on the computer now and then, and my latest project was a single crystalline eye. Flawless. Exquisite. And blind.

The world pressed in on me, closing in on every side.

Suddenly my chest was too tight, the air not coming up through my airways.

Trying to suck in a breath only increased the pressure, making spots dance in front of my eyes. The towel half-wrapped around me, I collapsed onto the cold tile floor on my hands and knees. This was it. I was going to suffocate while wide awake and aware.

The needle of my brain scratched again and again, my neurons stuck on repeat.

Some small corner of that broken brain recognized what this was: a panic attack.

I'd suffered more than one before. After I'd admitted to them and before I'd refused to attend any more sessions, Dr. Mehta had given me tools to deal with them. Tools to calm myself down. Tools to get my mind off the circling panic.

But I couldn't think of any of those tools today. Only one

thing filled my mind: *darkness*. The same darkness that was even now cramping around my skull, squeezing my brain, making the tiles blur and vanish in front of me.

Blind, I was going blind!

I came to consciousness to find myself naked and shivering on the bathroom tiles. My wet hair stuck to my cheek, dripped down my neck, fine black veins against the aged cream of the tiles. A faint scent teased my nose, evoking memories of summer and laughter, but slipped out of my grasp when I tried to hone in on it.

I could breathe now.

My brain had literally shut down my thought processes in order to give my autonomic nervous system space to function. Shame was a sob caught in my throat that I couldn't release, gritty eyes that couldn't cry.

Shuddering, I forced myself to get up.

One glance at the mirror gave me the timeline of my involuntary shutdown. Steam was yet a soft filter on the edges. I wiped my finger through the condensation to confirm it *was* that and not a phantom image created by my crystalline eyes.

The pad of my finger came away wet, a streak on the glass evidence of my trespass.

Shifting away from the mirror and my shame, I walked into the bedroom damp and cold. The room was frigid, the embers of the previous night's fire having long since gone dark. Reminded all over again of the oblivion that awaited me, I rubbed my hair and body dry with hard, rough motions that left my flesh red and angry—but I was still naked when the handle of my bedroom door began to turn.

"Not decent!" I yelled out at once, too late recalling what I'd forgotten in my alcoholic haze last night: there were secret passages in this house. The door might not be the only entry into my room.

Someone could be hiding in the walls watching me right now.

The door handle stopped moving, but there was nothing else. No apologetic call from one of my friends. No sound of footsteps moving away. Or if there was, I couldn't hear it through the thudding of my heart.

Infuriated by the renewed sense of panic that threatened to strangle me, I wrapped myself in the towel as I ran to confront whoever it was.

28

I wrenched open the door to see Vansi heading up the final part of the stairs. *Up*, not down. Also, if it had been her, she'd have yelled back that she'd seen it all before. We'd gotten changed into our bathing suits together plenty of times, neither one of us uncomfortable doing so in front of the other.

Now, my friend glanced over with a questioning raise of the eyebrows. "Nip slip, girlfriend."

Hitching up the towel without checking to ensure I'd covered the offending nipple, I looked up and down the corridor, saw no one. "Did you see anyone by my door just now?"

"No." Vansi looked around. "Did someone try to get in? They probably made a mistake and got embarrassed. All these doors look the same."

"Still, they should've said something." After all, it wasn't like we were strangers. "This way, just creeping off, it's . . ."

"Weird?" Vansi completed. "This entire house is fucking

weird." A loud whisper, though she obviously wasn't worried about Darcie or Ash, because she didn't look over to their door.

Which, I belatedly realized, was open. "Darcie up?"

"Came down a few minutes ago. Suitcases under the eyes, poor thing." That was my friend, born with a well of empathy so deep that nothing could suppress it. "Don't think either one of them slept well."

I felt for Darcie, but I was more worried about another member of the group. "How is Kaea?"

Pressing her lips together she shook her head. "Sick. Nothing crazy, and we did manage to get a third of a can of sugar-loaded soda into him—we have to see if he keeps it down, and if he can do the same with the soup Aaron's making. Any liquid is good, and we'll take junk calories if that's all he can stomach."

She turned toward one of the narrow windows that lined the staircase, the line of her profile delicate against the charcoal light. "This trip, this place, it was an adventure in the sun. Now all I can think about is that there's no chance a helicopter could get through the wind and the rain, and that our only way out is a road that Ash mentioned is prone to slips. So who knows if *that's* even open."

I kept my mouth shut.

There really was no point in spreading that piece of bad news. Soon as it stopped raining however, I planned to drive out to the site of the slip and leave a giant sign telling them we were stuck out here.

Hell, I'd make an arrow with fallen rocks if I had to; the isolated road was unlikely to be a priority, but a survey—most likely aerial—would be done to make a note of the damage so they could plan for the work involved to clean it up.

"Go listen to one of your true crime podcasts," I said to Vansi.

"You've had a hard morning. A little murder is what you need to cheer you up."

"Ha ha." She fought off a smile. "It's research. So I don't end up serial killer bait."

"Very important in New Zealand, that hotbed of serial killers."

This time she did laugh—that warm, hiccupy-sounding laugh that was one of the most beloved sounds in my life. "Shut up. What are you going to do?"

"Grab breakfast, and volunteer to help Aaron." I could chop vegetables for lunch prep or do the dishes, whatever he wanted. That was how we'd done things at the flat when Aaron cooked. We'd do the cleanup, or buy any special herbs or spices he needed. None of us had wanted him deciding it was too much work to bother cooking for us.

"Aaron's a great guy." Vansi's hand clenched on the rounded top of the banister at the landing. "If only I had the hots for him instead of for Phoenix." A tightness to her features, her skin stretched thin. "Sorry I snapped at you yesterday morning. I just don't know what's going on with him—but that's no reason for me to lash out at you. Forgive me?"

I couldn't do it, couldn't keep this secret from her. "He's smoking again," I blurted out. "I caught him on the veranda. He's been hyping himself up to confess, but with Kaea and all, he'll probably let it slide for the time being. Anyway, that might be why he's acting shifty."

Vansi stared at me for a long moment before bursting out into a huge smile. "Oh my God, Luna." Running over, she gave me the biggest hug, squeezing the life out of me. "All this time I'm thinking he's having an affair or just doesn't love me anymore, and all the man is doing is surrendering to an old bad habit."

Tears shone in her eyes when she pulled back. "I'm so happy. I never thought I'd say that about Nix smoking, but compared to everything I've been imagining, I'm ecstatic."

"I'm sorry I didn't tell you straightaway. Nix was feeling so bad about it and I knew he wanted to tell you himself."

"I understand." She squeezed my upper arms. "I can deal now that I know what's going on. Thank you, thank you, thank you." An enthusiastic kiss on the cheek before she all but skipped down the hallway toward their room.

I was happy for her, but I wasn't so sure that that was all that was going on with Phoenix. The smoking was a symptom, not the cause—because Nix just wasn't the type to break promises. Particularly one he'd made to his wife.

Vansi had to know that, too. But blaming their issues on his guilt over smoking might at least allow her to enjoy the rest of our time at the estate. The truth—whatever it was—would no doubt come crashing down soon enough.

Shutting the door, I wrapped my towel more securely around myself, then began to check every single wall of my room with methodical precision. I knocked lightly, listened to see if any wall sounded hollow, pressed every inch I could reach in an attempt to trigger a hidden catch—including inside the wardrobe. But as far as I could tell, the walls were apparently just walls.

Still not satisfied, I dragged over the delicate chair by the writing desk, climbed onto it with the intent to check the ceiling. I couldn't reach. Jumping off, I looked around. My eye fell on the slim folding umbrella I'd left sitting outside my suitcase. After living in Auckland, then London, I tended to pack one automatically. Now, I pulled the handle out to its fullest length, and began to tap the ceiling using that end.

A shower of dust, but no movement, no indication of any hidden trapdoors.

Hot from the exertion and with dust on my damp hair, but a fraction more certain of my privacy, I nonetheless took my clothes into the bathroom to change. No guarantee it was safe, of course, but all the tile made a hidden door much less likely.

I dressed as fast as I could.

A pair of thick black leggings, over which I threw on a short-sleeved thermal top in the same color and one of my favorite sweaters. Slouchy, falling to midthigh, it was made of fluffy blue yarn and felt like a hug in physical form.

My brother had knitted it for me.

Cable, pro athlete and heartthrob to the masses, was still young enough to be embarrassed about his knitting, but he also loved it too much to consider giving it up. Instead, with a rare few exceptions, he did it in secret, then gifted the items to those he trusted. His most recent project was tiny hats and socks for the premature babies born at our local hospital.

My baby brother had a gorgeous soul.

Smiling, I sat down on the bed and pulled on a pair of tight woolen socks, black with fine green stripes. Another gift from Cable, they were the warmest socks I owned—and I definitely needed them in this place. The staff might've cleaned it to a shine, but they could do nothing about the cold.

I frowned.

Would the caretaker think to check on us? But even if he did, how would he get through? His house, along with those of his few neighbors, lay beyond the landslide.

No, we were stuck here until the storm passed.

Dressed, I brushed the dust out of my hair but left it down so

it could dry, then stepped out after pulling on my sneakers. I'd
take them off if we decided to set up in the living room for most
of the day; unlike the dusty wine cellar and passageway, the main
areas of the house were spotless and it was more comfortable being shoeless while inside.

I looked in on Kaea once downstairs, saw that he appeared to
be resting relatively peacefully. Relieved, I tiptoed past the living room door to enter the kitchen via the separate hallway entrance.

Grace had beaten me down, was stirring something on the
stove. "Aaron decided to add old-fashioned oatmeal to the menu,"
she said with a smile, "complete with dried fruits and berries. I'm
having mine with brown sugar and cinnamon on top."

A sudden bright burning in my eyes, so sharp and painful that
I had to look away.

"Hey." The clatter of a spoon being put down on a saucer.
"What did I say?"

Making myself look at her, I replied past the knot in my
throat. "Bea used to have her oatmeal that way."

"Oh," she said softly. "I'm so sorry you all lost her. From what
Aaron's told me, she sounds like a woman I'd have loved to have
as a friend. The kind who'd get cocktails with me for Sunday
brunch, but also be happy to get muddy on a bush adventure." A
slight questioning tone to her words.

"Yes, that was her," I confirmed. "And she was so *happy*. She
loved making others happy, too." That was why I had such trouble believing Darcie when it came to Bea's mental health problems.

"Were you two close?" Grace began to stir the oatmeal again.
"You don't have to tell me if it hurts."

"No, it's good to talk about her." The pain inside smothered by a wave of remembered love, I said, "The thing with Bea was that we all thought we were her best friend. She was good about that, about letting everyone believe that they were her favorite."

It could've come across as manipulative or facetious, but the interest had been genuine on her part. She'd had so much love inside her, been ferocious about sharing it. And I'd never minded; I'd known my place in Bea's life and that it was one no one else would, or could, ever occupy—not even Ash when they married.

"She was the center of our group," I said, because it was the truth. "The one that organized the picnics and the nights clubbing, and who kept the group chat alive. Afterward . . . we drifted, like unmoored buoys on the ocean."

At first, I'd put the increasing distance between us down to graduating uni and going our separate ways into adult lives, but it was more than that. Our friendship had died with Bea, fracturing from that point outward until, now, we were casual acquaintances held together by the memories of the past.

A rare few bonds between individuals had held—mine with Vansi, Kaea's with Ash—but the group? We called ourselves friends, but we were more the ghosts of friends past.

"I hope we'll drift together." Grace's smile was shy. "I feel like the new kid in primary school saying this, but do you think we could be friends?"

It was an odd thing to hear in adulthood, but touched by Grace's vulnerability, I said, "Yes," and opened my heart for the first time in forever.

Grace's face lit up. "Oh!" she said a second later. "I almost forgot. Could you grab dried apricots from the pantry? Aaron asked me to get them soaking in warm water."

She raised her shoulders to her ears and gave a sheepish smile.

"I have no idea why he wants them, but I assume it'll be delicious so it's in our best interest to do as he's asked."

It wasn't until I was about to walk into the pantry that I remembered the vandalized painting, the eyes weeping bloody tears.

29

Aaron pinned a sheet over the creepy painting," Grace said from the stove, a shudder in her voice. "I refused to go in there otherwise."

Stomach unclenching, I nodded, and walked inside. I couldn't help glancing over at the painting, but Aaron had used a black sheet to ensure it was fully blocked from view, so there was literally nothing to see.

More relieved than I wanted to be, I got to hunting through the groceries for the apricots. But the painting loomed large in my imagination, a cold kiss on the back of my neck. Because the vandalism? It couldn't be explained away as easily as the doll. Someone had taken the time to deface Clara's art in a way designed to frighten those who saw it; there was nothing good-natured about it, nothing that could be put down to a prank.

I went to the sheet, my hand fisted on one end to pull it off.

But in the end, I decided there was no point. Looking at it

again wouldn't answer the question of why one of us—or Grace and Kaea's mysterious unknown intruder—would do this. It also didn't align with the theory of it being Darcie's stalker. Anyone who knew Darcie knew she hated cooking.

No stalker who'd done their homework would count on her entering the pantry. Yes, there was the secret passageway, but even we hadn't known about that until yesterday. And the painting had already been defaced when Aaron, Grace, and I exited into the pantry. Could one of us have managed it in the highly limited available window of time? Maybe, maybe not.

My eyes fell on the bag of apricots even as my mind circled the topic.

As I reached for them, I realized they were on the shelf that hid the secret passageway. No cans on there now—Aaron or Grace must've moved those to other shelves.

The plastic crinkled under my hand as I stood there, frowning.

Not sure why, I pushed open the hidden catch that I'd noticed last night when I was the last to leave the pantry. I'd pushed it shut instinctively, seen where it snicked into the wall to become nothing more than another shelf.

The door swung toward me with silent grace.

I stared at the hinges.

That was it. That was what had been bothering me. Everything in this house creaked and groaned. But this hidden door didn't make a sound when it should've creaked the loudest of them all.

Forgetting the apricots, I took out my phone and used my trusty flashlight app to examine the hinges.

Shiny. No hint of dust.

And when I reached out my finger and wiped it on the metal, it was to feel the slickness of oil between my fingertips.

Someone had taken care to make sure that these hinges wouldn't make a noise. Darcie? But why? Who else could it have been? Perhaps Jim, the caretaker? But that seemed unlikely. The man would have no reason to go searching for secret doors, and from what Darcie had said, he was the practical farmer type. Get in, get the job done, and get out.

"Did you find it?"

Jolting at the sound of Grace's call, I yelled back, "Got it!" and pushed the door shut again.

Once more, it closed in eerie silence.

The quiet disturbed me more than all the creaks and groans in the house.

It wasn't until I was using the kitchen scissors to open the bag so I could soak them for Aaron that I realized one other thing: cobwebs.

Aaron had walked into cobwebs.

That didn't mean no one else had used the passage. We hadn't thought to check for footprints in the dust—and at a lanky six three, Aaron was the tallest person in the group by several inches. A shorter individual could've traversed the entire tunnel without disturbing the cobwebs at the top. Especially if that shorter person hunched to make themselves even smaller.

Why? Why do any of this?

Knowing the right question, however, didn't give me the answer.

I had to fight my wince when Darcie joined us for breakfast in the lounge. The shadows under her eyes had turned into purple bruises, her cheeks hollow, and her stunning hair in a fuzzy braid that looked slept on.

She wore the same oversize gray sweater as the previous day.

"Bad night?" I murmured. It was easy to do so privately—she sat next to me on a wide couch, with Ash on her other side. He, however, was involved in a conversation with Phoenix, who sat in an armchair kitty-corner from him.

To my right was Kaea, with Grace and Vansi seated near him. All three were chatting, while Aaron had just got up to put on a fresh pot of coffee. Vansi and I had offered to do it instead, told him he'd done enough, but Aaron had insisted. Knowing the kitchen was where he decompressed, I'd let it go.

"My head felt like it had a drum in it." Darcie moved her spoon in her oatmeal but didn't eat. "The painkillers must've worn off at some point. I spent the rest of the night in a kind of half-awake, half-asleep daze. Had the weirdest dreams."

Her lips turned downward. "Ash said I screamed Bea's name at one point. Sorry if I woke you."

"I heard nothing through the wine drunk and no one else has mentioned it, either." I angled my head to look at the back of hers, saw only the fuzzy silk of her hair. "Is the wound healing?"

"Nix examined it before Ash and I came down, and he says that while it's swollen, it doesn't seem to be much of a cut. I guess it's true, head wounds just bleed like crazy." She tried out a faint smile. "Vansi shared more of her magic pills with me just before, so hopefully I'll start to feel a bit more human soon. Especially after all of Aaron's delicious food."

Ash said something to her then, and the conversation drifted. I didn't take too much part, content to listen. Content to think. The oiled hinges continued to niggle at me, until I took the opportunity to ask Darcie, "Does Jim maintain the secret passageways in the house?" It didn't seem likely when she'd said the passageways had always been her and Bea's private secret. "Does he even know about them?"

"Hardly." Her eyes were brighter now, her laugh fuller. "Not worth the potential liability. He could get trapped in one of the passageways, and the next thing I know, there's a dead body on our family estate." She shuddered. "No one who comes to work on the estate knows about the passages, but still, I make sure they're locked up."

As she finished speaking, Phoenix asked Kaea how he was doing, got a thumbs-up in return.

"This hasn't exactly worked out as I hoped," Darcie said to the group after accepting a top-up of her coffee from Aaron with a smile of thanks. "Do you think we'll laugh about this one day when we're old and gray? The disaster of a reunion I organized in the middle of nowhere?"

Aaron chuckled and poured me some coffee, too. "It hasn't been that bad."

The others all chimed in, and since I didn't want to be the rain on everyone's parade, I said, "I have thousands of photographs already—it's a fantastic place to shoot inside and out." Which reminded me. "With the rain and all, I thought I might explore the house a bit more, if that's all right with you, Darcie, take more internal photographs."

"Go for it," Darcie said, her fingers curled around her mug and her smile fading as she looked down into the dark liquid. "Sometimes, I think it'd be better if I just got rid of this place. Too many memories, you know? If I do end up making that choice, it'll be nice to have photographs to look back on."

"Big decision," Grace murmured. "Wouldn't it be tough to lose touch with such a solid piece of your legacy?"

Darcie's fingers tightened on the mug. "I swim between two extremes. Cling to all that once was—or start brand-new. No haunts trailing in my wake."

"I guess it's your decision to make." The edge to Grace's tone caught my attention, had me focusing on her.

When Darcie shot her a sharp look, Grace blushed. "Gosh, I'm sorry." She ducked her head. "I grew up rich, but I'm adopted—from one of those infamous Romanian orphanages.

"My entire history is what I remember from the time I was old enough to form memories. Even my parents' wealth doesn't help when it comes to finding my birth family—they're ghosts in the system. I guess I'm jealous of you having access to over a hundred years and more."

Darcie's face softened. "God, that must be so hard. I never thought about it that way."

I knew what was coming even before she glanced at me. "Luna's adopted, too."

I'd never hidden that. But for some reason, I didn't like how casually Darcie shared an intimate part of my history. Or maybe I was just irritable because I couldn't stop thinking about those oiled hinges.

"Aaron told me," Grace said before I had to answer, and I wondered then if that was part of why she felt so comfortable with me. "He said your family is amazing."

My heart softening toward this girl who'd clearly not been as lucky in her adoptive family, I plucked at my sweater. "My brother knitted me this."

Everyone exclaimed, and then we were talking about siblings. Darcie didn't mention Bea.

Afterward, while the others were involved in another conversation, I shifted to stand by the fireplace with Grace. "So, your family? Not too great?"

Her face became pinched around the eyes and the mouth. "My mum was sweet and kind. But she died when I was seven, and my dad . . ." A shrug. "He only adopted me to make her happy. My stepmother bore him his *real* children. He's thrown that in my face over the years, that I'm just a foundling with no past and that the only reason I have a future is because of the trust fund my mother left me."

"My God." I wove my fingers through hers, too angry for her to keep my distance. "What an asshole thing to say."

She squeezed my fingers. "Sadly, that's not even the worst of it."

After shooting a quick glance at the others to make sure no one was paying attention she lowered her voice and murmured, "I lost it for a while, to be honest. Drugs, the whole thing. I just . . . was lost."

My heart hurt for her. "You're a strong person, Gracie." Aaron's pet name for her just slipped out. "It would've been so easy to become bitter and hard after that kind of treatment."

"I met a friend while I was at my lowest," Grace told me, her voice choked up. "Someone kind and wise. They helped me find my way out, made me see my own value as a person."

"I'm glad. Are you two still close?"

Grace nodded. "That bond, it was formed at the worst time in my life and it's forever. You know what I mean?"

"Of course." That, I thought, was akin to my relationship with Bea. It had been formed in joy rather than in pain, but it was forever.

30

No one took me up on my offer to roam the house, which gave me an idea. After breakfast, I went upstairs to grab my equipment—and I made sure to give everyone plenty of time to set themselves up with whatever they were doing for the day. At which point, I crept back downstairs as stealthily as possible.

Should anyone bust me in the kitchen, I planned to say I was grabbing a snack to take along. But luck was with me and I found the kitchen warm but empty. The woodstove murmured away in the corner, but that was the only activity.

The dishes had been done—Vansi and Ash had volunteered for that—and the counters wiped down. A couple of cans of green jackfruit sat on the counter. Aaron had told me what he intended to do with those, but he wouldn't be starting on lunch for at least three hours yet.

He was in the living area with the others—I just barely caught the mellow tenor of his voice, followed by Kaea's deeper tones.

The part of me that liked to be involved, to know what was going on, was tempted to join them, but I had bigger fish to fry today.

Opening the kitchen door, I slipped outside, taking care to pull it quietly shut behind me. It didn't take long to get to Kaea's boots. I would've far rather taken them up to my room, but didn't want to be caught with them and have to explain what I was doing, so instead I took them around the corner to one of the alcoves I'd noticed on an earlier walk outside.

I'd borrowed Grace's small flashlight for my roaming, so didn't have to rely on my phone as I examined the shoe that had given way. At first glance, it appeared that the leather had simply torn away from the sole. Except that made no sense for a shoe from a major hiking brand that was designed for rough use.

I squinted in an effort to see more clearly.

A pounding behind my eyeballs, a silent and insistent reminder that I couldn't just *think* my eyes better. Especially in this light that cloaked the entire world in impenetrable gray.

Forcing myself to release the squint, I closed my eyes and took a deep breath, held it.

Once. Twice. Three times.

Dr. Mehta would've been proud of me, I thought as I opened my eyes once more. And that was when I saw it: a cut mark on the *inner* sole, next to the stitching. My heart thumped.

The saboteur hadn't touched the outside of the shoe, had done nothing that Kaea would've noticed during his routine checkup of the boots prior to use. Instead, whoever this was had taken great care to go inside his boot and cut away the glue and stitching *just* enough that it would hold for a while.

A failure engineered to take place in slow motion.

The cut I'd spotted must've been a mistake, a tiny slip of the blade.

Lowering the boot to the ground, I considered when the sabotage could've taken place. He'd gone hiking with Vansi and Nix prior to our arrival at the estate, and his gear had been in the back of the vehicle after that. And this kind of delicate sabotage would've taken time. It wasn't a quick grab and slash.

No, it had to have been done after we reached the estate.

Perhaps even before Kaea had organized the hike. This insane weather notwithstanding, it would've been a good bet that Kaea would end up on a trail within the first few days of our time here.

As for how . . .

We'd been all over the place that first day. Kaea had hauled firewood with Ash, for one. And he might've decided to take a long shower later—the way the pipes clanged, it wouldn't have been hard to figure out when he was in there.

"What exactly are you thinking, Luna?" I challenged myself.

There were only two options: one of us, or the stalker-stranger Kaea had posited.

It was tempting to shrug off the latter as fantasy, but from all Kaea had said, that break-in at Ash and Darcie's place had been vicious. Abnormal. The person behind it *could* be disturbed enough to come here, lie in wait for them. Not difficult to discover where they were going if they had their flight tickets on their nightstand, for example.

Ash liked to print things out—or he had back at uni. Never satisfied with an electronic copy. Or it could be as simple as notes jotted into a day planner. Darcie liked physical planners and diaries, had always kept lovely ones. Thanks to her social media, I knew she did that to this day. Neither one of them was a last-minute planner, either. They'd have made any necessary bookings back when we'd first agreed to the reunion.

No need to follow the couple here and get caught. Just come first, and wait.

Why Kaea, though?

He'd been with them that night, and if the stalker had been watching, they might consider him complicit with Darcie and Ash.

Goose bumps broke out over my skin.

"Stop telling yourself horror stories," I muttered and, after checking the coast was clear, stashed the boots back in the hiding spot that had protected them thus far.

And though fear crawled a cold snake in my gut, I didn't return to the safety of the group. I began to search the house under the guise of taking photographs, looking for any sign that we weren't alone in this sprawling manse with endless dark corners, hidden rooms, and corridors that looped in on themselves.

My lungs worked overtime when I eventually made my way up the narrow and winding steps to the turret that we all called "the tower." Once at the top, I bent over with my hands on my knees until I could catch my breath.

The circular space was empty, the view from the windows breathtaking.

I forgot the danger for several minutes and took image after image of the black clouds riven with lightning, the rolling thunder background bass. Though I was shooting in color, I knew the images would come out in a palette of blacks, grays, and white. Because that was all there was beyond the old glass.

By the time I let the camera fall to rest at my abdomen, the strap a familiar weight on the back of my neck, I'd all but convinced myself that it had to be an intruder. I couldn't imagine any of us hurting Kaea, I just couldn't.

I see you're not thinking the same thing about my big sister.

Bea's ghost, whispering in my ear in that sharply amused tone she could get at times. I winced. She'd always been too clever, seen too much. And today, her ghost was one hundred percent correct.

Darcie had a way of pushing people.

I could well imagine that she'd irritated the wrong person, and that person had decided to get back at her, with Kaea collateral damage. Interesting that Ash hadn't been targeted—but he looked like hell anyway, so whatever he yet felt for Bea, he did love Darcie enough for her pain to affect him.

Mind swirling, I made my way back down the stairs and outside, my goal a spot that'd give me a vantage point of the ruined wing. In preparation, I flipped my hood over my head, made sure my jacket was zipped, then took a clear plastic poncho from my pocket and threw it on over the top.

I'd carry my cameras inside the poncho, then arrange the plastic cape to protect the equipment from the elements while I took multiple rapid-fire shots. I did the latter in quick succession, shooting the ruined wing while the rain pounded at my head and back, and drenched my jeans.

I could already tell that this series would turn out brilliant, moody and striking at the same time. I had the choice of leaving it dark, obscured by a veil of rain, or add light to pinpoint the fractured glass, the burn marks on the wall.

Gothic or horror, romantic or dangerous.

Smoke and mirrors.

I'd always liked that about the camera, the awareness that

photographs weren't a true impression of reality. So much of it was art. The photographer's eye, the photographer's mind and heart.

Except for Bea.

I'd never fiddled with her images except to correct a mistake.

Never needed to.

My camera forgotten under the poncho and fine streams of water dripping down my neck, I stared at the rain. I could see Beatrice dancing within the crashing droplets, her dark hair dazzling against the golden grass and her skirts flying around in a burst of color. She'd gone through a boho phase at one point, her entire wardrobe hippie skirts and floral headbands. I'd called her a fey goddess.

Lovely and sensual and beautiful and bright.

She should be here.

She should be laughing with us and tasting the wines from the old cellar with me.

She shouldn't be dust far, far from home.

Why hadn't Darcie let us say goodbye?

No matter her explanations, the question haunted me, a thorn embedded in my soul. I couldn't help gnawing at it. And as, chest tight, I turned to walk to the graveyard to take images of it under the storm sky, all I could see was the headstone that wasn't there.

That was when I realized: by cremating and throwing Bea away, Darcie had also erased her from their family history. Two hundred years from now, any curious soul who walked this grave-yard would find only a grouping of three when it came to their nuclear family, the inscriptions long since worn away.

No sign that there'd been a fourth.

No remembrance of Bea.

31

A shiver rocked my chest.

    I woke out of my frozen daze to realize that I'd been standing there staring unseeing at the gravestones.

My teeth clattered.

That was it. I sloshed my way inside the estate house, pushing at the doors until one swung open. The place had so many entrances and exits; the idea of a stranger slinking around seemed more and more viable with every second that passed.

This door spilled me into an unfamiliar section of the house.

After locking it behind me, I wiped off my shoes as well as I could, took off the poncho and scrunched it into a pocket, then walked down the dark-paneled hallway lit by only a weak little light. I wondered who'd unlocked the door, turned on the light, couldn't help darting my eyes to the pools of shadow.

"Logic says one of the others went for a walk and wanted to step outside for a bit," I said under my breath, frustrated with my own fear. "Maybe Nix, sneaking a smoke. Forgot to turn off the light because this place would be grim even without the weather."

I couldn't make myself turn it off, either. Everything was too dark, the lights too dim—and the artwork straight out of a haunted mausoleum. My jeans and socks were drenched, but I had no idea where I was; might as well take my time finding my way back. Because while uncomfortable, I wasn't—yet—in any danger of severe repercussions from my state.

The paintings were standard formal portraits of ancestors dressed in more modern clothes compared to Clara and Blake. My eye caught on the painting of a tall blond woman who stood with a dark-eyed man in what appeared to be their wedding finery. That smirk of satisfaction . . . I'd seen it before.

Oh.

The girl whose name I didn't know.

Blake and Clara Shepherd's only surviving child.

Sole heir to the Shepherd estate.

Just like Darcie.

"If it was only one of us, they wouldn't ever have to work. With two, we're not exactly paupers, but not set up for life, either."

I couldn't remember which one of them said that to me. It must've been an offhand comment, or one made on a drunken night out. Money, of course, was a motive repulsive but powerful.

But Darcie didn't murder Bea.

She'd just murdered her memory.

Once we were gone, who would remember Bea? Would Darcie even talk to the child in her womb about the sister who'd been a part of her life for nearly two decades? Or would she brush Bea under the rug, treat her as a forgotten embarrassment?

Jaw tight, I carried on down the hall. The most disturbing thing in this part of the house wasn't actually the artwork. No, that honor went to the black-and-white photographs. Of people sitting motionless, no expression or life in their faces.

Dolls in human form.

It couldn't be explained by the technology of the time. If I was right about the vintage of these images, camera equipment had advanced to the point that people no longer had to pose in a frozen position for minutes at a time.

One particular image made my blood go frigid, my breath shallow.

Clara.

Her gaze was flat, her face round and pretty . . . and a softer version of Beatrice's. The genetic legacy was far more potent than in the painting above the entranceway. Her eyes an endless paleness, her dress dark and stiff around her neck.

A collar, choking her.

Everything in the image spoke of containment.

Her body imprisoned by the buttons that marched down her throat and chest. Her face a master class in self-control. Or perhaps it had to do with the hand on her shoulder. The man who pressed down that hand, his thin fingers with their big knuckles curling into her soft flesh, was tall and gaunt, with hollows in his cheeks.

No children in the image, but it was clear this had been taken years into their marriage. Long enough for Blake Shepherd to lose not just a significant amount of flesh from his bones, but also his sanity. Madness blazed in the eyes that looked out from the photo.

What had Clara suffered in this house?

And though I hated what I was seeing, I lifted the camera to my eye and took a photograph of a photograph. My equipment was good; the copy would come out crystal clear. I didn't know if I'd ever again examine it, but I felt a compulsion to make a record of it. Perhaps because half this house had already burned down.

A legacy of ruin.

Clara's eyes followed me as I walked down the hallway, and I had to fight with myself not to look back over my shoulder. When I did turn, it was off to the right and out of the line of sight of Clara and Blake and their sole surviving child.

It niggled at me, that mirror of past and present.

Summer sunshine and peach blossoms.

I froze in place. And though I knew the whisper of Bea's scent was a figment stirred into being by my thoughts of another devastated family, I felt my throat thicken, my eyes burn. "I miss you so much, Bee-bee," I whispered under my breath, realizing now that it was the same scent I thought I'd smelled this morning in the bathroom.

My mind tumbling unbidden into the past.

Because Bea wouldn't have hesitated to run into my bathroom if she'd heard me fall, would've comforted me after I came out of it. I wanted so desperately for her to be here that I was creating my own magical world where she'd never ended her own life, never left me.

Even knowing the harsh truth, it was tempting to turn, look for a beautiful laughing girl who'd never again smile at me while daring me to take a risk, take a chance.

Somehow, I made myself walk on.

I snapped countless photos of the details in the walls, of the shadows thrown by the diffuse light coming in through the windows, of the dust that floated in the air. Anything and everything, the lens through which I looked at the world a talisman to hold back the dark.

And all the while, I searched.

Looking for any hint of a ninth person on the estate. A ninth person who could never be Bea, no matter how much I wanted that to be true.

White.

I blinked, glanced back through the small window I'd just passed. I hadn't imagined it. The rain had turned to snow.

"Fuck!"

This had happened a few years earlier, too, while Cable was down here for a game with his university team. A polar blast straight from Antarctica that had thrown the country back into a sudden and hard winter for three or four days. And in large parts of the South Island, that didn't just mean a dip in temperature.

It meant *snow*.

Cable had sent me images of the playing turf covered in white, and of him and his teammates sledding down slopes that had gone from spring to winter in the space of a single night. The blast had killed lambs just born, destroyed crops when they were at their most vulnerable—and trapped people when roads became impassable without warning.

I kicked the wall, and then hopped around cursing myself for giving in to temper.

I hadn't realized I'd been holding on to hope of getting out of here soon until I saw the snow. Because there was no way in hell we were escaping the estate anytime soon now. None of our vehicles had snow tires and I didn't know about Darcie and Ash, but the rest of us weren't used to driving in snow.

I hadn't even driven for years! I took the Tube or the bus!

Gritting my teeth, I lifted my camera. If the kitchen was Aaron's "zen," as he'd once put it, being behind the lens was mine, and I desperately needed to find that zen. And say what you would, this estate was fascinating.

At one point, I found myself stymied by a locked door. Taking a step back, I stared at it, wondering why that door of all doors was locked. An entrance to a secret passageway? No, it couldn't be. It was right out in the open.

Yet it was locked.

"Probably where the family stashes their valuable antiques," I said to myself, but my mind kept snagging on the pricey paintings I'd spotted on the walls. Then again, perhaps Darcie was so rich that the ones on the walls weren't pricey in comparison.

I jiggled the door once again, even considered trying to pick the lock, but the closest I'd ever come to picking a lock was seeing it done on the television screen. I took a photograph of the door instead, the wood dark but with a gloss to it that said it had been cleaned prior to our visit.

I was about to walk away when something made me bend down, peer through the keyhole. It was an older type with a lot more open space than a more modern keyhole.

Rows of books on the wall.

Papers on the floor.

I contorted this way and that—enough to work out that the room was anchored by a large desk, and that papers sat literally everywhere.

A study.

Rubbing my lower back, I rose. And thought about Clara's diary entry, the one that had spoken about her husband's "secret room." Could this be that room? But if so, why keep it locked up like a shrine?

Or maybe, it's out of superstition that the evil within would escape.

Chilled, I moved on. I'd ask Darcie about it. Why not? Maybe it was nothing sinister. Might even be something as sad as that the office was one her parents had used while down here. An office she hadn't had the heart to tidy up.

After all, she hadn't exactly been complimentary about Blake Shepherd. I couldn't see her preserving his papers or treating his study like a historical artifact.

When a chill rippled up my body again, I realized it wasn't only because of the ghostly echoes in this building. My toes had begun to go numb. The temperature had dropped precipitously with the snow and not only wasn't I dressed for it, I was still wet.

My stomach rumbled.

Glancing at my watch, I saw that I'd been wandering around for three hours. No wonder. At least I'd managed to wander into a vaguely familiar area, and now aimed myself in the direction of the living area and our rooms.

I emerged into a section I knew well not too much walking later—near the door to the wine cellar. Remembering to avoid looking at the painting with the obliterated faces, I carried on.

Right past the tapestry that hid the entrance to the secret passageway.

I paused, half tempted to take the shortcut, but I couldn't get the image of Darcie's crumpled form out of my head. Would anyone think to look for me in the passageway should I have an accident?

Or what if someone else, that elusive ninth person, was already in there?

Tugging my outdoor jacket more tightly around myself, I walked on. Until at last, my eyes sensed a glow on the polished wood of the floor—a spillover of the light from the living area. I could also smell cocoa in the air, along with what I was certain was fresh baking.

Deciding to grab a mug of cocoa to take upstairs with me, I was smiling as I passed the staircase.

Someone yelled—not a scream. A yell of surprise, of shock.

The thud when it came was loud and somehow "thick."

It was followed by the crash of glass.

32

My eyes locked on Phoenix's crumpled form.

He lay broken against the wall opposite the bottom of the stairs. Glass shards from the fallen painting cut slices into the skin of his face, the blood beading and spilling over with excruciating slowness, but Phoenix wasn't crying or yelling.

Phoenix wouldn't be doing anything ever again.

Not with his neck at that angle, his eyes staring unblinking into nothingness.

"Nix! Nix!" Vansi's anguished cry jolting me into motion, I raced forward.

Suddenly, it seemed everyone else was on the scene at once. Grace arrived from the direction of the kitchen, while Vansi ran down the staircase and Aaron and Ash erupted from the living room.

"What happened?" a wild-eyed Aaron demanded as Vansi attempted to take her husband's pulse.

"I don't know." I looked up at the steep incline of the stairs. "I was still behind the stairs when he fell. I saw him hit the wall."

"That stupid rug." Grace's voice wobbled. "He must've tripped."

"No, I rolled that up," I reminded them.

"Vansi was up there with him. She'll know." Ash, talking to Darcie.

She hovered in the doorway to the living room, her eyes huge and sunken.

"Nix, please, wake up. *Please.*"

I knelt beside my best friend, putting my arm around her shoulders. "He's gone, V." I couldn't make myself look at Phoenix's shocked and broken face, was suddenly piercingly aware that he'd been my friend. A lost friend, but a friend nonetheless.

"No! No!" Vansi screamed and struggled, but I held her tight until she finally collapsed in my arms in a shudder of sobs.

I didn't know how long she cried, but she did so into exhaustion.

Darcie came, took Vansi from my arms. "Luna." A meaningful glance at my cameras, her gaze more alert than earlier.

I nodded. "Go with Darcie, sweetheart."

My friend's face was scarily blank as she allowed Darcie to lead her into the living room. She mumbled something.

"What did she say?" I asked Darcie.

Darcie frowned. "That she was only a minute behind him. Told him to go ahead because she realized her period had started. She was getting a tampon."

Everyone looked at each other. But when Aaron would've gone upstairs, I stopped him with a hand on his arm. "I need to photograph everything before we move Phoenix." Because we were stuck out here with no reception, and couldn't leave his body where we'd pass it every single time we wanted to go up or down the stairs.

He swallowed, his Adam's apple moving in a jerking lump. "I want to cover him."

"Not yet." It hurt me to speak, but one of us had to be rational, had to think of a future when Vansi would want answers. "Not until I've documented everything."

With that, I put the camera to my eye and began to shoot without *seeing* him. Just a mannequin, I told myself. According to Vansi, who'd gained the knowledge via her true crime podcasts, that was what people who'd found bodies often initially believed—that they'd stumbled upon an abandoned mannequin.

The human mind trying to protect itself from horror.

Just a mannequin.

Not Dr. Phoenix Chang. Not V's Nix. Not secret smoker Phoenix.

Just a mannequin.

I lowered the camera after who knew how long, having taken a photo from every angle I could think of—on two different cameras, to guard against the failure of one set. "Where are we going to put him?"

Ash, who'd stayed—as had Grace and Aaron—while Darcie took Vansi away, said, "Ah, fuck." He thrust both hands through his hair, squeezed his eyes tight. When he flashed them open, it was to say, "There's another cellar under the kitchen pantry. It's empty. And with the snow, it'll be freezing."

"You serious?" Aaron said. "Under the kitchen?"

"They needed it back before fridges." Ash's voice was flat, without affect. "We can take him to the wine cellar, but it's a mess of dust and cobwebs. The cellar under the pantry is kept clean, because if the power goes out, it can be used to store goods that need to be cold. We treat him with respect, wrap him up and put him in a safe place."

"He's right," I said, ashamed at myself for being surprised by Ash's raw empathy.

Our friend was dead. We had to care for him. "Before we do that, though, why doesn't someone go up to the tower to see if we can get a signal? If we can get through to the authorities . . ."

"I'll do it," Ash offered.

"I'll come with you." Grace held up a phone encased in a sparkling case. "My phone's new, seems to get a signal when everything else fails."

"I'll stay with Nix." Aaron's voice held a tremor. "Lu?"

"I'll finish doing the photographs." With that, I turned and walked up the stairs.

The floor runner that had almost tripped me up that first night lay tangled at the top, half on the landing, half on the first step.

It hadn't been there when I'd last been on this landing.

Cheeks burning but gut cold, I began to photograph everything. I made sure not to touch the runner as I walked around to photograph the hallway on either side. For good measure, I even took shots of each of the doorways, whether open or closed.

And, after a slight hesitation, I went into Vansi and Phoenix's bedroom and captured every inch of that. I saw the fallen box of tampons as soon as I entered the bathroom. The white tubes rolled around the floor near the sink, while the box itself had fallen into the sink.

As if Vansi had been opening it up in order to take one out, but had dropped it and run when she'd heard Phoenix cry out.

I'd have to tell the others that this room was off-limits. As far as I was concerned, this was evidence that she was in no way responsible for her husband's fall.

"Cops always suspect the spouse," she'd said to me more than once. "Half the podcasts I listen to where it's a spouse murder, it *is* the husband or wife. Ugh."

"Not this time," I muttered, certain that Vansi wasn't responsible for Nix's death. If I knew one thing in my life, it was that Vansi loved Phoenix more than her career, more than her family, more than life itself.

I'd pull the door to the room shut behind myself, leave it as it was for the police. Vansi could borrow my clothes for the duration and I had a spare box of tampons. Though I did stop by her open suitcase and grab her bag of underwear. Probably shouldn't have, but my friend was already hurting. I wasn't going to make her feel worse.

I was about to walk into my room when I realized I needed to photograph *everyone's* rooms, including mine. Flushing at the oversight, I got to it, and felt no guilt in walking into everyone's private areas.

Nix was dead. We could all deal.

Every single inch of this part of the house now recorded on my camera, both in stills and on video, I stared at the rug again. It seemed clear that Phoenix had become tangled up in the rug and taken a fatal tumble. The stairs were steep. That he'd broken his neck wasn't a surprise. The best possible result would've still included a broken bone. It just so happened that he'd been unlucky enough for that bone to be in his neck.

My insides churned.

I looked to the left, then the right. The walls. I hadn't photographed the walls around the staircase. I did so closely, but saw nothing. Not even when I zoomed in. There was no evidence of anything other than a terrible accident.

We'd have to disturb the scene and roll up the rug before it took another life, but I couldn't make that call myself. I'd talk to the others. In my mind, the safest option seemed to be to stay put in the living room. One of us could be assigned to come upstairs, get everything.

Probably me, since I'd already been up here.

My self-imposed task complete, I went and got the box of tampons I'd thrown into my bag without any real thought, just mechanically following my travel checklist. I put the box in Vansi's underwear bag. I wouldn't need any for at least two weeks and if we were still in this hellhole at that point, then I'd have worse problems than my period. I also changed out of my wet clothes and into fresh, warm gear.

When it was time to go down the stairs, I took extra care.

Aaron was seated on the second-to-last step, his head in his hands and his shoulders shaking. Taking a seat next to him, I put my arm around his thin shoulders and held him as he cried.

My own eyes were hot and dry. Brittle.

It was difficult not to look at Phoenix, given our location and his, but I tried my best, was actually grateful for my fuzzy peripheral vision. But it didn't matter if I didn't look at him. I'd seen him right after the accident and the image was now seared into my memory banks.

"This will destroy his parents." Aaron's voice was husky as he used his upper arm to wipe off his eyes. "He is . . . was their pride and joy. Their doctor son. The embodiment of their dreams, the cherished reason for all the sacrifices they made to get to this country."

"The rug's there, and it's all tumbled up," I said softly because I couldn't think about the Changs; I didn't know them well, but I'd met them at the graduation party they'd thrown for Phoenix when he officially became an MD.

The two had beamed like twin small suns.

"Yeah?" He rubbed his face with his hands. "Grace was right, then. Accident."

"But I rolled up and put that rug away, Aaron."

Forehead furrowed, he said, "One of us must've decided to put it back out. I don't want to ask who—they'll feel bad enough when they realize what happened."

Unlike Aaron, I wasn't so certain it had been a stupid mistake. But what evidence did I have of anything else? "I saw tampons scattered in their bathroom." Private information but information that needed to be known so no one would even think that Vansi'd had anything to do with Nix ending up at the bottom of the stairs.

"That's good." Dull voice, but tears silent and heartbreaking rolled down his cheeks. "I don't think his parents could take it if Vansi was involved. They adore her, you know. His mother's flat-out said that she doesn't think Phoenix would be on the road to being a surgeon if he didn't have a dedicated and supportive wife."

"You know them well."

A shrug. "Nix and I, we've been buds for a long time." He looked around. "Don't tell Vansi, okay? Don't tell anyone. But I can't keep it inside anymore, not now that he's . . ."

33

My heart thundered. "What is it?" I was ready to hear about the affair Vansi had feared, take that knowledge to my grave.

"He was having second thoughts about being a surgeon." Aaron pressed his lips together, shook his head. "All those years, all that backbreaking work, and he wanted to walk away from not just surgery, but medicine altogether. But he didn't know how to tell Vansi or his parents. They're so proud of him."

Of all the things he could've said, that was the one I'd have least expected. "Wow."

"Yeah, shocked me, too," Aaron said. "I only know because we went to another friend's stag night. Phoenix actually got drunk, if you can believe it, and spilled—the next morning, he asked me to never mention it to anyone. I haven't even told Grace."

"I won't say a word," I promised, and this secret, too, I'd take to my grave. "There's no point now." Let my best friend and

Phoenix's parents remember him as an accomplished doctor who would one day have become a stellar surgeon.

Aaron stared down at the hands that hung between his knees, his elbows on his thighs. "After Bea died, I didn't know how to handle it. I never knew anyone who died by suicide. Nix was the one who talked it through with me, who made me see that it wasn't anything I'd done or hadn't done—because I was going over and over that in my mind. Should I have reached out? Should I have done more to find her after she vanished?"

"I had the same thoughts." *They haunted me to this day.*

"Nix said he did, too, but he'd also started a psych module at the time, and he'd gone and spoken to the professor, and he shared a lot of his professor's advice with me. He was a good friend. A good guy."

A small sob escaped his throat. "He always said that when he was a surgeon and swimming in money, he'd invest in my restaurant. Not as a loan, as an investment—because he knew I'd make a profit." His voice shook. "He meant it, too. Nix didn't joke about finances."

The two of us just sat there leaning into each other until we heard footsteps approaching from the other end of the house. One look at Ash's and Grace's faces and my stomach dropped.

"Nothing," Grace said, her voice small. "No bars. No data. Dead air."

Hands on his hips, Ash paced in a tight square. "I keep telling Darcie we need to get a satellite phone for out here, but we've never quite got around to it." Anguish was another square, then another. "It's too fucking late now."

Grace touched his forearm. "No one could've prepared for this. And the snow, the storm, that came out of nowhere. No one's to blame."

Ash's eyes were red, and I realized he'd been crying, too. "We should take him to the cellar." His eyes went to Aaron. "Before V . . ."

Aaron moved his head in a jerky nod.

"I'll go find some sheets." Grace moved off in the direction of the linen closet without waiting for a response.

"I'll photograph the move," I said. "Just to cover us." Then I shared what I'd found upstairs.

Ash blew out a breath. "We should've thrown away that runner the first time someone tripped."

He seemed to not even have heard that I'd rolled and put it away, and I decided now wasn't the time to ask questions on the point. Because chances were that it was either Ash or Darcie who'd unrolled the rug—just putting things back to how they usually were in their house. They might even have been irritated that one of us had made the unilateral decision to alter the décor.

Ash nodded toward Phoenix without looking at him. "Shall we . . ."

"Wait." Rising with Vansi's silk underwear bag in my hand, I walked into the living room.

My friend sat hollow-eyed not with Darcie but with Kaea, who'd got himself into a seated position and was cuddling her against him. He looked like death, his cheeks gaunt and his eyes having a yellowish cast.

Shit, looked like he was getting sicker, not better.

Darcie, meanwhile, was by the fire, pacing back and forth.

"V," I said, my voice gentle. "I got you what you need. I don't think any of us should go upstairs."

She looked blankly at the bag I was holding out.

Touching my fingers to her cheek, I leaned down to whisper against her ear. "I put the tampons inside."

A shudder rocked her, and then she was rising to throw herself in my arms. I held her tight, my best friend who'd been in love with Phoenix from the first day she'd seen him. The best friend for whom I'd stood as maid of honor. The best friend at whose bachelorette party I'd drunk so many margaritas that I'd sworn off tequila.

I didn't know how long we stood there, but Vansi was ready to go take care of herself by the time we were done.

I glanced at Darcie. "Can you show V to a bathroom?" Because no way was she going out into the hallway while Phoenix lay there.

Darcie swallowed, nodded. "We can go through the kitchen and out via the veranda to reach one." Her face quivered. "We won't freeze if we hurry."

I waited until the two women had left before looking down at Kaea. "How are you doing, Slick?"

"Bad." His eyes were heavy lidded, his voice as heavy. "Like my insides are being scraped by a serrated blade. I need a hospital." He turned his head toward the hallway. "That wasn't an accident, Luna. I don't care what the fuck it looks like. Something is *wrong*."

Heat burned off him when I touched his shoulder. Delirious from fever? Possible. But he was also a criminal defense lawyer and a successful one. Sharp. Used to seeing what people wanted to hide.

"We'll find out. I'm photographing everything."

He gripped my wrist, his hold stronger than it should be. "Promise me you won't let me have an accident, too."

My skin flashed between hot and cold. "I promise," I said, my throat rough.

He didn't let go. "Lunes." Wild eyes. "I saw an angel while you were all gone before. All in white. She stroked my hair and told me I'd be okay." A shudder rocked his frame. "I don't want to die, Lunes. Tell the angel I'm not ready to go with her yet."

Fuck, he was hallucinating. I knew that was bad. It meant the fever was affecting his brain. "I will, Kaea," I told him, not sure he was capable of listening to reason. "I'll keep you safe—no one will take you."

It took me several minutes to convince him to lie down, close his eyes.

Panic was a trapped butterfly inside me as I walked out. Because I didn't know if I could keep that promise. Things were escalating. Someone was *dead.* I might've convinced the logical part of myself that it had been an accident, but my hindbrain was hyperventilating, seeing monsters out of the corner of the eye.

"Thanks for waiting," I said to the others when I reached them.

Grace stood beside a small pile of bedding. "Should we . . . wrap him up here?" she whispered hesitantly.

Everyone looked at me. I didn't know when I'd become the person making the decisions, but this one wasn't hard. "Yes," I said, hoping that was the best way to keep any evidence on him intact.

Then I lifted my camera.

And took photographs of my friends rolling another friend into a white sheet. They were careful, but Phoenix was still dead weight and my stomach lurched with every thud and roll.

The sheet was scarlet around his face by the end.

"I'm going to be sick." Ash staggered backward with his forearm over his mouth.

But he returned after a few seconds to help finish the task.

Together, we made the call to further wrap Nix in a blanket to protect his body from postmortem injury—and though none of us said it, to hide the blood that had soaked the sheet.

His heart might've stopped pumping, but there was still so much *red*.

I took photographs of every step of the progress, including when Ash and Aaron lifted him up and how they carried him. I also captured images of the painting that had fallen off the wall— that disturbing photo of Clara and Blake after their wedding, no happiness in either of them—and made a mental note to clear away the shards of glass after we got back.

"Fuck, he's heavy." Aaron grunted. "He always looked light to me."

Dead weight.

"Should I—" I started to say even as Grace parted her lips.

But the two men shook their heads. "We have it," they said almost in unison.

Thus began our slow, solemn march to the cellar. It felt like it took forever, and the tears I couldn't shed, they turned into a lump cold and rigid inside my chest. Painful. My tears calcified.

Grace and I did have to help Ash and Aaron get Phoenix down the stairs to the cellar—the access door for which lay between the kitchen and laundry. I'd taken it to be a storage closet.

Just a mannequin, I repeated silently inside my head.

Not our friend.

Not Nix who'd been Vansi's husband.

Not Dr. Phoenix Chang.

Just a mannequin.

Grace's sniffled tears were a counterpoint to my grim silence, her face wet with the fluid I couldn't produce.

By the time we reached the cellar floor, my heart was thumping from the effort of ensuring I didn't slip up, allow Nix to fall.

"Over there." Ash nodded to a spot below a narrow and high window that let in smudged gray light, partially as a result of the weather and partially because of the layer of dirt on the glass.

"Outside wall," Ash explained. "Probably the coldest place in the entire cellar."

Because Nix was a creature of the cold now, no warmth to him.

After we put him down with as much care as we could, Aaron massaged one hand with the other, the motion too hard, too fast. "He went to church. Not all the time. But enough. He had faith."

Without a word, we clasped our hands in front of our chests and lowered our heads, eyes closed.

Aaron spoke the Lord's Prayer in a voice that trembled.

"Go with God, my friend," he said at the end, a single tear rolling down his face.

"Go with God, Nix," I echoed, even though I wasn't religious in the least. But it seemed right that I support his final journey in the way he would've wished. "Thank you for all the scrambled eggs you made me over the years, all the talks we shared late at night on our camping trips while everyone else slept"—a fact I'd near forgotten—"and most of all, for being who you were: a good husband, a good son, and a good friend."

The others murmured their own goodbyes, with a crying Grace saying, "I wish I'd had longer to know you. The glimpses I did have of you showed me a man kind and loving and loyal, and I'm so happy you had such a beautiful life with Vansi. I wish you peace in your next journey."

Ash's goodbye was rough, short, and broken, Aaron's heartfelt and the most personal of all of us.

"I'll miss you, Nix," he said through his tears, one hand on Phoenix's body. "You were the best friend a guy could have. Thank you for standing up for me when I was a skinny twelve-year-old and for standing by me through life. I was going to ask you to be my best man—and you still will be. No one will take your place. No one could."

He spoke his next words in his parents' native tongue, a private goodbye between two boys grown into men who'd never stopped being best friends.

Then it was done.

And for all that I hadn't wanted to handle his body, it was hard to leave my friend in this cold and lonely place. I lingered at the end, lifting my camera to my eye to take one final shot.

"Come on, Lu." Aaron held out a hand from higher up the steps. "Nix is gone to our Father in heaven. What remains is the shell he occupied on this earth."

I envied Aaron his faith at that moment, because I wasn't so sure that Phoenix was at peace. That look of shock and terror on his face . . . No, I didn't think Nix was at rest.

But I allowed Aaron to take my hand and lead me up and out.

Grace didn't look askance at his grip when we appeared in the cellar doorway. Instead, giving me a teary smile, she took my other hand. Her hand was as fine-boned and small as Aaron's was long-fingered and scarred over with the small burns accumulated over a lifetime by a man who loved to cook.

"It's hard to leave him there, isn't it?" Grace said. "It feels wrong."

I nodded, my eyes burning as hot and as dry as the Sahara.

34

Darcie had already swept away the broken glass by the time
we got back. "I convinced Vansi to lie down," she whispered. "Gave her a sleeping pill I had. Just over-the-counter stuff.
She didn't resist—I think she wanted to shut out the world for a
while."

Her eyes searched Ash's face.

Walking over, he ran his hand down her braid. "You did the
right thing."

The pinched look disappeared from around her eyes, her lips
less taut.

Grace spoke then, but I wasn't paying attention except to note
that Ash replied to her.

Leaving the two couples to their quiet discussion, I went into
the living room to check on Vansi and Kaea. I didn't like the fact
that Darcie had knocked Vansi out; I could've sworn that my

friend had found herself again in the moments before we'd left with Phoenix's body.

But what was the point of Darcie lying? Vansi would wake sooner or later, and then we'd all know whether she'd chosen to take the pill or not. And this wasn't like any other situation V had faced in her life.

I couldn't presume to predict her emotional responses.

I saw Kaea first as his sofa was closest to the door. He shifted feverishly in his sleep, his skin so hot that I didn't even have to touch him to sense the heat coming off his body. "Kaea." I shook his shoulder gently, was shocked at the burn of his skin.

No response. To my voice or a harder shake, a stronger call.

He was in trouble.

My heart pounding, I checked quickly on Vansi. Her breathing was even, her rest appearing peaceful. I couldn't wait for her to wake—not just to see that she was okay, but because she was a nurse. If we needed anyone right now, it was Vansi.

"Kaea has a dangerously high fever," I told the others from the doorway of the living area. "Do we have anything to help bring it down?"

Everyone glanced instinctively toward the spot where Phoenix's body had crumpled.

The doctor in the group.

The one who'd been looking after our friend.

His startled, broken face flashed into my mind, a jigsaw outlined in red.

Jerking away my head, I found the others doing the same. We started talking all at once, but soon realized that the only thing we had was paracetamol—the kind anyone could buy at the grocery store or chemist, nothing stronger.

"Then we give him that," I said. "It might help a little at least."

Some small grain of knowledge at the back of my head said that a fever wasn't dangerous only because of what it signified in terms of what was happening within the body—but of its own accord. Did it really heat up the brain? Or was I making that up?

Vansi would know, and even tortured by grief, she'd help Kaea. That was just who she was. Which was why I found it all the more surprising that she'd taken Darcie's pill. "Vansi didn't say anything about Kaea before she took the sleeping pill?"

Darcie flinched before squaring her shoulders and jutting out her jaw. "I didn't drug her, if that's what you're implying." Words thrown out like bullets. "Do you think I'm behind everything?" Her pitch was too high, hurtful to the ear. "That I smashed my own head and put that cursed doll on my bed?"

"I'm sure Luna doesn't think anything like that." Aaron, always the peacemaker.

But I was through with peace. Especially given the intensity of Darcie's reaction. I wanted answers. "You're the one who brought us all together." I refused to break eye contact. "We're in your house. You know every single secret room and passage. And how could anyone *but* you have Beatrice's doll? Only *you* saw her after she died. Only *you* had access to her belongings. Only *you* got to say goodbye."

If my other statements had been bitter accusations, my final words were a broken softness. "Why didn't you let us say goodbye, Darcie?"

Her face went white, so much tension to her body that she appeared like one of those gruesome "medical artworks"— humans preserved without flesh, just bone and tendon and muscle. "Why do you care so much?" she screamed. "You were nothing to her. Just a pathetic puppy dog who followed her around. She used to laugh about you!"

If Darcie expected to cow me with that "revelation," she didn't know me at all. I'd never reacted well to emotional manipulation—and I knew exactly what I'd had with Bea. That treasure box of stolen tchotchkes? I still had it. I also still had the complete file of the nude photos Bea had asked me to take of her "while I'm young and beautiful, Nae-nae, so I can look back on them during my grandma years."

I'd been the keeper of Bea's secrets since the day we'd met and she'd slipped me a chocolate bar to hide in my jacket because, for a period, Mr. and Mrs. Shepherd had been militant about no refined sugars in the house. We'd later shared that chocolate bar while lying under a tree in the park, staring up at a blue sky patterned with leaves.

She'd turned, smiled at me, and I'd thought she was the most beautiful creature I'd ever seen. A bird with dazzling blue eyes who was meant to soar high while I watched from below to ensure she didn't fall.

"Listen to yourself." My voice was as cold as Nix's skin. "We all know Bea was too kind to *ever* mock a friend that way. So not only didn't you give us a chance to farewell her, you're now trying to assassinate her memory!"

Ash attempted to step in, speak, but Darcie yelled over him. "I was grieving when I made my decision about Bea!" Red spots on her cheeks, a hard glitter in her eyes. "I'd just said goodbye to the last member of my family. I didn't want spectators to my grief! Why the hell don't you understand that?"

"So you sent her off with nothing?" Bea's necklace burned against my skin. "Was that your final revenge on a sister who was brighter and more popular than you?" It was a truth none of us had ever spoken aloud, a silent contract of friendship.

Because though both sisters were stunning and accomplished, it was only Bea who carried within her the special spark that made people gravitate toward a person. Only Bea who glowed with charisma. Only Bea who could walk into a room and stop all conversation. And only Bea who Ash had loved with a mad devotion.

I didn't look at him, not cruel enough to dig at that wound. But the knowledge hung in the air, a silence so shocking that Grace's eyes had gone huge and round, Aaron a statue beside her.

"That's enough, Luna." Ash's golden skin held a pink undertone, his hands fisted at his sides. "I know you're distraught, but that's no reason to attack Darcie."

I barely heard him; this wasn't about Ash or Aaron or anyone else. Stepping forward, I faced Darcie with only inches between us. "Why did you cremate Bea instead of burying her in the family plot beside your parents? Why did you throw her away so far from home?"

Ash, in the process of raising his hand as if to push my shoulder so I'd back off, went still . . . then lowered his hand.

And waited for his wife to answer the question.

Darcie looked from me to him . . . and screamed. Just threw back her head and *screamed*. When she looked at me afterward, it was with the bite of venom in her gaze. I'd seen it before. Not often, but enough to understand that Darcie would make a bad enemy.

"Since you refuse to accept what I've already told you," she said with icy precision, "I cremated my baby sister because the rope that she used to hang herself had rubbed her skin raw, and her face was all puffed up. Nothing of her looked like Beatrice. She also wasn't found for a few days—there were maggots involved."

Even as Grace uttered a shocked cry and put a hand to her mouth, Darcie curled up her lip. "Happy now?"

But, forewarned by her earlier description of going to see Bea's dead body, I was ready this time. "Beatrice would've never hung herself." Quiet. As precise as her own diction.

"She told me once that of all the ways a person could die, suffocation was the worst." I didn't blink as I held Darcie's gaze. "She always said that if she ever had to do it, she'd take a poison that'd put her to sleep. Painless oblivion."

A flicker in Darcie's eyes, a skittering.

35

I wished that my vision was better, that I could be sure, but it wasn't and so what I saw could've been real . . . or nothing but a dance of shadows.

I gritted my teeth.

"My sister was mentally disturbed." A quiver in her voice, a liquid shine to her eyes. "I wouldn't put too much stock in what she said before."

Ash stepped between us, physically breaking the line of sight. "Enough," he said once more, and this time there was a sense of authority in his tone. "We are not going to start fighting between ourselves when we're already dealing with a horrific situation."

He glanced at Aaron. "Do you think you might be up to making us tea or coffee?"

"Sure, of course." A fervent desperation in this friend who was as gentle as Darcie was hard. "I'll make grilled cheese, too. It's way past lunchtime."

Ash pinned me with gray eyes gone as flat as steel. "I think it might be a good idea for you to sit down and go over your photographs. Take a bit of time out."

This was the reason I preferred to live life at a distance, behind the lens of a camera; because when my emotions did emerge, they were too big, too wild. It was why my parents had put me in therapy after my adoption at age three. No one knew what had happened to me in the years prior, but I'd come to them with a black rage within.

No one would've blamed them if they'd given me back like an unwanted dog.

But they hadn't. Instead, they'd been my parents. They'd gotten me help—and the therapist had taught me to regulate my emotions. Until now, I couldn't cry even when I wanted to.

I'd regulated myself to bitter dryness.

"I need to get my laptop from upstairs." My voice was as brittle as my eyes, a thing arid. "But I don't think anyone else should go up there. I've already contaminated it with my presence, so I can take a list and collect whatever people want. It's the only way to make sure we don't disturb the floor runner."

I glanced at Aaron and Grace, two people I was sure would back me in this. "I also think we'll be safer together, whether against the snow or . . ."

No one pushed me to finish that sentence, put our fear into words that we couldn't dial back.

I carried on. "The living area is already warm and we can keep it that way, and the sofas are plenty big enough for us to rest on. We can also drag in mattresses from the lower-level rooms."

Pretending Darcie wasn't there, I spoke only to Ash. "Assuming there are any downstairs mattresses that are safe to use?"

A curt nod.

Shifting, he took Darcie's hand. "I think Luna's right on this point." A brush of his fingers over her cheek, but he wasn't quite looking at her. "It's going to be impossible to heat all the rooms to the extent needed against snow. We'll have to take shifts feeding the living room fire as it is, to ensure it never goes out."

"Kaea's so sick, too," Grace blurted out. "The person on fire watch can keep an eye on him at the same time."

Darcie had looked over when Grace spoke, now gave a hard nod without ever glancing at me.

"Tell me what you want," I said to all four. "I'll get it from your rooms."

This time, Darcie's glance was cutting. "The rest of us can also avoid the runner, Luna. We're not blind." Spite, out in the open, striking a blow she didn't even realize. "I'd rather you didn't paw through my belongings."

"I'll go." Ash squeezed Darcie's hand when she would've spoken again. "I'll mirror your footsteps, Luna, avoid the runner."

"I don't mind if you get my things." Grace's smile was awkward, a woman caught between forces she had no way of comprehending. "Sweetheart?"

"Yes, same. Lu, you can grab my stuff."

The other couple gave me a short list before they headed to the kitchen cloaked in an air of haste. I didn't blame them. The atmosphere in the hallway was thick with tension vicious and ugly.

Darcie glared as Ash and I walked up the staircase.

He didn't say a word to me until we'd reached the landing and moved past the twisted runner, and could no longer be seen from downstairs.

A glance back, a pause, then he was looking directly at me.

I expected anger, even a repeat of Darcie's venomous sting, but his shoulders sagged, his face . . . sad. Just sad. "I loved Bea. God, how I loved Bea." Throat muscles moving, eyes blinking rapidly. "But I also love Darcie. We're about to have *a child*."

He jabbed a finger into the air toward me, but . . . there was nothing powerful about it, not like when he spoke of Bea. As if he was playacting what was expected. "I asked you to keep an eye on her, and you do this? Jesus, Luna."

Hell no. Ash might be acting the concerned husband out of guilt at his continued love for Bea, but Darcie wasn't going to snake out of this by playing the victim. And no way in fucking hell would I allow her to smear Bea's name with impunity. "Is that what she's told you all these years?" My nails cut into my palms. "That Bea hung herself?"

"I never asked." His hands trembled as he shoved his hair back once again, the strands abused golden silk. "I didn't want to know. I've always preferred to imagine her fading away in a drug haze. Beautiful and bright and happy." His voice caught. "Just falling asleep and never waking up."

"Bea didn't do drugs." She'd only ever done lines that one time and no one else knew about it.

"Nothing hard; the odd joint. Usually with Kaea."

"That doesn't count." I wasn't into drugs, but I wasn't preachy about them, either—because I'd battled my own vices. Wine, beer, vodka, there'd been a time I'd have overdone any poison that'd blur the edges of my world, make me feel more *normal*, less like an error in the code.

A year into my time at university, during a weekend when Kaea, Vansi, and Aaron were all away for reasons I couldn't remember, I'd woken to find I'd smashed every glass item in our kitchen, and that my feet were bleeding and studded with glass.

I should've gone to the emergency room.

Instead, I'd sat on the floor of our bathroom and used my makeup tweezers to pull the glass out shard by fine shard. I could still remember the sting of the antiseptic I'd wiped over the torn-apart flesh in the aftermath, the smell of iron rich in the air, and the crunch of glass as I swept it up.

I'd gone cold turkey for six months after that, and never again dropped that far into the abyss. Not even during Vansi's bachelor-ette party. Because blurring the edges wasn't as important as maintaining control. I hadn't shared the incident with anyone, had just spent the rest of the weekend hobbling around charity shops finding replacements for our mismatched glassware.

No one had noticed.

"I just liked the mental image." Ash's confession was raw. "Imagining her slipping away in peace. It brought me comfort. Now that's gone forever."

I felt for him, but not enough to shroud the truth. "Bea did not hang herself."

"Fuck it, Luna. *Please.* I'm begging you, don't pick at that wound. You saw how Darcie was after Bea's suicide—mad with grief."

Again, a flatness below the apparent emotion. Or perhaps I just wanted there to be, wanted him to be loyal to Bea, to be the devoted lover Bea had believed him to be, rather than Darcie's human-shaped doll.

"There was no logic or reason to her actions," he added, "so don't look for those things."

Swiping out an arm to cut off any words I might've said, he

shifted on his heel to walk into their bedroom. "I'll meet you back here in a couple of minutes."

I moved mechanically to grab my daypack, putting into it my laptop, wallet, and house keys. Everything I'd need if I had to leave the estate in a hurry. I also threw in a fresh set of clothes, plus some extra warm layers to share with Vansi, and was done.

I headed to Aaron and Grace's room.

Ash was crouched by the floor runner when I returned to the hallway—but had stayed far enough back that there was no chance of disturbing it. "It's too close to the stairs," he murmured. "I would've noticed if it was this close to the stairs. I pull the damn thing back all the time when we visit, but Darcie refuses to get rid of it because her mother bought it."

"I watched a documentary once," I said, even more convinced that Darcie was the one who'd unrolled the runner. "It was all about suspicious staircase deaths. They're really difficult to prove one way or the other."

Ash rose to his feet, his thighs pressing up against his pants. The beige material bore a small streak near the left hip pocket that could've been dirt—or dried blood. Nix's blood.

I didn't say anything.

I had no fight with Ash, didn't want to make him any more uncomfortable. Because though he'd ended up with Darcie, he'd always remain Bea's. If she walked back into his life right now, I had not a single doubt that he'd dump Darcie in a heartbeat.

And Bea . . . she'd loved him.

A sigh in my mind, a memory of Bea's luminous brown hair escaping from under her knit cap as she stared out at the crashing winter ocean. "I slept with Ash."

"Beatrice." I'd pressed my hands into the cold black sand on

either side of my body, and shaken my head. "You know Darcie has a thing for him."

"I know . . . but the way I feel about him, Nae-nae." She'd flopped all the way down onto her back. "As if I have fireworks inside me. I'm actually waiting for his texts and calls, can you believe it? Me? Waiting on a guy?"

I'd known of Bea and Ash's relationship long before the others. She'd told me all of it, safe in the knowledge that that was where the information would stop. Ash had no idea how much I understood about his love for Bea. He might wear preppy clothes for Darcie and pose as she wanted for her social media, but he'd have burned down the world for Bea.

I'd often wondered if the true reason he'd ended up with Darcie wasn't shared grief, but because she was the only living link to Bea, a shallow stand-in for the scalding flame of a woman who'd smashed all our hearts to pieces when she chose to leave us.

I said none of that as we walked down the stairs.

Neither one of us looked at the wall opposite the staircase at the bottom, a wall that now bore a slight dent—but we saw it all the same. The photograph was missing, too, I realized dully. Darcie must've put it away somewhere when she swept up the glass.

Stepping to the right off the final step, we both made a beeline for the living room.

Darcie stood by the fireplace, and Vansi hadn't moved since I'd last seen her, but her breathing was deep and even and she showed no visible signs of distress.

Kaea, meanwhile, seemed to have fallen into a peaceful sleep devoid of agitated movements. "How's his fever?" I asked Grace, who sat on a chair next to him.

"No real change." Twisting out the washcloth she'd just dipped into a bowl of water on the coffee table, she smoothed the cloth over his forehead. "My mamé—my mum's mum—used to do this for me when I was feverish. I figured it couldn't hurt."

I nodded. "Yes, my mother did that for me, too." And right now, Kaea could use all the help we could give him. "I grabbed the stuff you and Aaron wanted." Having put it all in a duffel I'd found in their room, I placed both it and my pack near the coffee table. "I'll go scout out mattresses on this level, see what's suitable to drag in here."

Darcie, who'd been whispering with Ash, said, "I'll come with you. I know which rooms were cleaned." Clipped, tight, hostile.

I wanted to tell her to leave it be, that I was more than capable of opening a few doors, but this was her house, after all. And who knew? Perhaps, in her brewing anger, she'd reveal the truth about Bea.

Ash made a move as if to come with us, but Darcie shot him a look.

Something unspoken passed between the couple, and then we were leaving. From the faint noises that filtered through from the kitchen, Aaron was still in there. I felt a piercing moment of relief that he was here in this place at this time; Grace was a sweetheart, but still a relative unknown. Aaron, however, was the one person on the estate that I *knew* I could trust without question.

The one person I couldn't?

She walked beside me as we headed into the shadows of a long and echoing hallway.

36

Is that what you think of me?" Darcie demanded once we were out of earshot of the living area. "That I'm an evil, vengeful bitch who kept you all away from Bea on purpose?"

No longer in the grip of rage, and conscious I couldn't alienate her if I wanted any semblance of truth, I rubbed my face with one hand. "I just wanted a chance to say goodbye, Darcie. Part of me can't forgive you for taking that away from me. From us. We loved her, too."

A long silence as she led me into a bedroom in which lay a mattress without sheets. We pulled it off to the floor and managed to get it out the door by dragging it sideways.

"I'm sorry." Quiet words from Darcie, who was at the far end of the mattress while I'd taken the front. "I wasn't thinking at the time. I just wanted it to go away. Like if I pretended it wasn't happening, if I got rid of her body, then she wouldn't be dead."

A shaky breath. "Such a stupid, childish instinct and I *hate* myself for giving in to it. Because now, I can't visit with Bea like I do with my parents, and I'm so ashamed, Luna. All the time. The shame eats at me. That's why I was hateful to you. Each and every day, I drown in regret for what I did to my baby sister, to the girl I spent my life protecting."

I stopped, my heart breaking. Of all the things Darcie had ever said about Bea's death, this struck me as the most real. Darcie had become a child in her grief, hiding from the horror by putting her fingers in front of her eyes.

If true, it was something I could forgive.

My throat hurt, my eyes so gritty it felt as if they had tiny stones within.

I lowered the mattress to the floor. Darcie let go of her end at the same time. It landed on the floor with a soft thud.

"I'm sorry, too." Crossing the distance between us, I wrapped her up in my arms.

She folded against me like a reed bending in the wind. "I'm sorry," she said again, her breath hot against the shell of my ear. "I wish every day and every night that I'd buried her in the cemetery behind this house. With my parents. So she wouldn't be alone." Hot wet soaked my shoulder. "*I* did that, I made her alone, when Bea was never alone."

"Grief can make us do terrible things." I rocked her, but couldn't make myself take the next step and tell her it was all right that Bea didn't have a gravestone, that we didn't need it to remember her.

The latter was true for me.

But I'd be gone one day, and so would Darcie. Who would remember Bea then?

Even as I comforted her, I couldn't help but note that she'd said *my* parents rather than *our* parents. A simple slip of the tongue? Or an indication of the psychological war she'd begun to wage the day of Beatrice's birth? The day on which Darcie had gone from being the apple of her parents' eye to being eldest sister to a new baby who'd enchanted everyone.

"None of that now," I said when she began to hyperventilate. "You have to take deep breaths, relax." I almost said that being overwrought wasn't good for the baby, remembered just in time that I wasn't supposed to know about the embryo in her womb.

Ash's DNA intermingled with hers.

If this had been a war, Darcie had won.

"Hold my hands," I said even as the cold thought passed through my mind. "Follow my breaths."

She did as I asked, and as I looked into her eyes—wet and ringed with red, broken blood vessels fragile rivers in the white—I felt like the worst person in the world.

The snow continued to fall in the hours that followed, and it nudged us into higher gear in setting up camp in the living area. Since Darcie still hadn't found her phone, I helped her look for it while we were moving things around, figuring it had most likely fallen into an odd spot like between the arm and seat cushion of one of the sofas.

"There's still plenty of firewood," Ash said at one point, but he was frowning.

A short discussion later, he and Aaron decided to fetch more from the barn in case the snow turned into a blizzard, and all our attention switched to them.

"We don't know how long we'll be stuck here," Aaron said to

Grace as he pulled on work gloves that Kaea had picked up from the barn during that first firewood run. "Better to overprepare than under."

"Be careful." Grace, her expression pinched, tugged his hood tight around his face.

Like her, I wasn't sure about the two of them walking out into the snow, but they were right in saying that at least the precipitation was currently manageable. Even a small increase in intensity and it might turn into a deadly whiteout.

"Make sure you tie a rope line to the barn." Grace lowered her eyebrows. "I mean it. Don't think that you can't get disoriented. I've lived in snow. I know what can happen."

"Grace is right." Darcie passed Ash his gloves. "I think there's a bit of rope in the laundry. We use it as a temporary drying line when we come down in better weather."

She was back with it within a couple of minutes.

Then, for the first time since I'd returned to the living room, I left Vansi and Kaea alone to go stand on the kitchen veranda with Grace and Darcie, all three of us focused on the men struggling against the snow and the wind.

I took a couple of snapshots and thought of how quickly we'd digressed to traditional gender roles. Then again, Aaron and Ash together were stronger than the three of us. But if it looked like they were beginning to get dangerously cold, I was going to make one of them stay in the kitchen to warm up, while I did a round, and then we'd swap.

I had a feeling Grace would back me on that; every muscle in her body was taut, her eyes narrowed as she fought to keep Aaron in sight in the low visibility. "I can't see them anymore," she said just then. "Darcie? Luna?"

I shook my head; I'd lost sight of them long before her.

"No, they've gone too far." Darcie pointed at the bright pink rope tied to the veranda railing. "It's taut. They're still unrolling it as they go."

Grace exhaled long and slow—and kept on glancing at the rope. Until too much time had passed, our cheeks burning with cold and our lips chapped. "Why aren't they back yet?" she demanded.

"Let me check the rope." But when I tugged on the roughness of it, it was to a sense of laxity. No tension. Either they were stacking firewood onto the wide wooden cart that Ash had told us Jim kept in the barn for that purpose, or something had gone wrong.

My mouth grew dry. "How long should we wait?"

Darcie responded first, her answer pragmatic but her gaze trained in the direction of the barn. "The snow's deeper than it looked from the inside. They're probably having trouble pulling the cart through it. The wheels aren't designed to navigate snow and it'll be heavy weighed down with firewood."

She had a point.

But Grace was a shivering, wild-eyed mess nonetheless. She began to gnaw on her fingernails. "Sorry." She hid her hands behind her back when she saw me glance at her. "Bad habit. Can't stop when I'm nervous."

"I get it."

Aaron's voice emerged from the white at the same moment.

We called back in unison, and as soon as they got in sight, we bounded out to help them pull the heavily laden cart as close to the kitchen steps as possible. Then all five of us pitched in to carry the wood inside and to one corner of the kitchen. It'd be easy enough to take logs into the living area as needed.

The guys did two more runs before we decided we had enough to get us through the next two or three days.

My bones ached from the cold from just standing on the veranda and the quick exposure to the snow when I'd helped unload, and I didn't begrudge Ash and Aaron their prime positions in front of the fire as they tried to thaw themselves out in the aftermath.

Grace plied both men with mugs of coffee while fussing over Aaron.

"We're such city folk," Ash muttered after he'd stopped shivering. "Jim would take one look at the lot of us and be ashamed at the youth of today." He glanced up at the array of dead stag heads. "We haven't even added a single animal head to the walls. Disgraceful."

"No stuffed small creatures, either," Darcie inserted, her tone as dry as the pelts of the unfortunate animals in this space. "Especially after I committed the cardinal sin of throwing out a pair of moth-eaten stuffed possums with green marble eyes."

Aaron folded his arms. "You're making that up."

"Scout's honor. One of my ancestors took up taxidermy for a hobby—only he wasn't that good. The possums kept falling over because he stuffed them lopsided."

Laughter, the rest of us teasing Darcie about her trophy-hunting-obsessed ancestors, and teasing one another about our descent into soft adulthood . . . until suddenly it was as if we remembered what had happened, that one of us was dead.

The silence that fell was so big it crushed.

We separated without discussion, each claiming an area of the living room as our own. Mine was against the right wall not far from the fire, the space defined by a double mattress that Grace had dressed with a floral bedspread.

A pile of spare blankets sat on an unused armchair.

We weren't in danger from the cold here, but the same couldn't be said for the rest of the house. Place would be an icebox. I wasn't looking forward to visiting the toilet, and hoped I could hold it off as I sat cross-legged on the mattress, my eyes on my laptop . . . and another page of Clara's clandestine journal, the words hidden among the images throwing me back in time.

> *It has been a season of beauty. I should not dismiss that. This land, it takes my breath away when the grass becomes a sea of gold, the morning frost the prettiest lacework in all the land. I have spent many a dawn chasing my children through that frost, their laughter as bright as the song of the bird that lives near the orange grove.*
>
> *The locals call it a tui. Its plumage is blue-black with a rainbow shine and it has a little white ruff at its neck. Mattie says the bird looks like it's wearing a tuxedo and he wonders whether it's off to a party.*
>
> *Such a lively imagination he has, my son.*

A tiny drawing of a tui sat at the end of the line, the image a decoration on a bowl that spilled over with grapes.

I'd never met Clara, would never meet her, and yet I felt a deep well of joy that she'd known some happiness in this cold and inhospitable land so far from her home. But not enough, I thought as I took a break to check on Vansi and Kaea.

No change.

Telling myself that was good news even as their stillness gnawed at me, I returned to my spot and to Clara's diary.

Blake is . . . lost to me. I have attempted to hold on to hope through the years, have attempted to be the wife he needs in the belief that it would draw him back. He was never the young lover I dreamed of in my girlish days, but, on our wedding day, he was a man proud and intelligent.

When I entered the estate house, he showed me to a salon he'd had created just for me, with furniture he'd had shipped from England. Furniture like that in my parents' home. So that I would have a piece of England in this land on the edge of the world.

I could've loved that man.

But he is gone and the one who lives in Blake's skin now is a creature disturbing. I would not worry so if it was only my life, but our children, our precious children, how can I protect them against the spreading taint of his madness?

Already, Elizabeth talks to herself when she thinks I am not looking. And she does not talk as children do, to friends created out of air. No, she talks in a way secret and dark, and even more troubling, she looks at her siblings with contempt. They adore her, wish to emulate her, and she wants nothing to do with them.

My Lizzie, my firstborn, she breaks my heart.

"Elizabeth," I mouthed, finally putting a name to that smirking survivor. And though my bladder had begun to protest, I didn't stop reading. *Couldn't.* My heart was tight, my pulse too fast.

Lizzie hurt Diana today. My baby girl is so small and so much in love with her big sister, and Lizzie burned her. She says it was an accident and that Diana stumbled into her while she was making a candle as she likes to do, but I fear I do not believe her.

The circular burn on Diana's soft little palm is too perfect, too precise. As if something was held to it until it seared the flesh through and through. I wish my wee babe could speak to me of it, but she does not have the words yet. She just holds up her hand and cries and I cry with her.

It is a terrible thing to write . . . but I am scared of Lizzie. No mother should ever say that, but I cannot squelch the fear inside me. When I look at her, all I see is her father's madness—but where Blake cannot hide it, is a creature possessed of rages and whispers, Lizzie has a cunning to her that chills my blood.

I will never again leave her alone with her brother and sisters.

I couldn't help looking over at where Darcie sat curled up in an armchair with a book. Elizabeth's direct descendent. Linked by a bond of blood to a woman I was now certain had murdered her mother and siblings.

37

F*ire.*

   So much of the Shepherd family history had been written in fire, I thought as I gave in to the urging of my body and closed my laptop to chance the temperatures outside the living room.

The frigid air beyond hit like a slap.

Hugging my arms tight around myself, I raced to the toilet and did my business as fast as possible while telling myself not to turn into a conspiracy theorist. Not only did I have no proof that Elizabeth had set the fire that had left her as the only Shepherd heir, I had zero reason to believe Darcie anything but sane.

Just because my feelings for Bea's sister were complicated didn't give me the right to shoehorn her into a psychopathic frame. Because Bea, loyal, beautiful, kind Bea, had shared the same blood.

I never intended to pause by the wall where Nix had died, but an inner niggling made me stop, look up the stairs. Something didn't make sense to me. If Phoenix had tripped and begun to fall, why hadn't he been able to stop himself by grabbing on to one of the railings, or just slow himself down by slamming his foot against the wall?

He'd been fit, strong, with fast reflexes—and he'd have known that a wrenched shoulder or fractured foot was a far better outcome than what awaited him if he tumbled all the way down.

I couldn't help but think about that documentary on staircase deaths.

Vansi was the one who'd made me watch it. I'd groaned, but found myself reluctantly fascinated. Especially during the part where the reporter had showcased the results of experiments on the damage caused to a body by an accidental fall as opposed to one where a person was pushed.

It had stunned me to see that the outcome could be near identical.

A push didn't leave much of a bruise if any. Even if there *was* a small mark, how would anyone notice in the plethora of bruises and cuts that resulted from a fall from such a height?

My nose threatened to drip.

Realizing I was half-frozen, I used a tissue from my pocket to mop up the cold-induced drip before returning to the living room. Phoenix was dead, and I wasn't a pathologist. They'd do a full examination, find what there was to find. The only one to blame—if we wanted to go that way—was the person who'd unrolled the rug.

And we'd never know their identity unless they confessed.

"How is he?" I asked Aaron, who was now sitting by Kaea just holding his hand.

"Ash and I managed to rouse him enough to get two crushed

paracetamol and soup down him." Aaron chewed on his lower lip. "He was groggy, not responsive to questions, but he did swallow the medicine and food, so that's a good sign."

What *wasn't* a good sign was that Kaea had shown no indications of needing to use the bathroom. I knew that from helping Vansi study for her exams, hoped desperately that the lack was just because he was sweating out all the liquid, nothing more.

Leaving Aaron to his silent vigil, I went to Vansi. Her breathing hadn't altered, her pulse slow and steady.

Darcie walked over to me.

"How much did you give her?" I was careful to keep my voice easy, nonconfrontational.

"Just one tablet," she whispered. "It's not that strong, honest. I've woken up before when there's a storm and a branch bangs against the window."

Frowning, I went to put my hand on Vansi's shoulder, shake, but she stirred before I could touch her, letting out a huge yawn and mumbling.

I dropped my hand to my side as Darcie exhaled. "Oh, thank God," she muttered. "I was starting to freak out that she had an allergy to the medication or something like that. She wasn't exactly in the right frame of mind when she took it."

"Let's leave her to it. Better she emerge into consciousness at her own speed."

Darcie nodded before making her way back to her armchair. Ash was missing from his, probably in the kitchen.

He walked through the connecting door some ten minutes later.

Unable to make myself return to Clara's writings, I'd been editing photos on the laptop while waiting for Vansi to wake; I had a hunch that she'd already broken out of sleep, but wasn't yet ready to face the world.

Who could blame her?

When she did finally open her eyes, her gaze was dull but rational. "Where did you put Nix?" she asked me when I went to kneel beside the sofa on which she yet lay.

"A cellar under the kitchen." I knew my friend, understood she was ready for the cold truth. "Let me get you a mug of tea."

Shaking her head, she sat up. "I need to see him."

I didn't tell her that she shouldn't remember Phoenix like that. I knew exactly why she wanted to see him. Because she wouldn't believe it until she did. Just like some part of me didn't believe that Beatrice was dead.

"It's freezing outside this room." I'd have pointed to the snow beyond the windows, but it was too dark now to see the flurries of white. "I brought your outdoor jacket from where it was hanging in the laundry. Put it on. And here, take this beanie, too."

While she did that, her motions slow and gaze blank in the way of a woman who didn't want conversation, I went into the kitchen and poured her a mug of tea from the pot Ash had made earlier. It was tepid by now, but that just meant she could guzzle it down.

I added a huge teaspoon of honey before I took it to Vansi. "I know you said you didn't want it, but it'll wash out the fuzziness from your mouth." While I had no experience with sleeping pills, I was sensitive to a particular hay fever medication—one of those people who shouldn't drive or operate heavy machinery while on it.

I only ever took a pill when nothing else would work—and I slept like the dead.

As Vansi threw back the tea, I turned off my laptop and pulled on my own jacket. I'd given my best friend my beanie, but my jacket had a hood that I tugged over my head. The others had realized what we were about to do, gone silent.

Ash walked over. "You sure this is a good idea?" he murmured under his breath.

"She needs to say goodbye on her own terms." I glanced over at where Vansi was robotically swallowing tea. "Otherwise she'll tie herself in knots wondering if he's just badly wounded and we've hidden him away somewhere. She wasn't rational when he died. She is now."

Ash, his hands on his hips, ducked his head.

When he lifted it back up, his eyes held knowledge stark and painful. "I wish—" An abrupt cessation, his jaw working.

He'd been about to mention Beatrice.

The lover he'd never seen dead.

The friend who'd simply vanished one day.

Unable to help him with his demons when mine yet howled, I walked over to Vansi. "Ready?"

"No." But she rose, her hands shoved into the pockets of her jacket.

The air outside the lounge was shards of ice in our lungs.

"Jesus, you weren't kidding." Her eyes snapped to the windows, which showed a scene of impenetrable darkness. "Why does everything feel muffled? Is it still *snowing*?"

My chest expanded on a rush of relief. My friend was back. "No break since it started." Predicting what she'd ask next, I said, "Ash and Grace climbed up to the tower, couldn't get a signal. We'll have to wait until the weather clears to try and get some help."

"What about that spot on the bridge that gets a signal?"

"According to Darcie, it's not as reliable as the tower. We can try tomorrow morning if the snow stops—no point attempting it in this weather."

"Too late for Nix," Vansi said softly as I led her to the cellar door. "I'm so glad he and I made up. We had sex right before he left the bedroom and it was like before—passionate and full of love and happy." A wobble in her voice, but she swallowed it back. "We were so happy."

My friend wasn't one to share such intimate details of her life. But I understood her well enough to guess that she wanted someone to know they'd been in a good place, a beautiful place, that their last words to each other had been of love. "I'm glad, V."

"I don't know what I'm going to do without him. He worked so much that I used to joke I was a singleton—but I wasn't. I always knew that he'd turn up in our bed sooner or later, snuggle up to me. Coming home to me was the best part of his day.

"He told me that so many times and you know how he was. Not mushy. But the way he said that . . ." Her breath caught as we stopped by the cellar door. "Will you give me time alone with him?"

"As long as you want. There's a light—switch is just inside the door." I touched my fingers to her arm. "We had to wrap him up. If you want, I can go down and make sure you can see him. I know you need to see him."

Vansi's nod was jerky.

When I opened the door to the cellar, it was to find that we'd never turned off the light.

Good.

I didn't like the idea of Phoenix alone in the dark.

Where before I hadn't wanted to touch his body, now I was just sad. It was much easier to unroll him from the blanket than I'd thought it would be. Almost as if he was helping me. The sheet took longer, especially as I wanted to hide the bloody section.

I was breathing puffs of white air and sweating inside my jacket by the time he was ready for Vansi. His face was still, his skin tinged blue, but the sheet had soaked away the blood and so he appeared battered . . . but oddly at peace.

That was the first thing Vansi said when she knelt down beside him. Brushing Nix's hair off his face, she said, "Hi, baby. You look like you're sleeping."

I left without another word, going up the stairs to sit with my back against the wall beside the door. The position put me opposite a wall with another one of those old-school paintings.

Thankfully, this one was just a paddock of sheep.

I considered reading more of Clara's diary on my phone, but didn't have the heart for it. Not now. Not with Vansi saying goodbye to Nix, who *shouldn't be dead*. There was no logical reason for him to be dead.

But he was.

The lights flickered.

And I realized I had another reason not to read on my phone. I had to conserve my battery. Who knew if the generators were designed to function in this kind of temperature? If they went out, we'd be reliant on the light from the fire and whatever flashlights or candles there were in the house.

Another flicker . . . and the house plunged into darkness.

38

That the outage lasted a short two seconds didn't stop my mouth from drying up, a scream building in my throat. Despite that, I was worried about something—*someone*—more than I was afraid of the dark.

Carefully opening the cellar door, I went to ask Vansi if she was all right, but caught the low murmur of her voice as she spoke to Nix, and knew I'd only be intruding.

I closed the door without a word and returned to my silent vigil. The knot that sat on my chest was a spiked ball that hurt with every breath. Today, I was glad that Beatrice wasn't here. Beneath her wicked outer persona, she'd been as soft as a crab without its shell.

Darcie had thought to hurt me by calling me Bea's puppy dog. She didn't understand. No one did. *Bea* hadn't been the one in control of our relationship. If she had, we'd have ended up in bed, ended up touching in the way of lovers.

In not wanting Bea that way, I'd gained a subtle power over her.

I'd never exercised it, never wanted to exercise it, but that it existed was enough to tilt the balance between us. Because Bea had trouble comprehending someone who loved her simply for existing, for being such a wild spark in the darkness.

No wonder Darcie had always felt as if she was in competition with her sister. In any other family, Darcie would've been the shining light. She was stunning, academically gifted, and goal-oriented to the extent of making five-year plans even back in high school. She should've been the Shepherd star.

Then had come Bea.

I'd once told Bea that she could be a great actress or powerful politician. "You have presence. People react to that."

Eyes solemn for once, she'd looked at me and shaken her head. "It's not a good thing, Nae-nae." Soft words, bruised gaze. "Sometimes, people want me too much. It's like they want to eat me up and keep me inside them. It's terrifying."

As I stared at the long grains of wood in the wall across from me, her words kept tumbling around and around in my head. What must it have been like to grow up so wanted that it became a weight on your shoulders? A curse.

"People fall in love with me," she'd added that day. "And they want me to love them back. It's not enough to be my friend anymore. Not after they fall in love. They want me in a way I can't give to everyone."

It's not enough to be my friend anymore.

I frowned, manacling one wrist with the fingers of my other hand. What had she meant by that? Was she referring to someone in our group? Had one of the others hit on her?

Ash I disregarded. Bea had felt the same for him as he had for her.

Aaron? No, I couldn't see it. He'd always been too intimidated by Bea. "Goodness, no, Lu, she'd swallow me up." A laughing confession while we were prepping a tomato salad together in the kitchen one summer's day, and I was attempting to get the identity of his crush out of him.

I'd thrown Bea's name out as a joke because the two had no chemistry whatsoever.

"There's a hunger inside her, don't you think?" He'd glanced out the window to our tiny back lawn, where she laughed with Vansi. "Truth be, she scares me sometimes, with that wild energy of hers. Energy that frenetic needs fuel to feed it."

I rubbed my fingers over my wrist, turning the skin red.

Nix, as far as I was aware, had never been that close to Bea, while Vansi was about as heterosexual as they came. She'd been boy crazy since we were fourteen. If anything, she'd been jealous of Bea.

Who did that leave?

Kaea.

The same Kaea who was horribly sick, his skin now holding an ashen tinge.

Forcing myself to let go of my wrist, I stared unseeing at the wall. I could've sworn that Kaea had simply never looked at Bea that way; of the two sisters, it was Darcie who was Kaea's type.

No, I just couldn't see it. Bea had likely been talking in the abstract.

Pain shot up my arm, and I realized I was once again gripping my wrist. So hard that I'd probably given myself a bruise.

Forcing my fingers to release, I rubbed at the skin until the blood began to flow again, and I wondered what I was trying to prove. That this was all an interconnected conspiracy? That it wasn't about Darcie's stalker anymore but Bea's memory?

Obsession.

The ugly word bloomed in my mind, my face smack-bang in the center of it. I didn't look away. Because it was true. I *was* obsessed with Bea. Her death had been and still was a defining point in my life.

"So you imagine phantoms where none exist," I muttered aloud, rubbing my palms over the tops of my thighs. Because Nix could've just had an awful, unstoppable accident. Kaea could've just made a rare mistake in what he'd eaten on the trail. And the first sighting of the doll could've been a well-intentioned mistake on the part of a cleaner, the second a prank gone horribly wrong.

There were innocent explanations for every single "suspicious" incident. Except . . . Darcie's head wound. I'd forgotten that. Another accident. What were the chances we'd suffer two bloody accidents in the space of mere days? That was when I remembered Kaea's shoe, that slice that had been a cut, not an accidental tear or a manufacturing fault.

A creak on the steps behind the door.

I stood up so fast my knees protested. But I was glad of my rapid reaction when Vansi emerged from the cellar. She walked straight into my arms, held on tight. No more tears now, just a sorrow so profound that it had altered the geography of her face.

"Will you help me put him back to rest?" She spoke against my shoulder. "I want to be gentle with him."

"Of course," I said roughly, the scent of her hair a familiar mix of vanilla and citrus. She'd used the same shampoo since she was fifteen. A drugstore brand that she swore worked better than any fancy formulation on the market.

I hugged that scent to me as we walked down the stairs, but I had no need of the armor. Phoenix hadn't begun to decay. It was too cold.

This time, I didn't attempt to roll him. If I did, I'd expose the bloody part of the sheet. Instead, I suggested we just tuck the blanket over and around him, covering his face and sheet-clad body. "This way, you can come and see him anytime you want."

Vansi nodded, but when it came time to cover Nix's face she hesitated and touched his cheek with trembling fingers. "See you in the next life, my darling." She took great care when she folded her end of the blanket over his cut and bruised face.

I'd ended up with the far longer edge, now folded it over him once.

"He loved the snow." Vansi didn't move, her gaze on the blanket. "We were hoping that he could get enough time off next winter that we could do a ski trip. It's been two years since we got to hit the slopes—winter's such a busy time at the hospital." Her breath caught.

Rising, I reached out to help her up, too. "It's too cold to stay here any longer, V. Nix wouldn't want you to get sick."

"He could be so overprotective, couldn't he?" She wiped the back of her hand over her eyes. "One time this winter, he literally put a scarf around my neck while muttering at me like a mother hen." Her lower lip quivered. "No one is ever going to love me like Nix did."

Her legs trembled as we walked away. But she kept on glancing back every few steps until we were at the very top and Phoenix's body lay in the darkest shadows. "Can we leave on the light?" she asked, her grief a weight palpable.

"Of course." Gently walking her out, I closed the door behind us. "Remember your first date? How awkward he was?" I'd been shanghaied by her into making it a double date because she was so damn nervous.

My "date" had been Kaea.

Vansi's smile was wet. "He crushed all the stems on the flowers he'd brought me."

"And dropped his ice cream."

"And the whole while, you and Kaea pretended not to see any of it." Her cheeks creased. "You were both such kind friends to us that day."

Soft laughter. "We had a good life, didn't we, Luna? Some people never find the love of their life and I found him in my teens. We had more than a decade together."

"Yes, you had a wonderful life." Wrapping one arm around her waist, I hugged her close. "He loved being your husband. I'll never forget how he looked at you on your wedding day."

It had been the epitome of a "big, fat Indian wedding" full of sparkle and gold, but the most luminous things had been the bride and groom's smiles. It had been clear to all and sundry that they were delighted to be together. Not a single tear had been shed on the bride's part during her leave-taking ceremony—an incident that one of her elderly aunts had termed "disgraceful!"

We were still smiling and murmuring about the wedding when we walked into the living room to find it devoid of anyone but Kaea and Darcie. Kaea slept peacefully enough—though that he'd been asleep for the entire day was worrying in itself—while Darcie stood near the fireplace staring down at the flames.

"Where are the others?" I didn't like that we were all separated again. Bad things happened when we were separated.

"Ash went to the tower," Darcie said, wrapping her arms around her middle. "He thought the snow was letting up a little, figured there might be a signal."

I couldn't see anything beyond the windows, the world outside a black void, and didn't entirely trust Ash's judgment. It struck me more as hope than reality. "And Grace? Aaron?"

"Grace is in the bathroom—she's got a bit of a stomachache. Probably nerves. Said she gets like that when stressed. And Aaron must be in the kitchen. He was here, then I looked up and he wasn't anymore."

Leaving Vansi to warm up by the fire, I poked my head into the kitchen through the connecting door. The large space was empty, but bunches of fresh herbs lay on the counter, next to a wooden board on which Aaron had already chopped up tomatoes and onions.

Vanilla, warm and lush, scented the air.

"Aaron?" Walking properly into the kitchen, I turned to check out the pantry.

I didn't realize I was half expecting the entrance to the secret passageway to be open until I found it neatly shut.

The items on the shelf that concealed the door lay undisturbed—even the small glass bottle of spice mix that someone had thrust in there between my last visit to the pantry and now. The haphazard way it was balanced, it would've no doubt fallen if he'd pulled the door shut behind him.

A chill crept up my spine.

Where was Aaron?

39

"Hey, you're back."

I jumped around, my hand flying to my heart. "Jeez, Aaron!"

Holding out his hands, palms out, he winced. "Sorry. I stepped outside for a second. Was hoping that the weather wasn't as bad as it feels in the unheated parts of the house." He brushed white powder off his shoulders. "I was wrong. It's worse. I think my nose is going to fall off from the cold."

Walking over to the coffee he must've put on earlier, he poured himself a fresh mug. When he lifted the carafe in my direction, I nodded. "Lots of milk and sugar. I want to drink it like dessert. Same for Vansi."

Face solemn, Aaron doctored two mugs, one for me, and one for Vansi, then took a sip of his far less milky concoction. "I'm stress cooking. Got a vanilla cake in the oven, and I'm starting on a homemade sauce we can use for pizza tomorrow."

"I'm not complaining about cake," I said. "And it's not like we're going to run out of ingredients. The pantry is overflowing with staples that last forever."

"Jim," Aaron said. "He grew up around here, knows the weather can be brutal. Darcie says he has a thing about ensuring the pantry has enough food to keep an entire family going for weeks. Just in case."

Grace came bustling into the kitchen from the hallway, her face flushed and her nose pink. "God, it's freezing in the bathroom, but would my insides hurry up?" Spotting me the second after the words were out of her mouth, she pressed her palms to her cheeks. "Oh, wow, Grace, way to be embarrassing. Just announcing your unmentionable business like that."

My lips curved, the sadness banished for this moment of life mundane and precious. "We lived together for a while," I reminded her. "There was many a night when I screamed down the house because my butt ended up on cold porcelain—Aaron and Kaea had a habit of leaving the toilet seat up."

"Mea culpa."

Laughing softly at Aaron's confession, Grace walked over to him. "I can confirm he's much better now." She smiled. "I hope Ash doesn't turn into an ice block in the tower. Has to be a fridge up there." She stole some of Aaron's coffee, and he kissed her on the nose.

Adorable.

Picking up my mug as well as Vansi's, I inhaled deeply before walking back into the reality of the day. A day on which I'd helped wrap a friend's body and put him in a cellar cold and dark.

A day on which my best friend had become a widow.

"Darcie," I said as I entered the living room, "I wasn't sure if you wanted a coffee."

"I've already had way too much. You guys drink." She paced to the hallway door, opened it to look out before ducking back inside. "I wish he hadn't decided to check on a signal. He knows there's going to be nothing, is just antsy. Next thing you know the lights will go out, and he'll be stuck stumbling around in the dark."

"I'm sure he'll be fine." To be honest, I was starting to wonder if Ash had decided to head out to get away from Darcie's jittery energy. I'd never seen her like this. So nervy I'd have said she was on drugs if I didn't know better. "How long has he been gone?"

She looked over at Grace, who'd just emerged from the kitchen. "He left before you, so twenty minutes?"

Grace scrunched up her face. "I think closer to half an hour." She rubbed her stomach. "Um, let's just say I needed to take my time."

"That's not very long," I said to Darcie. "Tower's a hike."

"Luna's right." Aaron walked in with a loaf cake on a wooden board. "This hasn't been out of the oven more than five minutes. I should really let it sit, but I have a craving for warm vanilla cake with butter, so let's all dig in while we wait for Ash."

He somehow got even Darcie to sit down, though she only picked at her cake.

Vansi accepted a slice, then just stared at it. "Nix didn't like cake except for—"

"—red velvet," Aaron completed. "I can't even remember how many red velvet cupcakes with cream cheese frosting I made for him over the years."

Vansi's lips tugged upward. "He'd hoard them each time you

did. It was the one snack he told me he wouldn't share . . . but he always did, my Nix."

As the snow fell outside, we fell into conversation about our lost friend. Having Grace there wasn't awkward—it actually helped. She didn't know the stories, her reactions new and bright, her interest genuine.

"Nix was always the smartest one in the group," Darcie said at one point. "None of us were slouches and Bea was right on his heels, but Phoenix . . . he was one of those kids who would've gotten into medical school even without trying."

"But he did try," Vansi continued, picking up the thread of the story. "He worked so hard when he could've coasted. Had a memory like Luna's—except where Luna remembers images, Nix remembered *everything*. He never had to memorize study texts. He had perfect recall."

My mind hitched on that, chewed—and was so absorbed by the thought that I almost missed Vansi's next words.

"He was determined to be the best surgeon in the country, not for clout, but because his patients deserved that. Nix never took shortcuts." She wiped away a tear. "But no matter all his professional accomplishments, he put so much time and effort into our marriage. Trust and commitment, he always said, that was the foundation."

I locked gazes with Aaron. And we made a silent vow: we'd keep Nix's secret till we turned to dust in the earth. To do otherwise would be to destroy everything Vansi believed of her marriage.

I had no doubts that Nix would've eventually spoken to her about his desire to change his career. But he'd never had the chance. And now it was too late. Saying anything about it would only brutalize an already devastated Vansi.

Darcie looked at her watch, glanced at the door, but didn't interrupt. Instead she went into the kitchen and put on a fresh pot of coffee that no one had requested. Then she rejoined us to stare unseeing at the fire.

Her stillness was so pure that we all jumped when she jerked to her feet fifteen minutes later. "I'm going to get Ash. He'll freeze if he stays out much longer."

"I'll come with you," Aaron and I said at the same time.

"Come or don't come. I don't care." Darcie went to grab her jacket where it hung on the back of an armchair, an unexpected burst of pink in among all the browns and greens of the living area. "I just want to make sure he's all right."

"Grace, V, you two okay staying with Kaea?"

Vansi nodded. "We need to get more food into him," she said, her voice a rasp but her professionalism evident. "I did a physical exam while you were in the kitchen, and I don't like how nonresponsive he's become. Our first task will be to attempt to rouse him to some degree."

Grace stood. "Should I go warm up a cup of the soup Aaron made? It's mostly liquid—he mashed up the vegetables, then blitzed it all."

Nodding, Vansi reached out to touch my hand. "I'll be all right, Luna. Go find Ash. Darcie's right in saying he's been out in the cold too long."

Darcie walked out the door, flipping up the hood of her jacket as she exited.

Not wanting her to end up alone, I grabbed my dark brown jacket and rushed out, Aaron doing the same beside me. We both snatched flashlights from the small grouping on a side table—I ended up with Grace's slender one out of chance, the cylinder fitting neatly into my palm as I jogged after Darcie.

She didn't go the way I would have. Hardly a surprise; this place was a labyrinthine puzzle.

This time, after a rapid-fire walk that was near to a run, Darcie led us not to a hidden passage but to a narrow set of stairs sheltered so deep in an alcove that I'd walked past it multiple times without ever realizing they existed.

The stairs were only wide enough to accommodate a single person at a time.

Aaron, bringing up the rear, said, "Does Ash know about these stairs? Only I'm thinking he might've gone the other way and we might miss each other."

"If he's not in the tower," Darcie said, "then we'll go down the other way. We'll either run into him along the way—or find him waiting for us with V and Grace." Her words were puffs of white as she took the steps at a speed that strained her lungs.

They strained mine worse, and not only that, I was having trouble seeing. The weak lightbulbs meant to illuminate the area had been spaced so far apart that they created more shadow than light.

My eyes couldn't adapt to the dappled effect, the world a shaky mirage.

I kept my hand against the wall on one side while gripping the railing on the other. "Why did they build such dangerous stairs in the olden times?" I said to hide my fear of the strangling dark.

It was Aaron who replied. "I've always wondered that, too. Didn't they have maids and other staff constantly coming up and down with food, water, laundry?"

We might've continued to chat, but Darcie surged on at a relentless pace. Though Aaron was having no difficulties, I couldn't keep up and talk at the same time. He patted me on the back a couple of times in silent encouragement.

Kaea would've slapped me on the shoulder and told me I was losing my conditioning.

Such different men. Both my friends.

A loud creak and I looked up to a burst of light.

Blinking against the spots in my vision, I barely made out the image of Darcie haloed in gold pulling open a door.

I made it the rest of the way on instinct. The bulb in the tower was brighter—golden—perhaps because Darcie and Ash used it often in order to download messages and the like, and I gave myself the time it took me to catch my breath to adapt to the change in illumination.

My vision was shaky even at that point, but I could tell the tower was empty. No mistake. The place had a couple of chairs and that was it. Nothing to hide behind.

"He's not here." Darcie spun toward the main doorway. "Come on, we have to go down the other set of stairs."

My vision still unstable, I hung back as Aaron followed her.

He paused, glanced back. "Lunes?"

Thinking fast, I lifted my phone. "Let me grab a couple of photos. Not sure I'll have the energy to come back here later. Ash is probably already in the living room."

He nodded in agreement. "Catch up to us soon, though, okay?"

"Will do." I collapsed into one of the chairs the instant after they left, my eyes closed and my breathing a conscious process designed to calm.

I could see again when I finally lifted my lashes, but the only thing to see was this room cold and grim and lonely. The door we'd come through had shut on its own, leaving only a seamless gray wall.

No life. Nothing but ice.

Mouth suddenly dry, I whipped my head around, certain I'd heard a whisper, seen a flicker out of the corner of my eye. But of course I was alone. It didn't matter; I raced down the stairs after the others. I didn't want to be alone anywhere in this house.

As it was, I spotted Aaron and Darcie on the far end of the hallway after exiting the stairs. "Aaron!" I began to jog toward him.

Darcie kept on walking, while Aaron hung back.

No longer panicked now that I had them in sight, I waved him on. "Stay with her! She's not thinking straight."

My cheeks were hot. Not from exertion but due to embarrassment at the foolishness of my earlier fear. I'd wandered all over the house today, come to no harm. Yet I still put a rush on it when Aaron disappeared around the corner.

Even with the distance between us, there was no mistaking the fear in Darcie's jagged motions as she half walked, half ran over the polished wooden floors while her ancestors looked on with painted eyes.

She slammed into the living room. "Where's Ash?" I heard her demand even before I reached the doorway, my breath painful enough that I had to brace myself against the doorjamb.

Vansi was frozen with a spoon halfway to Kaea's lips, while Grace sat behind him, attempting to hold his lolling head in place. Now, the petite blonde's eyes grew wide. "You mean you didn't find him?"

40

Darcie dropped to her knees, began to look under sofas, as if Ash was a child who might've crawled beneath, but what held my attention was the creeping terror in Vansi's dark gaze.

All at once, fear seemed the rational choice. "You two stay with Kaea," I said to her and Grace. "Ash might've decided to wander around in another part of the house. We'll go find him."

"Darcie." Aaron's voice was firm as he went and grabbed her hand, pulling her to her feet. "You know the house the best. We need you to tell us where to search. Is it possible he tried to use a secret passage and got trapped?"

Darcie shoved a hand through her hair, tugging out even more strands from her frizzy and already unraveling braid. "He only knows two of them. I showed him one before, and then there's the one where he and Luna found me. We didn't spend enough time here for him to bother learning the rest."

Shaking off Aaron's hand, she ran out the door, with the two of us in her wake.

My heart was thunder, my breath hard and cold, but I managed to keep up as Darcie led us first to the passageway behind the tapestry.

We went all the way to the pantry, the pace fast enough that I didn't have time to think about my terror of the dark. But when we tumbled out into the pantry to a crash of glass—that misaligned spice bottle—it was without Ash.

Instead of going out to the living area, Darcie took us back through the passage, then off in a zigzag run through the house that ended at the top of a flight of stairs. Where, face red and her own breathing unsteady, she pulled aside another tapestry to reveal a door.

"This one. Ash knew this one." She pressed a hand to her side for a moment before digging in her jacket pocket. "I put the keys in here after . . ." The bundle emerged in a jangle of metal, and she got the door unlocked on the first try.

But I grabbed on to the back of her jacket when she would've rushed in. "Calm down, Darcie." It was hard to sound firm when I was panting like I'd run a marathon, but I didn't release my grip on the soft puffiness of her jacket even when she tried to wrench away.

"I can see stairs." I shook her. "You go rushing in helter-skelter and we're going to end up with another body to lay beside Nix's."

She flinched as if she'd been slapped, but then gave a jagged nod and said, "Flashlights. We should take flashlights. The lights in there haven't been changed for years. It'll be a miracle if they're still working."

"We have them," I reassured her.

Aaron stepped ahead of Darcie at the same time. "Let me go first. You're in no state to lead us." Careful, gentle.

Darcie didn't argue.

Aaron switched on his flashlight. The resulting beam was strong enough to light his way . . . and tell us that no one had walked here before us.

The dust on the floor was a coating of gray fur.

Undisturbed. Uniform.

We should've shut the door, walked away—but Aaron stepped in, followed by Darcie, then me. A ritual to lay Darcie's doubts to rest, make sure she wouldn't be haunted by nightmares that murmured "what if" in her ear. Simply because something was illogical didn't mean it couldn't feel very real to her.

Darcie and I both sneezed while in the passage and after we emerged into another unfamiliar section of the estate house, while Aaron coughed. Cobwebs covered his curls and clothing. I dusted off my jacket sleeves, while Darcie wiped dust-coated hands on the front of her jacket. She ignored the resulting streaks.

The wood in this part of the house was the darkest I'd seen, the single light that had come on when Darcie touched a switch just before we exited the passage buzzing at a frequency that irritated my brain—as it emitted a weak circle of light that did nothing to penetrate the thick curls of shadow.

My eyes were teary from my sneezing, my nose stuffy, but I didn't protest as Darcie began to run again. "Stick to her," I told Aaron. He was faster than Darcie, while I was just slow enough that she might duck into another nook or passage while I was still out of sight.

And then she'd be alone.

As Nix had been alone when he fell.

As Darcie had been alone when she got that knock on the head.

As Ash had been alone when he vanished into thin air.

Her breathing—loud, close to sobs—echoing against the walls, Darcie led us through various doors and hallways that Ash might've taken had he become disoriented. "He's not as familiar with the house as I am," she said at one point when she finally had to stop.

Hands digging into her sides and her jacket unzipped at the neck, she sucked in air. "We stayed in that front section the times we came down here"—gasped words—"and he's always been more interested in the bridge." A wince, her fingers digging into her left side. "Did a ton of the work to bring it up to current safety standards."

She was moving again two seconds later, pushing open doors as she yelled Ash's name.

Silence. Over and over again.

Until Darcie was shivering so hard that her teeth clattered, and my ungloved fingers had gone cold enough to hurt. I managed to take her hands in mine nonetheless. "Could he have stumbled onto a secret room or passage and decided to explore it?" Maybe he'd had the same thought as Grace and I about a hidden stalker, but hadn't wanted to worry Darcie.

"He doesn't know any of the others," she said in a very small voice.

"He could've accidentally found one," Aaron suggested.

"Aaron is right. We should check—and we can clear the rest of the house as we do it."

"We have to be organized." Aaron tapped something on the screen of his phone. "Tell me the areas we've been through already. I'll add to that list as we check more parts of the house."

Pupils huge against the blue of her irises, Darcie began a dull recitation that named "the back salon" and "the mahogany gallery" among multiple other specific names, alongside more generic descriptions of various hallways or shut-up rooms whose original purpose had long since been forgotten.

I had the gut-deep sensation that the nursery had been in the ruined wing.

Darcie's energy was lower, her replies monosyllabic when we restarted the search, but she didn't falter. A few of the hidden doors proved to be stuck as a result of long disuse, while cobwebs crawled across every inch of the entrance for two more.

Aaron and I decided it was safe to discard those—but only after we checked both ends to ensure Ash hadn't gone in one side and become stuck or incapacitated in the middle.

One thing became rapidly clear: this house had far more secrets than I would've ever guessed.

Some passages were short. Others longer and more twisted, but all in all, there proved to be ten—that Darcie knew of, at least. "My father showed them to me, and he thought he'd forgotten a couple. Three of the keys I have don't fit into any door in the place, so he did probably forget."

As for the number of rooms, I had no idea. A few of those rooms were narrow and stifling—quarters for the servants, I assumed—the rest relatively large and impressively flush with windows for the time period in which this place had been built. But the vast majority of the rooms held air musty and stagnant, the furniture draped in dustcloths and the bed frames naked.

Our search yet incomplete, we nonetheless eventually circled back around to the living area.

Darcie's face collapsed when we entered to find no sign of Ash.

I wrapped an arm around her, wasn't sure she was even aware of me.

"Grace, you go help them finish searching," Vansi said after we'd updated them on the current situation. "It'll go faster with an extra pair of eyes. I'll stay with Kaea."

"Are you sure?" Grace touched her fingers lightly to Vansi's shoulder.

My friend, her heart full of empathy and her face worn, nodded. "Just swing by every so often to let me know how things are going."

I folded my arms. "I don't like any of us being alone in this house."

"I'm not alone." She wiped a damp rag over Kaea's sweating forehead.

"Vansi."

"I'll be fine, Luna." A tired smile. "There's no one here but us and the worst luck in the world." She held up a hand before I could open my mouth. "But, in case we do have a secret bogeyman creeping around—no one can approach me in this massive space without me spotting them a mile away. And if it makes you feel better, I'll keep a heavy skillet handy."

Even though I could see she was humoring me, I went and got her that skillet—a cast-iron one that would work better than any baseball bat—and put it right by where she was sitting as she watched over Kaea.

The faintest smile. "You goof."

"You'll be careful?"

"I promise." Smile fading away to nothing, she followed us to the hallway door.

When I turned back several seconds later, she was still watching after us as we headed off to search another part of the house.

And we did.

We searched.

Every level—including the attic and the cellars, as well as the upstairs bedrooms I'd initially asked that no one touch. In an effort to keep the area as undisturbed as possible, Darcie and I were the only ones to climb the stairs this time.

"Maybe he decided to take a nap," she said with sudden brightness halfway up. "God, I'd feel so dumb getting worked up if that's all it is."

Only, there was no sign of life upstairs, their room so cold that frost had begun to form on the inside of the windows.

He wasn't anywhere on that floor of the house.

Darcie went silent. Didn't speak again in the time that followed.

I was the one that took a quick look in the cellar where we'd left Phoenix, but his body lay undisturbed, and there was no one else in the frigid box.

"Nothing," I said, for what felt like the hundredth time.

Grace and Aaron, who'd been searching the rooms just down the hallway, emerged, shook their heads. And we kept on going. When we came to the locked study I'd found during my solo wanderings, Darcie shook her head. "Blake Shepherd's study. My dad had a key to it, but we never found it after he died. Ash wasn't interested in my ancestor's demented papers"—her voice trembled—"and I'd already satisfied my curiosity as a kid. Just didn't seem worth the bother of organizing a locksmith to come all the way out here."

By the time we'd combed through what felt like every inch of the house, Darcie was all but catatonic, hugging herself and rocking back and forth while she mumbled things under her breath. I caught scattered whispers, heard, "my fault, this is all my fault," before she rambled off on another tangent.

Taking her shoulders, I squeezed. "This is *not* your fault." I made my voice firm, channeling my old maths teacher from high school. "Is there any other place that Ash would've gone?"

She stared blankly at me.

"Darcie." I shook her. "Is there any reason for him to have gone into the ruined wing?"

Darcie's breath jerked as she shook her head. "He doesn't like that area. Says it's a hazard and we should get it pulled down. But it would cost so much and I didn't want to waste the money. Oh God." Her hand flew to her mouth. "What if—"

That was when Aaron said, "What about the vehicle?"

Letting go of Darcie, I swiveled to stare at him. "What vehicle?"

"That's right." He ran his hand over his hair. "You were taking photos in the house when Ash mentioned it. Jim has a heavy-duty farm vehicle parked in the large outdoor barn—same place we got the firewood from. Ash was thinking it might still have snow tires on it, since Jim switched to using his personal four-wheel drive soon as the winter snows melted away."

My heart thudded hard enough to drown out my own voice as I said, "Was Ash dressed for the snow? Would he have gone outside to the barn on his own?"

41

H ands on his hips, Aaron looked at the ground a moment before shaking his head. "No. He was wearing his coat, but nothing else. Beanie, gloves, outdoor boots, they're still in the kitchen by the woodstove. That's where we left them after the firewood run."

He squeezed his eyes shut, pinched the bridge of his nose. "Going out as he was dressed? No."

Opening his eyes, he shook his head again. "Ash is too smart to be impulsive that way. If he'd wanted to check it out now instead of waiting till tomorrow and hopefully a break in the weather, he would've grabbed me and we would've done it right, like we did with the firewood."

I agreed with him—with a coda: Ash *had* been impulsive once. But only with Bea. She'd made him open his world, consider taking risks. He was the opposite with Darcie. More set in his ways, less apt to go off the beaten path.

I'd picked up the change even in our sporadic interactions on the group chat.

Darcie's Ash was part of an established firm of engineers, ate a diet recommended by Darcie, and went on vacation to polished destinations twice a year. No trace left of the muddy boy who'd carried an equally muddy Bea across a creek while they both laughed so hard he'd almost fallen flat on his face.

No, the Ash of today wouldn't have gone out into the storm on his own.

But where else could he be? We'd searched literally every nook and cranny of this house.

Once again, I thought of the ruined wing—but didn't say anything aloud this time. Instead, I nudged Darcie back into the living area, settled her in the sofa, and left Grace and Vansi to minister to her with hot cups of tea that she ignored.

Angling my head at Aaron as the two women rubbed her hands and back, I met him in a far corner, away from the baleful gaze of all those dead animals above the fireplace. "We have to check out the ruined section," I whispered. "Remember that staircase Darcie told us led to that section?" She'd only checked that the door at the top was locked, and left it at that—because the only key was in her pocket.

"I was thinking the same." A quick flick of his gaze toward Darcie before he lowered his head to mine again. "He has to be there. No place else left."

"Darcie's too fragile. We have to slip away, check it out on our own." I hissed out a breath. "But first we have to figure out a way to get the key from her."

Aaron made a subtle motion. And I saw that Vansi had

convinced Darcie to take off her jacket, and was now hanging it over an armchair out of Darcie's line of sight.

I'd slid over and was sneaking out the keys before I could second-guess myself. When Vansi lifted an eyebrow, I just put a finger to my lips. She looked over at where Darcie sat rocking, and nodded.

"We should go now," Aaron whispered when I returned to him. "Before she comes to her senses."

Grace glanced over as we were about to slip out, and Aaron hitched his thumb over his shoulder to indicate our intent.

Murmuring that she was going to the washroom, she excused herself from the other two women—and met us in the hallway. "Give me one minute and I'll fill up an insulated bottle of coffee for you." Her voice, too, was a whisper. "You'll freeze in this house otherwise."

I wanted to rush, but she was right. We'd need the extra heat at some point. "Thanks, Grace."

She quickly vanished into the kitchen via the hallway entrance, and was true to her word, returning a short while later with one of those tall and skinny double-walled bottles I'd seen in the shops but never bought. "It's from the pot Darcie made earlier. I reheated it real quick on the stovetop."

She made a face. "Not appetizing, I know, but fast." A glance at me. "The bottle is Aaron's," she said after putting it into his hand. "But I figured you two wouldn't mind sharing."

"Thanks," I repeated, thinking of all the drinks we'd shared back at uni. Aaron had never been much of a drinker, and I'd usually ended up finishing his drinks. Probably should've taken that as a sign I had a problem, but sometimes I needed things to punch me in the face.

Aaron tucked the bottle inside his deep jacket pocket, then kissed Grace on the cheek.

"Wait, I got these, too." She thrust a small ziplock bag of cookies into my hand. "You still have flashlights?"

"Yes." Shoving the cookies into a pocket, I checked my phone battery, saw it was at fifty percent. Safe. "We'd better go."

"Good luck."

As soon as she shut the door to the living room behind her, we began to jog, moving rapidly through the house to get to the blocked-off set of stairs.

"Lu," Aaron said as we moved, "I was thinking. If Ash *is* on that side, then he or someone else would've required a key."

"Darcie's had them in her pocket since after she hit her head." I didn't huff as I spoke; Aaron was keeping the pace to one I could handle. "And that jacket's been either hanging in her room, or on the back of an armchair. There would've been times it was totally unattended."

Aaron suddenly halted.

I skidded to a stop. "What?"

"That means the key might not be in that bunch." His jaw worked. "Darcie only checked the door was locked. She never looked for the key."

"Shit." I rubbed my face. "We won't know until we try to unlock it. If the key *is* on her key chain . . ."

". . . then someone returned it after—what? Locking Ash on the other side?"

The two of us stared at each other, then turned to run on in silence.

But the words unspoken, they were a bass drum between us.

There were only five of us left who could've done it, and unless

Darcie was a grade-A actress, we could leave her out of the equation. "Why would anyone do something to Ash?" I finally blurted out, unable to keep it inside any longer.

Aaron pulled a knit cap from his jacket and tugged it on and down until it covered the tips of his ears. "Who the fuck knows?" The harsh word was an unfamiliar sound on his lips, a scratch on a smooth record. "I have no idea what is going on. Do you?"

I thought about whether to share what I'd been thinking, went to part my lips, shut them before the words could escape. I trusted Aaron, but the truth was that I didn't know him any longer. Not as I'd once known him.

Deciding to go for another truth, I said, "I think the best-case scenario is what Vansi said—that we've just had a run of bad luck. I mean, no one could've predicted the insane weather. Without it, we would've driven out by now, got a signal, and called for help for Kaea. We would've never been here for Phoenix to fall down the stairs, or for Ash to get lost in this enormous house."

The floorboards groaned under our feet as we reached the narrow corridor that held the internal staircase to the ruined wing. We didn't stop. Not until we'd climbed all the way to the top and stood shoulder to shoulder in front of the locked door.

"What if Ash is behind that door, Lu? That would change everything."

I got the keys. Immediately lost hold of them, my fingers tiny frozen sausages.

The metal sticks fell to the landing in a discordant cacophony. "Damn it."

Aaron was already grabbing them and handing them over. "Before you start to try them, let's take a breath. Just . . . settle."

My fingers tingled sharply as I flexed sensation back into them, my mind a rabbit that raced from one thought to another. "Good idea."

"We can drink a bit of this, too, warm up." Taking the sleek bottle of coffee out of his pocket, he unscrewed the lid and winced. "I think it's black. Grace must've forgotten you like your coffee to be hot milk with a dash of coffee."

I punched him lightly on the arm. "Smart-ass. You can have your bitter water." Black coffee might as well be tar as far as I was concerned. "I'll grab a drink when we go downstairs. And I've got the cookies for when I need an energy hit." I patted my pocket. "No use letting the coffee go to waste when Grace went to the trouble of packing it."

Aaron nodded and took a deep gulp of it, after an initial sip to test that it wasn't too hot. After he was done, he put the bottle back in his pocket and exhaled. "Okay, let's do it."

I took out the keys.

One.

Two.

Three.

Four.

Five.

The lock snicked smoothly open.

42

Aaron's pupils were tight dots when he glanced at me. "I really hope he's not there."

Swallowing hard, I nodded and stepped slightly back so Aaron could push open the door. It flowed into the darkness beyond, no hint of a groan or creak, no sudden shower of dust. My chest compressed in on itself, my heart a drumbeat that wouldn't slow down. I licked my lips with my tongue, tried to swallow. It stuck. I was glad that I hadn't decided to eat one of the cookies.

"Look." Aaron pointed down.

When I cast my gaze that way, I saw not footsteps but a wide streak that wasn't clean, but had obviously been disturbed—brushed to swirl all the dust and remnants of ash from the fire together.

But why? It was obvious that—"Oh." My gut clenched. "It's so we can't tell the size of the shoes that walked through the dust . . . and how many pairs there were."

Aaron moved the beam of the flashlight around the darkened space. This particular area had no windows, so all we saw were charred beams and furniture distorted and damaged by the fire. Macabre sculptures in the dark.

"I didn't realize they just . . . left it all here." Aaron crossed himself. "All that suffering and pain allowed to fester for generations."

I shivered, but not in fear. Now that I was here, I knew I'd been right not to believe what Ash had told me about Darcie saying Bea was the reason for the ruin; the entire scorched setup was *too* nineteenth century, not an inset power plug or even slight indication of modernization in sight—every shred of surviving fabric could've come straight out of some English country estate.

I couldn't guess why Darcie had even made up the tall tale—perhaps part of her ongoing war with Bea, even now that Bea couldn't fight back—but her lies meant Aaron was right about the suffering, the miasma of death.

Yet . . . to a photographer, the frozen firescape was fascinating. Eerie and draped in mystery, no scent to the place at all. The latter was explicable, given the passage of time and the fact that the building was open to the elements in multiple places, but it still felt "off" to my brain.

We had no time to linger, however, and carried on after a quick but careful look to ensure Ash was nowhere in this room.

"Be careful." I touched Aaron's back. "The floor beyond this point could be dangerous. Test before you step."

He nodded, and we moved with slow care until he paused at the next doorway. There was no door there, but the structure itself looked solid enough, as did the floor beyond it.

Aaron still tested it with one foot before putting any weight on it. "I think I know which part this is from the outside. It's at the top, back section."

Inside my head, I flipped through the photographs I'd taken. "Then we're in luck. That area seemed relatively stable." Quite unlike the devastated front section.

We continued to take extreme care regardless, still following that wide streak in the dust and ash. When I glanced backward, my flashlight beam picked out our footprints, ghostly echoes all that remained of our passing. Everything was black and white, as if the fire had sucked all color out of the world.

I turned forward, my movement rapid. And my vision wavered. I'd have to talk to my specialist about that, I thought as I waited for it to settle again. He hadn't warned me of this kind of disruption. He had, however, advised me to find ways to alleviate the level of stress in my life.

Said I needed to learn to meditate, do yoga, whatever helped me keep my blood pressure even. I'd still been in the denial phase and hadn't asked him if it was because my blood pressure could impact my vision, or because he was worried I'd have a heart attack from holding everything inside.

But what if he *had* been talking about the health of my eyes?

Maybe all this pressure within was causing my vision to degenerate even faster.

I took a deep breath, immediately regretted it. The searing cold of the ambient air burned my lungs.

Shivering, I looked forward . . . and realized that most of the right wall was just gone. No wonder the air felt like shards of ice.

Small piles of white sat below the jagged remnants of the wall.

"The track with the brush marks seems to turn here." Aaron moved the beam of his flashlight to the left. It wobbled.

"Sorry," he said in a voice that held a tremor, "hit of vertigo. Can't stop thinking that the wall to our right is barely hanging on."

"Wigs me out, too," I admitted. "I'm behind you, don't worry. Stuck to you like glue. Try to lose me and I swear I'll run screaming after you like a banshee."

Chuckling, he turned left to follow the streak on the floor. The furniture around us lay upturned—as if the fire had thrown it around. A possible explosion? Like in that movie I'd seen a few years back about firefighters being blown back right after they opened the doors into rooms that boiled with fire.

Aaron's hand banged hard against the back of what might've once been an armchair. Before I could ask if he was okay, the same hand crumpled partially under his arm as he went down hard on one knee. His flashlight hit the floor with him, the beam bouncing wildly until it settled, the light pointing back the way we'd come.

"Aaron!" I grabbed instinctively at his shoulder. "Did you trip?"

"My . . . head." He leaned forward, his breath erratic pants. "Swirling."

Wondering if he was having a panic attack, I knelt down and put my hand on the back of his neck. "Just breathe, slow and easy."

He tried—I could see him fighting to concentrate—but he collapsed onto his hands and knees moments later, would've gone to the floor if I hadn't slipped my arms under his and helped him to a seated position against the burned-out armchair.

"Go . . . look for . . . Ash," he managed to get out, his words emerging in slow motion. "I'll just . . . just . . . catch . . . my breath."

I didn't want to leave him, but knew he was right. The faster I did this, the faster we could leave. "Don't move." Leaving him with the bigger flashlight by his side, beam on, I used my smaller one to sweep the area while fighting the claustrophobia that was my lack of vision anywhere beyond the narrow strip of light.

When it passed over a pair of legs, I almost didn't see it. My brain, hitching. Snagging.

A delayed reaction.

I swept back the beam, barely stifled a scream, and a split second later was rushing over to Ash. He lay slumped on his right side, part of his face pressed to the dust and blackened debris of the fire, and his skin so white that I was certain he was gone.

Hand shaking, I put my chilled fingers to his throat.

His skin was the same temperature as mine, and as still as death. No, wait—

After blowing on the tips of my fingers to warm them up, I pressed them against his throat once more . . . and wondered if I was imagining it. "No, it's there." A pulse too deep and far too slow. "He's alive!" I yelled to Aaron.

"Thank God." Lethargic but understandable.

Trembling, I began to check Ash for injuries. Had he hit his head?

My fingers were so cold once again that I didn't even feel it when I touched something sticky on his back. It was only when the beam of my flashlight caught my hand that I saw my fingers were coated in red.

Perhaps it was shock, but I didn't panic. I just shifted so I could look at his back.

A mass of darkness spread over the camel brown puffer.

Holes—so *many* holes—in the fabric, the filling that spilled out a dull pink from his blood.

"He's been stabbed."

No response from Aaron.

Heart kicking, I crossed back to him. "Aaron!"

"Lu . . . ?" My name a slurring attempt that faded into nothing as his eyes fluttered shut. He fought to open them. "Wh . . . wh . . ." Another exhale, this one quieter and somehow more peaceful.

Then, nothing.

I took hold of his narrow but strong shoulders, shook hard.

When I got no response, I didn't give myself time to think—I slapped him on one cheek. Hard enough that it stung even my mostly numb palm.

No response from Aaron.

The skin of my cheeks burning hot, then going ice-cold, over and over again, I had to focus to check his pulse. It beat steadily, in a far better rhythm than Ash's.

The realization did nothing to stop the screaming inside my head—because he was unconscious.

They were both unconscious.

In a part of the house so frigid that we might as well be outside in the snow; it was a miracle Ash hadn't already frozen to death.

I had to get them to safety.

"Think, Luna. *Think*." I gave myself thirty seconds to run through the breathing exercise Dr. Mehta had taught me, just long enough to stop the skittering in my brain and regain some semblance of control.

I looked at Aaron, then angled the flashlight at Ash.

One tall and lanky, the other slightly shorter but more built. Neither one small or light in comparison to my own body. And right now, both incapable of helping me.

Dead weight.

I shoved away the whispering reminder of Nix's body, how hard it had been to handle him.

Biting down hard on my lower lip, I decided my priority: to get them out of this section exposed to the snow and frigid external air. It wasn't too far to the other side of the doorway, all of it on a flat surface.

If I could stash them in a corner, the walls would provide protection from the cold air, and their bodies could share heat. I'd then find blankets, rugs, whatever I could to insulate them from the cold.

I decided to try to move Aaron first, since he was closer to the door—and healthier. My mind was working now, and I had an excellent idea of what was wrong with him. If I was right, then while Ash's chances of survival were low, Aaron had a good chance of making it as long as I could keep him warm.

My thoughts felt cold, inhuman—but I wasn't cold at all.

Everything burned, fear a shriek inside my head that repeated Vansi's name over and over again.

Because my best friend was in the same room as the person who'd stabbed Ash and left him here to die.

43

Shoving away the thought before it could paralyze me, I tucked the flashlight into a pocket of my jacket at an angle that did enough to illuminate the area in front of me that I could see where I was going. My eyes hurt from the effort, but there was nothing I could do about that, so no point focusing on it.

Managing to push the burned armchair behind Aaron far enough back that I could slide my hands under his armpits, I began to drag him in the direction from which we'd come.

"If you can hear me at all"—I grunted and twisted around a fallen chair—"try to take some of your weight off me." Maybe it was my imagination, my brain trying to make things easier, but I could've sworn I felt a renewed tension in his body, a determination to assist. "Thanks, Aaron. That's it. We can do it."

I had to stop multiple times, my back sending out warning shots and my breath hard gasps of frosted air. I couldn't even think about if the damaged floor, the nails exposed in places, might be cutting through his jeans to gouge his skin. I didn't have the capacity to move *and* protect him.

His cheek scraped against a serrated edge on a twisted piece of the doorway. "I'm so sorry," I said, glad to see that the cut appeared minor.

Sweat trickled under my arms, cold and wet, my nose threatening to run. I kept on going, sure that if I stopped, I'd never again move.

Just one more step, just one more step.

And though I'd intended to place him on this side, I realized it was still too exposed, too cold.

I kept going.

Until I finally reached the door that led to the stairs. Putting him down, I went to open it. My arms screamed. I had no idea how I was going to do this a second time around—but I'd face that problem when I got to it.

"Just a little farther," I said, and dragged Aaron through the door to prop him up against the wall of the landing.

It was much warmer here in comparison to the other side, more survivable. The biggest danger was that he'd move without conscious volition and tumble down the stairs, but I had to take that risk. To leave him on the other side would lead to exposure and certain death within a short period.

"I'll get blankets after," I said, then ran back to Ash.

The trip was much, much harder this time around. He was true dead weight. And though shorter, he was more muscled and thus noticeably heavier than Aaron. I collapsed at one point, my knee throbbing from the force with which I hit the floor.

My eyes burned, stabbed, gritty and dry, my pants spotted with red where Ash's back made contact with me. I wasn't sure if he was still bleeding, or if that was transfer from what had soaked into his lacerated jacket, but hoped it was the latter. Because if the bleeding hadn't stopped or slowed down . . .

Forcing myself up despite the protests of my knee, I hooked my arms under his armpits and began to drag. Half a step at a time now. My body close to giving up. Sweat pasted my inner top to my back, dripped in runnels between my breasts, and beaded on my temples to roll down my face.

"Just a little farther," I said, not sure if I was talking to Ash or to myself.

My shoulder slammed into the first doorway. "Fuck!"

Somehow having retained my hold on Ash, I kept on going—and tried not to think about the streaks I'd spotted on the floor while I was on my knee, my flashlight beam low.

He *was* bleeding. Maybe I should've left him where he was instead of reopening his wounds, doing more damage. Too late now.

I reached the door to the staircase.

Arms quivering, I managed to get him through and prop him up against an immobile Aaron, then second-guessed my decision. Would it be better if he was on the floor on his back? On his side in the recovery position? Aaron, too?

That was when I realized there was no room on the landing to stretch either one of them out. *Fuck!*

There was no choice.

Leaving Ash braced against Aaron, I then locked the door, shutting out the shades of death and loss that, as Aaron had said, festered beyond. That done, I took the double-walled bottle of coffee from Aaron's pocket and put it in the opposite corner to the two men. "I'm going to find blankets," I said aloud, in case Aaron could still hear me.

My task proved harder than I'd assumed.

This part of the house might have anemic yellow light in the form of those flickering sconces, but it hadn't been opened or made up for use anytime recently. There were no mattresses, much less sheets and blankets. I'd begun to hyperventilate by the time I burst into a furnished room swathed in dustcloths.

I grabbed one of the cloths. Rough but warm. And clean on the underside. It'd do.

Pulling as many pieces off the furniture as I could handle, I dragged them upstairs to my friends, covering them as best as I could. I did three trips, until the fabric was a thick swaddling around their bodies, with only their faces peering out. I tugged Aaron's knit cap down securely, then flipped up the hood that came with Ash's jacket.

Streaks of red everywhere, Ash's lifeblood dripping out of him.

"He's still alive," I said to myself.

For how long, Luna?

I refused to listen to the voice in my head. If I did, this was all over.

After picking up the bottle of coffee, I went downstairs to the same room and hid it underneath a huge old bed with a moldering mattress, rolling it hard so it banged to settle against the far wall.

I had to protect the only physical evidence I had.

Because I could think of only one reason why Aaron had collapsed and I hadn't. Unless he'd had a heart attack and I was just too stupid to realize it, he'd been drugged. And the sole thing he'd consumed in the past two hours that I hadn't was the coffee.

Grace had packed that coffee for us, but Grace wasn't the one who'd made it.

It was Darcie who'd made the coffee. As it was Darcie who'd invited us all to this godforsaken place. What was her plan? To kill us all? Why? And even if she hated the rest of us for an unknown reason, why would she stab Ash?

The only thing that was clear was that she was dangerous . . . and she'd been alone with Grace, Kaea, and Vansi this entire time. "Please be okay, please be okay," I chanted under my breath as I began to run once again.

A stitch formed in my side, my breath sharp and cutting.

I had no idea how I was going to get Aaron and Ash to the warmth of the living room. There were too many stairs, too long a distance. I didn't even know if it was safe to move Ash that much . . . or who was alive to help me.

Slowing down only when I was within a short distance of the living room, I paused to catch my breath. My inhalations and exhalations were so rough and loud that I couldn't initially hear any other sounds.

It was a thin, piercing scream that penetrated.

"Oh God," I gasped, and slammed through the doorway.

. . . just in time to catch Bea's falling body in my arms.

44

"Nae-nae." A breath of sound, the scent of summer sunshine and peach blossoms, the feel of fine cotton and gauzy lace. "I tried to—"

Her eyes fell shut, her head lolling on her neck.

I was frozen, locked in time in this moment, my brain broken.

Bea was dead.

Bea was *dead.*

Bea was so light in my arms.

Another scream, this one without air, barely gasped out.

But enough to snap me out of the slip in time that had brought Bea back to life.

I looked up.

To a sea of red splashes.

On Kaea's skin, on Vansi's face, on the floor, sprayed on the wall.

Terror shredding me, I tried to make sense of what was going on.

Vansi, collapsed on the same couch as Kaea, was spotted with red.

Kaea was the same . . . and he lay so motionless that I couldn't tell if he was even breathing anymore.

Grace and Darcie, however, staggered on either side of the fireplace, one bloody hand on the mantel each and the other clutching at their wounds.

Darcie's stomach was a blur of red, her sweater a Rorschach painting. But her horrified eyes were on me, on *Bea*. "She's dead!" White face. A voice shrill with fear. "There was a funeral. I paid for a casket." Gasped-out words. "Suicide. There's a d-death certificate."

Releasing her grip on the mantel—leaving behind a smeared handprint—she pressed both hands to her stomach. "Grace is—" she managed to get out before she lost consciousness so fast that I had no way to catch her even if I hadn't been still holding the woman who looked like Bea.

It was pure luck that Darcie's head didn't crack on the sharp edge of the brick footing that bordered the hearth.

Still upright but pale, Grace threw down a large butcher knife she'd been holding, its blade slick with scarlet. "I had to use the knife," she sobbed as blood dripped from a wound on her side, enough blood that a droplet hit the hearth in front of me. "She was about to stab Vansi. I had to do it, Luna!"

I looked from the unconscious Darcie to the conscious Grace.

Before I could speak, however, Grace staggered, looked at me with a startled, devastated expression, then fell to her knees with a thud that couldn't have been faked. It was too brutal. Hard enough that my own knee throbbed in remembered pain.

Then she kind of toppled over in slow motion until she lay unmoving on the ground.

The entire series of events couldn't have taken more than thirty seconds, but it felt like an endless lifetime.

A crackle from the fireplace.

I began to move because I had to move. *Don't think, Luna. Just do. Don't think.*

First, I put the woman in my arms gently on the floor on her back. Only then did I notice that the white of her dress was saturated with blood all down her front. Streaks splattered her chest and neck, too. A droplet marred her jaw.

Don't think. Just do.

Shoving up her dress without regard for her modesty, I checked for wounds. Nothing. Her skin flawless but for a small birthmark shaped like a crescent moon on the curve of her waist.

I dropped the blood-soaked dress back down.

Stumbling past the unconscious woman with Bea's face and Bea's birthmark, I wiped the blood off Vansi's cheek—and realized it wasn't her own. Her skin was as smooth and unmarked as that of the other woman, her body clear of visible wounds. Fingers trembling, I checked her pulse. Steady like Aaron's.

"Drugged," I decided, only then noticing the bloody steak knife half under the sofa.

Stomach threatening to spasm, I kicked it deeper underneath.

Kaea wasn't feverish any longer, and he did have a pulse, albeit weaker than Vansi's. Because Vansi had spent the day caring for him, getting food and medicine into him. Only, she'd been sabotaged by an invisible enemy who had to have been dosing Kaea's food or drink with *something*.

My foot hit an object.

I jumped, half expecting another fucking blade—but it was Vansi's skillet.

Taking the makeshift weapon in hand, I walked to Grace. Her pulse was stronger than I'd expected. Not about to be caught flat-footed, I forced myself to pinch the skin on the soft underside of her arm with vicious intent. No reaction. She really was uncon-scious.

I made sure the butcher knife—Jesus, a *butcher* knife—was far out of her reach regardless.

Then I checked on Darcie. She was so clearly unconscious that I didn't bother with a pinch. Her wound looked far worse than Grace's, but for all I knew, Grace was bleeding out on the inside.

Putting the skillet on the old fur rug, I sat down with my hands gripping my hair. "Fuck! Fuck! Fuck!"

What was I going to do? What the hell *could* I do?

Especially with the snow.

Jolting upright on a sudden thought, I ran to the window. Enough light from the room fell beyond the glass to reveal that the heavy sheet of white had turned into slushy rain.

The polar blast had passed us.

With the temperature rising, the layer of snow on the ground might be all but gone by tomorrow. Except I didn't think most of the people on the estate would survive till dawn.

Chest painful with the scream I couldn't release lest I go mad, I ran to find clean towels—and took both knives with me, drop-ping them in a hip-height ornamental vase on my way to the laundry.

I was careful, never allowed my bare fingers to touch the weapons.

After returning to the living room—where, contrary to my

fears, no one had moved—I pressed a thick white towel to Darcie's stomach, the other to Grace's side. Since I couldn't keep pressure on them both, I went to the junk drawer in the kitchen. I'd found it while in there with Aaron.

The roll of duct tape was right at the back.

I taped the towel around Darcie, then Grace, as tightly as I could. Hopefully I wasn't causing harm by compressing their guts, but what use were guts if the two women bled to their deaths?

Duct tape in hand, I sat back again, my gaze going from one to the other.

It had to be Darcie. Grace was a stranger, a person with no reason to hurt us.

Someone who had *nothing to do with Bea*.

But . . . Grace was a stranger. And Darcie's horror at the presence of the woman who looked like Bea had been real.

Darcie also had no reason to stab Ash. Ash was her golden prize, the man she'd wanted since the day she'd laid eyes on him. No, Darcie would've never stabbed Ash.

But Grace was wounded. And Darcie had been trying to tell me something about Grace.

Grace had also been holding a butcher knife.

Jaw set, I pulled Darcie's hands behind her back and taped her wrists together so strongly that escape was impossible.

I did the same to Grace.

I didn't trust my instincts. Everything was a mess. None of it made sense.

Worried that one or both might throw up while unconscious—especially if one of them had been drugged—I put both into the recovery position, then did the same for Vansi and Kaea.

It would've been child's play to drug Vansi. She might look

together, but her grief was a wound as bloody as Darcie's. A drink offered by a friend and she would've accepted it with thanks.

Either Grace or Darcie could've doctored Kaea's soup with whatever it was they were using to poison him. The risk of anyone else taking a bit of that sickbed soup would've been low to negligible.

No, the ugly stuff had made its way into its target.

Having got everyone into the best position I could, I forced myself to go to the woman with Bea's face. And I made myself look at her. *Really* look at her. Thinner than the Bea I'd known, but with the same full lips, the same gentle roundness to the jawline. The same thick hair, so silky and such an intense shade of chocolate. Brushing it away from her left ear with trembling fingers and lungs compressed until there was no air in them, I counted the holes in her earlobe.

One at the top. Two at the bottom.

The tiniest blemish where she'd had a stud put into the inner part of the shell one year before deciding she hated it.

I sat back. Stared. And decided to check her feet.

My feet are weird. Do you think boys will care?

A conversation from a lifetime ago, a world of crushes and school dances and notes passed in hallways.

Tugging a white sneaker off her left foot, I encountered a thick woolen sock. Neither went with the lacy dress that was more Darcie than Bea, but it made sense in this house. My brain liked that. At least something made sense.

I pulled off the sock without really looking at her exposed foot. First, I put the sock beside the sneaker; next, I retrieved a mental photograph of Bea's "weird" foot; and then I looked down. A second toe that was at least half an inch longer than her big toe.

A little toe that was half the size it should be to be in proportion but still had a nail painted in Bea's favorite shade of plum.

My eyes burned, dry and hot.

I wanted to believe.

Don't think. Just do. There's a lot to do.

Once I'd put her sock and sneaker back on, I forced myself to get a can of Coke from the kitchen, along with several granola bars. I checked the seal of each and every one before I took a sip or bite.

I ate without tasting anything, my only intent to fuel my body.

I couldn't just sit here and wait. Many of my friends would die, become corpses cold and blue. Shoving the base of each palm against my closed eyes, I gritted my teeth, tried to work out how to move Ash and Aaron here, where at least it was warm.

There was nothing.

I'd break their backs dragging them down the stairs.

And though the snow had stopped falling, and I'd put them on the landing instead of beyond it, it remained bitterly cold. Ash would die before dawn, I was certain of it. As for Aaron . . . hypothermia could kill, and his system was already vulnerable, depressed by the drug that had stolen his consciousness.

I dropped my hands from my eyes, a half-eaten granola bar in my grip.

Spots of blood had bloomed on the towel I'd taped to Darcie, and while Grace's remained white, she hadn't stirred since she went down.

I didn't have to be a doctor to know that wasn't a good sign.

Vansi and the woman with Bea's face might be all right if they hadn't been overdosed, but Kaea's breathing was so shallow I kept expecting to hear it stop altogether.

Giving up on the food, I gulped the sweet soda that stuck to the back of my teeth, and I made my decision: I had to try to get help. I couldn't live with doing nothing and waking up to at least two dead friends, likely more.

If I decided to head out into the snow, it was only my own life I'd be putting at risk. They'd all still be in the same position as if I'd sat on my hands. Bleeding. Freezing. Dying.

My gaze landed on Grace and Darcie once more, flicked to Vansi and Kaea.

Shit. I couldn't leave Grace and Darcie here. I didn't trust either of them. What if the one behind the horror of the past days woke while the others were still unconscious? What if that person managed to escape their bonds?

I could wrap them up even tighter, but what if Vansi woke and they talked their way out of their bonds? What if the *wrong one* talked her way out? Leaving V a note wouldn't be a slam dunk— *especially* as time went on, and her soft heart began to bleed at seeing badly wounded people incapacitated on the floor.

All good reasons, but the real one was that I couldn't walk out the door while these two remained with my unconscious, vulnerable friends. I'd panic halfway down the drive, turn back.

As for *her*.

Leaving her behind had never been an option.

"None of it matters unless you can get out, Luna."

Maybe the sugar in the soda rebooted my brain, but the first thing I thought of was the farm vehicle Aaron had mentioned. I didn't know what "farm vehicle" entailed, but it was time I found out if I could drive it out of here.

45

I went to Kaea's pack.

I'd need more than my jacket if I intended to go outside.

Kaea didn't let me down. He'd packed thermal gear, including gloves. After stripping off to the skin but for my bra, I used a spare towel to rub off any remaining bits of sweat, then began to layer on clothing as he'd taught me once, prior to a snow-tramp.

I even wrapped a scarf around the lower half of my face.

The last thing of his I used was a thin woolen cap. After pulling it on, I shrugged into my jacket and flipped up the hood over the cap. My face was flushed, my skin prickling with heat, but that wouldn't last once I stepped outside.

I checked one more time to make certain neither Grace nor Darcie could get out of their bonds. Logic said I should tape up the woman in the bloody white dress, too, but I couldn't do it. Not when she had Bea's birthmark and when she'd called me "Nae-nae."

As it was, when I checked on her, it was to find her respiration and pulse unchanged. She was as unconscious as Vansi. Vansi, who was helpless. If I was wrong and this woman did wake, this woman with so much blood on her dress . . .

Just think of her as an unknown, Luna. Don't look at her face. Don't think about her birthmark.

Dry sobs racked my frame as I made myself turn her, tape her hands together behind her back.

Mind threatening to crack and breath jagged, I headed into the kitchen, grabbed what I needed. My next stop was the back door.

Taking a deep breath, I pulled it open.

The cold bit like a ravaging beast, but with most of my face protected by Kaea's lightweight scarf, I didn't hesitate.

"Hesitation kills you dead in cold weather, Lunes." Kaea, zipping up my jacket during that long-ago trip. "Think on your feet and keep moving."

Tugging the kitchen door shut behind me, I went down the steps and found the bright pink rope that Kaea and Ash had used as a guideline.

When I tugged, it held firm.

No way for me to grip it securely, however, and still hold on to my flashlight well enough that it didn't end up lost in the snow. Tucking it into a pocket created the same problem—and it seemed a pointless risk when the light barely penetrated the sleeting darkness.

Deciding I should conserve the battery power for the barn itself, I made myself switch it off.

I was blind.

Bile burned my throat, but I'd come too far to crumble now.

But at least if I died out here, whether from a panic attack or the weather, I wouldn't have to do it watching my friends die one after the other.

A good trade.

What about her?

I can't think about her. Not now.

Breath sharp and hot in the folds of the scarf as I fought not to listen to the manic voices in my head, I zipped the flashlight safely in my jacket, then stepped out into the slush and sleet proper. One hand over the other, never losing total contact with the rope. My feet threatened to slip on the wet snow multiple times, and the rain that was partly ice and all frigid pounded at me from all sides, but I refused to let go of the rope.

As I refused to look at the dark.

I closed my eyes. This way, I could pretend that I'd be able to see when I opened them.

One more step.

Bea's voice, the words those she'd spoken on that snowy hike. I could imagine her ahead of me, holding back a hand to help me up. "Come on, Nae-nae, don't be scared. I'm here."

Her voice was so vivid that I wondered if I was having an aural hallucination. If I was, I didn't want it to stop, didn't want to be alone in this brutal landscape where the dark surrounded me on all sides, a crushing embrace.

Just a little farther. You're almost there.

My foot twisted to the right.

I corrected myself before I did serious damage, still wasn't fast enough. The area throbbed. But it held when I put my weight on it.

One hand over the other. One foot in front of the other, shoving against a wall of cold wetness. Nothing but ice. I thought I was crying, but the grit in my eyes told me I wasn't.

Frigid droplets against my skin. Ice tears gifted to me by the sky.

Fucking poetic, Luna. At least you'll die making good use of your life of art and poetry.

So many evenings we'd spent in the flat drinking cheap beer and wine. At some point, one of the others would inevitably ask me to read poetry. I didn't know why. It was just a thing we did. Never while sober, only while drunk. Bea and I alone had enjoyed poetry while sober.

I loved the form for its clean precision, while Bea loved listening to me read it.

She'd lie with her head in my lap, her eyes sparkling up at me and her hair a caress of rich chocolate brown across my legs, and she'd *listen*. No one in my life had ever listened to me as Beatrice did; as if I was the center of her universe.

I had loved her with every breath in my body.

I would still love her on the day the undertakers put me in the earth.

There was nothing I wouldn't do for her.

Why hadn't she told me she was still alive?

I literally ran into the barn. Would've probably done so with my face if I wasn't wearing a heavy jacket and reaching forward to grab the next part of the rope. As it was, with my momentum, I took the hit on my arms and part of my chest.

"Oof." Rope in a death grip in my left hand, I searched with my right for the door handle.

Oh, bless Ash and Aaron.

They'd tied the rope around the door handle itself, leaving just enough slack that I could push the door partially open and slide in. Shutting the door behind me the instant I was out of the relentless assault of nature, I just stood there for close to a minute, so cold by now that I couldn't tell if there was a difference in temperature or not.

I was also still blind.

That panic subsumed by the bigger panic facing me, I went to grab my flashlight, but my fingers were numb despite the coverage provided by Kaea's gloves. The metal cylinder slipped out of my hand to land with a thud on the invisible ground.

A dry sob caught in my throat, I dropped to the ground on my knees, began to scrabble around . . . and remembered my phone just in time. Forcing myself to stop my frantic search, I took off my gloves as I fought to breathe air that was too black, too heavy.

Tiny lights sparked in my damaged eyes as I shoved the gloves in one pocket, then took extreme care in removing my phone from the other pocket.

The glow of the screen was a beacon in the dark.

Air filled my lungs, my brain able to function again, the jolt of fear a hard reset.

I didn't allow myself to think about a future in which I wouldn't be able to use light to search for an item I'd dropped. I just grabbed the fallen flashlight, turned it on, then put away my phone. At which point, I began to swing the flashlight in wide arcs while walking in a straight line.

Light shone off metal about ten steps later.

I bent over in sheer, bone-melting relief. I'd been worried "farm vehicle" meant a tractor, but before me was a Toyota Land Cruiser. An 80 series. No, I was no genius at identifying vehicles.

I just knew Land Cruisers thanks to my maternal uncle's obsession for them.

A man who lived off the land in the back of beyond, he wasn't officially a farmer, but he owned a huge sprawl so rugged that it was half rock. Despite the constant and repetitive hard use, he'd been through only two Land Cruisers in twenty-five years. These things *lasted*. Per Uncle Frank, the old-model Land Cruisers might as well be tanks, they were so heavily built.

I had no idea whether those were snow tires on it or not, but they *looked* like what I imagined snow tires must. As if they'd eat up the snow and spit it out without even noticing.

I almost ran to the driver's side door.

No key in the ignition, but I found it tucked into the sunshade. Of course. Who was going to come all the way out here to steal a car?

I inserted the key, then stopped, closed my eyes, and said a prayer to Aaron's God. I might not believe, but he did, and his life was on the line, too, so perhaps his God would have mercy on us all.

Lifting my lashes in the aftermath, I turned the key.

The roar of the engine almost blew out my eardrums. Only then did I realize how used I'd become to the howling quiet of the estate. Rain, endless rain, wind, and nothing else. Not even any voices now but for my own.

Shivering, I crossed my fingers, then glanced at the fuel indicator. Over halfway full. I dropped my head back against the headrest on a deep exhale. That was plenty enough to find out if there was any chance of getting to help.

"Okay," I said to myself, both hands on the steering wheel. "Okay."

There was really only one choice. I'd try for a signal on the bridge, though I had little hope of success. If I could get to the location of the slip, on the other hand, I could judge the weather at that point, decide on if I could walk to the small settlement beyond.

It wouldn't be easy, but it *could* be done if I prepared myself.

My plan assumed I'd be able to clamber over the slip itself, but I had to assume that, or I might as well give up now and watch my friends gasp their last breaths one by one. "Not an option."

Decision made, I left the engine running so that it could warm up—another lesson imparted by my uncle—and jumped out to open the huge barn doors. The rain was needles against my face, but it no longer held even slushy ice. The chill remained murderous.

Break down in this and I'd freeze to death.

Just one more victim of an incomprehensible massacre, my body to lie cold and wet and decaying under the spring sky.

46

After getting the big doors open wide, I glanced over at the far smaller door through which I'd come.

How was I going to get to the house without a guide rope? The snow might've turned to rain, but that made no change to the visibility as far as my eyes were concerned. There just wasn't enough light, the world a smeared blank.

In the end, I made the call to drive the Land Cruiser out, decide my next move from there. Once through the doors, I turned immediately left, so that my headlights pointed in the direction of the house.

All I saw at first was rain, a delicate haze of it. As if it was aglow with candlelight. Wondering if I'd switched on the wrong lights by accident, I fiddled with the switch—but couldn't amp up the wattage.

"Shit." I squeezed the steering wheel . . . and came to the

startling realization that my eyes reacted better to the glow than they did to light bright and biting.

I picked out the tree first, a smudged outline in the fog with waving octopus arms. "Gotcha." I grinned, scrolling mentally through all the images I'd taken in back of the property.

If I was right, the distinctive tree was positioned halfway to my destination.

I began to roll the car slowly forward. It moved without problem over the snow. This vehicle wasn't going to slide off the road into a ravine. Not unless I made a mistake.

My shoulders were stiff and my fingers white-knuckled by the time I reached the tree. Stopping, I searched the rainy darkness for any hint of the house.

I couldn't see any—No, there it was. I hunched over the steering wheel, my eyes narrowed. Was I imagining the twin glimmers of light . . . my headlights reflected back on a window?

Deciding that if worst came to worst, I could always retrace my steps by following the deep grooves in the snow—the rain wouldn't wash those away that fast—I drove forward at a snail's pace, my abdominal muscles held so tightly that it hurt. But the reflection of light grew brighter and larger, until I was parked at the bottom of the back steps.

Mouth dry, I jumped out of the driver's seat—literally jumped, the Land Cruiser's height not making for an easy step out—without turning off the engine. I wasn't about to risk the engine seizing from the cold.

I didn't bother to take off my boots before running into the house.

What I saw in the living room firmed up the decision I'd already made to take Grace and Darcie with me: Grace was partially conscious, and had managed to crawl to the edge of the fireplace's brick base. I knew what she wanted to do—scrape her taped wrists against the edge until the tape gave way.

Though I was ninety-nine percent sure Grace wasn't the problem, I couldn't be certain beyond all doubt. She'd had a knife in her hand; I had only her word that it had been in self-defense.

Her body slumped into a lax state again right then, and whether she was faking or not, I took the opportunity to find a piece of paper and scribble a note for Vansi.

Taking farm 4x4 to see if I can get help. Darcie and Grace with me. Stabbed each other. Cause of blood in living room. Don't know who was aggressor. Ash wounded and Aaron likely drugged at top of staircase leading to ruined wing. Check on them if you can. Don't eat or drink anything you don't make yourself, or that doesn't come from a sealed can or package. I'm going to try my hardest to get us out safe. —L

Below my scrawl, I sketched a rough map that'd lead her to Ash and Aaron. If she woke soon, she might be able to keep them alive until Aaron roused enough to help her bring Ash down to the warmth of the living area. *If* Ash was even still alive.

Best-case scenario: he was and they all got to the living area. If Kaea had been dosed, he should start to emerge out of it in the coming hours, which would leave Ash as the worst off. The others should be safe; there was plenty of firewood and food to get them through until help got there.

I didn't mention the woman in the white dress because there was no way to explain her without sounding delusional myself.

Finished, I taped the note to Vansi's wrist with duct tape. Obvious enough that she'd notice, but not on her hand, where she might groggily rip it off. Especially as I'd put the bulk of the note under her sleeve, with only the duct-taped section poking out.

Then, I did something I shouldn't have done—but I could no more stop myself than I could stop the world from turning. Racing upstairs, I went into Darcie and Ash's room. When I came out, it was with one of Darcie's floaty dresses in hand. Not white but an ethereal green.

One of the brand-new ones never linked to her online, the tag still on it.

I ran out to put it carefully into the back of the Land Cruiser.

Once inside again, I looked at the three I needed to get into the vehicle. Making the call that Grace wouldn't be able to free herself in the time available even if she *was* faking unconsciousness, and that the woman in the bloodstained dress was as deeply out as Aaron had been, I picked Darcie up with my now familiar grip under the armpits and dragged her to the kitchen. The task was nowhere near as difficult as with Ash and Aaron, but it wasn't exactly easy, either.

She was light for her height—but that height put her several inches above me.

I didn't bother with a jacket for her. She'd only be exposed to the outside air for the minute or so it'd take me to get her into the Land Cruiser, and I'd already turned on the heat in the vehicle.

I still grimaced at the icy slap of the air when we exited.

Grimaced again when her feet clanked on the steps. But she was wearing shoes. The thudding slams wouldn't hurt her. Those same shoes scraped twin grooves into the snow as I dragged her to the Land Cruiser. I had to lay her down for a second to open the back passenger door and hoped it was quick enough that the wet didn't really penetrate her clothing.

But right before I would've manhandled her into the seat, I changed my mind and dragged her to the front passenger seat. Darcie was the worst injured, the one least likely to have the energy to lunge at me in a sudden surge of violence.

And better for my concentration not to have the woman who might be Bea next to me.

With how high the Land Cruiser sat off the ground, it was hard to wrestle Darcie into the seat. In the end, I braced her back against the open edge of the door, then got into the vehicle and literally pulled her up into the seat. I took as much care as possible, but I was sure I still inadvertently hurt her in the effort. My own back gave several unhappy twinges.

After finally managing the task, my face hot and breath steaming, I slapped the seat belt across her limp form.

Inside the house, Grace was in the exact same position as when I'd left, so she had legitimately lost consciousness again. I had no trouble getting her out; she was the smallest person in the entire group. Her curls gleamed shiny and golden below me, and for a moment, it seemed impossible that someone like her could've stabbed another person.

I didn't bother with extra duct tape once I had her belted into the back seat. She could hardly break out of the tape with nothing sharp in the vicinity, and with me keeping an eye on both her and Darcie.

My last passenger was lighter than she should've been; her bones needed more flesh, her skin lacking a familiar glow. It hurt me to see her in such a fragile state, but her lack of weight made it easier to get her into the vehicle. Right behind me.

I'd rather that than have Grace at my back. Because while this woman's dress was covered in blood, Grace had been holding a butcher knife.

I should've left then, but I went back.

Kaea's pulse was so faint as to be a whisper. "Just hold on a little longer," I pleaded. "Please, Kaea."

After pressing my lips to his pallid cheek, I moved to Vansi. Strong pulse, warm skin. "I'll see you soon, V." What I didn't vocalize was that if I didn't, I hoped she wouldn't be left alone in a house full of corpses.

47

For a short while, I maintained my sense of direction by keeping track of the glowing kitchen windows using my rearview mirror. I didn't have the night vision to make out the entire looming hulk of the estate but I could well imagine how the turrets speared against the storm sky, needles stabbing into nothingness.

Poor Clara. What must it have been like to be trapped here with a mad husband and a psychotic child? Perhaps not psychotic in the true sense, but from all I'd read, there'd been something very wrong with Lizzie. Normal older sisters might get irritated at baby siblings, but they didn't *burn* their tiny palms.

Darcie had come from that bloodline.

So had Bea.

Gritting my teeth, I drove on. By the time the safety of the warmly lit kitchen vanished into the rain, which seemed to have intensified since our departure, I knew I was *maybe* a quarter of the way to the bridge. A long way left to travel across formless grassland, with my vision limited to the tiny area in front of the Land Cruiser's dim headlights.

I swallowed, stopped, searched for any possible landmark.

The light was bad. I shouldn't be driving. Truth was, I probably wouldn't be able to renew my driver's license when it expired. But all that meant nothing here. I searched again, looking for anything that'd anchor me.

A sharp shadow poking up out of the snow on the very edge of my field of vision.

"Old guardhouse!"

I knew where I was now, felt confident enough to go forward until I sensed an upward slope. Good. The day we'd arrived here, we'd climbed a gentle slope from the bridge, come down the other side. Now, I was doing it in reverse.

It still felt as if my bones were crunching against each other with the force of my grip as the Land Cruiser crawled through the snow.

"You can do it," Bea whispered in my ear.

I jolted. "Bea?"

Nothing. Silence. And when I twisted in my seat to try and see my back seat passengers, all that met me was a thickness of shadows. No change in their breathing. No indication of consciousness. And yet I could swear I'd heard Bea's voice.

It was a madness, no doubt, the stress crushing my brain, but I didn't care.

I had *missed* Bea for nine long years. Half the photographs I'd taken of shadows disappearing behind corners had been attempts to look for her.

Turning back to face the front, I started forward again. A minute later, the Land Cruiser began to move downhill.

I brought the car to a halt, staring ahead in an effort to spot the bridge even though I knew I couldn't fucking see in the dark!

Just go, Nae-nae. Take the leap.

I had no other choice. I rolled the Land Cruiser downhill.

And almost ended up in the crashing waters of the creek ten creeping minutes later. I stopped, sucked in gulps of air. I'd made it to the water, but the bridge was nowhere in sight. I was either too far to the left or to the right. But at least I could just follow the water in one direction, then the other.

My neck was iron, my fingers like claws by the time the headlights picked out jutting metal arches. *Finally.* Chest expanding, I angled the vehicle until it faced the bridge.

I thought my eyes were playing tricks on me at first, but no, the bridge swung to and fro in the wind, its creaks the groans of a dying man. Even worse was the water that roared over the platform, a surge of snow and ice from the mountains turned liquid.

I stared blankly at the sight.

I'd been prepared for a swollen creek, but this . . .

Not that it changed the choices available to me: forward or back. That was it.

Getting out into the slamming rain, I walked to the last safe spot on this side of the bridge. While the water did surge over the top of the bridge platform in violent pulses, the waves weren't high. The Land Cruiser could get through.

If the bridge was strong enough to hold the vehicle's weight after the pounding it had been taking in the storm.

Guess I'd find out. I'd made my decision, would carry it through. No turning back. And no point in trying for a signal, but I did so anyway just in case.

Nothing.

Wading back through the slushy snow after stowing my phone back in my coat, I jumped into the vehicle. The warmth was a blast that I knew would make my frozen fingertips hurt as they thawed out.

"The bridge is underwater." A soft voice from the back seat.

My heart kicked so hard that it was in my mouth, a slippery lump of muscle that threatened to choke. I swiveled after hitting the overhead switch for the interior light, saw Grace looking at me with groggy eyes. The other woman, the one I couldn't allow myself to believe was Bea, lay slumped in a drugged sleep. I struggled against the need to shake her, make her tell me what was going on.

Returning my attention to Grace with conscious will, I said, "How you feeling?"

"Hurts." A whimper. "You tied me up."

"It's tape," I said, as if that made it any different. "Sorry, I couldn't figure out which one of you started it."

Coughing, Grace nodded.

"Hold on." Exiting to go around to the back, I took four bottles of water from the stash I'd grabbed on my way out of the house; I threw three into the empty glove box, and opened the fourth. Then, going around to Grace's side of the Land Cruiser, I unscrewed the bottle and held it to her lips so she could sip.

After she pulled back, I screwed the top back on and put the bottle beside her. Not that she could get to it, but it would make it easier for me not to mix up which bottle belonged to which person.

Grace spoke again after I was in the driver's seat. "I have no reason to attack anyone." Her eyes, lost and emotionally bruised, held mine in the rearview mirror. "I barely know most of you."

"Yeah." And yet I didn't offer to free her. "Do you know the woman beside you?"

Grace shook her head. "She came in the door right before you did, but she was kind of wobbly on her feet. I thought she was going to fall." Swallowing hard, she looked at her fellow passenger. "Oh, no. She's been stabbed, too."

"It's not her blood." Turning off the interior light, I struggled to make sense of what Grace had told me.

I couldn't.

Just do, Luna. Think later.

My eyes having finally adjusted to the sudden lack of light—or as much as they *could* adjust, I looked ahead to the bridge. "We have to get over that. You might be hurt less than Darcie, but you still have a stab wound that's continuing to bleed." I'd spotted hints of red on the towel when I'd given her the water.

"Bridge is . . . dancing."

She was right—the bridge was continuing to sway this way and that in the wind, and every so often, it'd *ripple*. I watched the movements, and I watched the water, and I saw the pattern. If I could make it across between one ripple and the next, I'd avoid the biggest of the waves that crashed over the platform.

Snapping my seat belt back on, I said, "Here we go," and put the car into gear.

One. Two. Three. Ripple. *Go!*

The groans as we drove on were hollow and deep, and I didn't dare think about what was going on beneath the tires. I kept my eyes not straight ahead but angled slightly to the left. So I could see the metal of the struts, use that to orient myself in a straight line.

The tires scythed through the water, the Land Cruiser living up to my uncle's love for it. It was as solid as a block of steel.

It was also heavy.

I thought I heard a crack, forced myself not to panic. There was nothing I could do if the bridge was collapsing under us. I had to outrun the damage—yet not go so fast that I spun us out of control.

Water smashed onto the driver's side and over the windscreen, blinding me a second time over. The bridge's sway took on a new twisting motion at the same instant.

And I realized I hadn't outrun the oncoming ripple.

Teeth gritted, I bent over the steering wheel and squinted. The barest blur of light glancing off metal, and my own sense of direction. That was all I had.

"You're too far to the left!" Grace cried. "We're about to hit a girder on this side!"

No peripheral vision.

"Now?" I said after correcting.

"Yes, good."

"Tell me if it happens again. I'm not exactly a four-wheel-drive champion."

"You've got this," she said, her tone warm. "I couldn't drive in this."

My mind pounded with the thunder of the water, the howl of the wind, the groans and cracks of the bridge. Sweat pooled under my armpits and in between my breasts. I should've taken off my outdoor jacket before attempting this.

I'd do it after we reached the end. It had to be soon.

This bridge wasn't infinite.

Though it felt exactly that on this dark and stormy night straight out of a horror flick.

You've got this, Nae-nae.

How appropriate that Grace had unknowingly said exactly the same thing Bea had said to me so many times over the years.

Because this all came back to her. I knew that in my gut. Somehow, it all began and ended with Beatrice.

"Go right," Grace said. "Just a bit."

"Now?"

"Yes, that's good."

Something bumped under the tires and I had the sudden thought that we'd hit the girder . . . but no, we were rising up and away from the bridge. "We made it."

Lungs tight with the breaths I hadn't taken, I brought the car to a standstill, wasn't sure my hands weren't actually claws by now I'd gripped the steering wheel with such force.

My desperate gasps of air filled the silence.

"I've always hated theme park rides." Grace's laughter was all nerves and relief. "Good driving there."

Shrugging off my jacket but leaving it trapped between me and the seat, I said, "Thanks for the help."

"Team effort."

"We should be able to follow the line of the trees and stay on the road," I said and began to creep forward . . . and felt the uneven bite of gravel under the left tires. The right continued to plow through snow.

"Tree canopy must've protected the left side of the road from the snow," I said aloud. "Tell me if I start to float too much from the left." That was the safe side, the side with the trees.

On the right was a ravine. We wouldn't survive the fall.

"I will." I could tell from the sounds in the back and the faint, shadowy shape of her in the rearview mirror that Grace had twisted in her seat to better watch that side of the road.

Guilt nipped at me. "Sorry about the tape. It won't be for long." Now that we'd navigated the bridge, I felt more hopeful of making it out. I'd still have to climb the muddy, rocky bulk of the slip, but Grace and Darcie and . . . Bea would be safe inside a warm car in the interim. I'd leave the windows down enough for ventilation, but not enough that they'd be in any danger from the cold.

And I'd try not to think about her. About Bea.

Because it was Bea.

My mind might be gibbering chaos, but I knew her too well to make a mistake on that front.

"You have to believe me," Grace pleaded. "Darcie lost it. She gave Vansi a cup of coffee and Vansi got real drowsy. I figured it was shock, you know? She's been so strong all day, worried about Kaea, and I was sort of waiting for reality to hit her."

My throat thick at the memory of Phoenix's body so alone in the cellar, I nodded. "Nix and V, they were each other's first and only love."

"Aaron told me," Grace said softly, even as I thought I heard Darcie's breathing alter. "He said Nix told him on his wedding day that he couldn't imagine going through life with anyone else."

"You should tell V that once she's had more time to grieve." It'd matter to her, especially given the problems she and Phoenix had been having of late. "Why did Darcie attack you?" I shot Darcie a quick look, didn't spot any visible change.

"It was weird. I talk nonsense when I'm nervous, and I was worried about everything, so I started babbling about that TV drama that was on recently. You know, with the twin sisters? Where one turns out to have murdered the other one?"

I was about to say I had no idea what she was talking about when I remembered seeing a promo on a billboard in the city.

"Did the posters have one woman on them, half in light, half in shadow, with a mirror image behind her?" The poster had disturbed me for reasons unintended—I'd thought it was my eyes making me see double.

"Yes, that's the one. I was saying how I didn't buy the cold-blooded nature of the murder when the writers of the show had spent the entire season building up the bond between the twins." Grace's words picked up speed. "If we were to believe that, then we had to believe that by killing her twin, the survivor was killing herself—and yet we see her walk off into the sunset to live the perfect life."

"Go on."

"There's nothing else—that's when Darcie began screaming."

I caught Grace's bewildered headshake in the rearview mirror, the movement clear enough that I could make it out even in the gloom inside the vehicle. The instrument lights barely penetrated the thick dark of it, but I couldn't risk driving with the interior light on—my vision wouldn't be able to cope with the different light levels inside and out.

"She asked me if I was accusing her of killing her sister, and how dare I . . . and honestly, I don't remember the rest too well. I know we were in the kitchen for the start of it. That's when she must've grabbed the knife and I must've panicked and taken one, too."

Grace's voice trembled. "I was so scared, Luna. I screamed at her to stop after she chased me into the living room, but she wouldn't, and then she tried to hurt Vansi and I had to fight—I didn't mean to stab her that hard!"

She was sobbing by the end, her breathing jagged and broken.

A sound from the front passenger seat, a stir.

48

I dared a glance and saw that Darcie's eyes were fluttering. "Darcie?" I said sharply, even as I returned my attention to the windscreen and the blurry gold of my headlights in the rain.

Darcie's answer was a groan.

"Don't let her convince you it was me," Grace begged, her voice wet. "I know she's your friend, but I didn't do anything except defend myself. She's probably the reason this woman is unconscious. Darcie probably gave her something, too."

Darcie's voice was a rasp low enough that it would've been inaudible if I hadn't brought the Land Cruiser to a halt when I sensed her trying to straighten up from her slumped-over position. "Sh . . . she . . . 's lying."

"I'm not!" Grace kicked the back of Darcie's seat. "You crazy bitch!"

"Grace! Stop it!"

A sob. "Sorry, I'm sorry. I just can't stand her anymore. She hurt Aaron, too, didn't she? That's why he didn't come back with you."

"He's fine. Just unconscious." I didn't add any information about Ash.

Then Darcie said, "Ash?" in a voice that was a tremor.

"He's fine, too," I replied, because the last thing I needed was for her to dissolve into hysteria, feigned or real. "Just fell through a rotten board and hit his head. I left him and Aaron together in a warm place."

Darcie's cough was painful, a scraping kind of thing. "Grace stabbed me." The words were firmer this time, even though her face was white from lack of blood, her lips almost bluish. "She's crazy."

"I don't even know you!" Grace yelled. "Any of you! You're Aaron's friends!"

"Luna . . ." Another rasping breath. "She's right. We don't know her. We know nothing about her."

A chill spread through me at that simple statement that echoed my own earlier thought. Grace might not know us, but we also didn't know *her*. But there was a much, much bigger elephant in the vehicle. "Darcie," I said, "why is Bea in the back passenger seat?"

Darcie seemed to jerk. "I th-thought I imagined . . ." Rustling, as if she was struggling to look into the back. "Scam, it's a scam," she rasped at last. "Bea's *dead*. They sent me an official death certificate. My Triss is dead, Luna."

She sounded so shaken, her tears so savage that I found myself wanting to believe her. But that woman *was* Bea. Yet if Darcie hadn't known of her continued existence . . . then what? Where had Bea been all this time? Had she somehow fooled Darcie into believing her dead, then just left us for so many years?

My heart threatened to implode from the pain, but I had to face it. If Bea had been alive the past nine years, then she'd *chosen* not to contact me.

"G-Grace is insane. Came after me with a cleaver after I started to worry why Vansi was so deeply asleep. Said she'd tell me why while she was gutting me."

"Luna, don't listen to her!" Huge tears rolled down Grace's face as she jerked forward against the seat belt, coming close enough to me that the blur of darkness vanished and I could see her. "She's getting into your mind. That's what she does! *She's* the one who made us all come to this horrid place!"

Darcie took several breaths to reply, as if gathering her strength. And in that time, I decided to continue driving. I didn't know how long it'd take in this weather, or how much longer either woman would survive. Because while Grace had seemed feisty when she'd lunged against her seat belt, I'd noticed that the whites of her eyes were scarily pale.

She was losing blood. A lot of it.

"It's funny," Darcie said at last. "I almost forgot. It was Aaron who suggested we meet up. Said he wanted to introduce Grace to his oldest friends."

I could imagine Aaron doing just that—after Bea, he'd been the one most likely to organize group events. "Who chose the estate as the location?"

"Me," Darcie admitted. "We'd otherwise have had to pay for a place and it was big enough."

"See?" Grace said. "She's the one who brought us to this hellhole."

Grace was right—but if Grace had nudged Aaron into bringing up the idea of a reunion, then the Shepherd estate would've
been by far the most obvious option. I didn't keep a permanent
residence in the country, Vansi and Phoenix had an apartment in
a building close to the hospital, Kaea's was a small bachelor pad,
while the two other couples owned homes in the suburbs. Nice
enough homes but not set up to accommodate eight for what was
meant to be a vacation.

We could've hired a place, but it had never come up because
Darcie had offered the estate right off. Even if she hadn't, *someone*
would've asked if it was available and still in a habitable state.
While we'd never visited it, we'd heard all about it the years we'd
been friends with her and Bea. We'd always talked about doing a
big weekend there, never quite got around to it.

The pathway would've always led to the estate.

"Luna." Darcie's quiet, pained voice. "You know me. I've never
been violent."

No, Darcie wasn't violent. Darcie was manipulative, far preferred to get her way through more underhanded methods. If
anything, Bea had been the violent one. I'd once seen her lash out
at Darcie over some slight, literally haul her into a hair-pulling
fight. But they'd been teenage girls then, their hormones running
amok.

"I'm not violent, either." Grace's tone was brittle. "But she's
your friend and you don't know me. You don't know that I draw
hot baths for Aaron after he's had a hard day. You don't know I
drive a cute red car that's my pride and joy. And you don't know
that I spoil our puppy so much that I cried when we left him with
the dog sitter."

Something flashed in front of the lights.

Braking hard, I searched the dark. "Did you see that?"

"What?" both women said, one a sharp question, the other a mumble.

I looked hard, but whatever it had been was gone. Probably an animal. A possum? Did they have deer in this region? I didn't know, took extreme care when I started to move again. "Grace, do you remember the exact location of the slip?"

"No." A single sullen word. "Maybe forty-five minutes away at regular speed?"

I frowned, tried to think back to our discussion. "That doesn't sound right. We'd be well past the settlement by then."

"Maybe it was thirty minutes then? My brain's all fuzzy." The strength in Grace's tone was dwindling rapidly, and I could imagine her face coated with fine threads of silver. Imagination was all I had right now, because she'd pushed back into her seat and been enveloped by the pillowy shadows; I could see large motions but no detail of her face or expression.

Her dullness of spirit and hazy memory worried me for what it implied about her level of blood loss.

As I drove, I chewed on my lower lip, attempting to see through Grace's and Darcie's words and coming up against the same hard wall of fact: they'd admitted to stabbing each other. I just had no way to tell which one had been the instigator.

"I'd never hurt Ash." Darcie's whisper was a sepia photograph as faded as Clara and Blake's wedding image. "That woman pretending to be Bea . . . she has blood on her dress. Did she do something to him? Did Grace?"

I'd been trying not to think about that, to focus just on the situation with Grace and Darcie—neither one of whom had blamed Bea for their own stabbing. So where had the blood come from?

Grace snorted. "Your husband didn't come back because he can't stand to be around you."

"You don't know him. You don't know us."

"Aaron told me about Ash and your sister, and I saw the truth on his face when he found that doll. He still loves her. He was the one tormenting you with it, you know. You really think he's going to stay with you now that she's come back from the dead? And how about that? I thought you told everyone *she was dead*!"

"Grace," I snapped, intending to tell her to knock it off.

But Darcie said, "Ash would never do that to me," at the same time.

"I saw him with the doll the morning of the hike! I figured he was just being a dick and it wasn't my business to interfere in your fake picture-perfect marriage."

"I don't beli—" Darcie's words cut off as she began to cough, harsh and raw.

"You need water?"

But she shook her head. After half a minute, the cough cleared away in short spurts.

In the silence, I listened for Bea's breaths . . . and heard them. Deep and steady, her sleep drugged and dreamless.

She was alive.

Bea was *alive*.

And I couldn't think about that if I wanted to stay sane this night and get help for Kaea and Ash, Aaron and Vansi, all four of them trapped in that house stained by violent deaths past and present. The question of Bea would swallow me up if I permitted myself to fall into it.

"Your husband hates you," Grace said from the back, her tone more spiteful than I'd have imagined Aaron's adorable fiancée

could ever sound. "Surely you know that. The way he looks at you
when you can't see him, it's not like a loving husband. He looks
at you as if you're someone he's never seen before. As if you're a
monster hidden under the skin of his wife."

I should've spoken up, should've defended my friend, but I
needed to hear Darcie's reaction.

"Ash doesn't hate me," Darcie said, but her voice was tremu-
lous, lacking in conviction. "I've never done anything but love
him. Why would he hate me?"

"Yes, why?"

Grace's quiet question raised the hairs on the back of my neck,
had me throwing Darcie a measuring glance before I returned my
attention to the road. "He has been a bit edgy," I said, thinking
back to that conversation at the top of the stairs that hadn't quite
settled right in my gut. "You two have a fight?"

"I thought he was happy about the pregnancy, but . . ." Her
voice faded off into a piteous whisper.

And suddenly, I felt like the most raging bitch on the planet.
I'd forgotten that she was pregnant. Pregnant and wounded and
in apparent shock over Bea, and now Grace was forcing her to
confront relationship issues that didn't need to be confronted.
Not here. Not now.

"Enough, Grace," I said when she inhaled as if in preparation
for further verbal blows. "Both of you stay as still as you can,
don't do anything that might increase your blood flow. I don't
know how long it'll take me to get past the slip and return to you
with help."

Silence from the back seat, but Darcie said, "Do you think
Ash hates me, too, Luna? Do you think he's still in love with Bea?"

I couldn't do this to her, couldn't hurt a friend who'd been in my life for over a decade and a half. "He actually asked me to keep an extra-special eye on you because you were pregnant," I said, avoiding the question without seeming to avoid it. "He said for me not to spill the beans, but he wanted someone else to know."

"Oh." A smile in the word itself. "Thank you for telling me that."

The rain thundered hard against the windscreen in a sudden surge, as if we'd passed right under a huge thundercloud. A lightning flash followed, illuminating a large section of the road ahead of me. No blockages up ahead. Just a winding curve I knew had to lead to the slip. Even with my speed, we'd gone too far for it to be otherwise.

With that knowledge in mind, I took extreme care as I rounded the corner, ready to stop at any moment . . . but the road carried on uninterrupted, only a few scraggly broken branches scattered across the tarmac.

49

I tried to straighten my back from its hunched-over position. I'd miscalculated badly. And though I just wanted to stop, have someone else take control, make things better, I carried on through the increasingly slushy and slippery snow.

"I think I'm bleeding again. It pulses." Grace's voice was ragged. "Seriously, please undo my hands so I can press them to the towel. You can even tape them up in front rather than at the back."

My fingers clenching on the steering wheel, I hesitated.

And Darcie whispered, "Don't fall for it, Luna." Her voice kind of . . . bubbled, as if she had blood in her throat. I hoped to hell that wasn't the case.

"If she has her hands in front of her," Darcie managed to breathe out, "she can throw her arms over the headrest and strangle me from the back."

"Do you see now? How she thinks?" Grace demanded in that voice devoid of its punch. "She's lost it. All I want to do is put pressure on my wound. And meanwhile, she still hasn't explained what her dead sister is doing in the back seat with me."

Swallowing, I stopped the car and angled my body to look at her. From what little I could see, Grace did appear pale and sweaty, her face set in a wince. "You should be able to put pressure on it if you lean over hard against the door. It won't be as comfortable, but it's doable."

Even as I shifted my gaze forward again, my attention on the wet landscape partially aglow in the Land Cruiser's lights as we began to move again, my mind raced. It hadn't escaped my notice that it was Grace attempting to escape her bonds, while Darcie had accepted my decision to incapacitate them both.

On the flip side, Darcie was in worse shape than Grace—even with Grace getting weaker—and might just be worried Grace would retaliate against her if given the chance. And Grace was also right on the point of Bea. But Darcie's expression when she'd seen Bea, it had been the terrorized fear of a woman seeing a corpse risen. Surely Darcie wasn't that good an actress? Especially when bleeding and in pain?

The lights gleamed against the melting snow up ahead, the engine revving as it started up an incline.

"Where are we?" I muttered. "I don't remember a hill except right after the settlement."

Neither woman said anything, all attention on the road as the Land Cruiser crept up and up and then we were at the top of the ridge, and I thought I saw a bright dot in the distance.

Frowning, I tightened my abdomen and switched off the headlights. The decision threw us into pure darkness but for those pinprick flashes behind my eyes, and at first I thought that was what I was seeing through the rain. Nothing but misfires from my brain.

But the flashes didn't fade or flicker out. They resolved into tiny golden squares.

"That's the settlement."

Realization crept over me in a cold swell.

"Oops." A single soft word from the murky black of the back seat. "At least I can call you Nae-nae now. Bea gave me permission, said to tell you she said it was all right."

Even as my brain struggled to comprehend the impossibility of her words, she said, "Sorry about what's going to happen next." Words coated in sorrow. "But she has to pay."

She jolted forward out of her seat, her arms somehow free.

Reaching around the headrest, she hooked one forearm against Darcie's throat while gripping the wrist of that with her free hand so she could tighten the suffocating embrace to a brutal vise. This close, I could see her expression. Her teeth were bared, her eyes intent, no evidence in her features of the frailty she'd put into her voice only minutes ago.

All of it so fast that I was still belted into my seat.

It locked into place as I attempted to rush her. "Grace!" I struggled to undo the belt. "Stop!"

Darcie's eyes were bulging, her face red and hot by the time I got free. And Grace, she was so strong. I couldn't break her grip, my hands having no effect on the ropy lines of her tendons.

Climber, she was a climber, like Aaron.

That was where they'd met. In a club for climbers.

Grace was strong.

I'd forgotten that, gotten used to seeing her as petite and cute. *Think, Luna!*

A flash to the past, to a self-defense course Vansi and I had done in high school. Not much had stuck, but I did remember one thing that had grossed me out so much I'd had a nightmare about it.

Shifting so that I was kneeling on my seat, I thrust both my thumbs into Grace's eyes with all my weight behind it, as if I wanted to dig into the slippery orbs.

My stomach lurched, liquid pooling in my mouth.

Grace's scream was a shrill thread in the darkness. Falling desperately back into the murk of the back seat, she pressed her hands to her abused eyes.

I tried not to think about the wetness on the pads of my thumbs, or if I had caused permanent damage to her eyes. Those most precious organs.

While she was still whimpering, I crawled into the back by going in between the two seats. Too late, I realized I should've switched on the interior light. All I could see was the vague shape of her. It would have to be enough—and since there was a fucking high chance that she was the one who'd murdered Nix, stabbed Ash, and poisoned Kaea, I forced myself to hit her hard in her wounded side.

I needed time to think without fear of attack.

Blood bloomed in a clogging viscosity of scent and she screamed again.

About to vomit from my own actions, I used the opportunity to pull her arms tightly behind her back. When I used my belt to lock her arms together, I did so with a tightness that meant she had no movement at all. It probably wasn't safe for the long term and the belt wasn't fully secure, but with the settlement in the distance, it only had to last a short time.

That was when I felt the scrap of tape that clung to one of her ragged nails, and remembered her habit of tearing at her nails.

Apparently the resulting edges had been sharp enough to slowly, stealthily cut through tape.

Hauling her upright, I slammed her back against the seat. Only then did I realize that she was still belted in. Figured. My belt locked me in, while hers had allowed her to stretch out enough to get to Darcie.

"Nae-nae," she began.

"Shut up." My jawbones crunched. "Just *shut* up."

Summer sunshine and peach blossoms.

Bea was so close, my knee pushing into her thigh. It would be so easy to turn, bury my face in her hair, pretend none of this was happening. Like I'd been pretending for a year that I wasn't going blind. I was an expert at pretending. But I did that tonight and more people would die.

Crawling back into the driver's seat before I surrendered to my need to cradle Bea, just hold her and listen to her breathe, feel her heart beat, I finally threw on the interior light, then looked at Darcie. She was breathing like an asthmatic, a fine whistle sounding as she attempted to suck in air, her eyes bloodshot. "It won't be long until we get to the settlement," I told her. "Conserve your strength."

I had to start the engine again—the Land Cruiser had jolted to a halt when I jumped into the back seat without putting it into neutral. Pure luck I'd already pulled the parking brake or we'd have rolled backward and down into the ravine.

Above the renewed roar of the engine came a voice from the back seat that had a new roughness to it, as if Grace had damaged her throat when she screamed. "No, don't conserve your strength, *Darceline.*" A sinuous kindness to her tone. "I think Luna wants to know what you did to her Bee-bee. Will you tell her? Or shall I?"

50

I twisted, putting myself in a position where I could see both their faces.

One an effective stranger, the other one of my oldest friends.

Grace, her eyes bloody and teary, was staring at the back of Darcie's head with a rage that should've been impossible given that they, too, were strangers. Darcie, meanwhile, had started to breathe in a different way. Faster, shallower.

"She's insane," she finally managed to rasp out. "Don't listen to her."

But I shook my head with slow deliberation. "No." Putting the vehicle in neutral, I pulled the parking brake I'd only just released. "We'll stay here as long as it takes to uncover the truth. Because that's Bea next to Grace, Darcie."

"No, it can't be," Darcie insisted on another hard-won breath. "I'm hurt bad, Luna."

I looked at the growing stain on the white of the towel,

nodded. "You're bleeding again." Probably from having struggled against Grace. "You need help."

But I didn't move the vehicle, didn't head to the settlement and the assistance there. "So you better talk fast." I almost didn't recognize my own voice, it was so flat and callous. "Why does Grace want to kill you?"

"I told you!" A small coughing fit that I waited out, and that Grace didn't interrupt. "She's psychotic."

I locked eyes with Grace. "Are you psychotic, Grace?"

Grace turned to look at Bea with the tenderest expression I'd ever seen on her face. When she glanced back at me, her eyes were wet and her voice a whisper. "'Nae-nae, my fierce Nae-nae, she always loved me best. She never hurt me, never wanted anything from me except that I be me. I wish I'd told her about my wonky brain. I wanted to, was getting ready to, and now it's too late.'"

Grace's smile was sad, a portrait of aged grief. "That's what your Bea said to me. She told me other things, too, like about the black-and-white photo shoot in the studio with the piano. You can ask her yourself when she wakes up."

A million tears built up in my head until the pressure pulsed and pounded and threatened to crush me. "How—" I swallowed hard. "How do you know about the photo shoot?"

"Aaron!" Darcie cried out. "Obviously Aaron told her that. Bea must've told him and he told Grace! That woman *is not Bea*! She's dead! I can show you the death certificate!"

I didn't look at Darcie, my eyes only on Grace.

Her bruised, bloodied eyes swam with tears. "Bea never forgot that time at school when you swapped skirts with her."

A hammer slammed into my chest, cracking open my rib cage to expose my insides. No one else knew that. Not a *single* person.

Bea had been too embarrassed then, and later, it had become a memory shared only between the two of us. Of how we'd been two awkward teenage girls who thought the incident the end of the world.

She'd been thirteen, her period had come early, and she'd stained her skirt. Though I was older than her, I was shorter. Short enough that I could roll up her skirt at the waist and still not get in trouble for a uniform violation. Add in the oversize blazer I wore as part of the uniform, and we'd successfully masked the stain.

Our secret memory. Not to be spoken to anyone else.

I wasn't angry Bea had revealed it to Grace. I recognized the act for what it was: a message that I could trust Grace, that *Bea* trusted Grace.

"How do you know Bea?" I asked this stranger who wasn't a stranger after all.

Then I looked at Darcie at last . . . and had to accept the rest of it.

"What did you do to Bea, Darcie?" I asked before Grace could answer my question. "Don't lie. You could bleed out in the time you waste lying."

Darcie sucked in a breath, hung her head. Her shoulders shook, her sobs beautiful theater. "I did what needed to be done." With her hands taped, she couldn't use them to wipe away the tears and they dripped soft splashes onto her sweater. "I wanted to help her."

"Liar!" Grace kicked the back of Darcie's seat hard enough to rock it.

"*Grace.*" I shook my head in a curt negative.

Jaw shoving against her taut skin, she nonetheless sat back.

"She did it because she wanted Ash, who only wanted Bea," she bit out. "Darcie's hated Bea from the instant she realized who her sister was going to become. *She* was meant to be the golden child, Bea the one in her shadow—only it didn't work out that way."

"It wasn't like that." Darcie's eyes, so lovely and so blue, held a silent plea. "I told you she had mental problems. *Serious* mental problems. They began to intensify that year, but she wouldn't get help."

"I don't believe you." Because Darcie was implying a sustained decline at a level that would've begun to affect Bea's everyday life. I didn't care how good someone was at masking a condition, they couldn't hide that kind of a change from a friend who saw them day in and day out.

I closed my hand around the necklace I hadn't taken off since the day I put it on. "I dropped in on Bea without warning all the time. Not *once* did I surprise her in an unstable state."

"My sister was clever at hiding her fragmentation," Darcie sobbed, her gaze swinging to Bea, then back to me. "She was this dazzling butterfly around you and the others, and then when she was alone, she'd lie on her back and stare at the ceiling. She even cut herself. In places you'd never see. Been doing it for years. Had scars all down the inside of her thighs."

Grace laughed, a genuine belly laugh.

Darcie's expression flickered. "She's mad. Listen to her."

"No, Darcie. She's laughing because you had to push your story too far and now I know you're lying." Because that shoot in the studio with the piano? It had been the nude one.

Beatrice's skin had been flawless. "Bea had no scars on her thighs." She still didn't.

"She was very good at hiding it," Darcie insisted. "Makeup,

tanner, whatever it took. She was broken, Luna! I was just trying to help her!"

Grace jolted forward against her seat belt. "You tried so hard you had her drugged to the gills and locked up in a mental institution."

The silence inside the car was a voracious, grasping thing that dug its claws into my brain and cut bloody furrows. "Darcie?" My nails sank into my palms. "What is Grace talking about?"

"She needed help!" Darcie screamed. "She was spiraling. I was afraid she was going to really hurt herself. Then she did! She tried to kill herself!"

"Only after you'd locked her in that horrible place and thrown away the key!" Grace shouted from the back seat. "You shut her away from the entire world, from everyone she loved, when you knew that she needed the energy of the world and of her people to thrive."

It was at that moment that I accepted Grace truly knew my Beebee. Because that was what I had always understood about my friend. She was bright and lovely and beautiful—but she couldn't be alone. She needed people, needed our attention to fuel her spirit.

That was why I'd held the power in our friendship: I needed no one. Not that way. I could spend hours alone in perfect contentment. Bea hadn't understood that, had admired me for what she saw as a boundless internal well of strength.

"Grace, tell me all of it." When Darcie tried to speak up, I said, "Shut up." It came out quiet and calm. "I can't listen to any more of your self-serving bullshit."

The look on Darcie's face was one I'd never before seen—a primal terror that stripped away all vestiges of sophistication and turned her into a hunted animal.

Then Grace began to speak. "Most of the mental health institutions in this country," she began, "are linked to the public health service. Chronically underfunded and, yes, there might be the odd mistake in treatment, but those mistakes get caught by the strict oversight systems in place—there's little room for corruption."

I nodded; that was the impression I'd gained from media articles on the topic.

"But you see, Nae-nae, the rich don't like to air out their dirty laundry—especially when that dirty laundry might include children with 'defective' minds." Venom dripped from the last words and I knew she'd heard them directed at her.

"There's a small and very exclusive private hospital an hour or so out of Invercargill," she said, naming one of the southernmost parts of the country. "People in my father's circle send their kids there for discreet rehab. Drugs, alcohol, sex. The usual poor-little-rich-kid syndromes.

"But there's a high-security wing, too," she continued, "for those judged at risk of harm to themselves or to others. It's a place with cold walls, locks, heavy doors, and no way to get outside beyond two-hour walks in a fenced green space with no view and no flowers."

"No one could get away with forcing another adult into an institution." I frowned. "There are laws."

"Darcie had medical power of attorney over her sister in case she ever became incapacitated," Grace said. "Did you know that? Bea had the same over Darcie. Their lawyer suggested it since they were both adults and had only each other. It was meant to stop any red tape if one of them was ever hurt bad.

"Bea signed and promptly forgot about it—but Darcie saw it

as a weapon. Saw how she could use her influence with certain people to get rid of a sister who was so much better than her."

I trusted Dr. Cox, could really talk to him, you know?

The same Dr. Cox had walked her down the aisle in lieu of her father.

"A doctor couldn't authorize that alone," I said, working it through. "Especially if the 'patient' had the money to threaten legal trouble. Too much risk for a private institution that wants to stay private."

"Oh, dear Darceline got a nice shiny piece of paper from her pet judge, too. Confirmed that Bea was off her head, no longer able to make decisions. Darcie, as her closest relation, was appointed her 'welfare guardian.' What a joke!" Grace kicked the back of Darcie's seat again, and this time, I didn't rebuke her. "As if this piece of human garbage has ever cared for anyone's welfare but her own."

Reaching past Darcie to grab a bottle of water from the glove box, I twisted off the cap and drank down half the bottle before making myself look at this woman I thought I'd known enough to believe that she'd never harm Bea. Compete with her? Steal her lover? Sure. But to actively *hurt* her? To lock her up. No.

"Why did the judge listen to you, Darcie?" I asked in a calm tone that felt outside myself. "Please don't lie. It's too late for that. No matter what happens from this point on, I'll be alerting the authorities about Bea—and looks like I have Grace to give me all the information I need on that, so I don't even need to rely on you."

My blood was cold, my thoughts a glass lake.

51

Darcie's cheekbones pressed against her skin, blades that should cut. "Uncle Landis was a friend of my mother's."

One of her mother's old law buddies, a man Darcie really looks up to . . .

Not just an old law buddy. A judge. One whose name sounded oddly familiar. I'd probably met him at Darcie's wedding.

"He'd seen Beatrice at her worst," Darcie continued, "during an out-of-control episode that she had right before her specialist got her on the correct medication and her therapist made a breakthrough. Once Dr. Cox certified that she needed to be in care, Uncle Landis signed off on the transfer."

"He should have recused himself." The cold seeped from my blood into my skin. "Why exactly were he and Cox so firmly on your side if they saw Bea grow up, too? Why no loyalty to her?"

"I had a video," Darcie said, her eyes huge. "Bea lost it right before she went to the facility, was—"

"Bea told me about that," Grace spit out. "Said she thought you must've messed with her meds, or drugged her some other way. Your sister *remembered* you smiling as you videoed her." Tears in Grace's voice. "She cried! She loved you and you did that to her!"

It took everything I had to keep my voice calm. "That still shouldn't have been enough for a doctor and a judge. She could've been on a recreational drug trip, for one. Why no further investigation?"

Swallowing, Darcie ducked her head.

It was Grace who answered. "Darcie has a way of courting successful people who she might be able to use," she said silkily, the tears yet an echo in the thickness of her words.

I thought of Darcie's social media accounts, all the smaller profiles she was cultivating because they were linked to far more influential ones. Yes, Darcie knew how to play the long game.

"She started on the judge and the doctor when she was thirteen, fourteen," Grace added. "That's what Bea said when she learned how to cheek her pills and wasn't a zombie all the time. Darcie was always *so* interested in what those disgusting old men had to say, the perfect young acolyte."

Her lips were curved and her eyes narrowed on the back of Darcie's head when I glanced at her. "Bea never said it went further than that with the old men, but since Judge Landis Beale apparently has a thing for underage girls, I'll let you draw your ow—"

"You liar!" Darcie screamed with what energy she had. "Uncle Landis was never inappropriate with me! He just liked me better!"

Funnily enough, I believed her. Because Darcie wouldn't have sacrificed when she could manipulate. Massage an old man's ego as a pretty young woman while dropping seeds in their ear about her "unstable" sister and, when the time came, they'd do exactly as Darcie wished.

"What about the facility itself?" I asked with the same remote calm that had brought me to this moment. "Why did the doctors and therapists there not begin to question her diagnosis or her heavy drug regime?" Even Darcie couldn't manipulate that many people.

"Everyone in the insane asylum says they're sane." Grace's laugh was jagged. "Your friend and her lapdog of a doctor made sure Bea's intake forms were filled with words like 'delusional' and 'expert at masking' and 'incapable of accepting her diagnosis.'

"This wasn't a slapdash plan, Nae-nae. Darcie was meticulous, down to the extent of turning in a disturbing diary that Bea was supposed to have written. The doctors trusted the older sister who was so *worried* about Bea, and who a *judge* had granted authority over Bea."

Darcie's eyes overflowed. "I had to do it." A trembling plea. "I had to protect her the only way I could. Grace is twisting everything up. Bea was sliding downhill fast and I knew that could be dangerous. Everything I did was for her own good."

"Oh, was telling everyone she died by suicide when you *knew* she was alive for her own good? Or was it so you could fuck the man she loved?"

Grace's words were a bomb that spit out shards of frozen silence.

Plastic crackled, and I realized I was in danger of collapsing the bottle and spilling water all over myself. I shoved it into the map pocket on the inside of the door. "Darcie? What does she mean?" A brittle demand.

"I have the death certificate!" Darcie sobbed. "They told me she was dead."

"Twelve months ago," Grace said with a vicious smile. "The facility informed you of Bea's death twelve *months ago*. Before that, you paid all the fees for her prison cell out of her own fucking inheritance. Eight years. That's how long you knew Bea was alive while letting everyone else believe she was dead. *Eight. Years.*"

"I knew she wasn't going to come back." Darcie's words tumbled out one after the other in a rapid torrent—as if she could convince me if she spoke fast enough. "I knew she was too sick to ever come back. I just thought it'd be easier if—"

My hand stung from the force of the slap, Darcie's head slamming into the headrest then bouncing forward with a nasty jolt.

When she looked back at me, it was with a whimper, blood trickling out of her nose and fear a scared child in her eyes.

I should've felt bad.

I felt nothing.

The cold had gone beyond skin and blood and bone.

"You're the best actress I've ever known." I looked at her in true admiration. "I really thought you were grieving your sister the day you told us she was dead."

"I was! I knew she was too sick to ever recover!" Blotchy skin, blood trickling from her nose to her upper lip in a fine tributary. "I thought it was for the best that I left her to heal as much as she could, without any pressure—"

"Without any friends?" I wanted to hit her again, so much that I knew it was dangerous.

And right now, I wanted to know the truth more than I wanted to hurt her. But I wanted something else more. Turning to look at Bea, I said, "Grace, can you tell if Bea's still out?"

"Yes, she is," Grace said without hesitation. "I gave her a big dose. Nothing dangerous. Just meant to keep her under until I took care of her dear, loving sister."

My eyes locked with Grace's. I nodded slowly while ignoring Darcie's babbling about how Grace was a monster, how she'd just admitted to drugging people.

Shifting back to face the windscreen, I made myself clench my fists hard enough that my nails dug into my palms. Drawing my own blood instead of Darcie's as I spoke words flat and without anger. Without any emotion at all, so remote they could've come from another person altogether.

"She must've thought none of us cared." My poor Bea, who'd thrived in the sun of people's attention. "She must've believed that we'd abandoned her."

"She did." Grace's voice came out damp, whispery. "She cried in her room night after night, and all her sparkle, all that gorgeous, defiant light, it began to bleed out of her. She thought you'd all forgotten her, even you, her beloved Nae-nae."

The distance cracked, a serrated breach through which flowed agony. "Tell me she discovered the truth long before she escaped that place," I begged the swollen and reddened eyes in the rearview mirror. "Tell me she knew I didn't leave her, that none of us left her."

"Yes. Her psychotic bitch of a sister let it slip the last time she ever visited. She came to rub in the fact that she was now sleeping in Ash's bed, said that he'd leaned into her in his grief over Beatrice's suicide." Grace began to sob, a hard, wracking thing so violent that it took her three attempts to get out her next words.

Then she did, and the fractured glass fell in smithereens at my feet.

"Beatrice tried to kill herself that night."

All the pain, all the rage, all the *hate*—it rushed back into me in a punch that sparked stars behind my eyes.

When I could stomach looking at Darcie, it was to see that her expression held no outrage or anger. It exhibited only the desperation of a liar who'd been discovered.

"She trusted you." It was all I could get out, the enormity of what Darcie had done almost impossible for my mind to grasp.

"She was out of control," Darcie insisted. "She needed help. You never saw her lose it! Never saw—"

Her words were nothing but a formless buzz, my eyes attempting to make sense of this snake in human skin. Because even if I believed *every* word she'd spoken about Bea's mental health, none of it mattered. She'd lied about Bea's suicide, made us believe our beautiful Bea was gone when she'd been trapped and wounded and slowly dying.

Darcie had locked her sister up in a place far from all her family and friends . . . and then she'd twisted the knife into Bea by crowing over her "win." She'd broken my unbreakable Bee-bee.

"Please." Darcie's breath hitched, that more than her speech catching my attention. "My head feels faint. I'm losing too much blood."

I looked at her abdomen, realized I could no longer see any of the white towel.

I didn't care.

That was when Grace spoke. "No one will ever know." A murmur rough with the remnants of her grief for Bea. "If you let her bleed out. If you let her die like she tried to let Bea die. I'll never tell. Even if I lose my mind and spill my guts one day, I am certifiably mentally disturbed. No one will believe me."

She was right. In all of it.

I wondered what she'd done to end up in that facility with Beatrice, and found my mind filling with fragments of Kaea's report on the break-in.

Disturbing and ugly, unhinged.

Obsessed.

Stalker.

"Did you kill Dr. Cox?" I asked, my mind calm enough now to put together the pieces.

"Sure. Bastard deserved it." Grace shrugged. "I suffocated him after meeting him on a cliff where he thought he was going to get a blow job. Wasn't hard to dump him onto the rocks after that. Slight downhill slope. Release the parking brake. Easy.

"Getting those dark-web files onto Landis's computer, on the other hand, was a pain in the ass—I had to fuck him three times before he got a little too 'drunk' and I had hours of access—but I'm sure he'll be getting fucked in more ways than one in the prison to which he's headed."

"How did you know what to do? How to access the files and bury them in his computer?"

"No one ever said I wasn't smart. Just crazy." Grace's smile in the rearview mirror was sinister in its amusement. "I decided on my plan two years ago, the day I got out of the facility. That's a long time to learn how to do something. The trick is to *commit*."

Yes, I could understand why a person like Grace had ended up in the institution. Perhaps she'd stalked someone, or taken revenge on another person for either herself or someone else. But none of that changed anything she'd told me . . . or what she'd just suggested.

"No one will ever know," Grace murmured again. "If you turn

her in, she *will* get out one day. She'll breathe the free air she stole from Bea for *years*, and she'll live in the house that she stole from Bea, with the man she stole from Bea. All their inheritance, every cent of it, is in Darcie's fucking name. Helpful Uncle Landis again."

Darcie began to speak, sobbing, begging, but I couldn't hear her. All I could hear were Bea's sobs as she lay lost and alone. All I could see was the agony in her eyes as she decided to take the only way out open to her. "Did she try to hang herself?"

I felt no surprise when Grace shook her head. "She had a stockpile of drugs, took them all. She was almost gone by the time they found her."

My sweet Bee-bee.

Maybe she hadn't been as strong as she should've been, but not everyone was strong. As not everyone could bring light into the room with a smile. That had been Bea's gift. Kindness. Warmth. Joy.

For strength, she'd had me.

And then, she'd had Grace. "You kept her alive." I knew that because Bea *was* alive; she wouldn't have made it on her own. "Thank you."

"She's so . . . bright. Like sunshine." Grace's words glowed with devotion. "I couldn't let her light go out. I tried to inspire her by saying we'd get revenge, but Bea was so broken that it didn't matter to her. She's not like me—she's not driven by anger. Instead I made her think I'd die if she wasn't there with me. So she stayed. Not for herself. For me."

Yes, that sounded like Bea. Dazzling and a bit of a wild child with a penchant for petty thievery—and loyal. A friend who'd never let go if she thought you needed her.

"Even after I got out," Grace continued, "I kept it up, told her that if I didn't have the goal of getting her out of that place, I'd end myself. I know it was manipulative, but it was the only thing that worked. I smuggled a phone to her so I could stay in constant touch, make sure she never forgot."

"You did the right thing. You kept Bea alive."

Putting my hands on the steering wheel, I stared through the silver sheet of rain to the lights of the settlement a short distance away. So easy it'd be to say that we'd started out later than we had, or that we'd become scared at the bridge, hesitated too long. So long that Darcie hadn't made it.

No one would ever know.

52

Clara

Today is a good day. We are all to have tea in my salon. My haven of beauty and tranquility in this house full of secrets and loneliness. My children's laughter will fill the air, and perhaps even my husband will attend.

He was . . . more himself this morning when I asked him. More the Blake I married. Stern but kind. I know it will pass all too soon, but for today, he is that man and I hope he does join us. It will do good for the children to spend time with their father as he once was.

And Lizzie . . . Lizzie smiled with such innocent joy when I mentioned it. She did not argue against having to spend time with her siblings, even said that she'd been waiting for just this kind of an opportunity when all her siblings were together. She wishes to give them a surprise gift.

I am hopeful that my eldest has turned the corner, leaving behind the jealousies and anger of the past. That she has prepared a gift for the little ones, it fills my heart.

Oh, how I look forward to this afternoon when my entire family will be gathered in the sun.

53

It was surreal to think that twenty-four hours ago, I was stuck in a house on the edge of nowhere, my friends dying around me. Today, I sat in the searing whiteness of a hospital room, dozing fitfully in a leather armchair a nurse had draped with a soft sheet so that the cracked leather on the arm wouldn't catch at my skin.

When I woke with a jolt a few minutes after midnight, I saw that Kaea's breathing was even, his stats stable. The same nurse had taught me how to read those stats after I kept asking her about them, and I'd memorized the ranges she'd told me were good.

But Kaea wouldn't come out of this undamaged.

Grace refused to tell the doctors the exact drugs with which she'd dosed him, but whatever it was had done internal damage that might equal the need for a transplant down the line.

Per Grace, it was punishment for turning Bea down when she'd been sixteen.

I'd known Bea'd had a crush on him for about five seconds, also knew it had passed as quickly. Bea, I understood, would've shared the story with Grace as a humorous anecdote of childhood drama, a funny snippet of life to make them both laugh in that dark place where they'd been imprisoned.

It was Grace who'd decided that Kaea's gentle rejection—because Kaea wasn't cruel, *would* have let Bea down with tenderness—was a crime that deserved the death penalty . . . after plenty of suffering. I had the feeling his mind and legal training had counted against him, too. That ability to unmask liars, expose twisted truths—and zero in on unstable points in an opponent's psyche.

Grace, however, was far beyond simply unstable. Her name wasn't even Grace and she wasn't adopted, much less from Romania; she hadn't tried to keep up the lies now that she'd achieved her aim of exposing Darcie.

Rubbing my face with one hand, I decided to check in on the others. The hospital staff had been very kind, allowing me to stay in the rooms long past visiting hours. News of what had gone on in the house had spread through those caring for my friends, and the hospital had even sent a psychologist to talk to me.

He'd strongly recommended I "undertake a regime of therapy" after my return to London, "with the aim of staving off long-term PTSD."

I wanted to laugh.

I wondered what Dr. Mehta would say if I walked in and told her that I now had even worse problems than before my relaxing little vacation. Not that she'd be seeing me. I wasn't going back to London.

How could I when Bea was here?

After making sure Kaea's blanket was tucked in around him, I shoved up the sleeves of my oversize gray hoodie as I padded over to the next room. My sneakers were soundless on the hospital floor. The shoes and clothes were both courtesy of Detective Stu Ratene. He'd taken my own gear in as evidence even though I had little blood on me.

Procedure.

Though my eyes were tired this late into the night on such a limited amount of sleep, I could see fine; it was never fully dark in a hospital, not even at the darkest hour of night.

Too many machines with blinking lights, too much need for nurses and doctors to be able to rush into a room in an emergency without having to fumble to find their way. What existed in the hallways was a light bright enough to hurt, while within the rooms hovered a dark gray twilight somber and restful.

Despite the wires and the machines and the drugs, Ash was awake and staring out the window at the dark beyond. Tiny squares of light patterned his face, thrown from the windows of a neighboring high-rise. "Luna," he said when I walked in.

His face was sallow and thin, his eyes hollow.

As of my last conversation with the staff, Ash remained listed as critical. His family was out of the country, would land in New Zealand in the early morning hours. Until then, they'd given the hospital permission to share information with me.

"You saved his life," his mother had sobbed on the phone. "Please take care of him a little longer."

I almost hadn't been in time to save Ash at all; the kitchen knife his attacker had used when she'd lured him into the ruined part of the house with a cry for help had nicked a vital organ. He'd been bleeding out into his abdomen.

Ironically enough, it was the cold in the house that had saved him.

"How are you awake?" I came to stand beside his bed, my arms crossed. "You're meant to be under heavy sedation post-surgery."

"I have an irregular reaction to anesthetic—always wake up too fast." His words were a monotone. "Can't feel my stomach, though. No idea why. In fact, no idea why I'm in a hospital."

Had this been Kaea, I'd have touched him multiple times by now, but with Ash . . . I didn't blame him for falling for Darcie's strategy to oust her sister, and yet I did. "How are you feeling overall?"

His chest rose and fell as he turned his head toward me. "I dreamed that I was being held by a crying angel. I could smell blood, but I wasn't afraid. Funny, huh?"

A crying angel.

"About that . . ." I grabbed a lightweight plastic chair from the corner and moved it close to his bed. After taking a seat, I told him what I thought he could handle in his current state—and that didn't include information about Bea's return from the dead. Mostly, I focused on Grace's desire to get vengeance for her friend.

Not even a drop of surprise on his face.

So, Grace had been telling the truth. "It was you that put Creepy Bea in Darcie's daypack."

"Yes." He stared up at the ceiling. "Darcie freaked out after the doll appeared on our bed that first time. Total breakdown. All her filters gone. She said that no one should have had the doll, that the facility had disposed of all of Bea's belongings after she died."

His mouth twisted. "When I asked her what facility, she got this deer-in-the-headlights look that isn't in any way usual for my wife, and then she told me that Bea checked herself into a mental health facility before her suicide. She said Bea hadn't wanted any of us to know."

His hand flexed flat against the blue hospital sheet. "I knew at that instant that she was lying. Bea was a people person. She hated being alone. You know that. You spent hours with her just hanging out—I used to be jealous until I realized how much she needed *her* people around her, and that if I tried to take that away, I'd make her sad. So I never tried. I loved her enough to never try. Our Bea would've wanted visitors, an endless stream of them."

So Ash had decided to terrorize his wife. I couldn't judge him for that.

"I guess Grace must've taken the doll," he said. "Or Bea gave it to her. Place like that, they must've become incredibly close even after only a few months together."

That was when I realized that, distraught or not, Darcie had managed to hide *when* she'd thought Bea had died. She'd stuck to the original story, with Bea dead only months after her disappearance.

"I should've tried harder to find her." Ash's calm tore apart in front of me, his features twisting into a rictus. "I looked so *hard*, but I had no idea where she might've gone. I asked Darcie for help."

That flexed hand fisted to bloodless white. "She pretended to help me. Can you believe that? That bitch pretended to help me look for the woman I loved more than anyone in the world when she was the reason we lost her in the first place.

"I hate myself for ever letting her touch me, for betraying Bea by loving Darcie even as much as I did. I thought we were united by the same pain, but the whole time, she was crowing over what she'd done to my beautiful Beatrice. I'll rip her online persona apart, destroy that precious reputation of hers, then take everything in the divorce. Just watch me."

I touched him then, closing my hand over his fist.

He slipped into sleep with shocking suddenness, his injured body unable to maintain consciousness. I wondered if he'd even remember this conversation when he woke. I wasn't sure. But I knew that the Ash who had left for the vacation wasn't the Ash who'd come back.

Nothing would ever be the same again.

"Lu?"

I looked up to see Aaron in the doorway. A small white bandage marked the spot where I'd scraped his cheek against the door while hauling him to safety.

Angling my head, I invited him in. Ash wouldn't wake now, his breathing so deep and even that I knew it was unnatural, a result of the drugs in his system.

Aaron dipped out for a second to quietly borrow a chair from another room, put it down beside mine. Then he sat hunched over with his hands between his knees, staring down at the ground. I stroked his back, my heart breaking for him. Of all of us, it was Aaron who had the best heart, was a person who was just quintessentially *good*.

That was what had drawn Grace to him.

"I fell in love with him through Bea's descriptions of him," she'd told me the last time we'd spoken. "She always said he was the caretaker of the group, the one ready with a warm hug and a cookie if anyone was feeling down. No one's ever taken care of me that way before."

The doctors had worried that he had hypothermia, but it

turned out Grace had only given him a mild dose. He'd swum to consciousness an hour before the firemen who were the closest first responders finally got through to the estate; he'd figured out where he was and—after making sure Ash was as comfortable as was possible—had stumbled into the bloodbath of the living room.

It was Aaron who'd found my note.

His body quivered under my touch. "I'm sorry, Aaron."

He tried to breathe. It caught, broke. "I still love her. I'll always love her." Red blood vessels snaked through the whites of his eyes when he looked at me. "She's not . . . There's something fundamentally wrong with her brain, Lu. But she's loyal and she's loving and she can be so fiercely protective."

I had no argument with any of that. Grace had done what she had *because* she loved with obsessive, protective loyalty. "Did she tell you why she ended up in the institution in the first place?"

I'd shared everything I could with him the first instant I saw him. Uninjured as I'd been, I'd ridden back to the estate with the fire crew. There had been only one available fire truck. It had carried on to the estate, while Jim and a member of the fire crew trained in first aid took charge of the Land Cruiser and raced out to meet the ambulances that had been dispatched from the closest medical facility.

In a place that isolated, everyone pitched in, and decisions about limited resources had to be made on the fly.

The rescuers going to the estate hadn't wanted me with them until I'd pointed out that the house was a maze; the chances of them managing to locate Ash and Aaron, even with instructions, were dangerously low.

I'd also warned them about the bridge, but following an

examination using high strength flashlights, they'd made the call to go through.

Afterward, Aaron had ridden out with me in the fire truck—the fire crew had made the decision to load all remaining survivors into their appliance and power through the weather toward the one ambulance still heading in our direction. Vansi's breathing had been even, her pulse fine, but Ash and Kaea . . .

"Ambulance won't make it in time," had been the fire chief's grim determination. "Roads are still dangerous and the air ambulance remains grounded."

Aaron had listened to my words in unmoving silence, a shell-shocked frontline veteran of a war he hadn't even known was occurring. Now, I waited for him to tell me why Grace had ended up in the facility.

"Psychopathic personality traits," he said at last. "I looked it up, but the stuff I read doesn't fit her. It's all about cruelty and a lack of empathy. You've seen Grace. She has so much empathy.

"I think the shrinks just wanted a label to put on her. Something for her father to justify locking her up in that place. She'd still be there if he hadn't died, and her half brothers decided they didn't want to be on the hook for the fees to keep her locked up. They signed her out on the agreement she wouldn't contest the will—she's taken care of herself since."

Her father still being alive was another thing Grace had lied about. As for how she'd funded her life outside the facility without access to familial money, I had a feeling that a woman who could hack into a judge's computer with such stealth wouldn't have found it difficult to access money.

As for the rest . . . I wasn't so sure I agreed with Aaron. Because the Grace who loved Bea enough to avenge her was the same Grace who had pushed Phoenix down the stairs. The odd thing was that while she'd accepted the blame for Kaea's poisoning, and the stabbing of Darcie and Ash, she wouldn't admit to that push.

"He fell" was all she'd say when I'd asked. "You saw that rug. So easy to get tangled up in it."

Grace had stonewalled the police in the same way; oh, in between sleeps to heal from the wound Darcie had inflicted, she was talking plenty, giving the cops more than enough to get her committed to another facility for life. Except when it came to Nix.

And it wasn't like she was attempting to blame Bea, either. No, Grace had been clear that the revenge plot had been all her. "No one pushed Nix," I'd heard her say to the detective in charge of the case. "It was a terrible accident. He wasn't on the list of people I planned to hurt."

The question of why Phoenix had to die haunted me. Not just for myself but for Vansi, who was in a sedated sleep on a different ward. She'd snapped after learning what had taken place, begun screaming and screaming and screaming.

I wasn't sure if my friend as I'd known her would ever come back.

Meanwhile, the storm broken, the police were currently processing the estate.

It was an unmarked gray hearse that had driven Phoenix's body away from the cellar where he'd lain so cold and alone. But his peace wasn't to last. Soon, they'd cut him up in a search for the truth.

54

Did Grace say anything about Phoenix?"

I knew it was the wrong subject to bring up as soon as the words left my mouth.

Aaron's back went stiff, his spine rigid. "She didn't hurt Nix."

I knew he was wrong. The same way I knew that Aaron loved Grace as much today as he had yesterday. "I'm sorry, Aaron," I said again, because he was innocent in all this; all he'd done was fall in love with a woman who was funny and sweet and kind.

He didn't say anything else for a long time, but he stayed with me, the hushed sounds of the hospital at night and Ash's deep breathing our accompaniment.

"Vansi?" he said at last.

I shook my head. The doctors said my best friend had no severe traumatic injuries, but I knew the ones to her mind and heart might yet end her.

"I'm glad she didn't wake up in the living room," Aaron said softly. "The blood . . ." He rubbed both hands over his hair, dropped them in between his knees again, his forearms braced on his thighs. "I thought I was still asleep, caught in a nightmare. If I hadn't felt the crumple of paper when I tried to shake V awake and seen your note . . ."

"I should've left another one in an obvious spot." It infuriated me that I hadn't even considered that Aaron might be the one who woke first. Because I hadn't realized that, in her own warped way, Grace loved him. She'd never planned to cause him permanent harm.

"Not your fault, Lu." A sob he caught and held in his chest. "I have no idea how you did what you did, got to Jim's. And Bea . . . I went and prayed with her." He squeezed his eyes shut. "She was just like she always was when I wanted to do that—I know she doesn't believe, but she smiled and thanked me for thinking to do that for her."

"Because she knows you do it out of love."

We sat in another long spell of a silence filled with the questions I could never ask him—nor he ask me. The boundaries had been laid down, our friendship now bordered by fences that couldn't be scaled.

"I'm going to go back to sit with Grace," he said at last, rising from his seat. "The cops have been good about that."

I stood with him. "I'm glad." Though it wasn't too much of a surprise since, prior to answering the cops' questions, Grace had made the request for me and Aaron to be allowed to see her.

And, it wasn't as if she was a physical threat anymore. Not only was she injured, she was handcuffed to one rail of the bed, with an officer *inside* the room with her at all times. She was also her normal, bubbly self—so much so that it was an indictment on the state of her sanity.

I stumbled a little as we walked out from the nocturnal dimness of Ash's room and into the brightly lit corridor.

Aaron's fingers around my biceps. "Whoa," he said. "You're tired. Rest."

"I can't sleep." So much easier to blame tiredness for the stumble and not my eyes struggling to adjust to the rapid change in lighting. "I'll collapse at some point, but until then I can keep the others company. Ash was awake for a couple of moments just before—not sure if he'll even remember talking to me, but he was lucid at the time."

Aaron's face morphed, a roller coaster of emotion after emotion. "He's going to be devastated. I can't believe—" He pressed one hand against the wall, his fingers curling into a fist. "The way Darcie *cried* that day she told us that Beatrice had committed suicide."

"You know, there's one thing Darcie said to me that I don't think was a lie—how, that night, she *was* saying goodbye to her sister. Because Darcie never planned to set Bea free."

Aaron slumped against the wall. "She couldn't have kept her locked up forever."

"No. I don't think she ever expected Bea to survive."

My friend stared at me, his throat moving convulsively. "Grace saved Bea."

"Yes," I said, then hugged him.

He hugged me back as hard, before breaking off to lope to Grace's room, his long legs eating up the hallway. I didn't follow, instead taking a seat on one of the hard plastic chairs bolted to the wall. Detective Stu Ratene came out of Grace's room as Aaron went in, the two exchanging glances but no words.

Spotting me farther down the corridor, he walked over.

I raised my eyebrows. "You're working late."

He gave me a one-sided smile, his face that of a boxer who'd taken a few too many hits, his skin pockmarked by youthful acne, and his body a wall of muscle on a tall frame.

Man oozed sex appeal of the rough-and-tough kind.

"This case is so twisted, I can't even think about sleep," he muttered, before walking over to the nearby coffee machine. "You want?" He dug out his wallet. "It's not bad for machine coffee. Less like barely flavored water than usual."

I went to say no, but realized I was cold on the inside. "Hot chocolate if the machine has it."

"Coming right up."

He waited until both drinks were ready, then carried over the disposable white cups. "Here you go, milady." As he sank down into the seat next to me with a groan, his blazer opening around him and his thighs pushing up against his jeans, I saw one of the night-shift nurses shoot him a "come ask for my number" smile.

His returning smile reminded me of Kaea. Not because they looked in any way similar. No, it was that charm. Paired with a wickedness that was playful rather than cruel. Kaea had never been cruel and I knew with certainty that Bea had long ago forgiven any teenage grudge she'd held against him.

Grace, however, saw only in black and white.

A loyal friend who would do anything for you. But who had no concept of degrees when it came to what she considered a crime.

I cupped my hands around the warmth of the hot chocolate, the steam bathing my face.

Leaning against the chairback and kicking out his feet, Ratene said, "You mind if I ask you a few more questions?"

"Ask as many as you want. I want the truth of what Darcie did to Bea on the record."

"The woman you know as Grace," he said, "she say anything to you about Judge Landis Beale?"

I'd had time, had thought this through. "No. Who is she?"

"He," Ratene corrected. "He's the judge who signed the papers that gave Darcie guardianship over her sister."

"You've already tracked down the records?"

"It wasn't hard with the details Grace gave us." His eyes narrowed, and suddenly he wasn't the good-looking man the others in the vicinity were fawning over—he was a hard-eyed cop. "Legal sleight of hand to strip a woman of her life."

"Grace didn't mention him. But I think *Darcie* maybe mentioned an Uncle Beale once." I frowned. "At her wedding possibly." My words were insurance against being found on the same guest list; it was unlikely Ratene would make anything of that, but I didn't want him to have even a tiny reason to question my veracity when it came to what I knew about the judge. "I didn't pay too much attention—it was a chance to catch up with my friends, and we mostly hung out together."

"The judge was a friend of the Shepherd family," Ratene confirmed. "My sources tell me he's now gotten wind of Grace's arrest and he's saying she targeted him, that she's the one who loaded up his computer with hundreds of frankly sick and *very* illegal images."

I snorted. "Sounds like he's clutching at straws. Grace is smart, don't get me wrong, but she'd have to be a hacker genius to get into a judge's computer."

The trick is to commit.

Ratene's eyes bored into the side of my skull, but I'd prepared for this. The tiredness helped. I just zoned out, my expression a blank stare at the facing wall.

"He probably is," he said at last. "Technical experts say his digital fingerprints are all over the laptop. Plus, he has no photos or other evidence to prove he ever met Grace. Texts and calls went to a prepaid phone that's now dead, and the number is listed in his phone directory as 'Bianca.'"

Clever, clever Grace.

"His defense can still try to bring Grace up at trial, but prosecutor says the fact she's so unstable will make that a useless argument. Plus, he'd just be calling attention to his lack of ethics in not recusing himself from the application to do with Beatrice Shepherd."

Not a good look if Judge Landis Beale wanted the jury to see him as an upstanding citizen who'd never think of looking at such vile material as had been found on his computer.

"What does Grace say?" Because she would've said *something*; she was too clever to simply deny that Beale had been on her hit list.

"Says she planned to poison him, but couldn't figure out how to get close enough to do it. Then she heard about his arrest and decided to leave him to fester in the mess he created for himself. No need to murder him when he'll get brutalized in jail."

I smiled within.

"What about Dr. Cox?" Ratene continued. "She mention him?"

I nodded. "She murdered him. Promised him a blow job, but suffocated him and sent his car off a cliff."

"You don't sound disturbed by that."

"I feel numb. Doctors say I'm suffering from shock. If I am, I don't want out of it."

Ratene was quiet for a beat. "Yeah, I can't blame you on that, Luna." Several beats later. "There was money involved with the doctor, by the way. Shouldn't be telling you, but what the hell. Darceline Shepherd gave Cox an extremely generous gift eighteen months after Beatrice was committed."

"Patience."

"Yes. But for Cox to wait that long, it wasn't only about the money."

No, it had been about Darcie's ability to manipulate and mold people into doing exactly as she wished. "It can't just have been the judge and the doctor involved," I said. "Surely others must've questioned why Beatrice was in the facility?"

"We've just begun digging there." He shot me an assessing look, then gave a short nod, as if coming to a decision. "Did you have any idea they stood to inherit two million dollars each when they turned twenty-five?"

My mouth fell open.

"That's what I thought." He finished off his coffee with a grimace.

"Where did that money come from?" The Shepherds hadn't been poor in the least, but they hadn't had millions lying around, either. At least that explained how Darcie had been able to easily pay the private hospital fees year after year.

"Life insurance," Ratene said. "Parents' wills were structured in a way that meant that should a payout ever occur, it'd go into a trust until Darceline and Beatrice were of a certain age. To be released early only if the rest of the estate wasn't enough to support their daughters."

"Beatrice didn't know." It was a certainty inside me. "She was still in high school when they died. A minor. Darcie handled all the paperwork."

Crunching his empty cup in one hand, he threw it at a nearby trash can with pinpoint accuracy. "Knowing about the money, you still think this is about Ash Wakefield?"

I sipped the last bit of my sugary drink. "Yes. But only because he was Bea's, not because he was Ash. Do you see?"

A slow nod. "They always compete?"

"No. That was the problem. Bea just shone brighter—she never had to compete, didn't even understand that Darcie saw her as a threat."

"Ah."

I handed him my cup. "Can you make it two for two?"

He winked, lined up the shot and—"Boom." Rising in the aftermath, he held my gaze with his own. "Being numb might feel good now, but don't allow it to consume you. Numbness leads to a kind of quiet death."

Poor Ratene.

He'd believed me.

Truth was, I wasn't in shock.

I was at peace.

55

After Ratene left, I considered whether to go lie down in the spare bed the nurses had found for me. My other options were to doze in the armchair in Kaea's room, or the one in Bea's.

Then Aaron exited Grace's room.

Back to me as he headed in the direction of the toilets meant for visitors, he didn't see me. The police officer on duty inside Grace's room came out at the same moment, stretching his stiff shoulders as he ambled to the coffee machine.

I got to my feet. "Is it okay if I go in to see her?" My heart thudded, my mouth dry.

"She's asleep, so it should be okay." His face was round, his smile kind. "And I checked the handcuff before I left. Any issues, just holler. I'm not going any farther than this machine and a cup of joe while I stretch out my legs."

"Thanks." I closed the distance to Grace's room before he could change his mind. "Grace," I hissed the instant I entered. *"Grace."*

She startled awake, her eyelashes flickering and her eyes dazed. "Nae-nae," she said sleepily several seconds later, a soft smile on her face. "Can I call you that even though it's only for you and Beatrice? She gave me permission, but I want yours, too."

I nodded, because even though she was a very dangerous individual, one with a gift for murderous obsession, she'd also been there for Bea at the most awful time in Bea's life. Grace was also the only reason we knew the horror of what Darcie had done; I could never dislike her.

I told her that point-blank. "I'll consider you a friend for the rest of my life."

Big green eyes searching my face. "Even after what I've done?"

"I've always loved Bea best." Quiet words. "More than I've ever loved anyone else."

A smile that lit up her face. "I wouldn't have hurt you. Just like I wouldn't have hurt my Aaron. If it had gone according to plan, I'd have taken care of Darcie, then run up to find you both. I would've kept you warm, safe."

Brushing back the soft silk of her curls, I nodded. "I know." I also knew she'd planned to pin the blame for everything on Darcie, and that if her plan had failed, with her unable to best Darcie, Aaron and I would've frozen to death.

"But, Gracie?" Taking the hand that wasn't locked to the rail, I wound my fingers through hers. "I need to know about Nix for my own peace of mind. It'll haunt me forever otherwise."

Grace went motionless, her gaze swimming around the room. "No one is here and I'm not wired."

Grace held my gaze, then moved her mouth . . . but made no sound. I missed the words she shaped the first time around, had to bend down with my ear right by her lips so she could whisper them to me. I had no fear that she'd bite or otherwise attack me. Grace and I, we had a bond unbreakable.

"He remembered me from a time when I wasn't Grace."

"When did you meet?"

"Before the institution. Before I knew Bea. In Zurich. Just one night at a party thrown by the son of a family friend. He met them on a hike. So long ago. I forgot all about it, about them."

But Phoenix never forgot anyone. Even if it took him time to place the recollection, he always did in the end.

I'd teased him about it being Zurich. Had I jogged his memory without realizing it?

My heart hitched.

"Make sure Bea knows I did everything." Another whisper, Grace's gaze boring into me. *"It's all on me."*

Nodding slowly, I touched her curls once again. "You're a good friend, Grace."

The sound of a nearing footstep.

I rose just as the cop walked in, coffee in hand.

When I looked from him to Grace, she'd closed her eyes. Pretending to sleep. This conversation was over. Never mind. We'd talk again. I'd visit her in the next place where they locked her up.

I slipped out with a smile for the officer, then grabbed my outdoor jacket from Kaea's room before heading off the ward and down the hall to the section that held patients considered stable, in only for observation.

How ironic that Grace's intricate plan had begun to fall apart due to a chance encounter. Every other thing, she'd planned. Including her choice of target to gain entry into our friend group.

That she loved Aaron, I didn't question. He was eminently

lovable. But he was also the most vulnerable to a beautiful, sweet woman who wanted all the same things he did—which she knew, because Bea had known. Bea who, in her prison, had shared everything with the only person she felt she could trust there.

Including the details of a grand old house with secret passages, complete with a map drawn with crayon during an "art therapy" session that showed Grace the locations of those passages—and where Bea had hidden her keys.

Grace had never counted on Bea being physically present when she set her plan in motion.

"It was just icing on the cake when Aaron told me about the suggestion we go there," she'd shared with me in the Land Cruiser. "I had plans for Darcie in the city, but it was so much better out on the estate. I could make her so much more *afraid*. I looked up the weather on our way to the estate, prepared to make use of it, but I had contingency plans in case the storm never landed."

Darcie and Ash had been her two main targets.

Kaea's injury and later suffering had been enough to satisfy her for the time being, though she'd planned to kill him at some point in the future, but the rest of us would've been safe enough unless we got caught in the cross fire.

Phoenix had been collateral damage.

I struggled with myself. Nix had been an innocent victim, as was Vansi, my friend a broken shell that might never be repaired. *That*, I finally understood, was why Grace refused to confess to Nix's murder. And why she was willing to confess to everything else, be committed for her crimes.

Penance.

Because some part of her had the capacity to feel shame.

My chest tightened.

I felt shame, too, but not for what I'd done. For being willing to forgive Grace for the choices she'd made. Because without Grace, we'd have soon been commiserating with Darcie on her miscarriage, and hoping for the best for her—for a life that she'd gained on the back of her sister's corpse.

As I walked along the wide corridor between wards, I saw nothing of the cold hospital tile, heard none of the medical chatter. My mind was back in the Land Cruiser, the rain slamming onto the metal and glass and Darcie bleeding out in front of me.

"No one will ever know."

"She's pregnant," I'd said, accepting in that moment that I'd have let Darcie die had she not been responsible for the embryo within.

Grace's laughter, so amused. "Oh, Luna—I can't believe you fell for that. She's a *liar*. Her and Ash were having trouble before a sudden birth control failure and pregnancy, weren't you, Darcie?"

"I wouldn't lie about that."

"So you mean that wasn't your husband who walked into a divorce lawyer's office three months ago? Couple of weeks before you 'discovered' your pregnancy?"

Darcie's face draining of what little color it had retained, her eyes round orbs and her voice mute.

"Yes, I watched you," Grace had whispered with cheerful glee. "I watched all of you. So I know you haven't been to the doctor once in the past two months. Surely, a woman in the first trimester of pregnancy should be under the care of a physician? I think I'll send Ash an anonymous text telling him to take you to the doctor for a blood test."

Desperation in Darcie's gaze. "Please, Luna, don't let her tell him. I just need a bit more time. I'll get pregnant. We'll have a baby and it'll make us like we were before. We'll be happy again—and you can be an honorary aunt like we always said."

I'd just stared at her, wondering if she'd taken another hit to the head. "Even if you confess, even if they put you in prison," I'd said when she went silent at last, "it won't be for long. Nowhere near enough for what you did to Bea . . . and what you did to the rest of us."

We would've been better people with Bea in our lives. I wouldn't be this broken, hollow being who didn't understand her place in the world. Bea had been my sun, had fed energy into me simply by existing. It was all I had ever wanted from her. Just that she exist.

When I'd thought her dead, I'd begun to wither on the vine.

"She was the only person I've ever fallen in love with," I'd said gently to Darcie. "You murdered me when you took her from me."

"She was unstable. She tried to kill hersel—"

"Stop, Darcie. You knew *exactly* what you were doing when you had her locked up. You knew that she'd never make it."

And then I'd done . . . nothing.

Four of us in that Land Cruiser as the rain beat down and Darcie bled. I'd asked her about Professor Hammett with a kind of distant curiosity. "Kaea said you lied to us and it had to do with the professor."

Faint with lack of blood and eager to please me, earn my forgiveness, she'd told me. So tawdry. A failing grade turned into a high pass after she caught him kissing his boyfriend. Two quiet men. Happy to be together. Except one of them was married. The lie Darcie's joyous celebration of how she'd aced the class.

I'd wondered how Kaea had found out, hadn't cared enough to dig any deeper. I'd just listened to the rain as Darcie's pleas faded off into a whispering silence.

No one will ever know.

Only Grace.

And Grace would never tell. Because Grace knew how to be loyal. Yet Grace had also killed an innocent.

But . . . her life was done; she'd spend the rest of it behind locked doors, no threat to anyone else.

No one will ever know.

Grace wasn't the most reliable keeper of secrets. But even if she told, even if anyone believed her, there was no way to prove that I'd taken my time getting to Jim's. No way to prove that Darcie had begged until her voice failed.

No way to show that I'd watched her die.

I'd wondered if I'd be haunted by her slow death, but that wasn't what haunted me. No, it was the thought of Bea curled up in an institutional bed crying because she thought we'd all abandoned her.

For Darcie . . . I felt no guilt at all.

Did that make me a psychopath, too?

56

Unconcerned by the idea that I might not be as sane as I believed myself to be, I pushed through the ward doors. It was far quieter here, and most people were in shared rooms with only curtains around their cubicles. No need for an excess number of nurses and orderlies when the vast majority of these patients didn't require much beyond a regular check to ensure they remained stable.

Many would be discharged tomorrow.

Bea, however, had a room of her own. Must've been Ratene's doing. So he could have a private space in which to talk to her. As it was, he hadn't gotten his wish, with the doctors pronouncing her too drugged when she'd arrived—and then, he'd been busy with the scene at the estate. Later, it was Grace along with me who'd commanded his time.

"I haven't, but that's fine," Ratene had said during one of our talks, when I'd asked him if he'd managed to speak with Bea yet.

"Grace has admitted she kept Beatrice drugged the entire time Grace was at the estate, because Beatrice never agreed with her plans of revenge.

"I mostly need to talk to her about her unwilling detention at the facility, start the ball rolling on that investigation. But it's not like I don't have enough to do with business at the estate. The facility can wait."

Bea was a victim.

As such, there was no cop outside her room.

I pushed inside the small space to find her bedside lamp on as she lay in bed with her eyes wide open. "Nae-nae. I was waiting for you." She patted the sheet.

Toeing off my new sneakers, I managed to fit myself on the hospital bed, the two of us lying face-to-face, our breaths intermingling. She didn't stop me when I touched my fingers to her cheek, reassuring myself that she was warm, that her blood flowed in her veins. "You're alive."

A smile that wasn't quite right. "I'm not the same. I couldn't always avoid the drugs there—and they didn't give me the right ones until Grace got out and hacked the system, changing my assigned meds."

The trick is to commit.

A year into her freedom and Grace had managed to create fraudulent paperwork good enough to convince Darcie that Bea really was dead. She'd gone to the extent of making a phone notification, the number spoofed to make it appear it came from the facility, and she'd sent invoices for a casket and a cremation.

Later she'd sent that official-looking death certificate.

Darcie *had* been horrified to see Bea standing there, alive and well. That part, at least, hadn't been an act.

Darcie's belief in Bea's death—and the resulting destruction of Bea's property on Darcie's command—was also why Grace had stolen her phone. So that Darcie couldn't even attempt to call the facility's unlisted number, a number saved on her phone alone; she'd certainly never shared it with Ash.

"Grace," I said to Bea, "told me you asked to stay inside when she could've got you out six months ago." After making Darcie believe Bea was dead, Grace had taken over the fee payments and all communications with the facility—in Darcie's name. However, even with all the skills she'd learned, it had taken her several more months to arrange for Bea's release. Only for Bea to ask her to wait even longer.

"I wrote the release paperwork on the judge's stationery," Grace had said with a grin back in the car. "Same man who put her in now ordering that fucking prison to let her go. Seemed poetic."

"My new regimen of drugs was working," Bea whispered in the soft, almost dreamy light of her lamp. "But I wasn't me yet. I had to wait." She was the one who stroked my face now, the bandage around her right palm a searing white. "I'm still not me, Nae-nae. I don't know if I ever will be again."

"You're alive. You breathe. That's all I ever wanted." My own breath caught. "Forgive me for not finding you."

"How could you?" She touched her forehead to mine. "You trusted Darcie. So did I. I have no memory of being admitted to the facility—I went to sleep one night, and I woke up there. I don't blame myself or you. Only Darcie."

I stroked her wrist. "Let's go for a walk." I didn't think this room was being monitored, but we couldn't take the risk.

Bea's eyes held a thousand secrets as she rose. Her hospital gown was loose, the slippers into which she slid her feet institutional. The police had taken the dress in which she'd come into the ER, and all her other stuff was at the estate.

"I'll buy you some clothes," I said as we padded out of the room. "Your favorite pink jeans and a sparkly unicorn T-shirt."

Sudden laughter before she tucked her arm through mine. "I'll have you know that was ironic high fashion at fourteen."

We didn't speak again until we were outside the ward, in the wide-open corridor with no one else around. As if even the staff had gone to sleep. A false silence, but in this moment, we walked alone. "Grace said it's been a month since she got you discharged." Me and Grace, we'd had time to speak in the Land Cruiser.

Bea nodded, her slippers making *hush hush* sounds on the hospital tile. "She picked me up, took me to the estate. Already had clothes and other supplies, even my favorite perfume. I wanted to get on a plane and come to you, but I was afraid, Nae-nae. When you've lived in a cage for so long, the outside world feels like it'll crush you—and I didn't know who you were anymore."

Baby steps, Luna. One at a time.

Dr. Mehta, her wisdom infinite. "I understand. The estate was a safe place to heal, decide on your next steps."

"Yes, and I had my secret room to hide in if the caretaker came by."

"Cops don't know about that room."

"Even Darcie didn't know where it was. I found it as a kid, used to hide there when she got annoying." Bea looked up at me, a question in her expression.

"Far as cops are concerned, you stayed in one of the main bedrooms until we arrived, then hid in a remote part of the estate after our arrival—until Grace began to drug you so you were malleable and she could walk you to places she knew we wouldn't or couldn't look." Blake Shepherd's locked study, for example. "She'd then give you another dose so you'd lose consciousness."

No one was going to test Grace on her stated ability to pick locks, not when they were dealing with murder and attempted murder. "Your secret room can stay a secret." There might be nothing in there for the cops to find, but why take the risk?

"What about my things?"

"Grace's told them you didn't have much, that the bag will be around somewhere. She can't quite recall the last place she shoved it. Ratene's good, but cops have budgets. They can't hunt endlessly for a victim's belongings when they have the perpetrator and the necessary evidence to put her away."

Reaching the end of the hallway, we turned right, continued on to another. A harried doctor passed us in a half jog, two nurses crossed ahead of us, then the world went quiet again.

"I didn't know you were all coming to the estate until you arrived," Bea said. "Grace hadn't told me. I panicked, hid. But then I saw Darcie with Ash and I got so mad."

"Creepy Bea."

"It was the one thing she didn't take from me. Said I could have the ugly monstrosity." A sigh. "Does it make me evil that I enjoyed hearing her scream when she found it on her bed?"

"No. I'd have done worse."

Elevator doors opened, disgorging two orderlies with a patient on a stretcher. "Evening, ladies," one of them said, while the other smiled.

We smiled back at them before they headed off in the opposite direction, and we came to a stop at the glass wall at this end of the corridor. It looked down into a dark carpark, the lights of the nearest town glimmering in the background.

"Bea?" I untangled our arms so that they hung side by side and I could weave my fingers through hers. "You know the rest of what to say to the police?" I'd visited earlier, while Ratene was still at the estate, and we'd walked that time, too, our conversation more desperate.

Looking at me with those blue eyes that weren't desiccated and burned but vividly alive, she said, "Grace drugged me when I realized what she was doing to Kaea, when I argued with her about her plans for vengeance. I didn't want any of it—but she'd become obsessed with the idea of avenging me and wouldn't stop."

"Yes." I squeezed her hand. "You somehow made it to the living room the night of the fight."

"Grace was late in giving me the dose. It hadn't quite kicked in when she left me alone." Her fingers tightened on mine. "She really was late."

"I know. Why do you have cuts on your hands?"

"I got in between Darcie and Grace in an effort to stop their fight."

"What if anyone asks why you came in wearing Darcie's dress?" We had to prepare for that on the off chance the police went to the trouble of tracing its provenance.

"Grace gave it to me. She must've stolen it to mess with Darcie."

"Good. That's all you know, all you remember, your memory is foggy."

Rain in my mind again, a ferocious drumming on the roof of the Land Cruiser. A silent Darcie, her heart still beating but her body shutting down—and Bea in the back seat with the blood-soaked dress. "We need to get her out of that dress," I'd said to Grace.

"I'll help you."

As it was, I'd managed to strip Bea on my own. But afterward, Grace, weak as she was, was able to help stand her in the rain behind the warmth of the car's exhaust while I poured bottles of water over her as fast as humanly possible.

Bea, naked in the dark, runnels of what would've been pink in the sunlight racing down her lax body to become lost in the water that was the world as the skies continued to thunder down.

No more blood on her face, on her chest, under her nails. Her hair rinsed and rinsed again.

Then, putting her in Darcie's dress and allowing that to get wet, too—but only after we'd smeared it with Darcie's and Grace's blood. No underwear, but she was a woman who'd been drugged and barely conscious of her actions.

Plausible deniability.

Rain, so much rain, a waterfall of sound in my ears as the world blurred.

Placing Bea back into the Land Cruiser, then using my belt to bind a seated Grace once more.

"No one will ever know," she'd said again, and we'd both understood that she wasn't talking about Darcie anymore.

"There's a missing knife. It wasn't beside Ash."

A shake of her head, her words starting to slur as she said, "No. It's in the kitchen drawer. I washed and bleached it."

I hadn't known what to do with the bloody dress or the tag from the one on Bea, had stared around me as I stood with the small bundle scrunched in my hand. I couldn't just drop it in the ravine. Too high a chance it'd be seen.

"Bury it." Grace's weakening voice. "In among the trees. Ground's wet."

Easy to dig.

I'd turned and hiked up into the thick and tangled forest that loomed over us, while the rain erased my footprints from the mud behind me. I hadn't been able to go far, not with my vision. I couldn't risk becoming lost in the dark. But it hadn't mattered. I'd found a fallen branch, used it to dig a hole near the roots of a forest giant. Afterward, I'd covered that area with leaf debris until it looked exactly like the rest of the rain-lashed area.

The rain had cleaned my hands and body of all evidence of dirt, but my boots had been muddy. No one cared. I'd hiked to the barn by my own admission, and I'd gotten out to check the bridge before we made it out. Jim, the first person to see us, hadn't even questioned why three of us were wet when we turned up.

Such a stormy night, after all.

The perfect night to bury secrets.

"I was so angry at Ash," Bea whispered. "But I remember holding him to me, rocking him. Then . . . I was in the living room, and I saw you."

"Grace says she stabbed him." It might even be the truth, Bea only stumbling onto the scene in the aftermath.

The bandage on her hand flashed white in the light as she stared at it.

She dropped it after a while, said, "I know what to say to the police." A glance at me. "Grace . . ."

"For Nix," I said softly. "She's made her choice."

"I never wanted him hurt. Or Kaea."

I didn't follow that thread, didn't ask her who she *had* wanted hurt.

"Is that—" She pressed her face to the glass with startling suddenness, staring in the direction of an iconic fast food restaurant sign that glowed against the night.

I laughed. "You want a burger? A cop got me one, said it's the only place around here open twenty-four hours."

Eyes lighting up, she rose on her toes like a child. "You don't mind?"

"For you? Never."

First, however, I walked her back to her room. She yawned as she got under the blanket and lay down. "I'll nap so we can talk again after you come back."

Her eyes were already closing as I went to shut her door behind me. A faint smile curved her lips, my Bee-bee so dazzling and bright that she had the power to hold the world in the palm of her hand.

Shutting the door, I reached up to straighten the nameplate one of the staff had slid into the slot: *Beatrice Clara Shepherd*.

I ran my finger over her middle name. Had I known that? Yes. I frowned. But it had been way back in high school. She'd never used it, and I'd never once remembered while reading Clara's hidden diary.

Tonight, the sight made me smile.

The outside air was cold and crisp with a slight bite to it. It surged into my lungs, snapped life into my cells. And made me think of a long-ago night when I'd drunk a bottle of champagne with Bea deep in the heart of a city park. She'd known my fear of the dark, had brought along candle-shaped lamps that we'd put all around.

We'd gone through her nude photos together in the faux

candlelight, choosing the best ones for the final file. But I had all of them, every outtake, every blurred image where she'd moved too fast or begun to laugh while in motion.

Because I loved her best.

I shifted, began to walk. And though I could've stayed in the brightly lit environs of the pathway that led eventually from the hospital complex to the modest outdoor mall that held the fast food restaurant, I turned toward the sidewalk wrapped in darkness. It was inside me now, that darkness, a sinuous knowing of what I was capable.

Luna, please. Please, please. I'm so sorry. Please. Please Luna.

I was the whisper from under the bed, the monster hidden within the folds of the night.

Would you bury a body for me?

I'd do far worse for you, Bea.

My vision telescoping to a pinprick, I walked into oblivion.